THE HOUSE OF LOST WHISPERS

JENNI KEER

B
Boldwood

First published in Great Britain in 2025 by Boldwood Books Ltd.

Cover Design by Alexandra Allden

Cover Images: Shutterstock

A CIP catalogue record for this book is available from the British Library.

Paperback ISBN 978-1-83656-077-7

Large Print ISBN 978-1-83656-076-0

Hardback ISBN 978-1-83656-075-3

Ebook ISBN 978-1-83656-078-4

Kindle ISBN 978-1-83656-079-1

Audio CD ISBN 978-1-83656-070-8

MP3 CD ISBN 978-1-83656-071-5

Digital audio download ISBN 978-1-83656-074-6

This book is printed on certified sustainable paper. Boldwood Books is dedicated to putting sustainability at the heart of our business. For more information please visit https://www.boldwoodbooks.com/about-us/sustainability/

Boldwood Books Ltd, 23 Bowerdean Street, London, SW6 3TN

www.boldwoodbooks.com

Ann Warr-Wood
Best friend and a second mum all rolled into one

PART I

BEFORE THE WAR

1

SUNDAY 14 APRIL 1912

The unprecedented sales of his last book, *The Mystery of the Broken Violin*, had afforded Mr Jasper Davenport and his wife the finances to sail across the Atlantic Ocean on the largest, most luxurious steamer in the world. It was to be truly the trip of a lifetime and, with public readings at various literary societies lined up in several large American cities, a potentially profitable one to boot.

The Davenports, however, were devastated when their only daughter presented with a blotchy rash the week before their departure. The doctor confirmed what they all suspected: thirteen-year-old Olivia had contracted measles. Selina Davenport was all for cancelling but was eventually persuaded by her husband that they should go ahead because the child had battled the worst of the illness before they were due to set sail. Besides, he pointed out, by being on the maiden voyage of the RMS *Titanic*, they were certain to go down in history and, as an author of adventure novels, it was an experience he couldn't afford to miss. He already had in his mind an idea for a story set aboard a great ocean liner, so he planned to treat the trip as research.

From the moment they stepped foot on the ship, they were in awe of both the size and magnificence of this engineering marvel and, as first-class passengers, they were treated like royalty by the crew. Their Louis XVI triple-berth stateroom was the height of luxury, with electric heaters, horsehair-stuffed sofas and marble washstands. Rich Axminster carpeting had been laid in the first-class reception area, the Georgian smoking room boasted a carved Italian marble fireplace, and the grandeur of the main staircase was unparalleled.

Eager to remember every detail, both for the novel he was planning, and to share with his daughter upon their return, Jasper made extensive notes on everything from the bevelled mirrors and fine Irish white linen, to the quirky characteristics of his fellow passengers. Thomas Andrews, the exceedingly amenable Harland and Wolff naval architect who had designed the ship, was on board and was happy to talk about the construction and outfitting of the vessel. Captain Edward J. Smith proved incredibly helpful with his polite enquiries as to the procedures followed should someone pass away whilst they were at sea. Jasper even chatted to some of the children playing shuffleboard and quoits on deck, wondering who his daughter might have befriended had she been present.

All of the information was carefully written up in his leather-bound notebook, and although it wouldn't make up for Olivia missing this most momentous of journeys, sharing this with her when he returned home was the least he could do.

On the Sunday morning, the Davenports attended the church service, led by the captain, in the first-class dining saloon. Afterwards, Jasper set to work outlining his next novel at the small table in their room on A deck. The room itself had inspired the fictional setting for the grisly murder of a wealthy Manhattan heiress, and he could already picture the scene: her dark-red blood pooling into the thick carpeting and an ivory-handled dagger sticking from her back. One of the more talk-ative stewards, who regularly answered the bell push above the bed and served them their morning tea, had been earmarked as a possible character in the book. A particularly theatrical fellow, Jasper could quite see him being the one to discover the body, running down the corridor with his hands in the air and wailing like a woman.

That afternoon, he helped his wife secure a deckchair on the promenade. She sat with a tartan steamer rug across her knees to read a book; not one of his though – she complained that they were rather too violent for her tastes, centring as they did, almost entirely around men. He then took himself off to the first-class smoking room and settled in one of the leather-uphol-stered armchairs, where he engaged some of the other passen-gers in a lively political debate.

That evening, the couple dined on oysters, filet mignon, roast duckling and peaches in Chartreuse jelly. The temperature dropped sharply and by eleven o'clock, they were tucked up, snug in their four-foot-wide bed, complete with its impressive ornamental brass bedstead. Selina placed her cold toes on her husband's bare legs and he chastised her, before relenting and allowing her icy feet to remain.

At exactly 11.39, he rolled over in his sleep and flung his arm across his wife. On the ship's deck, unbeknownst to him, look-outs Frederick Fleet and Reginald Lee were in the crow's nest, ninety-five feet in the air, alert for hazards in the water. The air temperature had fallen to near freezing, and below a clear sky, punctuated with sparkling stars, the ocean was as calm as a millpond.

But, at precisely that moment, an anomaly in the magnetic field surrounding the earth allowed radiation from the sun to enter the atmosphere and shoot along every vein of metallic ore that ran through the planet. The resulting vibrations disrupted the very fabric of space and time and, inexplicably, a duplicate earth was formed as the reality of this world cleaved into two. Few people noticed anything amiss as it lasted the tiniest fraction of a second. A jolt in our physical existence. A juddering of time. But those magnetic ripples were felt through every deposit of copper and seam of iron that ran from the molten core of the planet to the earth's crust.

For most of the 1.8 billion people going about their lives, this involuntary wrinkle was not even noticed. But on that night, at that exact moment, when the very survival of over two thousand passengers was at stake, every fraction of a second made a difference to the tragic sinking of a luxury liner somewhere in the North Atlantic Ocean, four hundred nautical miles from its intended destination.

On that night, in that exact location, that ripple mattered...

2

TUESDAY 16 APRIL 1912

It was beyond beastly. Olivia Davenport was stuck in her bedroom recovering from a rotten case of the measles, and under the care of a woman called Ruth, whom her father had hastily employed before his departure. The highly efficient and no-nonsense young lady had contracted the disease in her youth and so was well placed to supervise the convalescence of the irritable and somewhat overdramatic child.

Olivia had been running a dangerously high fever the previous week, and everyone had been genuinely concerned, almost to the point of her mother cancelling their trip. Thankfully, however, she was now out of danger, but isolated from the remainder of the household, and was under strict instructions to continue with a period of bed rest. The only thing that had seen her through the mind-numbing boredom and crushing disappointment of being unable to travel with her parents was escaping into swashbuckling adventure novels, Gothic novelettes and her father's collection of penny dreadfuls. The result of such reading matter, however, was her tendency to lean towards the melodramatic.

'I am utterly convinced that I witnessed a heavenly host of angels sweep to earth in my darkest moment to take me to heaven, because I heard their sweetly singing voices call to me,' Olivia said, from her sickbed.

'I'm not sure you were *quite* that ill, young lady.' Ruth adjusted the pillows and raised a serious eyebrow. 'In all probability, you heard Bessie humming to herself as she went about her duties – and she strikes me as no angel. Come now, miss, drink up. You must have plenty of fluids.' She passed her charge a small glass of water.

Ruth was kind enough but Olivia was heartily sick of eating nothing but 'restorative' broth and enduring tepid sponge baths – although the latter had succeeded in bringing down her temperature.

'If only I hadn't caught this wretched disease, I might be with my parents now and have met with my future husband on the voyage. Perhaps some rich, young American who found me engaging and we might have begun an exchange of correspondence over the next few years, until he returned to this country only to find me all grown-up and breathtakingly beautiful...' Olivia was convinced that she would grow into her looks '...and now he shall meet someone else and I will be destined to remain a spinster for the entirety of my life.' She threw her hand across her forehead in her misery.

'You're rather too young to be thinking about husbands, miss,' Ruth scolded. 'I strongly suspect being an only child has necessitated such a vivid imagination. Cook says you had a make-believe friend when you were younger. I am one of eleven and had no time for such frivolous nonsense.'

'Sophie,' Olivia confirmed. 'And she wasn't make-believe; it was simply that no one else could see her. Had she still been around, I know she would have agreed that they should have postponed their trip until I was well. Fancy having such a grand adventure without me when I was so looking forward to travelling to a whole new continent. Catching measles is absolutely and unequivocally the worst thing in the world that has ever happened to me.' And with that dramatic pronouncement, she collapsed back into her pillows.

Ruth smiled and swept up the young girl's wrist to check on her pulse as her patient wittered on.

'It's really quite the thing to see the names of the passengers printed in the newspaper, and the tragedy of it all is *my* name isn't there. Think how jealous the girls at school would have been.' She sighed. 'Life is so dreadfully unfair. Daddy promised to write letters but it's hardly the same.'

The sound of a motorised vehicle drifted through the open window and the nursemaid stepped over to look out at the driveway.

'Who on earth can this be?' she muttered. 'The housekeeper will have to inform them that the Davenports are away.'

Olivia slipped out of bed to join her and peered outside. It was such a grey afternoon and she couldn't think why someone would be calling on them. But when the smartly dressed figure stepped from the shiny, black motor car, she recognised him. As he placed a silk top hat on his ginger head, she wondered what had brought Sir Hugo Fairchild, her godfather and a baronet no less, to their Suffolk home.

The ladies had a good enough view from the first-floor window to see the deep frown across the man's forehead as he tucked a newspaper under his arm and headed for the front door. Olivia was confused. Surely, Sir Hugo knew that his dearest friend, Jasper, was currently sailing to America and so would have no reason to visit them, especially when there was a case of measles in the household. The pair exchanged a nervous glance as the doorbell rang.

* * *

It was Ruth who broke the news to Olivia twenty minutes later, having been summoned downstairs by the housekeeper. She returned to the bedroom, closing the door behind her slower than Olivia had ever seen anyone close a door in her entire life, but the girl was old enough to know that an unannounced visit from her father's oldest friend was a portend of bad tidings.

It was headline news – the possible sinking of the RMS *Titanic* in the early hours of the previous day – but reports were conflicting and details few. The ship had collided with an iceberg, and the fate of the passengers and crew remained uncertain. Everything was still such a terrible muddle and, with the *Carpathia* still en route to New York with the survivors on board, it was almost impossible to get accurate information. Sir Hugo had already sent numerous telegrams but so far had been met with unsatisfactory answers.

All they could do was wait.

And, as a distraught thirteen-year-old girl lay curled up in the white cotton sheets of her sickbed, her mind racing with a million possibilities, and very few of them cheery, she reflected that perhaps getting measles hadn't been the worst thing in the world, after all.

3

THREE MONTHS LATER

It was early July and Olivia peered out the windows of Merriford Manor at the immaculate lawns, dotted with elegant topiary, and perfectly symmetrical borders of summer flowers. Even in her wildest imaginings, she had never anticipated living anywhere this magnificent; if only the circumstances that had seen this turn of events hadn't been so unbelievably tragic.

This was now her home and would be so until she was of age, as her father had named his oldest school friend as the person who would give his daughter the best care should anything befall him and his wife. Perhaps, she thought cynically, Sir Hugo's extraordinary wealth and enormous house were also factors, but the Fairchilds were kind people, and the extended Davenport family was small, and alarmingly unreliable.

Her godfather had employed a governess for Olivia as it had proved impossible for her to continue studying at the girls' day school in her home town when she'd moved to the village of Merriford Lode. (The word 'lode', she'd been told, meant seam of iron.) Lady Fairchild was particularly keen that her new charge should benefit from the very best education, even though the public boarding school that her boys attended was not an option for Olivia's sex.

The governess, a quiet but efficient spinster, had assessed the young girl and found her to be exceptionally bright for her age. It was she who had suggested to Sir Hugo that lessons were in the morning and then the child was encouraged to spend time outdoors in the afternoons. The woman was convinced that fresh air, good food and time would help Olivia heal, and she was right. Wandering free throughout the extensive grounds, sitting by the boating lake, climbing up the large oak trees... Olivia's irrepressible imagination had quickly resurfaced. Pretending to be someone else, an intrepid explorer or a cursed princess, helped her to forget the pain of who she really was – a thirteen-year-old orphan, plucked from her safe and loving world, to be surrounded by people she didn't know and living in an unfamiliar house, so grand that it had taken her a whole afternoon to understand how the staircases were linked.

The manor itself was an impressive Jacobean red-brick house that boasted thirty-five acres of gardens, over forty staff and twelve family bedrooms. During the course of the eighteenth century, two wings had been added to the front of the ornate rectangular property: one incorporated the kitchens, utility areas and servant quarters, and the other contained stables, a brewery and various workshops. The house consequently appeared U-shaped, with two hexagonal brick towers where the wings met the main building. To Olivia, these towers epitomised the escapist fairy tales that she so enjoyed reading, and, joy of joys, both contained spiral staircases – now that really was the stuff of valiant knights and imprisoned princesses.

That particular morning, Olivia was in the long library, situated on the first floor of the main building, browsing the hundreds of books. This room ran the length of the house and had five ceiling-height windows that overlooked the driveway. When she heard the door at the east end open, she ducked behind one of the high-backed sofas. Fearing it was one of the Fairchilds' sons returned for the summer, she was relieved to hear the voices of the generous couple who had taken her in.

'I was very concerned those first few days when she was so quiet,' Lady Fairchild said. They were mid conversation and Olivia was clearly the subject of their discussion.

'Yes,' her husband agreed. 'But the young are so resilient and her ability to rally has been a lesson to us all. I can only put it down to the ridiculous nonsense that fills her head. There is no doubting that she is the daughter of an author.'

Olivia heard them walk past her hiding place and settle in the large armchairs that faced the marble mantelpiece.

'And such an alarmingly tactile child,' his wife mused. 'I didn't know what to do when she rushed at me that first morning, flinging her arms about my skirts like that.'

Olivia remembered the moment well. All she'd wanted was someone to hold her tight, but Lady Fairchild had patted her head as though she were an overexuberant dog.

'And now we have this bold request to sleep in the east tower – clearly a result of her fascination with castles and princesses. The thought of her being so far from us at night concerns me. I don't know what to do for the best, Hugo, really I don't.'

It had taken Olivia a week to leave the sanctuary of her new bedroom, but she never could stay gloomy for long – something she'd inherited from her mother.

'After every raincloud, the sun is sure to follow, and what a shame if we allow ourselves to remain shut inside when we could be outside basking in its warmth,' Selina Davenport would say to her daughter when she bemoaned some tragedy of Greek proportions, like the time she'd tried to iron her curly

hair straight and merely ended up with considerably less hair to
fret over.

'If she wants to be in the tower, after all she has gone
through, even if the request is somewhat... unusual, can we not
accommodate her?' Sir Hugo said.

'And what do you suggest we do with your late father's
orchid collection, which currently occupies the upper floor?
One of the garden hands currently sleeps in there to deter
thieves. It's hardly a space fit for a young girl.'

'The plants can be moved and the young man can return to
the bothy with the other gardening staff. The west tower has
always proved convenient for housing the grooms and coach-
man, and I see no reason to change that arrangement, but I have
no use for the east tower. They were romantic whims of my
grandfather and are of little practical use. They're technically
neither part of the house nor the wings, and were merely an
aesthetic addition to balance the architecture. With a thick rug
and some solid furniture from the guest rooms, the space could
be made quite homely.'

It had been brave of Olivia to make such a request, but then
she'd never been backwards in coming forwards. Perhaps, being
the only child of indulgent parents, she had an elevated sense of
her own importance, and she'd been somewhat intimidated by
the immense wealth and status of the people who were now
taking care of her. They were very kind, but Lady Fairchild was
forever 'just passing' her current bedroom and trying to engage
Olivia in conversation. It was as though the older woman knew
she had a duty to step into a motherly role but was nervous of
how she might achieve that.

All Olivia had craved during those first few days was the
tight embrace of another, but Lady Fairchild had sat tentatively
on the end of her bed, trying to ease her suffering with a

constant flow of meaningless platitudes and intrusive enquiries, when it was physical touch that so eloquently said the things that really needed to be said: *You are safe, we care for you, and no one expects you to talk until you're ready.* She needed to be separate from their smothering concern, somewhere she could find solace inside her head, and escape into worlds where none of the pain existed.

'But she's so young. I don't like the idea of her being so far from us at night – the time I feel she is at her most vulnerable.'

'She's thirteen, Cynthia. Some girls her age are already out at work and she's always had an independent spirit. Can we not grant her this one request?'

'Ruth will have to sleep in the tower with her.' Lady Fairchild had employed the woman who had seen Olivia through the measles, hoping that a familiar face would help her settle.

'That can easily be arranged. The boys will be back soon and we can tell them the tower is out of bounds. We don't want them smothering the poor girl.'

It had been fortuitous that Olivia's arrival had been during term time, allowing her to move in without gawping adolescents asking uncomfortable questions – although the oldest two Fairchild sons, Clarence and Louis, were at Cambridge, so they were technically men, and intimidating ones to boot. Clarence, heir to the estate, had a long, white scar under his chin that, to her melodramatic mind, always made him seem extra dashing but slightly scary. Louis, the next in age, was dreadfully blunt and somewhat of a cold fish – occasionally upsetting her on previous family visits.

The younger two, Howard and Benji, fourteen and nine respectively, were at boarding school and, despite over a decade between the oldest and youngest brother, the family resemblance was unmistakable. They all had the strong Fairchild nose and fair hair, save Howard, who had been almost ginger when they'd been younger, like his father, but was now a more respectable auburn, and his wide face was scattered with pale freckles that made him look like he'd been sprinkled in chocolate. Despite being closest to her in age, he'd never shown any interest in his father's godchild, whereas Benji had always followed her around like an eager puppy, asking endless questions. Being so young, and more gentle in nature, set him apart from his brothers. He didn't belong to the pack – and it was a pack Olivia was not looking forward to seeing again.

'Very well, then I will see to the arrangements,' Lady Fairchild said. 'I believe it to be an indulgence but appreciate that if anyone deserves to be humoured, it is her. Let's hope she doesn't attract too many fire-breathing dragons and handsome knights when she moves in.'

'I am certain she would handle both with admirable fortitude,' her husband replied, and they both laughed.

4

Within the week, Olivia had moved into the tower. The lad who'd been living there was apparently quite put out but was not in a position to argue. The head gardener, Mr Rowe, oversaw the transfer of the priceless collection of orchids to one of the conservatories at the back of the main house, although Olivia understood that Lady Fairchild was not enamoured of the plants and it was only the rarity of the collection and pleas of the head gardener that had persuaded her to keep them. Ruth was given the room on the ground floor, so that anyone wishing to call on Miss Davenport would have to get past her first; not exactly the dragon protector of fairy tales, but certainly someone capable of challenging visitors and keeping her safe.

Olivia had watched the young gardening lad from the nursery window as he'd moved his belongings out and found herself quite taken with him. He was a serious-faced individual, with green eyes, a suspicious gaze and unruly, black hair. She rather thought his looks suited those of a tragic romantic hero and so it became his furrowed brow that bent earnestly towards hers in her escapist fantasies, as he swept her onto his majestic black steed and galloped from the battlefield into the blazing sunset.

The change of bedroom marked a new start for Olivia and allowed her to move on from her grief. She could so easily have perished on the *Titanic*, even though as a child of first-class passengers, her probability of survival would have been high. But she felt lucky to have escaped the horror of it all, and decided forthwith to spread joy and live a life her parents would be proud of.

For days, she'd held on to the ridiculous hope that they'd swum to safety or been picked up by a passing fishing boat – a daring escapade worthy of her father's books. But as she gleaned more about the unfathomable tragedy from the papers, and concerned adults gently nudged her towards the awful truth, she realised no one could survive more than a few minutes in the icy waters of the North Atlantic Ocean, and it was simply not a place that smaller vessels would happen to be bobbing about. By the June, when their bodies were not amongst those recovered by the vessels contracted by the White Star Line to retrieve the dead – she'd finally accepted there would be no burial either.

One warm July afternoon, having packed her father's old knapsack, and wearing a battered Homburg she'd found in the boot room, she took herself to a small copse near the boating lake and draped herself across the thick bough of a sycamore. She was on her stomach, with her eyes closed, when a voice jolted her from her daydreams.

'Why are you sleeping up the tree?'

Olivia looked down to the ground, where the youngest Fairchild son was gazing up at her through a pair of thin wire spectacles, wearing a tweed jacket and knickerbockers, and clutching a leather satchel.

'Benji?' She heaved herself upright and swung her right leg over the wide branch, wrestling to straighten her skirts as she did so. 'I didn't know you were back from school.'

'My term finishes before Howard's. Mother said I wasn't to bother you and that we had to be extra kind because...' He didn't need to finish the sentence and wisely chose not to, his cheeks colouring up as he realised his error, and his eyes drifting slowly to the ground as his words tailed off.

'Girls don't climb trees,' he eventually said, to fill the silence.

'I'm not a girl; I'm Sir Walter Raleigh, battle-weary and taking the opportunity to rest a while on top of this misty mountain.'

'But it's not a mountain; it's a tree,' he astutely pointed out. 'And you're not Raleigh.'

Olivia slid down the wide trunk and sighed. She didn't particularly want to engage with this young boy, who she felt was somewhat of a baby compared to herself.

'I can be anyone I want to be. Yesterday, I was Rapunzel, locked in a tower, letting down my hair for the handsome prince to climb up. Today, I am an intrepid explorer and charming privateer. Since six o'clock this morning, I have fought alongside the Huguenots and explored the Americas. This afternoon, I shall present Queen Elizabeth with tobacco and endeavour to discover the lost city of El Dorado. By nightfall, I'll have been executed for treason.'

Benji narrowed his dark-blue eyes and shook his head slowly from side to side. 'But not really, you're not. It's just pretend.'

'That rather depends on how you decide what is real. The scenes I hold in my head are real for the moments I choose them to be. Our brains allow us to live many lives other than our physical existence. Ones we can't control, like in our dreams, and ones we can, like our deliberate thoughts.'

The young boy looked up at her face in wonder.

'Mother says you're a strange one, but we shouldn't draw attention to it because your parents are dead.' He'd completely forgotten his earlier attempts to avoid the delicate subject. 'And then I thought I'd be sad if my mother and father drowned at sea, so I decided you might like some company.'

'That's sweet but I'm quite happy on my own.'

'Please let me play. I'm very good at swishing swords about. I have an old one of Howard's made of wood. Only don't tell my brothers when they return. They always rib me for being childish because they're too big for play-acting now.'

But Olivia didn't want to include Benji in her make-believe world, because you couldn't explain all the wonderful things you saw in your mind's eye to someone else and, if you tried, it took you out of the moment. The whole point of her escapism was that it was a solitary activity. If she wanted to scamper down a grassy hillside to attack a fierce Viking army one minute, but be running from a fire-breathing dragon towards the mounted figure of her would-be saviour the next, then she didn't have to explain the change of game to anyone. She was certainly not prepared to let Benji come to her rescue, when she was planning on a green-eyed, dark-haired young man fulfilling that role. Her imaginary worlds were intensely personal and not to be shared with a curious nine-year-old.

'What's in your satchel?' she asked, trying to be kind by angling the conversation towards him.

'Just stuff.' He shuffled from foot to foot and blinked several times.

She slid from the tree and collected her knapsack from the base of the trunk, swinging it up in the air. 'I have all the essentials in my bag: a hearty lunch, a small telescope, a compass and a catapult. I'm a mean shot,' she admitted. 'My father taught me.'

'I have pencils with me,' he said, deciding he could trust her. 'And paper. I like drawing things.'

She remembered Benji sitting quietly in the corner of the vast morning room when her family had visited back in December, contentedly scribbling in a sketchbook, whilst his brothers spent most of the day playing battledore and shuttlecock in the high-ceilinged entrance hall, with their mother continually apologising for the noise. The afternoon had ended with a broken chandelier and Clarence and Louis being reprimanded by a furious Sir Hugo. To see them with their heads bowed in front of their father was a reminder of what an important man the owner of Merriford Manor was.

Not long afterwards, Clarence had sauntered into the morning room, snatched up the pad and called his baby brother 'our little Cubist'. This, she understood, was a slur on his artwork, although quite what he expected a nearly nine-year-old to be producing was anyone's guess.

'Come on. Let's walk back to the Japanese gardens and you can sketch the dragon?' Olivia said, recognising Benji was not going to leave her alone any time soon. Besides, she'd gone off the idea of being beheaded by an angry King James I.

* * *

The oriental gardens at Merriford Manor fascinated Olivia. The pond had a bright-red arched bridge at one end and, right in the centre, stood a five-foot-high stone dragon that continuously spewed water from its ferocious open mouth. There were screens of bamboo dotted about that made the space seem larger than it was, and the air was filled with the sweet, fruity scents of jasmine and honeysuckle.

Benji settled down with his sketchbook balanced on his

knees, the tip of his tongue sticking out in concentration. Olivia lay back on the neatly clipped bank of grass and stared up at the bulbous clouds drifting by. She imagined boxing hares and jumping horses in the twisting shapes of the cumuli above her head, happy to lose herself in this whimsical activity and provide silent companionship to a lonely little boy for a while.

Their peace was disturbed by the rumble of a wooden barrow being wheeled over the bridge. Benji put down his pencils and stood up to wave.

'Ahoy there, Tanner. I'm back.'

It was the emerald-eyed object of her romantic imaginings, and the young man grunted, his eyebrows heavy over his face, as he slipped on a pair of waders.

'Afternoon, Master Benji,' he begrudgingly acknowledged in a soft Norfolk accent. 'How was school?'

'Horrid. I don't like the other boys in my dorm or any of the lessons. Numbers always confuse me and I get picked on because I'm small for my age.'

'Be thankful for an education, young man. The learning you're doing now will reap rewards when you get to my age. You won't be slaving away all hours, undertaking back-breaking work, for the sake of a few shillings.' He looked at Olivia, who had now seated herself upright, as he stepped into the water. She shielded her eyes from the sun with her hand. 'Young Miss Davenport, I assume?' He nodded in deference, and then turned back to the barrow, reaching for the long handle of a wide pond net.

'This is Tanner,' Benji explained, belatedly realising the two had not been introduced, but then the worlds of a relatively wealthy orphan girl from the main house and an undergardener were quite removed. 'He's always been kind to me, and some-times lets me help with deadheading the roses, or seed planting in the greenhouse. He can't help being grumpy. That's just his way.' The young boy shrugged.

Olivia tried not to smile at his lack of tact, and Tanner raised his eyebrows at the candid description of him but didn't comment. Perhaps he knew it was a fair assessment. Instead, he returned his focus to the task of skimming the blanket of bright-green duckweed from the surface of the water.

'I'm sorry that you had to move from the tower.' Olivia felt the need to apologise, but there was also a part of her that wanted to engage the young man in conversation. At a guess, he was perhaps six or seven years older than her – to her mind, the perfect age gap for any romantic couple.

He shrugged. 'Don't matter, miss.' But the way he avoided her eye suggested it did.

'Well, it was kind of you,' she persevered and cleared her throat. 'I, erm, found a small bone-handled penknife on the window ledge of my new bedroom – the right-hand room on the first floor. Shall I see that it is returned to you?' she said.

'That's far more likely to belong to young Master Howard, who is always finding himself in places he shouldn't be. I had the room on the left.'

He gave a nod and a half-smile, perhaps in an effort to dispel the accusation of grumpiness. There was no more to say, so he returned to the job in hand as she watched Benji shape and shade his mythical beast for a while.

A wasp buzzed around Tanner's face but he swatted it, inadvertently shooting it towards himself. A moment later, he cursed, whipped off his shirt, and she could see the red welt forming where he'd been stung. Olivia's mouth dropped open, unable to believe her luck at seeing a real-life man briefly naked from the waist up. Tanner swore under his breath again and dressed himself. How brave, she thought, as he carried on without a fuss until he'd completed his task and, with a barrowful of lime-coloured weed, climbed back onto the path.

'Would you like to see my dragon, Tanner?' Benji asked, scrunching up his eyes as he assessed his handiwork and twisting the paper from side to side. 'I'm not sure it's any good. It looks a bit like a snake with legs, or a very thin horse.'

He held up the sketchbook and the gardener walked over to them, taking the time to consider the young boy's efforts. 'That's wholly splendid, young man. You've really captured the eyes. Very fierce. I certainly wouldn't want to meet it on a dark night. Much better than I could do. You've a gift, and if you keep practising, I can see you becoming quite the expert.'

'Clarence said I'm rubbish and that a blind chimpanzee could do better.' Olivia noticed how he hung his head as he spoke.

'Older brothers always pick on younger brothers. They're scared that one day, you'll be bigger and better than them. People who criticise others are often unhappy with their lot in life, and lashing out makes them feel better.'

The difference between this young man's encouragement and Clarence's scathing remarks did not escape Olivia. Benji sat up straight and suddenly looked more self-assured.

'You not drawing, miss?' Tanner asked. He was making an effort, she recognised, probably because Benji had called him out as grumpy.

'Olivia doesn't do drawing,' Benji answered on her behalf. 'Her pictures are in her head. She does play-acting and pretends she's Sir Walter Raleigh fighting the Spanish, or Rapunzel locked up in a tower. And, for a girl, she's absolutely top drawer at boy things, like climbing trees.'

Olivia suddenly felt hot and uncomfortable. She didn't want Benji sharing this information with the gardener in case he thought of her as a child, and she wasn't – not really. Yes, she still wore her hair down and her skirts were off the ground, but she was developing curves and had an awareness of herself as a young woman... and an eye for handsome young gardeners.

'Ah, daydreams.' Tanner walked back to the wheelbarrow. 'You'll grow out of them, miss. Being a grown-up is knowing that the only way to be happy is to accept the cards you've been dealt. There's no point escaping into worlds that don't exist or wishing life was different. We all have our sorrows to bear and pretending you're someone else for a few minutes won't make your troubles disappear.'

But she wasn't having that. The lad was wrong. Her father had built his whole career on people escaping to other worlds. He had told her repeatedly that one of the best things about being an author was the knowledge that his stories brought joy to the ordinary man, allowing him to escape his dreary life, even if just for a few hours. If your existence was a monotonous round of work and sleep, then delving into a world of adventure, where the lowly triumphed, anyone could be a hero, and evil was punished, would lift your spirits. Books offered hope, as well as educating you, and possibly even inspiring an individual to greater things – assuming you could read, of course.

'Isn't that even more reason to lose yourself in a daydream?' she said. 'When life doesn't turn out how you expect, you can at least imagine that it has.'

'And what good does that do? Thinking about things you can't have and places you'll never visit? I'm fully aware of my lot in life. I don't dream of being King of England because it won't happen. Sum of my ambition is to keep working so that I have a roof to keep me dry and food on the table. I'll keep my head down and do this job to the best of my ability until I can lift a spade no more.'

He doffed his woollen cap at them both, grabbed the handles of the barrow and headed for the little curved bridge.

'I say,' Benji said, when he'd disappeared from view, 'don't go getting him into trouble or anything, will you? He has always been awfully kind to me. I overheard two of the maids whispering about him once, and saying how his sweetheart, Annie, had run off with another man and that's bound to make someone prickly. Although I generally find girls a nuisance – not you, of course,' he added hastily, his cheeks tinged pink. 'You don't count... as a girl, I mean.'

'Charming.' Here she was, trying to navigate her way into womanhood, when Tanner clearly thought of her as a child, and Benji didn't consider her sex at all. That was the problem with play-acting – she was always so many people that she wasn't sure *she* even knew who she truly was.

Her cheeks, however, remained warm from her interchange with Tanner and her heart was beating slightly faster. He had done nothing to dispel her romantic notion of him as her knight in shining armour. In fact, quite the contrary, she had marvelled at his bravery with the wasp, and admired his strong, tanned forearms as he'd pushed the barrow of duckweed. When she crawled into her bed that night and closed her eyes, he would be by her side in her wild adventures – whether he liked it or not.

5

The following week, Olivia was mortified to be caught trying on one of Her Ladyship's silk evening dresses the afternoon before a large dinner party. It had been an impulsive act – the young girl imagining what it might be like to be the lady of the manor, as she'd walked past the open bedroom door and seen the gown lying across the bed. Eyes closed, and waltzing around the room in the arms of an imaginary Persian prince, she had been jolted from her daydream by the older woman's voice.

'Olivia! What on earth are you doing?'

'I... I was attending a masked ball in the hope of stealing a priceless jewel...'

How ridiculous it sounded spoken aloud.

'Play-acting? I don't understand. You have lots of pretty dresses of your own. You really shouldn't be in my room, touching things that don't belong to you.' Her tone wasn't unkind but she was certainly peeved. 'And my pearls too? They aren't toys, child; they belonged to Sir Hugo's grandmother. If the string should break, I would be quite distraught.'

Olivia bowed her head. She'd made a mistake and got

carried away with the romance of it all. What she needed in that moment was a pair of forgiving arms to wrap themselves about her, so that she could learn her lesson and move on, but they were not forthcoming, and she'd slipped out of the dress and run from the room in tears.

Sobbing into her pillows up in the tower, she reflected that the Fairchilds were very different to her parents, and the formality of their opulent lifestyle was unsettling. It seemed to the lonely young girl that the more money you had, the fewer emotions you were allowed to display. No one had embraced her since her arrival, and it was clear Lady Fairchild was not going to encourage her imagination as her own mother had done.

This contrast to her own family was brought home to her even more when, at the end of the week, the remaining Fairchild offspring returned from their various educational establishments, curious about the little orphan that their parents had taken in. Benji, who had become surprisingly chatty over the two days they had spent together, immediately became more withdrawn and Olivia, as an outside observer, wasn't surprised. Within the first few hours, Howard had ambushed his brother with a squirt gun from his hiding place in the boathouse, and Clarence had shouted at him for asking a visiting young lady whether she was hoping to marry the future heir to the manor.

Because the household was overwhelmingly large, and there were so many bodies bustling about, she initially didn't encounter the boys very much, despite Lady Fairchild's optimistic endeavours to engage them all in games of croquet or suggesting they walked to the back fields to fly kites. It was only at mealtimes that Olivia found herself with Benji and Howard, as Louis and Clarence were deemed old enough to dine with their parents. After a few initial gawps across the dinner table, Howard found it easier to say nothing at all, rather than skirt around the very obvious and very large elephant in the room, and she missed more than ever the lively discussions of home.

The 'sinking of the unsinkable' news story, however, simply would not go away, and the British Wreck Commissioner's inquiry was concluded at the end of July. It had been set up to examine the circumstances surrounding the biggest maritime disaster, outside of a war, to befall the nation, scrutinising the actions of the crew, and interviewing nearly one hundred people. The findings were widely anticipated and Olivia knew her emotions would overwhelm her again when they were published, especially as it would surely highlight that the disaster was avoidable.

The horror of everything she'd gone through in April returned. There had been so much confusion in those first few hours and it had taken days to establish the full list of survivors. When the death of her parents was finally confirmed, people stopped talking about the *Titanic* in front of her, but it had been easy enough for Olivia to get hold of the newspapers. The dramatic language used in the articles, the vivid artists' impressions of that fateful night, and the harrowing eyewitness accounts had only added to her distress.

It was inevitable then, that summer, that her nightmares would return – images of a huge, upended ocean liner and lifeless bodies bobbing about in a black sea, as her mind repeatedly played through a long list of what-ifs. What if the iceberg had been spotted sooner? What if there had been enough lifeboats on board to save everyone? What if the *Carpathia* had been closer and could have reached the distressed vessel before she slipped quietly to the bottom of the ocean? So many factors had been against those on board that night, from the arrogance of the ship's designers, to a catalogue of human errors that could so easily have led to a different outcome.

Unfortunately, Louis, the second eldest Fairchild, was the only brother who failed to recognise the need for discretion. Olivia came across him in the library one evening, long after she should have been in bed, but Ruth had allowed her to return some volumes to the great library and choose something else to read.

'Sorry about the ship thing,' a voice said as she entered the long room. It made her jump and she nearly dropped the heavy, leather-bound volumes on the floor. She hadn't even noticed the gangly, blond lad seated by the middle window because she'd been wondering what it might be like to possess so many books, and was imagining herself to be a scientist or a doctor, perhaps in a world where women were welcomed in these professions.

'I rather liked your father,' Louis continued. 'He was a good sort. I didn't particularly take to his novels, though,' he added with a shrug. She thought it wouldn't have hurt him to pretend that he had, especially as the poor man had died such an awful death. She slid the books onto an empty table. 'I generally don't get on with fiction,' he offered as an explanation. 'It's so often distinctly lacking in facts.'

She frowned at him, wondering if he was teasing her, but his face reflected his earnestness and Olivia knew Lady Fairchild had high hopes for Louis. He was studying law and his mother had talked of his future career as a barrister, utterly convinced he would end up as a high court judge. He was, she insisted, the studious sort.

'I only read *The Mystery of the Broken Violin* because one of the chaps at college had it in his room and I belatedly made the connection to Father's old school chum. It was better than Jules Verne's stuff and nonsense about travelling to the centre of the earth, or that Wells fellow and his time machine, because I do struggle with things that aren't, and can't possibly be, real. It's why I couldn't study the Classics like Clarence – all that claptrap about the gods.' He rolled his eyes. 'I only deal in science and numbers, reassuringly reliable, and find the possible existence of God a ridiculous idea. Confirmed atheist, myself, but don't tell Mother.'

There was still no trace of a smile. He was a solemn and humourless individual, Olivia decided, as she quickly slid the first book back onto its correct shelf, desperate to return to the tower.

'Where exactly do you stand on God?' he asked, leaning forward slightly and raising his eyebrows. 'Have you been sucked into the nonsense of a divine being, creator of the universe and source of all moral authority?'

'My faith has been of great comfort to me since I lost my parents.'

He frowned, and then flicked over the page of whatever he was reading.

'I guess you need to believe they are in some heavenly plane, watching over you, but frankly, I don't think He's got much compassion if He let all those innocent people drown in the first place. If there is a God, He's pretty damn selective over whom He saves, that's all I can say. Because I have come to the conclusion that when people do not have the necessary scientific knowledge to understand a thing, they simply invent a god to explain it. Like Zeus and his thunderbolts. Greek gods aren't even particularly moral.' His eyes remained focused on his book and he didn't look up at her, almost as if he was talking to himself.

Olivia felt a lump rise in her throat. She didn't want to get involved in a theological debate and certainly didn't want to contemplate that the sinking of the *Titanic* had been merely on the idle whim of the supreme creator of the universe. Louis wasn't saying these things to be cruel, but she didn't want her faith challenged at this most difficult of times. She hastily returned the other two volumes to the shelves and started to walk towards the door.

'And that's another thing... I wouldn't have minded the east tower, away from Clarence's spiky temper and Howard's childish pranks, but you get given it because the unfortunate death of your parents somehow entitles you to special treatment.'

Olivia was mortified. In her shock, she turned, open-mouthed, as tears started to form in her unbelieving eyes. Finally, he noticed the horror across her face.

'Look here, I didn't mean to make you cry. I'm not terribly good at dressing my thoughts up with fancy words.'

'No, you really aren't,' she agreed, as she stomped out the room, trying to blink the tears away.

Ruth, who had been waiting for her on the ground floor with two mugs of cocoa, immediately realised something had upset Olivia, but the young girl didn't want to talk about it. It wasn't what Louis had said; it was the matter-of-fact way he'd said it.

It was only tucked up in bed a little while later that she felt overwhelmed by the return of the Fairchild sons and everything that the inquiry into the sinking had dredged up. She was clearly an object of curiosity and pity all at once, embarking on the journey to womanhood without her mother, and trying to navigate strange emotions and changes to her body that she didn't understand. Lady Fairchild meant well but she was confused by the orphan girl who was now part of her household. Her mother would have laughed had she found her daughter prancing about in an oversized dress, swept her up from the floor and waltzed with her. Now she had no one to waltz with.

In the tiny wrought-iron bed, under her single sheet and

snow-white candlewick bedspread, facing the rows of red bricks that divided her bedroom from her dressing room, in the tower she'd chosen as her refuge, it was suddenly all too much. The Fairchilds were well meaning but this wasn't her family. She'd been slotted into the busy life of an enormous household and would never be the focus, like she'd been with her parents. The very nature of their deaths would follow her around for the rest of her life – a sensational story that would never go away. The garden lad and Lady Fairchild had both made her feel silly for using her imagination, and now Louis was suggesting that there wasn't even a heaven. It was the tipping point.

What started as a few sobs punctuating the night quickly escalated to a crescendo of desolate misery. She could only find the sunshine for so long and, now that everyone was reminding her of the rainclouds, she'd lost her way. Once the tears started in earnest, she couldn't stop them falling. Either the ever-sensible Ruth couldn't hear her weeping from the room below or, more likely, she knew that comfort was the last thing Olivia needed in that moment. Sometimes, a good cry was cathartic and absolutely necessary, and she was grateful not to be disturbed. There were definite benefits to being away from other people in the sanctuary of the tower.

So, it came as a shock to realise that she was not alone on the first floor that evening, and someone not two foot away from her didn't seem to share Ruth's compassion, because as she continued to lament her misery at full throttle, a stern male voice came from the other side of the bedroom wall.

'For the love of God, who's in there?' There was a stomping of feet that faded away, and then the voice returned. 'Where are you hiding? Show yourself.' There was another pause. 'Either you leave or you stop making that racket. I need my sleep.'

The startling revelation that there was someone in the

adjoining room halted her tears. No one but herself and the housemaids had access to the tower. How had someone got past Ruth, and more importantly, why?

Now extremely angry herself, she threw back the bedding and ran to the adjacent room to give the perpetrator a piece of her mind. Where was his understanding of her situation? She didn't care what she looked like, with her bed-ruffled hair, in her long, cotton nightgown, and her face blotchy and swollen from the crying. How dare someone tell her to be quiet in the privacy of her own bedroom and pretend to be the injured party. How dare someone even be in the tower. She had personal items in that dressing room – undergarments and such – things she didn't want someone looking through.

She flung open the adjoining door but, apart from a small hanging rail and a split chest of drawers (which had been the Devil's own job for the footmen to get up the spiral staircase), to her utter bewilderment, there was absolutely no one in the room.

6

Not many moments later, Ruth climbed the spiral staircase, possibly hearing the banging of doors and stomping of feet and finally deciding to check on her charge. Olivia explained that she'd heard a voice, but Ruth assured the young girl that no one had entered or exited the tower through the main entrance, which only left the windows. Together, they checked the casement stays in the dressing room but they hadn't been tampered with. Had one of the Fairchild boys scaled the outside wall and called in through her open window? Howard, in particular, had a reputation for pulling silly pranks. She didn't know much about acoustics but thought it possible that a voice could be carried around the inside of the hexagonal structure, making it sound as though the speaker was next to her. After all, this was the basic principle of the whispering gallery in St Paul's Cathedral. But Ruth had another theory.

'Had you begun to drift off, miss?' she asked.

It was only too obvious that she was implying the voice was in Olivia's head. Perhaps it was. She understood that grief did funny things to you. Lady Fairchild, in her ongoing efforts to connect in some meaningful way, had passed over an article from one of her ladies' journals about loss. It had, rather alarmingly, highlighted the possibility of psychosis in extreme cases. Was it possible that the imaginary voice had been a result of her distressed brain struggling to cope?

'That must be it. I'm overtired and have allowed Louis's words to upset me.' She didn't want Ruth to worry. She'd carried on conversations in her head since she was a small child, but this was the first time someone had spoken to her out loud. Or her troubled mind had made her think someone had.

She returned to her room and silently slipped back into bed, too bewildered to shed any more tears.

* * *

'Louis thinks he might have upset you last night.'

Lady Fairchild had asked to see Olivia. The interview felt very formal, as the young girl sat on the sage-green sofa in the morning room, opposite Her Ladyship, who was fiddling about with some embroidery. Olivia was clutching a lace tablecloth and had a curtain ring on her finger because she'd been in the middle of her wedding to a returning general from the American Civil War when she'd been summoned, and she did so love to dress up.

The older woman's face was pulled into a worried frown but Olivia remained intimidated by this relative stranger.

Lady Fairchild tried to defend her son. 'He sometimes says things without thinking and has a habit of treating life in a very black and white manner, but you must pay no heed to my boys. They simply aren't used to girls,' she said.

Olivia nodded and forced out a smile. She looked down nervously at her clasped hands, longing for the arms of her mother or the wide lap of her father – always offered when they'd been worried about her. These kind people were doing their best, but no one had held her close in weeks. Even Ruth was not the sort to embrace another, nor would it have been appropriate for her to do so. Although Olivia suspected her maid was the reason she had been summoned. As someone now in the Fairchilds' employ, she was expected to report back, and would have informed her mistress about the rumpus in the night.

'Perhaps a little trip to the seaside will lift everyone's spirits and help us to feel more like a family,' Lady Fairchild suggested. 'We can go by train, which will delight Benji. A change of scene will do us all good – or maybe it's just me who needs a different outlook.' She tossed her embroidery frame onto the small circular table by her chair – the first sign that her privileged life was perhaps not as enviable as Olivia had imagined.

'Sir Hugo won't come, of course, even though he visits Haven-on-Sea often enough without us. But I shall insist all the boys attend, and may even invite the Dunn lad, when he comes over later, to make it a merry little band.'

'The Dunn lad?' Olivia queried. The name meant nothing to her.

'Clarence was into boxing at one time and Ernest Dunn was someone from the village he used to spar with in the holidays.' Her Ladyship rolled her eyes. 'Although my eldest son is more into horses and shooting now, and spends much of his spare time out in the stables, so I'm not sure why he perpetuates the friendship. After all, the boy's father is only a postal worker and Ernest a mere junior clerk for a shipping company.' Kind she may be, but she was also a snob.

'We shall go the week after next,' she concluded. 'And then the sea air can blow all your silly nonsense away.'

get on with the tennis. It's a game for four and he's just not big enough – he can hardly lift the racket. This is a sport for men.'

'You're not a man,' she shot back. 'You're fourteen. And not a particularly nice fourteen-year-old, at that.'

He raised his hands to calm her and looked across the net to where Clarence and Ernest were exchanging amused glances – although whether this was because Benji had been forgotten or she was putting Howard in his place, she wasn't sure.

'There's no need to get your petticoats in a twist. I forgot, all right? It was just a bit of fun and then I got distracted by the game. Look, he'll never survive senior school if he can't take a bit of gentle ribbing. I've had my fair share of teasing over my hair and got on with it.'

'Just because it happened to you, doesn't make it right. Have you not heard the expression "pick on someone your own size"? I'm nearly your size,' she pointed out, and it was true, although she didn't doubt he'd be shooting up to Clarence's height in the next couple of years. 'And you don't want to pick a fight with me, because I'd win.'

She spun back to the gate and left him open-mouthed as Clarence irritably requested that they resume the game.

* * *

Lady Fairchild organised a picnic for the youngsters on the back lawns to round off the day. Cook had rustled up a delightful selection of cold meats, pickles and jellies, and had even baked a fresh cob loaf.

'I'd forgotten Tanner worked here,' Ernest said, gazing across at the two gardeners who were weeding the flower beds. 'His mother lives in the village.'

'Poor devil.' Clarence rolled over onto his back and rested his head on his interlocking fingers. 'Went all peculiar after that girl he was sweet on disappeared last spring.'

'Women are so fickle,' Louis said. 'One of the many reasons I do not intend to marry.'

'Lucky to have the choice. One of my many unwritten duties is to produce the next heir for the manor.' Clarence sounded resentful.

'Oh, come on, Fairchild. You can hardly moan when you get to inherit all this,' Ernest pointed out, his hand sweeping across the view of the enormous house. 'And procreation is hardly a chore. In fact, I've always found it rather fun.'

'Young ears,' Clarence chastised and nodded in the direction of Benji and Olivia, who were together at the far end of the blanket, keeping their heads low and remaining largely silent, not wanting to give the four older lads any excuse to mock them.

'Odd girl, though.' Ernest's brow folded into a wrinkle. 'I found out, after she went missing, that I was the last one to see her. She was heading towards the station. Didn't they think she'd run off with a traveller?'

'We all know there's only one reason to run away and marry.' Louis raised an eyebrow.

'I should think it's being able to go to bed when you like and not get told what to do by grown-ups any more,' Benji mumbled, tossing pieces of sausage roll at an appreciative, and increasingly bold, blackbird.

Clarence scoffed. 'I think you'll find being married is ten times worse than living with your parents. Besides, of the four of us, I suspect only you will marry for love,' he mused. 'I shall marry for duty, Louis will be married to his job, and Howard will never settle down. He's too restless.'

'Howard's got some catching up to do,' Ernest pointed out. 'He's not even dipped his wick yet.'

'What does dipped—'

'Ernest!' Clarence interrupted Benji. 'Can you please watch what you say in front of the children. There's a chap.'

Resentful at being called a child again and, after a long and trying day, Olivia excused herself and returned to the tower, where her imaginary friends were infinitely more pleasant. The voice had not returned, although she thought she heard humming coming through the wall in the night, but rolled away and put the pillow over her head.

If Howard was up to his stupid nonsense again, she wasn't interested.

7

Summer was Olivia's favourite season. Long hours of daylight, Mother Nature offering up her bounty, and a kaleidoscope of colours everywhere you looked. It made her more determined than ever to focus on her future, and she made an effort to daydream less and pay attention to her lessons more. She'd been at Merriford for a couple of months now and felt grateful that she was fed and clothed, and was receiving a good education, when so many people did not have these things. Every day, she looked for reasons to be cheerful.

Another survivor had sold their story to the newspapers on the back of the *Titanic* inquiry, so her positivity helped to ease the resurgence of her grief to a degree, as did the gentle awakening of her womanhood. She would be fourteen that autumn and different things mattered to her now. For example, if there were young lads around, she cared more than was necessary about her appearance, but it was not the Fairchild sons who made her self-conscious; instead, it was the taciturn Tanner. With his emerald eyes and dark, wavy hair, he had the potential to look exceedingly attractive – if only he would smile, instead of wearing a crumpled frown every time she came across him. The frequency with which their paths crossed started to increase, because if he was trimming hedges down by the river, deadheading roses in the formal borders that edged the lawns, or digging up vegetables in the walled kitchen gardens, she deliberately chose to loiter nearby.

After the tranquillity of the Japanese gardens, the kitchen garden was one of her favourite places to be. It was, by virtue of being enclosed, a suntrap and a secret space, with espaliered fruit trees and neat rows of vegetables within equally neat beds of soil. Gravel paths criss-crossed the patch of land and a solitary wooden bench stood at the far end. The object of Olivia's affections was busy within the large greenhouse that stood up against the south-facing wall. She remembered Benji saying how he'd been allowed to plant seeds with Tanner so she walked over and stood in the doorway. Although not strictly a member of the Fairchild family, she knew her position was elevated enough to get away with disturbing him.

'What are you doing?' she asked, watching his nimble fingers work along the rows of dark-green tomato plants.

'Morning, miss.' He nodded but looked irritated to have someone questioning him. 'Pinching out the side shoots.'

She stepped down into the sunken space. Shelves of dense foliage and ripening red fruits towered above her, accompanied by the unique tomato plant aroma: a musky earthiness. The wrought-iron roof vents had been cranked open but it was still oppressively hot inside – lovely for the tomatoes but too muggy for people.

Tanner eyed her as she approached but kept his head facing forwards, his wide fingernails nipping the shoots as he worked swiftly up each plant.

'May I help? I promise to follow your instructions carefully.'

'I'm not sure it would be—'

'It's so hard having no close family left in the world. All I want is some quiet, and to occupy myself with some useful task to stop me dwelling on... things, as the Fairchild boys are too boisterous for me.'

'And yet Benji told me you fought the Spaniards and charged towards a maraudin' Viking army. You clearly embrace a boisterous side on occasion.' He turned his head to hers and raised one eyebrow.

'Please?'

There was an almost inaudible sigh to her right.

'Very well, miss. Start on the row afore you. You're looking for the titty-totty shoots between the main stalk and the leaf stems. Like this – see? Use your thumb and forefinger to nip them out. It makes the plant focus on ripening the fruit, rather than growing more leaves.'

He showed her what to do and she undertook her task in earnest, occasionally hearing grunts from him as she kept up a steady but nervous chatter.

When they were finished, she followed him outside.

'I reckon you'd best be off now, miss. I don't think the master would approve of you doing my job.'

She reluctantly made her way back to the iron gate just as Lady Fairchild entered.

'Olivia, what are you doing in here?'

'Tanner was showing me the tomatoes. He is always more than happy to have me follow him about.' The last part was a definite exaggeration, but she didn't want to get into trouble with Her Ladyship for bothering the young man.

The older woman glanced across at her gardener and then back to her, narrowing her eyes, as Olivia skipped back to the

house, wondering if it would ever be possible to fly an aeroplane
to the moon.

* * *

Benji was reading the latest edition of the *Boys' Own Paper*,
earnestly studying a section on how to make a canoe, when
Olivia sought him out later that afternoon. Howard would not
get away with picking on him, because she would go out of her
way to make up for the thoughtlessness of his brothers.

'Come on,' she said. 'We're going on a grand adventure.'

'Are we?' His face became quite animated, and he certainly
didn't need telling twice, as he leapt to his feet and all thoughts
of canoes vanished.

'Apparently, there's a castle not far from here. I was reading
up about it in a book from the library. Your mother was kind
enough to speak to the owners – who are personal friends of
hers. We're to have a private tour. One of the stable hands
helped me sort out two bicycles and Cook has made us some
sandwiches. You *can* ride?' she asked.

'Of course I can ride and I know of the place. But can we not
go out of the village past the shrieking pits, please? They're
haunted. Clarence told me Ernest has been scaring everyone
with his spooky sightings.'

'You don't need to be frightened of ghosts,' she said, trying to
reassure the young boy. 'My governess said the pits are just pools
of water along the lode where medieval people dug for iron.
Over time, they've filled up like small ponds.'

A vein of metal ore ran through the earth in Merriford, so
people mining this precious resource nearby made sense.

'But they do shriek,' he insisted.

'Only when the wind rushes over them, making a wailing sound, like when you blow across a bottle top.'

But Benji was having none of it.

'A madman haunts the pits, waving an axe and threatening anyone who comes near. He murdered his wife and the shrieking is her cries. I know Louis thinks it's all nonsense but I don't want to go near them.'

'We have no choice unless we go the long way round. Besides, I don't think we'll come across ghosts in the day. And, if we do, I can look after us.' She swished her arm in a figure of eight as though she was fighting off an opponent with a sword and Benji smiled.

Howard teased them over their planned outing when he saw them heading off, but Olivia suspected he was sore not to be invited. He might profess to find the pair of them too young to hang about with, but who wouldn't want a thrilling bicycle ride to a fifteenth-century castle, with sandwiches and fresh peaches thrown in? He was jealous, she decided, and it served him right.

In the end, despite moderate rain for most of their journey and Benji complaining that his legs ached every fifty yards, the pair had a lovely afternoon. The owners of the castle had instructed their housekeeper to show the youngsters around, and the lively old woman amused them with tales of derring-do. She even pointed out a delightful priest hole under the main staircase.

But when they returned, Benji was distraught to find the sketchbooks that he'd left on the nursery table had been defaced.

'I know it was Howie,' he said, trying not to cry. 'Look at these stupid faces drawn across pictures that took me hours.'

Olivia was incandescent. This bullying behaviour had to stop. She stormed downstairs and found out from the house-

attractive? Some girls liked fair hair, others dark; some thought a moustache the very epitome of fashion, and others were quite put off by them. And some found sour-faced, introspective gardeners really quite the ticket.

'Cigarette anyone?' asked Clarence, and a small group drifted out to the platform, away from the ladies. Howard went too, but he didn't smoke; he just wanted to be with the men.

Because Olivia was restless, it wasn't many minutes afterwards that she followed out of curiosity. As she stepped from the doorway, Howard's voice travelled around the corner and she was clearly the topic of conversation.

'...stupid girl who has come to live with us because her parents died on the *Titanic*, and everyone feels sorry for her – even Father, who's let her sleep in the east tower, like some entitled princess, until she's old enough to return to her own home.'

'Does she have some great estate to return to, then?' Ernest enquired. '*Is* she a little princess? A wealthy heiress waiting to be married off?'

'Nah, her father wrote stupid storybooks so probably as poor as the proverbial church mouse.' Howard had really taken against her and was implying she was some penniless orphan, but Olivia knew she would be comfortably off when she came of age. The very reason her father had been able to indulge his literary ambitions was because he was financially secure. 'You'd better not let me get lumped with her, Clarrie.' He was now addressing his oldest brother. 'Because I refuse to spend the day with a babyish Benji and an annoying girl.'

Olivia heard Clarence chuckle. 'You won't find girls annoying for much longer, little brother. They'll really start to come into their own soon.'

'Yes, young ladies really can be the most extraordinary fun,' Ernest agreed.

'I'd rather eat my own eyeballs,' Howard huffed, and she heard the others laugh as the stationmaster announced that their train was approaching.

The family climbed aboard the first-class carriage, as the footmen, accompanying the family for the day, and Ruth, undoubtedly chosen for her pragmatism, were dispatched to third. Two rows of variously excited people faced each other. Howard sat with both arms crossed and a sullen look across his freckled face, and the older lads began to chat about politics and hunting – neither of which interested Olivia.

She pressed her forehead to the cold glass of the window, as every join on the track gave a little jolt, and lost herself in the rhythmic chug-chug of the engine. The world whizzed past in a blur of green and gold: the flat Norfolk landscape and its endless fields awaiting harvest; centuries-old trees, thick with foliage; and the brown and white dots of livestock, idle in the heat.

'I shall visit the tropical gardens first,' Lady Fairchild said. 'And whilst I am there, perhaps the footmen will see to the hire of deckchairs, so that the younger three can build sandcastles and eat ices. Ruth can supervise those who wish to bathe. Olivia, I have purchased a swimsuit for you, to this end.'

'I will be going with Clarrie and Louis,' Howard said, all but stamping his foot. 'I have no desire to build stupid sandcastles. I'm not four, Mother.'

'And Olivia is hardly going to want to swim in the sea considering that's how her parents died,' Benji pointed out, and Lady Fairchild's hand flew to her mouth.

'Oh, my dear, how thoughtless of me. Why didn't you say something when I suggested the seaside?'

'Because I'm not afraid of the sea,' Olivia replied, aware all eyes in the carriage were on her. 'If I refuse to sail because of what happened to them, I will never leave these shores and then

finally walked back to the station at the end of the day. Even Lady Fairchild had a sparkle in her eyes and a giddy spring to her step as they boarded the train. Her face displayed momentary alarm when the sleepy head of her youngest son fell onto her lap, and she patted ineffectually at his small, blond head as his thumb found his mouth. Benji was simply too exhausted to contemplate the potential ribbing from his brothers.

Olivia was pleased to be homeward-bound and looked across at the slightly less stroppy Howard, but he still avoided her eye. She thought of his silly pranks and how he seemed to have taken against her and decided to confront him about the voice. It had to be him – it was the only logical explanation. His mother was giggling with Ernest, who was insisting Her Ladyship looked far too young to have grown-up sons, so Olivia leaned forward and hissed at her nemesis.

'Have you been larking about in the east tower at night, Sprinkles?' she asked, deliberately using the stupid nickname because he'd been a misery all day and she was fed up with his odd moods.

'Don't call me that,' he huffed.

'Just answer the question. Have you been pretending to be a ghost? Talking to me through the walls? It's all jolly clever and terribly amusing, but I'd really rather you didn't, unless you want to be locked in the privy again.'

He scowled. 'I know we're supposed to feel sorry for you, but voices through the walls? You're cuckoo.'

'Leave her alone,' mumbled Benji from his horizontal position, in an unusual display of sleepy confidence.

'Well, if it isn't you, then it must be a ghost.' All the talk of shrieking pits in the village and battles at the nearby castle had got her thinking. 'Do you know much about the history of Merriford Manor? Specifically, whether there were any murders or unresolved accidental deaths of a young man since the building of the towers?'

'The house was built three hundred years ago and there will have been numerous deaths. You'll have to be a bit more specific,' Howard said. 'Every ancestral home worth its salt has a few irate ghosts rattling around.'

'This ghost is called Seth.'

'That's Tanner's Christian name,' Benji volunteered, looking up from his mother's lap.

'He's not dead, you idiot,' Howard said dismissively, but Olivia was taken aback by this new piece of information.

Seth Tanner had been sleeping in the adjoining room when she'd ousted him back in July and he'd been none too happy about it. Now that she thought about it, the voice was similar to his in tone and timbre.

The question was whether the grumpy young undergardener was sufficiently annoyed to exact revenge by playing such an elaborate prank. And, as Olivia gazed at her own reflection in the window of the carriage, there was a small part of her that thought perhaps he was.

9

'I know you were unhappy to be moved from the tower,' Olivia said, as Tanner weeded the flower borders that led down to the boathouse the very next day. 'But I don't think it's very kind of you to pretend to be some mean-spirited ghost and scare me at night.'

It had been raining all morning and the air had the fresh vegetation and wet soil smell that was so wholesome in the summer. They were on a tree-lined sloping path to the lake, cast in shadow and not in view of the main house. In the silence that followed, she could still hear drops of the earlier rain falling from the canopies above and landing on the shiny, wide, dark-green leaves of the elephant ear below.

The irritated gardener looked up at her with a frown. 'I've no idea what you're talking about, Miss Davenport.'

'Coming up to my dressing room in the dark and getting cross with me through the wall.'

He sat back on his feet and the grooves of his frown deepened. 'Now look here...' His nostrils were flared and she could see a vein throbbing in his neck. He cast his eyes about to check there was no one else within earshot. 'I've been nowhere near the tower since I was asked to move from the room, and you can't go about accusing me of such things. It's wrong of you to suggest that I've been near your bedroom at night. This is serious.'

He got to his feet and she felt intimidated by his height.

'Look at me, miss.'

She tipped her head up to his, a curious, but not altogether unpleasant, feeling swirling inside her tummy. She'd been convinced he was the man she'd been talking to through the wall, but now, she wasn't so sure. He was extremely annoyed by the suggestion.

'I've already had Her Ladyship cross-questioning me about when you helped in the greenhouse. You may, or may not, be too young to understand the implications of her enquiries, and the unsavoury nature of what you are accusing me of, but I can assure you, *I could lose my job.*'

There was an even greater churning as she realised what he was saying. He was a nineteen-year-old lad, and she wasn't quite fourteen. If it was thought that he had been encouraging her, people would question his motives. In her defence, all her silly, escapist imaginings of herself with Tanner had been about what might happen in the future, when she was a young woman. Girls her age had silly fancies about older men all the time – that was simply part of growing up – but accusing him of coming near her bedroom at night was a whole other matter. She felt an uncomfortable prickle creep across her skin. Tanner was in danger of being thought of as someone interested in young girls in a most unnatural and disturbing way.

She swallowed hard and decided to explain herself. 'I've had a voice talking to me through the wall and I couldn't understand how the person was getting in. If it's not you then perhaps there *is* a ghost haunting the tower. Did you hear noises when you slept there?'

'No, I certainly did not,' he said with conviction. 'But my money would be on Master Howard. He knotted up my boot laces when I gave him an earful for trampling through the strawberry patch. Although, I can't prove it was him.'

'He promised me he wasn't behind it and, to be fair, the voice doesn't sound like his.'

'Then might I respectfully suggest one last option, Miss Davenport, and that's that you're imagining it all.' He really was quite cross now and tugged off his gardening gloves to toss them into the barrow of weeds. 'I've seen you chit-chatting to yourself on more than one occasion. We all know how much you like play-acting and dressing up.'

Olivia wriggled uncomfortably, realising that she'd probably been spotted by numerous members of staff as she played out her little dramas in the house and grounds. Were they all laughing about her in the servants' hall?

'Look,' he continued, 'my grandfather worked in these gardens years ago. He planted the orchard and every time I harvest the apples, I think of him, especially now that he's passed on. I'm lucky to have a position here, and it's only because he was so respected that I've been given the opportunity. Gardening is in my blood – and my grandfather's blood, sweat and tears are in the very soil of Merriford.'

Olivia already knew how important this job was to him.

'I realise that being in the employ of the Fairchilds, I've no right to demand anything from a member of the household, but I would ask you stop bothering me. I love my job, it's what keeps me going, and I'm not prepared for you to put that in jeopardy.'

She nodded her understanding and bit at her lip to prevent herself from crying. In that moment, she felt every inch the child he clearly thought she was. She'd been so sure the voice was his that she hadn't stopped to think through what such an accusation would mean for him. Embarrassed, Olivia excused herself and ran back up the path to the house.

* * *

Approaching the lawns, she was confronted by Howard. His arms were folded and his face was set in a frown.

'Please don't tell me you've been trying to befriend the staff,' he said snootily, as Tanner walked past them both, pushing the wheelbarrow, and disappeared into the distance. 'I know Benji still hangs about the kitchens talking to the scullery maids, but he's a child. There comes a point when you must realise that there's a them and an us. Some of us are born to lead and are given the education to do so. Others are born to follow. The undergardener went to the village school and I doubt he could even conjugate a Latin verb. Our worlds aren't meant to overlap.'

'Ernest isn't an us,' she pointed out. 'He went to the same school as Tanner. You don't seem to mind overlapping with him. In fact, you take great pains to impress him.'

Howard scowled, not liking her observation, which was obviously truer than she realised.

'He's more an us than a stupid servant. You have to admire a chap like Ernest, who has plans to better himself. That man—' and he nodded in Tanner's direction '—aspires to nothing.'

Cross with him for judging both her and Tanner, who despite his admonishing words, still made her heart skip about wildly every time she set eyes on him, Olivia told Howard an untruth.

'Tanner has this very afternoon informed me that he thinks of me as a friend. Not everyone sees class as a barrier to friendship – not that it's any of your business. In fact, he said I was always welcome to find him in the gardens and he complimented me on my dress. He added that I was extraordinarily pretty for my age and how it would not be long before I was as grown-up as him. So, stick that in your pipe, misery guts.'

Olivia strutted past her adolescent foe and headed back to the tower, leaving a red-faced Howard staring after her, and feeling her lies served him right for being such a total prig.

* * *

Over the next few days, however, Olivia made certain that any area of the grounds she frequented did not contain Tanner. She might have fabricated their conversation to annoy Howard, but she'd quickly realised it had not been wise to focus on a real person in her romantic fantasies, and she resolved to only dream of fictional characters from then on. The last thing she wanted was the gardener getting into trouble on her behalf.

A week later, and she was surprised she hadn't encountered him in the grounds at all, even accidentally. It was over breakfast in the nursery that she overheard Benji moaning that he missed his friend.

'Is he unwell?' she asked, trying to keep her tone light. That would explain his absence.

'He doesn't work here any more. Father got him a job with his cousin, Uncle Jonty,' Benji explained, as Howard looked up but immediately dropped his gaze when their eyes met.

Olivia felt her heart rate increase.

She tried to keep her voice light. 'Did he do something wrong?'

Howard poked at his eggs with the fork. 'Mother said the

new job was more suitable, but I'm not sure your infatuation helped.'

'You did spend quite a lot of time with him,' Benji pointed out, who was usually on her side but obviously felt slighted in this instance. 'Even after you told me you preferred to be alone.'

An uneasy feeling swirled around her chest. It wasn't just the gardening Tanner loved, but Merriford Manor itself, as he had a sentimental connection through his grandfather. What had she done?

'Is he still local?' she asked.

'Goodness me. Don't tell me you intend to track him down? You can't leave the poor fellow alone, can you? Such a ridiculous infatuation. You're just a child and he's staff.' Howard scrunched up his fist and rose from the table as her face flushed. It appeared he would never forgive her for locking him in the gamekeeper's privy and she'd made an enemy for life.

'You're so immature,' she shot back at him. 'He was an interesting person and was kind enough to teach me about plants. It was a simple friendship, which you wouldn't understand because you don't appear to have any. All your brothers bring chums to the house, except you. Is that it?' she asked, tipping her head to one side. 'Have I discovered the real reason for your annoying behaviour. You're lonely?'

'I say, that's a bit mean, Livvy.' Benji scrunched up his face and wrinkled his nose. 'Howard has friends at school. I'm certain of it.'

But Howard ignored her jibe and took a step closer to her, his freckled face wide with a smug grin. 'Well, he won't be loitering down by the lake for you to *accidentally* stumble across any more. Uncle Jonty's estate is in Cambridge.'

Olivia had heard enough. She pulled back her right arm and

10

The days remained unseasonably cool and everyone grumbled that they'd never known a summer like it. As the month drifted by, and the weather failed to improve, she noticed how restless and irritable the Fairchild boys were becoming, cooped up inside. Even Olivia's sunny nature and attempts to jolly everyone up were often met with scorn. Bashing out a stream of music hall tunes on the piano failed to raise a laugh from everyone except Benji – who thought that everything Olivia did was simply marvellous.

Clarence had a handful of chums over for a couple of Saturday to Mondays, and his mother got particularly excited about the possibility of a romance with the sister of an earl who was now part of his social circle. Louis returned from a military training camp that he was part of at university, and Benji filled two sketchbooks with drawings that he refused to show his brothers but allowed Olivia to look through. Every time she was asked her opinion of his artistic efforts, she remembered how Tanner's kind words had buoyed him up and endeavoured to do the same. Besides, he really was rather good for a nine-year-old.

Having decided that Seth was a ghost, she made use of Sir Hugo's extensive library and researched the possibility of the supernatural, but opinions remained divided. There was certainly an educated elite who believed in them but, equally, medical professionals who offered more rational explanations for the sightings, suggesting, for example, that they might be afterimages from overstimulated optical nerves. Whilst she was reluctant to abandon the refuge that was her tower, she felt decidedly less inclined to engage in her play-acting there, and uncomfortable that some ethereal spirit might even be watching her sleep. She still spent much of her time engaged in escapist daydreams and fantasy, but she did so in places Seth couldn't float out to observe her.

However, she continued to interact with the voice, always well after dark, and even though it was usually only a brief exchange. The conversation would begin with a weary sigh or groan from him, which alerted her to his presence, and she generally tried to jolly him out of his mood by offering uplifting platitudes.

'It's hard to be cheery when you've had a gutful of misery, betrayal and death,' he said.

It all sounded very 'gallant knight'. Had he led a rampaging army into battle? Perhaps some friend of his had become a spy for the enemy and been tortured on the rack. Maybe he'd witnessed his people fall victim to famine or plague.

'It can't be that bad,' she reasoned. 'Promise me that in the morning, you will stand in front of the looking glass and smile – the biggest one you can manage, even if you don't feel like it. You'll be surprised how it lifts your mood.' Could ghosts look in the mirror? she wondered. He seemed to think not.

'I'm not taking advice on how to live my life from someone who is dead,' he huffed.

It was the last straw for Olivia, who decided if he was so determined that *she* was the ghost, then she would play the part to the fullest. She jumped from the bed and swept up a wilting crown of gypsophila that she'd made in the gardens earlier that day, and grabbed the thin coverlet from her bed, placing it about her shoulders like a robe. Returning to the wall, she nestled close to the bricks and began a slow, mournful wail.

'You do not understand my woes, for I am a poor princess beyond help. My lover has treated me ill and caused me to jump to my death from this very tower in my misery.'

She put her ear to the wall, wondering if he was still lingering. She had no idea what spirits got up to when they weren't haunting exhausted thirteen-year-old girls. Perhaps he'd drifted to another part of the house and was terrorising the housemaids.

But after a beat, he commented, 'Your lover?' His tone was incredulous. 'You sound about ten.'

Something occurred to her for the first time. 'Can't you see me?' Surely, he was an ethereal mist able to pass through physical barriers such as walls, and could easily determine that she was not the age she was pretending to be.

He sighed. 'No, but I can damn well hear you, and that's more than enough.' He paused. 'Can you see me?'

'No, you're the other side of the wall.'

'I would say float through and let's have this thing out face to face, but I'm currently in nothing but a nightshirt and not in a fit state to receive anyone – certainly not royalty.' His tone was distinctly acerbic. 'And most definitely not a child.'

'I'm *not* a child.' She crossed her arms even though the action was apparently not visible to him. 'I am a princess who—'

'Yes, yes, tossed herself off the tower after putting on her parts.' She felt rather peeved that he was implying she'd had an unwarranted tantrum after such a dramatic betrayal. 'And yet, I remain unconvinced that you are old enough to have had a lover and am not rightly sure royals ever lived at Merriford. Was there even a house here in medieval times?'

'Absolutely. There was a Norman castle but it was demolished, and I was betrothed to the fair Lord... erm, Merriford, but he jilted me at the altar. In my misery, I climbed the tower, erm, which happened to be in the same place as this tower, and plunged to my death.' It was a complete fabrication but he didn't correct her. Perhaps he didn't know.

'Right,' he scoffed at her fanciful tale. 'Either you really are a crazy, lovelorn ghost, or my mind is in more of a muddle than I thought, and I think I prefer the first option. So, Princess Cordelia, if you've quite finished moaning about your love life – or rather lack of it – I'd appreciate you drifting off and wailing about it to someone else.'

'Fine by me.'

'Great.'

'Great.'

'And you definitely can't see me through the wall?' His voice took on a slightly anxious tone.

'I'll tell you what,' she said, 'you stay your side and I'll stay mine.' It was obvious neither of them wanted visitors, nebulous or otherwise.

'Agreed. Now, if you don't mind, I need sleep. Goodnight, ghostly girl.' He still sounded irritated but she knew that his humorous form of address proved that he was not as cross as he was making out.

11

As September prepared to nudge August to the side, Olivia acknowledged that Merriford Manor, despite its size, was beginning to feel more like home. Sir Hugo and his wife had done their best to accommodate her whims, and Benji was fast becoming the little brother she'd never had. There were places about the house and grounds that were now dear to her; climbing the grandfather oaks by the lake reminded her that she could conquer anything, and she was particularly fond of the library, appreciating that knowledge was power. How could you not feel the rush of excitement stepping into a room that could take you on a thousand adventures, stir up all manner of emotions, from sadness to joy, and give explanations on the working of everything, from the human body to the creation of a rainbow?

But now that she knew Seth couldn't float through the wall to watch her, it was the tower, despite the resident phantom, or maybe in some way that she hadn't fully appreciated, because of him, that she felt safest and she felt empowered. It was ridiculous really; a building couldn't care for you, and yet every time she stepped inside, she felt connected to something greater, something beyond its hexagonal walls.

After realising that Benji had been overlooked by his brothers for much of the summer, Olivia arranged for the pair of them to have a midnight feast in the boathouse. His exclusion wasn't out of spite, but it was easy for an older lad, like Ernest, to pop by and make up the four needed for so many of their sports. They didn't want a child for their tennis doubles, and they certainly didn't want a girl.

Benji warned her that Clarence often had late-night parties out there but, as he was in London with Sir Hugo for the week, they knew it would be theirs that night. They both enjoyed the furtive stealing of food items over the course of the day, and ensuring they had a working lantern, a warm blanket and the necessary crockery. She tucked them all behind one of the long-abandoned wooden canoes inside the building and had been quite surprised to find a pair of lady's undergarments wedged between the boat and the wall. They probably belonged to some young woman Clarence had entertained, and she hoped their removal had been connected to swimming and not any other activity. They were covered in cobwebs so she decided to dispose of them, as they'd clearly been long forgotten. The abandoned item was foremost in her mind later that night, however, when she told spooky stories by the flickering light. The boathouse, she whispered, was haunted by the ghost of a woman who had murdered her parents and then come to the lake, taken off all her clothes, and thrown herself in the water. A petrified Benji lapped up every word, as well as every crumb of their contraband cake, and she wondered if her tale had been rather too graphic for an anxious boy of nine, who still couldn't bring himself to cycle past the shrieking pits.

The two younger boys were set to return to school later that week when Howard sought her out. His conscience was clearly bothering him – that and the fact she'd subsequently called him Sprinkles several times in front of other people.

'Look here, I wanted to clear the air before I leave. I've not been the kindest to you since you came into our lives, but I admire you, really I do. You're the pluckiest girl I know and I'd like us to be friends.' He stuck out his hand in a gesture of reconciliation.

'Apology accepted,' she said, shaking it, and hoping this really was the end of his sulky behaviour.

'Benji absolutely worships you, even though I know he's sore that you get to remain here whilst we're all shipped off to school. Perhaps the truth is my brothers and I are slightly jealous of that.'

'Perhaps *I'm* slightly jealous that you get the very best education,' she countered.

Howard grinned. 'If you'd been born a boy, you'd have really been something,' he said, and then realised the implications of his words. 'Not that you *aren't* something, but you know what I mean. We all think the same; even Clarence said you've given Mother a lift. She hates the start of term, when her boys all leave home, and now she has you to keep her company.'

It felt good that the Fairchild boys had accepted her. She knew they'd all viewed her as somewhat of an oddity at the start of the summer, running around wearing old curtains as cloaks and haring down hills shouting, 'Charge!', but she would miss them and looked forward to their return in December. The first Christmas without her parents would be a difficult anniversary, but she knew that the Fairchilds wholeheartedly embraced the season, and the energy of their household and lavish scale of their celebrations would be a distraction.

The boys finally departed, after Howard had made her swear

she would never, ever, call him Sprinkles again, and she looked forward to being part of the harvest celebrations in the village over the coming days. The relentless August rains, however, meant it would be a poor one that year, but Olivia wouldn't allow the temperamental British climate to dampen her spirits, even when – during a particularly violent thunderstorm – an enormous crack of thunder woke her up in the middle of the night.

'Bloody hell!' The shout from behind the wall was almost as much of a shock as the bellowing rumble that had disturbed her sleep, although she was strangely pleased that the voice had returned, as she'd not heard from him for a while.

'Thunder can't hurt you,' she teased. *Especially as you don't technically exist,* she thought to herself.

'Oh, it's the tragic princess.' He sounded irritable. 'I'd hoped to be rid of you.'

So, he'd been listening out for her as much as she'd been listening out for him, *and* he'd remembered her fanciful tale.

There was a bright flash of lightning that illuminated the room and barely a beat before another thunderous roar. The storm was almost directly overhead. Powerful lashes of rain were beating against the windowpanes, like handfuls of gravel being thrown at the glass. She pulled the counterpane further up her body, even though it wasn't especially cold. It wasn't that she felt in imminent danger from the elements but instead was reminded that Mother Nature was a force to be reckoned with.

'I'm afraid you can't get rid of me that easily. I've been haunting Merriford Manor for centuries – roaming the grounds, looking for the duplicitous blackguard who betrayed me.'

She slipped back into her role as Cordelia, thinking that 'blackguard' was a good word – one she'd picked up from her father's collection of sensationalist penny dreadfuls, and she hoped it made her sound more historical.

'Hate to break it to you, Princess Whatever-It-Was, but your young man is long dead, and I strongly suggest that if you wish to be reunited with him, you ascend. Isn't there a bright light you can follow? A heav'nly host calling you? Walk to the light,' he urged.

At that moment, her whole room lit up with another dramatic white flash. The accompanying rumble was barely a second behind.

'Maybe not *that* light,' he said, proving that they were experiencing the same storm.

'You're funny,' she said. 'Annoying but funny.'

His comments reminded her, however, that for him to be haunting the tower, he had also met his death there, and something was preventing him from moving on. It might be prudent to discover what it was.

'Do you have anything in your life that is unresolved?' she asked. 'Some loss that you haven't properly come to terms with?'

His tone changed in an instant and it was obvious that he was no longer amused.

'You tossed yourself off the tower purely 'cause some lord decided he didn't want you. Some of us confront the unpleasant things that life throws at us and don't take the easy way out,' he said, bitterness lacing his voice. 'We plough on, even though our hearts are heavy, because others rely on us.'

She was upset by his presumption but could hardly defend herself as she'd led him to believe that she was a ghostly jilted bride. A part of her wanted to say she did understand, and to share the brutal circumstances of her parents' deaths, especially as he then said something that struck a chord with her.

'I don't think grief is properly understood by those who

haven't witnessed, or been affected by, a truly harrowing death. Dying's a part of life, granted, but people expect you to be over it after a given amount of time. I've tried, but it's still there, like a piece of nettle root, festering under the surface and waiting to poke its head through the soil and cause problems again, just when I thought I'd dug it all out.' His sigh floated through the wall. 'Meanwhile, my poor, traumatised mind conjures you up, because I'm not sure that I believe in ghosts – proof, if I needed it, that I haven't recovered from the horrors of it all.'

The horrors of what? she wondered, as they both lapsed into silence.

The rain continued to lash against the windowpanes and there was a further rumble of thunder.

'If this dreadful weather continues, I'll be shut up in this tower for the whole of tomorrow and will have to amuse myself with jigsaw puzzles and books,' she grumbled.

'Ghosts can't do jigsaws,' he pointed out. 'You can't lift up the pieces.'

'I can imagine I'm doing one,' she countered, cross that she'd momentarily forgotten that she was supposed to be a spirit. 'In fact, my imagination is my salvation. I often escape into a world of my own making, where good triumphs over evil and I can achieve all the things I aspire to.'

'What's the point of such nonsense? You have to face your problems eventually.' Which was pretty much what Tanner had said to her the day Benji had first introduced them.

'I create joy in my daydreams *because* I've experienced sorrow in my life.' As she said those words, she realised how true they were. Her fantasies had never been more important, carried more weight, than after she'd been orphaned.

Deciding to give a little of herself away, she told him part of the truth.

'I lost both my parents when I was young. They were drowned at sea and it hit me very hard.'

'Ah, but you were a princess. You led a sheltered life, cushioned by money and cosseted by all around you. You never had to toil for a living, work all the hours God sends for someone else, knowing your place in life and never aspiring to things you couldn't have.'

He was teasing her, but perhaps she had been a princess, in a way. As an only child, she'd been her parents' sole focus. Whilst the Davenports had not possessed the immense wealth of the Fairchilds, she had wanted for nothing. And by being taken in by Sir Hugo, this privileged existence had continued.

'That's nonsense and unbearably defeatist. Why can't you aspire? Why can't the boot boy become the butler? It happens. You can make opportunities for yourself, have dreams. Aladdin started off as a thief and ended up a king. Dick Whittington was a poor orphan who became the mayor of London.'

'They're fiction. And, no offence, but it don't sound to me like you started at the bottom of the heap.'

'That doesn't make my grief any less raw.'

'No,' he conceded through the wall.

'To lose any parent is heartbreaking. To lose them both, and without warning, was utterly devastating. And yet, I was able to cope with my sadness by embracing the truths they had taught me: life is short and you must always live it to the fullest.' She wriggled about in the bed to get more comfortable. 'How would they feel if I gave up and spent the remainder of my days feeling miserable and using it as an excuse for doing nothing? Why should I hide myself from the sunshine? She will still heat the soil and bring light to a dark world, whether I stay locked up inside or allow myself to bathe in her warm rays. The daisies on the lawn will still follow her journey from east to west, and open their glad faces when she shines. It didn't take me long to realise that if I could rally... if I could make something of myself... if I could be outside and smile at the flowers...' Her voice cracked. She might not be explaining this very well, but her emotions were true.

There was a silence.

'Can't say I recall any kings of England drowning,' he said, before his tone became more earnest. 'But your words are sage, indeed, for one so young. Well, young when you died. I'm guessing you're hundreds of years old by now.'

Olivia was regretting her fanciful tale because in that moment, she wanted to be honest with her new friend, so she compromised.

'Maybe I'm not technically a princess. I have what my mother always described as a melodramatic imagination, but don't you see?' She shuffled up onto her elbows, keen to get the importance of her point over. 'I found a way to cope, and it was by escaping into my dreams.'

'And then your lover dropped you like a hot potato, and you hurled yourself from a tower in your despair?'

Ah, she'd forgotten about that.

'A stupid, impulsive decision that I bitterly regret,' she said, embracing her pretence to be Cordelia. 'It was foolish to step from the tower. Think of the travels I could have undertaken and the experiences I could have had. I would so have liked to write books about it all. His betrayal cut me deeply, but I should not have let it overwhelm me. I am but a broken vase – and vases can easily be mended and still hold beautiful flowers.'

He laughed out loud. 'You're one crazy, mixed-up little thing, but I rather like chatting to you. It doesn't matter who or what you are: the ghost of a princess or otherwise. I don't need to know the details of your life, any more than I wish to share mine, so let's make a pact? We can provide each other with a bit of night-time cheer without prying into each other's lives. Deal?'

'Deal,' she agreed.

Not talking about her heartache, and embracing the frivolous role of Cordelia, rather suited her. She felt the same as him. Did it ultimately matter where the voice came from, when it was proving such an excellent distraction? Even if she'd fabricated him, he was serving a purpose and helping with her healing, much like the imaginary friend of her childhood. Sophie had bridged a gap between the security of home and the harsh realities of starting school, and when the young Olivia had grown in confidence, Sophie had faded away.

Seth, she now realised, was here to help her navigate her unimaginable grief and ease the turmoil of being uprooted from everything she knew. She had wrongly believed herself on top of everything, that her cheery spirit and vivid imagination would help her weather the storm, but perhaps her head knew better. This disembodied voice was her very own creation, manufactured to help her step into this new phase of her life.

He was here to help and then he, too, would simply disappear.

12

The next few months passed by uneventfully. Christmas was bearable, helped by the feeling that Olivia was part of a family once more, with Her Ladyship encouraging the boys to think of her as a sister. She revelled in the endearing chaos of the Fairchild household, which took her mind off things, and then found peace in the quieter moments with her night-time companion, even though she didn't know his personal circumstances – or, rather, her mind had not fabricated any. It was refreshing spending time with someone who didn't view her as the poor *Titanic* orphan, and instead thought of her as the plucky, if slightly unhinged, spirit of a medieval princess.

She noticed that Seth usually appeared very late into the night, long after she had retired, and maybe this was no coincidence. Was it possible her brain was, by that point, dancing between consciousness and her dreamworld, making her more open to an imaginary friend? Although, why her head had chosen to give him such a grumpy persona, she wasn't sure. Maybe she *had* unwittingly been influenced by Tanner, or maybe it made more sense for him to be crotchety if he was to be useful in relating to her grief. Whatever the truth of it, she continued to delight in teasing the voice whose spectacles were dark, because hers were tinted pink.

The comforting delusion of such a friend continued in the background of Olivia's life throughout the following year. Seth's prickly nature started to soften, which she suspected was part of her healing process, and things generally settled down for her.

At the manor, Clarence began stepping out with a lovely girl who was distantly related to the royal family. It was serious enough for Lady Fairchild to look out a diamond ring of her mother's and pass it over in the hopes that an engagement was imminent. Every school holiday, when the younger boys returned, Howard continued to annoy everyone *but* her, perhaps realising he'd met his match, perhaps out of sympathy. He tried the patience of his brothers with his endless pranks: packets of flour on the tops of doors, frogs in beds and desk drawers, and blacking on the eyepieces of Clarence's field glasses – although he received a sound thrashing when that particular jape was discovered.

She still escaped to her dreamworlds but chose not to race around the estate enacting them, and was less frequently found climbing trees and imagining them to be the towering ramparts of besieged castles. Instead, she was more often seen clutching a small, leather journal and frantically scribbling down the weird and wonderful scenarios in her head. These uninvited thoughts were just as dramatic, but she was simply choosing another way to express them, and her favourite place to do so was next to the sweet-smelling honeysuckle in the Japanese gardens. Thankfully, the weather that summer proved to be a vast improvement on her first year at the manor.

Outside of Merriford Lode, however, the nation was undergoing tumultuous times. The suffragettes ramped up their action in their fight for the vote, and the country was shaken by Emily Davison's heartbreaking sacrifice at the Epsom Derby. Olivia found common ground with Lady Fairchild over their sympathy for the brave women force-fed and ill-treated in their fight to give the gentler sex a voice. Meanwhile, Sir Hugo became increasingly concerned with the ongoing strikes, demonstrations and labour disputes that were affecting his various business interests. The alarming state of unrest in the country was one of his favourite grumbles, along with the thorny issue of home rule and Asquith's inadequacies as prime minister.

By 1914, everyone was aware of the growing disquiet abroad. Her own father, before his death, had written about the threat of an imperialist Germany in his espionage thriller, *The Mystery of the Broken Violin*, foreseeing the escalating tensions in Europe. His novel had centred around the battle to have the most powerful navy in the world, and she'd had to look the word 'militarism' up in a dictionary. Two years later and it no longer seemed like fiction.

By that July, the possibility of war was very real, although Olivia was more concerned with the upcoming church fete, and what she might wear to attract the attention of the butcher's son – a striking lad, who was the same age as her. She'd volunteered to run the coconut shy, hoping that, as a keen cricketer, the boy concerned would be tempted to test out his impressive overarm bowling on her stand. The assassination of some archduke she'd never heard of was nothing in comparison to her frustrations that her curly hair would never stay neatly pinned up and she always seemed to have grass stains on her skirts. It was only when there was a very real possibility of people she knew and cared for being involved that she began to appreciate the seriousness of the situation.

'The kaiser has been coming over here, shooting at Sandringham, competing at Cowes and pretending to be a great friend of this land,' Sir Hugo announced, tossing a newspaper across the breakfast table, with its headline announcing that Austria–Hungary had now declared war on Serbia. 'Whilst all the time he's been building up his armies and creating a battle fleet. Mark my words, it's only a matter of days before all of Europe is sucked into this – which is rather what I fear he had planned for all along.'

Lady Fairchild looked most alarmed. 'And my boys?' she whispered.

'When the time comes, they'll have to do their bit and do our nation proud. And then that bellicose fool will see who he's messing with.'

The thought that Clarence or Louis, or any of the young men she knew in the village, could be called upon to fight was not something Olivia had considered, and it preyed on her mind over the following days.

She had shared nothing of her real life with the voice through the wall since their pact and had maintained the charade of the jilted Cordelia since she'd first heard Seth two years previously. In fact, she'd created quite a detailed life for the ghostly princess: anecdotes of hunting and gaming, and fanciful tales of banquets and balls – all the things she imagined a medieval princess might have spent her days doing. Seth came to her intermittently and their conversations remained largely one-sided, as she only got grunts in reply from him or, if she was lucky, a blunt observation about the weather.

But one night, all this changed. The exceptional temperatures sweeping across the land were making everyone irritable – even Olivia. She'd been tossing and turning for hours when she heard her imaginary friend lump down on the non-existent bed with a belch, before bursting into a decidedly off-key version of a song about the 'good old summertime'. It wasn't a tune she'd ever heard and marvelled at how her brain had conjured up such complicated lyrics.

'Have you been drinking?' she moaned through the wall. 'Because perhaps you'd like to keep the noise down for those of us who are trying to sleep.' This had been *his* request when they'd first encountered one another, after all.

'Oh, hello there, Cordelia. Forgot about you.' There was a further squeak of bedsprings and she heard an empty bottle fall to the floor as he groaned. 'Sometimes, I think having a resident ghost is worse than being married. I get all the nagging but none of the benefits.'

Olivia blushed, her already pink cheeks getting even hotter. She was old enough to understand his meaning.

'As you are merely a figment of my imagination, it's lucky that marriage is not something you have to worry about,' she said. 'Although I'm still bemused as to why I didn't choose to resurrect my parents, instead of creating you. And if you're not a product of my grieving mind but are, in fact, a genuine spirit, then I'm equally frustrated that I'm being haunted by you, instead of being contacted by them.'

'And yet we both know that *you're* the ghost, Cordelia.'

But Olivia was done with the silly charade. There were bigger things going on in the world and the time for childish games was over. Sir Hugo was convinced Britain would enter the war any day now.

'I'm as real as the wall between us and you know it. I've only been pretending to be a stupid ghost because you kept insisting that I was one, and yet everyone at Merriford Manor knows my tragic circumstances because the sinking of the *Titanic* and deaths of my parents will follow me around for the remainder of my life. I'm grateful that you've helped me to navigate that, but it's time for you to leave me now.'

'The *Titanic*, as in the Harland and Wolff ship that made the news a couple of years ago?' Seth sounded confused.

'Yes, the one that hit an iceberg and sank to the bottom of the North Atlantic Ocean, with the loss of fifteen hundred lives, including both my parents.'

'What are you talking about? The *Titanic* didn't sink. It came darn close, granted, and about two hundred people *did* die – mainly crew in the cargo holds and boiler rooms – but it limped to Halifax and another ship took all the passengers to New York City.' He laughed to himself. 'Can you imagine the public uproar if the boat had actually sunk?'

'I don't need to imagine it because it happened!' She was angry now and heard her own voice crack as she ploughed on. 'Why would you pretend otherwise? What a cruel and unkind thing to do.'

It was Seth's turn to get cross. 'I may be many things, missy, but I'm not a liar. I have seen with my own eyes people who survived the accident. That ship did *not* sink.'

Olivia relayed the facts she knew so well, almost daring him to challenge her detailed knowledge of events.

'And I can assure you that it did. Frederick Fleet was up in the crow's nest and saw the iceberg at thirty-nine minutes past eleven, whereupon he immediately telephoned the bridge. First Officer Murdoch sent a telegraph to the engine room and ordered the engines to be reversed, and the ship's wheel was turned hard to starboard. The iceberg ripped through several of the watertight compartments, causing irreparable damage, as far too many were breached for the ship to stay afloat. It took nearly three hours to sink and there weren't enough lifeboats for everyone on board, so only seven hundred and five people survived. It was a catastrophic maritime disaster on an unprecedented scale.'

There was a pause before he responded. 'I'm pretty sure only two of them watertight compartments were breached and the front of the ship was crushed up, like a telescope. People were slammed into walls, thrown from their beds and anything that weren't bolted down was shunted towards the front. Nearly a hundred and fifty crew died, mainly firemen, trimmers and greasers sleeping in the ship's bow, and about sixty passengers.'

Olivia worked through the logic of his claim. Her own research over the years had suggested that there could so easily have been a scenario when her parents had survived. The whole tragedy was a catalogue of human errors, where so many tiny details were overlooked and every bad decision had conspired against them. This *could* have been the case, granted, but it unequivocally wasn't.

'No!' Olivia shouted. 'The lookouts saw the iceberg and the ship turned at the very last minute.' This was too cruel.

Seth remained calm. 'Well, it dint because the men in the crow's nest dint spot it in time. They had no glasses; I can't remember why – locked in some cupboard, I think – and it was pitch-black. One of them said there was this queer moment, when a shiver of something rippled through him. The newspapers loved that little detail and the headline was something like, "Lookout Senses Disaster Moments Before Impact".'

'I wish it were the case.' She took a deep breath. 'But it wasn't.'

There was a moment of silence and then he hiccoughed. 'Damn the drink. It's really messed with my mind, and I've got too much going on right now to deal with a quarrelsome ghost – real or imagined... I'm sleeping this off in the boathouse.'

'Fine,' she said. 'You do that. And don't bother coming back.

I thought you were here to help me but you're making every-thing worse. How dare you open this all up again. How dare you say such unkind things.'

There was a squeak of the bed and the sound of footsteps retreating into the distance, as Olivia rolled onto her back and stared up at the ceiling, totally bewildered by the conversation she'd just had with the voice beyond the wall.

She'd been so certain he was either something her mind had conjured up or a spirit that had failed to move on to the afterlife.

But now she was not so sure.

13

The following morning and Olivia was just as confused. There was no way she could have created such a convincing alternative scenario by herself. Or was there the tiniest possibility that the voice was telling the truth? It was only natural that she would want to believe that her parents hadn't perished in the icy North Atlantic Ocean but that would mean that Seth was a real person – and what? There was another version of this world somewhere in the universe, much like the world that Alice had stepped into through the looking glass in Lewis Carroll's children's fantasy? Was the wall somehow a bridge between them? For two years, she'd been convinced he was in her head, but could he genuinely have been the other side of the wall all this time? And then she chided herself for thinking such poppycock.

There was, she decided, only one way to put this nonsense to bed, and the following day, she persuaded Benji to spend the night in the tower with her, telling Ruth they were going to stay up all night sharing spooky stories – which was laughingly close to the truth.

'At least when I hear voices tonight, it will be a proper

conversation between you and Master Benji, rather than you talking to yourself,' the woman said, as she made up a bed on the floor for the youngest Fairchild boy. 'You woke me up last night with your shouting.'

Ruth was a sound sleeper and was rarely disturbed by Olivia's conversations with Seth, so she hastily reassured the servant that the night-time chatter had just been her play-acting.

Later that evening, she and Benji climbed the spiral staircase together, carrying mugs of cocoa and a plate of Cook's coconut biscuits.

'Do you remember when I wondered if the tower was haunted, back when I first moved here?' she asked him.

'When you thought Howard was pretending to be a ghost and started asking if anyone called Seth had ever died in the tower?'

She nodded. 'I still have that same voice talk to me from time to time.'

Not quite the wide-eyed, gullible boy of two years ago, Benji, however, still believed in spirits. She knew this because he always avoided the shrieking pits whenever possible, and had jumped at the chance to spend a night reading ghost stories – bringing his favourite book of spooky tales with him.

'And you want me to see the spirit too?'

'I've never seen him,' she admitted. 'I hear him. Through the wall. But yes, I think you're the only person who will take me seriously.'

Benji smiled, puffed up that he was the one trusted to share this big secret with Olivia.

'A real-life dead person. How thrilling!' He clutched his book closer to his chest.

But the pair were to be disappointed. No Seth spoke to them through the wall, even though Olivia remained awake until the early hours, determined to share the secret that she'd kept to herself for so long. At one point, she'd even banged on the bricks with her fist, calling for him to answer her. But there was no response.

Benji was bitterly disappointed.

'Honestly, Livvy, you really had me going there for a while, but you're as bad as Howard with his silly jokes,' he complained the next morning.

She could only conclude the voice had been in her head, after all.

* * *

A couple of days later and the situation in Europe was now on a knife-edge. Sir Hugo even cancelled one of his regular jaunts to Haven-on-Sea, such was his desire to remain near a telephone. Lady Fairchild was becoming increasingly anxious, wanting all her boys home during these uncertain times, and was relieved when Howard finally arrived back at the manor to complete the set.

Olivia hadn't seen the third-born Fairchild son since Christmas, as he hadn't come home at all that Easter, and had instead spent the holiday with a school chum who had a house in the south of France. He was also nearly a week later than Benji returning to Merriford Lode that summer because he'd been on a camp with the school's Officer Training Corps – or OTC. He stepped from the motor car that sunny Saturday and visibly froze as she skipped across the driveway to greet him. She, in turn, was shocked to find he'd grown another two inches and now towered over her.

'Gosh, Livvy,' he said, unable to hide the frown marching across his face. 'You've rather changed since I saw you last.' She wasn't sure if this was a compliment or a criticism. She may not have grown upwards, like him, but she would be sixteen in the autumn and knew her figure was changing; her hips were wider and her bust was filling out – even if her wild, fair, curly hair was just as untameable. Olivia knew she was on the cusp of womanhood and, even though she wasn't as obsessed by clothes as his mother, she certainly wasn't averse to wearing pretty dresses, especially when the butcher's son was around.

'So have you.' The pair studied each other in silence but neither could think of a sensible thing to say and eventually, Benji appeared and dragged Howard inside to see the watercolour of the boathouse he'd been working on that morning. They were all hurtling towards adulthood and Olivia had the strong sense that things would never be the same again. Even Benji was finding his own way. That evening, Sir Hugo begrudgingly admitted that the boy had talent, indulging his talk of one day studying art somewhere, like The Slade. Clarence's face was thunderous – Cambridge had been decided for him – but he said nothing.

Benji and Olivia, who had always enjoyed bicycling around the lush landscape of Merriford Lode together, crept out early one morning, before the family had risen, to escape into the endless fields ripe with grains, under the cloudless, blue skies. Nature, she generally found, nicely offset her worries – be they real or imagined.

Meadow browns and orange tips danced from flower to flower and the dusty smell of baked earth filled the air. The day promised to be pleasant, and she sat at the base of a huge sycamore, leaning back on the scaly trunk, as Benji peered through his spectacles and sketched the picturesque valley below. A colourful tapestry of emeralds, golds and umbers began to emerge as the sun rose over the gentle contours of the Norfolk skyline.

Olivia wrestled with all that had happened in the tower that past week. She hadn't heard Seth's voice since the night of their *Titanic* quarrel and she had to wonder if she'd simply come up with the fanciful notion of a looking-glass world, where her parents were alive, to counter all the bad things that were going on in the newspapers.

Their companionable silence lasted a couple of hours. Olivia closed her eyes and let her mind play out the adventures she might have abroad, should she be brave enough to travel when she was of age, until she heard the thunder of racing feet and felt the cool of a shadow fall across her face.

'Benji, Livvy, you're not going to believe this.'

Howard stood before them both, gasping for breath, his hands on his knees and his freckled cheeks red from the exertion of running.

'You two must have been up with the larks. No one knew where you were, but the most dreadful thing has happened: we've declared war on Germany!'

She gave him a disbelieving look. He had form when it came to telling tall tales to get a rise out of others.

'I wouldn't joke about something like this, Livvy.' He looked disappointed that she doubted him.

'No,' she acknowledged.

'It happened last night but is all over the newspapers this morning. It's an absolute shocker but Father is trying to convince Mother not to panic, and that it will all be over by Christmas. Louis is in the OTC and of fighting age, and Clarence used to be when he was at Cambridge, so chances are, if they're keen, they can get out there pretty darn quickly.'

'I can't bear to think of them caught up in this, even if it's a short-lived skirmish,' she said.

Her heart was beating wildly and she studied Howard's face, raising her hand to shield the sun from her eyes. He was only a few weeks off turning seventeen and all but a man. The sunlight caught the auburn hairs across his top lip and she could see now how his face had changed since he'd been away – his jaw was more prominent, his cheekbones more defined, and his face had lost the roundness of youth. How had this happened so quickly?

'Does that mean, one day, I might get to fight the Hun?' Benji said, closing his sketchpad and sliding his pad and pencils into his satchel.

'Unlikely.' Howard put out his hand, offering to help Olivia to her feet. 'Father says we won't need many men to wrap this whole thing up. We're the most powerful empire in the world, and we all know that Britannia rules the waves. The good old British Army will do its job in no time and put the jumped-up kaiser back in his place.'

'If it turns out to be another Hundred Years War, like when we tried to take the French throne, then we'll all have to fight eventually,' Benji said. 'Although, technically, that one lasted a hundred and sixteen years.' He gave an earnest nod as he delivered this fact. It wasn't difficult to guess what he'd been doing in his history lessons.

But as Benji's words filtered into Olivia's mind, she considered the possibility, however remote, that this conflict might last longer than anyone anticipated. As she was pulled upright, she locked eyes with Howard and recognised he was as uneasy as she was. He didn't immediately let her hand drop, and she felt something that she couldn't quite pin down pass between them. The slightest whisper of doubt floated in the air and her stomach gave a bilious flip.

PART II

THE GREAT WAR

14

The shock news that the country was at war slowly began to sink in as the newspapers cautioned against the stockpiling of food, young men examined their consciences with regard to doing their duty, and everyone was alert for spies. For the most part, life went on as it had always done, but Norfolk had concerns not felt by those who lived in the west of the country. Would the Germans attack their vulnerable coastline and sweep down to London? Could the war be coming to them? It heightened Lady Fairchild's anxiety but Sir Hugo insisted that the British Navy would defend our shores and that her panic was unnecessary.

However, Clarence's decision to be part of the great commissions rush at the start of the conflict soon sent his mother spiralling into another emotional whirlwind. Not many days after war was announced, Lord Horatio Kitchener – the new secretary of state for war – made a direct appeal for men who were, or who had been, cadets in the University Training Corps to take temporary commissions in the regular army. The oldest Fairchild son was one of the first to attest.

Olivia hadn't been in the room when he'd told his parents and, according to Louis – who was excellent at recounting precise conversations, even though the emotions involved clearly bemused him – Lady Fairchild had become quite hysterical. But Clarence was a man of twenty-three and there was nothing she could do about it. There was a shortage of officers, he told his mother, and his public school education had given him the qualities needed to fight this war: courage, leadership and a love for his country. He could not, in all conscience, stand by when he was needed.

'It will be a long time before I see any action,' he'd reassured her. 'I might be ahead of the regular Tom, Dick and Harry signing up, but I need to undergo more training and secure a commission before I'm deployed to the front. In all likelihood, the whole shebang will be over before I even make it out to France.'

'Lucky fellow, then you'll get a season's shooting without paying for a gun licence,' Sir Hugo had joked, but his wife had not found his comment amusing, giving him the most withering stare.

It wasn't long before Kitchener's face stared out from every newspaper, shop window and advertising hoarding, shaming any young man who didn't answer the call to defend those they loved. Sir Hugo bemoaned the appeal for big houses to release their male fighting-aged servants, as hundreds of thousands of men enlisted in the first couple of months, spurred on by a deep sense of duty. The numbers of the rank and file swelled nicely, but soon those trying to secure a commission far exceeded the posts available. The public schools had almost been too successful in their training of young men in both soldiering and sacrifice.

Whilst Clarence waited for his commission to come through,

Olivia spent more time with the Fairchild boys than she had in months. Perhaps it was the advent of war, perhaps a tacit understanding that they were growing up and things would inevitably change.

Lady Fairchild suggested the youngsters have a picnic by the lake and make the most of the lovely weather. Clarence immediately took control and duly ordered Louis to locate a table and some blankets, and Benji to beg food from Cook. It was all done in the same strident manner that an officer might command his men, and Olivia suspected he would be perfectly suited to military life, even though, as the eldest son, it had never been part of his plan.

Benji scurried off and managed to secure, amongst other things, egg sandwiches, chunks of cold venison pie and an assortment of sweet treats from the kitchens, and they all set off to the shady spot under the willows by the boathouse. Olivia had just royally thrashed Howard at croquet but had the uncomfortable feeling that he'd let her win, and that almost made her more cross than if she'd lost. He followed her to the blanket and placed himself behind her, out of her line of vision, but almost close enough to be touching.

Their truce of two years ago had held but she couldn't help but feel a cooling of relations between them, even if she couldn't pinpoint why. Whereas Benji had quickly assumed the role of adoring younger brother when she'd arrived at Merriford, her relationship with Howard had always been more complicated. Sometimes, he sought her out for tennis or chess, and occasionally sat quietly in the same room as her when she was reading, but contributed little to any conversation when she was around, and actively avoided her eye. If she'd done something to offend him, she wished he'd just come out and say it.

As the food was shared between the group, and everyone

revelled in the heat of such a beautiful day, the lads spoke of war and glory. It was all they ever talked of now. The conflict had even overtaken observations regarding the weather as the preferred conversational opening amongst the population at large. Foolhardy heroics and making the ultimate sacrifice were all very well, but Olivia knew that such acts were not much good to a dead man, nor indeed the family of one.

'All my friends have volunteered,' Clarence said, tossing a grape into the air and catching it in his mouth. He was leaning back nonchalantly on one arm in the manner of someone who knew he was commanding the conversation.

'Old Teddy Johnson's younger brother was camping with the Eton College OTC near Aldershot when the news broke,' Louis chipped in, looking slightly bemused by it all. 'They got sent home in all the chaos but he's determined to get out there as soon as humanly possible to whip the Hun into shape. I'm not sure what I'll find when I go back to Cambridge with this patriotic fervour sweeping across the nation. Soon the universities will merely consist of foreign men and those not physically fit to enlist.' He shrugged. 'I'm holding back for a bit. Total nonsense for everyone to up sticks and rush over to France when they'll all be back again within a few months.'

Louis was not the sort to get swept up by sentiment. Nor was he one to rush into things before he had the necessary information. He tended to employ more of a 'wait and see' philosophy, certainly where physical activities were concerned.

'Don't hold back for too long,' Clarence said. 'We have a family reputation to uphold. Both our grandfathers served, and that cousin of mother's made a career out of it until the Boers got the poor chap. We can't be seen to shirk our duty.' He tugged a further handful of grapes from their stalks. 'I'm not sure if the *pater* is pleased that he's too old, or a bit done, and wishing he could be out there, but he certainly doesn't much like the son and heir gallivanting across Europe when I should be taking over the reins of Merriford. A part of me, however, is pleased to be making my own decision about something at long last.'

'Not sure why Mother's in such a state about you going. She's practically produced a whole platoon,' Howard joked. 'If you bite the dust, old chap, there's a few of us in reserve. I might inherit yet, and I have grand plans for the old place.' He punched Louis playfully on the shoulder. 'Enlist, there's a chap.'

Clarence smiled but then looked more serious. 'There's a rumour that the horses will be requisitioned. Father's dreadfully cut up about it – I think he'll almost miss them more than he'll miss me – but with at least two of the stable hands already signed up, we soon won't have the staff to look after them.'

'I'll miss the horses too,' Benji whispered. He didn't ride but Olivia knew he was a frequent visitor to the stables, as were Clarence and Sir Hugo. His gentle nature had always preferred animals over humans. 'I hope they are treated kindly out there.'

'Most of the chaps I know are only getting the uniform so they can persuade their sweethearts into the bedroom,' Louis volunteered, as usual blissfully unaware of the inappropriate nature of his remarks.

'Oi, there's a girl present,' Howard reminded him and four sets of eyes turned to Olivia.

'Well, it's true. I'm sure she'll be the first to have her head turned by a handsome man in regimentals – after all, she was always banging on about dashing knights and the like.'

'She's only fifteen, for Christ's sake,' Howard muttered through gritted teeth, but Louis blundered on.

'What exactly does your girl think of it all, Clarrie? Is she happy that her fiancé is off to charge at the enemy with his bayonet fixed? Because, all our jokes aside, there's no guarantee you *won't* get killed.'

Olivia's insides withered a little at the brutality of Louis's words but the brothers had spent a lifetime with his frankness.

'She's not happy about it all but then women worry too much. She'll like me in my uniform well enough, but don't you be getting ideas about stepping into my shoes. I'm coming back as soon as we've shown the kaiser what for.'

Olivia could tell that Howard was becoming increasingly agitated. She turned to him and noticed that his fists were in balls. He gave a short snort. 'I don't understand the uniform thing. Men can be brave and chivalrous in other spheres. It's not a khaki peaked cap and a few brass buttons that makes you a man.'

'Worried it will all be done and dusted before you get a chance to do your bit? Or worried that you'll never get to experience the pleasures of the flesh?' Clarence ribbed, and smacked his brother affectionately across the head. A rough and tumble ensued and Olivia slid away from the jostling bodies. They couldn't help themselves – any opportunity to show off their strength and become top dog. Perhaps, she considered, the war would be a temporary outlet for the restless energy of thousands of frustrated adolescents across the world.

* * *

The whole thing finally became heartbreakingly real when Clarence left a fortnight later for training and, over the following weeks, alarmingly long casualty lists started appearing in the newspapers. Olivia witnessed Benji's silent tears as the horses were taken away, and people began to realise that the war was not going to be the jolly jaunt so many brave young men had convinced themselves it would be. She was later to learn that three-quarters of a million willing men enlisted in the first eight weeks, but the German war machine had been forty years in the preparation. And as the kaiser pushed through Belgium towards Paris, there was a growing unease that the enemy had been underestimated and the quick victory that everyone had predicted would not materialise.

She tried to communicate with Seth, partly to quiz him further over his wild claims that he existed in some place where the *Titanic* had not sunk and her parents might still be alive. But, more than anything, she needed to speak to someone who was not part of the Fairchild family and had no idea of what they were going through. How refreshing it would be to pretend the country was not at war. But there was no reply to her soft whispers of his name, and no scuffling feet or squeaking bedsprings when she pressed her ear to the cold bricks. Their interactions had always been sporadic at best and often a couple of weeks would pass before she caught up with her crotchety friend. And he *was* a friend now, whatever the truth of his existence and despite their quarrel. He may huff at her unrelenting cheeriness and grunt at her overly dramatic pronouncements, but he always made her feel safe and that her opinions were valued.

As the days passed, however, other things took precedence over conversations with a voice that she started to suspect she had finally outgrown. She still undertook her lessons in the mornings, but helped Lady Fairchild in practical ways with the fundraising for the troops in every spare hour outside of that, so that by December, and with the household preparations for Christmas now in full swing, Olivia realised that she hadn't heard from Seth for months. She had grown up so much since moving to the manor. Imaginary friends belonged to childhood and she no longer felt like a child, even if she was caught in that bemusing wilderness where she was also not yet quite an adult. Seth, she finally accepted, had merely been a product of her grieving imagination. He had helped her to settle, and now he had gone.

Because hadn't she long since decided that when she no longer needed him, her mind would simply let him go?

15

The country slipped quietly into the new year, but no one felt comfortable celebrating because war was now an unhappy part of everyday life. Abroad, the battle lines had been drawn and, from what Olivia understood, there was little movement in the jagged line of trenches that split Europe in two, from the North Sea down to the Swiss border. That January, when the Zeppelins dropped bombs on Great Yarmouth and the Norfolk coast, the shock of the war possibly coming to British soil frightened everyone.

The manor was struggling with a much-reduced staff as most men of fighting age had enlisted, leaving only the chauffeur, a stable hand who professed to be a conscientious objector, and one of the footmen, who was deemed medically unfit. The only other male member of staff was Mr Rowe, the head gardener, who was far too old to be considered for active service. Olivia knew how frustrated the women were, unable to serve abroad unless in a nursing capacity, when the people they cared most about in the world were in such danger. In the end, Lady Fairchild set up the Merriford Lode Women's War and Red

Cross Working Group, gathering local women together once a week to knit socks, gloves and mufflers, sew underwear and kitbags, and roll bandages. The social side of this lifted everyone's glum spirits, especially as tea, cake and occasionally sherry were provided, and they consoled each other that they were doing something, however small, for their boys on the front.

'You won't like this, Mother, but I've signed up,' Louis announced when he was home for Easter, fortuitously coinciding with Clarence's short spell of leave before being deployed to France. Olivia wasn't convinced Louis liked the idea of going to war much either, but questions were already being asked of young, fit men who were not serving.

Their mother threw her hands up in despair.

'So now I must bear the joint sorrow of Clarence shortly to be sent to the front line, and you imminently to follow? If the war drags on until the autumn, will Kitchener take Howard too?' She refused to ask her second born any questions about his enlistment from that moment, as though her denial would make it go away.

As the morning of Clarence's departure grew nearer, the atmosphere in the house shifted. Even the rowdiness of her sons settled down. Gone were the ribbing and playful shoves. Silence glided from room to room, her cloak covering all those she swept past. The time for jokes and false optimism was past. He was going out to do battle with the Germans and Olivia recognised that every name on the War Office's casualty lists was someone's father, someone's oldest brother, some *Titanic* orphan's friend.

Second Lieutenant Clarence Fairchild stood before them all the following morning, not even able to tell his family where he was going. All they knew was that he was sailing for France, where there was now a shortage of young officers – quite the reverse from the situation at the beginning of the war.

Sir Hugo instructed the chauffeur to take his oldest son to the station for the London train. Lady Fairchild had decided that seeing him off in a public place would be too much, so instead, the family gathered on the long, gravel drive outside the porticoed front door and said their goodbyes where no one other than the occasional curious housemaid peering from a window could see the stifled emotions of a family who remained uncomfortable weeping or embracing in view of others. Surely, Olivia thought, if there was any time for a mother to put her arms out to her son, it was now. But Lady Fairchild merely bent forward to kiss both his cheeks, and Olivia was not convinced her lips had even come into contact with his skin. Sir Hugo cleared his throat in place of words that he couldn't find, and shook his eldest son by the hand.

This could not be the extent of their farewell. Someone had to show Clarence how much he would be missed, and so without a thought, she threw her arms about his neck.

'Don't die,' she cried, saying what everyone else was thinking.

Clarence chuckled. 'I'll do my best, Livvy. And in the meantime, you take care of my family for me?'

'Olivia?' his mother questioned.

'She's the strongest one of us all,' her son pointed out. 'She confronts her emotions and talks about the things that matter.'

After the motor car had disappeared into the distance and the Fairchilds had retreated inside, Olivia stood alone on the shallow steps for quite some time, struggling to turn her feet around in case it was to be the last time that she ever set eyes on the future heir of Merriford. She'd experienced the raw grief of losing family, and this was her family now. How would she cope if something happened to Clarence or Louis?

Eventually, she walked to the east tower and climbed the spiral stairs to her room, pulled out her journal and tried to put her overflowing feelings into inadequate but heartfelt words.

* * *

A few days later and Howard returned home, having been first on an OTC training day and then staying with a school chum. He was sore to have missed his brothers by less than a week. Olivia was sitting in the Japanese garden, wrapped up warmly with a muffler around her neck, when he stumbled across her. The day was crisp but the maple trees and tall grasses sheltered her from the worst of the wind.

He stepped from behind the screen of bamboo and hesitated the moment he saw her, as though he wanted to turn and walk away, but she jumped up and ran over to embrace him. She felt his body stiffen but she needed an outlet for her emotions and one of her *nearly* brothers would have to do.

'Oh, Howard, isn't it simply awful that Clarrie is out there, and we don't even know where?'

She felt his head bow towards her as he buried his nose briefly in her hair, and then he pulled back, taking hold of her shoulders and gently pushing her away from his body. It wasn't aggressive but it was clear the intimacy wasn't welcome. He looked awkward and embarrassed. Perhaps he was too old for such embraces now. She must remember not to be so overexuberant, especially if he had friends over.

She fussed with her skirt as she sat back down.

'I've just seen Ernest Dunn at the house.' Howard didn't comment on Clarence. She understood; he simply couldn't. 'He's walked up from the village to call on Father.' He hitched up his trousers and joined her on the bench. 'Something to do with securing a commission. Clarrie always said he was a driven young man, and he's certainly making his mark at the shipping offices. It makes me realise how lucky we are to have the opportunities we do. I heard him say once that he would have given anything to study at university. Bright chap but lacking the necessary connections. Maybe the army will be the making of him – he certainly always knew how to deliver a punch. Makes me keen to do my bit. Get out there and have my innings.'

'Don't say that. It's not a game, Howie. The vicar's son has been quite badly wounded. Lost a leg, we were told. How long before the people we care about are injured or killed?' Her lip started to wobble and he reached out to pat her knee. 'I don't understand. It was all supposed to be over by now.'

'Don't worry about us Fairchild boys. We're made of stern stuff.'

'I just want straight talking,' she said. 'I'm sixteen, not six.'

He shifted uneasily on the bench beside her. His eyes flashed across her body before he stared intently at the stone dragon.

'I'm perfectly aware how old you are,' he said, a slight edge to his voice. 'I was just trying to protect you.'

'I don't need protecting, Howard. I've always been able to look after myself... Don't forget, you were once on the receiving end of my right hook.' She raised an eyebrow and he dipped his head to indicate that he remembered. 'And I have been fully aware of the harsh reality of death since I lost my parents. You of all people should know I'm not a helpless little girl.'

He sighed, accepting she would not be fobbed off.

'From everything I hear, we're locked into a deadly stalemate, and the reality is neither us nor the Germans are making any significant territorial gains. A couple of the chaps at school have fathers in the government and they pick things up. The unpalatable truth is that no one predicted the horrific numbers of dead and wounded, but the artillery fire and use of machine guns make this a war like no other.'

'Will it still be raging when you reach eighteen?' she asked. 'Will you get sucked into this too?'

'Obviously, I want the war over tomorrow and my brothers safely home in Merriford, but I can't deny there's a tiny part of me that wishes to prove my worth alongside them. Can you imagine how insufferable Clarence will be in years to come if he's some war hero and I've never even been shot at?'

'You don't have to prove anything. Not to Clarence, and certainly not to me.'

'Perhaps not, but there are things I need to prove to myself. I've spent my life in his shadow, and Louis's come to that. Clarence is the heir; Louis is the clever one. What am I?'

'You,' she said, leaning forward and engaging his eyes, 'can be anything you want to be.'

'Even Sir Walter Raleigh?' He was teasing her but she didn't mind.

'Exactly.' She gave him a wide smile and for the first time in months, he relaxed and smiled back.

'I'll still be joining up as soon as possible.'

'I don't understand why,' she said, shaking her head and getting to her feet. 'But we will simply have to agree to disagree. I'm heading back to the house. Are you coming?'

'I'll join you in a bit. I'm going to pick Mother a little posy of primroses from the banks of the boating lake. It's always covered in a swathe of lemon yellow this time of year. Maybe it will bring her some cheer. She had a letter from Clarence a little while ago. He's at the front now, but because he can't say where, it's done nothing to alleviate her worries.'

'Your poor mother. Yes, flowers are a splendid idea, so long as you don't put a frog in them.'

'I am fully aware that the time for such pranks has passed,' he said in a quiet voice.

There was a moment of silence where they acknowledged this truth and, unable to think of anything further to say, she took her leave. She walked over the red bridge and back to the manor, entering through the large French doors of the south-facing music room where her eager governess had occasionally tried to teach her restless pupil the piano. Momentarily blinded by moving from the bright sunshine and into the gloomy interior, Olivia realised Ernest was inside, as surprised as she to encounter one another.

'Goodness, Olivia Davenport, you've grown. I haven't seen you for over a year. Where did those curves come from?' he asked, giving her the biggest smile. 'You look absolutely enchanting.'

She was flattered that he'd noticed and, even though he was kind to everyone, she felt the heat rush to her cheeks. 'Enchanting' was such a grown-up word and she mumbled a thank you, before he gripped her hand with his and spun her around under his raised arm, as though they were in the middle of an opulent ballroom and she was the thing to be admired.

He bowed dramatically and then kissed her fingers, showcasing his gift of making everyone feel special whilst he was in their company. Despite her usual self-composure, Olivia's knees behaved rather badly and refused to communicate with her brain.

'Was Sir Hugo able to help?' she asked, torn between feelings of giddy foolishness, and her fear that yet another innocent young man was off to war and might never return.

Instead of answering, he spun her under his arm again and

then pulled her close, like she'd seen her father do when he'd danced with her mother around the drawing room, and she found herself pressed up against Ernest's body. Thrilled and embarrassed all at once, she looked up into his deep-brown eyes. He'd always had the look of the undeniably handsome matinee idol Maurice Costello about him. Although a fine face was not always a guarantee of character – Costello had been arrested for beating his wife a couple of years previously.

'How about a good-luck kiss for the brave local lad signing up to be a soldier?'

He gave her a cheeky smile just as the heavy, velvet curtain was flung back and Howard stepped into the room, surprised to find his older brother's friend embracing Olivia. It took him less than a second to register their intimate proximity.

'What the hell are you doing?' he shouted, dropping a small posy of pale-yellow primroses onto the top of the piano and launching himself at the older man, pinning him to the wall. Even though Ernest was taller and stronger than him, the poor chap looked quite bewildered by the unprovoked attack.

'I don't know what you think is going on, Master Howard, but I'm not about to seduce her. What do you take me for? She's just a girl. Seems as though someone is jealous, though.'

The lads glared at each other and Howard's freckled face turned the colour of strawberries.

'Have I hit the mark? Sorry, old chap, didn't know you had feelings for her.'

'Don't be ridiculous. She's like a little sister. I'm just looking out for her.'

Howard couldn't meet her eye as he stepped back from the older lad, but she'd heard enough. Ernest hadn't meant anything by the dancing – he was like that with everyone, even occasionally Lady Fairchild. It was obvious that Howard had overreacted.

'This is ridiculous,' she said. 'Fighting over nothing when your brothers are either facing the real enemy or preparing to. And you think *I'm* the child.' She glared at them both and flounced out the room. But once in the hallway, she lingered, wanting to hear the remainder of their exchange.

'Look here, old chap, I really didn't mean to offend her, or you, for that matter.'

'That's not how gentlemen treat ladies.' Howard's voice was unusually shaky.

'I'm sorry if you think my behaviour was inappropriate but it was merely a kindness. Do you not think young girls like someone older to take them seriously once in a while? I suspect the problem, dear boy, is entirely yours.'

From the thawing of her relationship with Howard only minutes before by the lake, a sharp frost was to creep back between them. For a long time after that, Olivia wished she had kissed Ernest that day, not because it would have meant anything to either of them but just to know what it felt like, and she couldn't forgive Howard for interrupting their moment.

16

By the May, Clarence had sent a couple of letters home, treasured by his mother and read aloud to all, even though the forced joviality of his words were apparent to everyone but her. It was a survival tactic, Olivia suspected, employed by Lady Fairchild, to blindly believe his claims of seeing very little action and that they'd got the Hun on the run, rather than contemplate the realities of his situation. Because the awful truth was filtering through now, for those who cared to seek it out. You only had to look at the growing casualty lists, or the number of women wearing black. As if that wasn't bad enough, one of the local dairy farmers had lost both sons in Ypres during the April, only four days apart.

The Germans' sinking the British ocean liner the *Lusitania* that month hit Olivia hard and naturally brought back the nightmares of three years previously. The circumstances surrounding both tragedies could not be more different but the similarity of both vessel and the numbers who had lost their lives made comparisons in the newspapers inevitable. It was noted that the wealthy sportsman Alfred Vanderbilt, who perished on the *Lusitania*, had been booked on the *Titanic* but not sailed, and Lady Duff-Gordon, one of the most famous of the *Titanic* survivors, had a ticket for the *Lusitania* but cancelled at the last minute. It was all such a painful reminder for Olivia of the capriciousness of life and the what-ifs that determined your destiny. Her tears that night were for her parents, not the twelve hundred victims of the torpedoed ship. And amidst the unrelenting flow of self-pity, she still hoped to hear the voice beyond the wall, grumpy or otherwise, offering a distraction. But it was not to be.

The summer passed in a blur, with Ruth surprising everyone by marrying an injured veteran she'd met through a friend.

'You don't need me now, miss,' she explained. 'I helped to bridge your move from Windy Acres to Merriford, but you'll be seventeen soon and have always been alarmingly independent.' She smiled to show she was teasing. 'And there is someone who needs me more.'

The reduced staff was still causing Lady Fairchild problems, and she was constantly moaning about overseeing a household with increasingly limited resources.

'I can't even ride over to see my dearest friend in Norwich,' she complained. 'They took our beloved saddle horses for the war effort and we are down to two cart horses, which are both needed to do jobs on the estate.'

'Then learn to drive the motor car,' Olivia suggested. 'If the actress Minnie Palmer can do it, so can you.' She'd imagined herself behind the wheel of such a vehicle on numerous occasions, haring through the countryside or undertaking some grand adventure across Europe. 'Think of all the places you can go. And without the need to ready a horse beforehand.'

'But motor cars are for men.'

'I'm pretty certain you don't have to grow a beard in order to be competent behind the wheel.'

'Oh, you are a tonic, Olivia,' she replied, with a smile. 'Perhaps I shall.'

And learn to drive she did – even though her husband swore she was an absolute menace on the road.

It was not until early October that Clarence finally got a short spell of leave, stressing he was luckier than most, as there were men who had been out since the start and not been home in over a year. The lavish preparations undertaken by Lady Fairchild were on such a scale, one might have thought the king himself was visiting. Benji and Howard were away at school until the Christmas holidays and Lady Fairchild was anxious all morning, snappy with the maids and fussing over tiny details that Olivia was certain the exhausted and battle-weary Clarence would not care one jot about. The curtains in his bedroom simply must be washed and it was imperative that fresh flowers from the greenhouses were placed in all the rooms.

At first, all was well. His face was gaunt, he had a haunted look about his eyes, and he was thinner than his mother would have liked, but he allowed himself to be fussed over and treated to the very best of everything – from the Royal Worcester, gilt-decorated tea set, to a ridiculous array of his favourite sweet treats and his mother's insistence he must try every cake – which made Olivia feel quite nauseous on his behalf.

'Have a madeleine, dear. Cook made them especially.'

He gave a weary smile and forced one to his lips, as Olivia recognised what his mother did not: he simply wished to be left alone, but he undertook his filial duty and bore her endless questions with good grace.

Her voice dipped to a whisper. 'Are you in very much danger out there? Your letters are so lacking in detail.'

'Honestly, Mother, I'm not sure what you imagine, but I've hardly been charging at the Germans non-stop since I arrived in France. We only spend a few days on the front line at a time and, even then, I'm largely dealing with my men's correspondence, answering the endless official enquiries delivered by the runners, or completing laborious daily returns detailing the quantity of ammunition we have and what's left in our trench stores...'

Lady Fairchild began to relax, convincing herself that Clarence was not being shot at by the Hun or dodging stray shells on a battlefield. He was an officer; he was safe. He was merely an administrator who happened to be working from a dugout in a bank of soil, rather than a cosy office in Westminster or Whitehall. But even Olivia was astute enough to realise the importance of what he didn't say, rather than what he did. He didn't say, *I never go over the top*, or *I am never in danger*.

'And you know how stoic the British are,' he continued. 'I hear more fuss made over the loss of a mouth organ or a tin of peppermints than I do over the loss of a limb.'

'Shall I add peppermints to your parcels?' she asked, focusing entirely on the wrong aspect of his words. 'That's something I can do, and it will make me feel useful. Would tinned kippers and oysters be welcomed? How about a bottle of cherry brandy, every now and again? And the postmaster's mother mentioned naphthalene balls for the lice.'

'If you must send me parcels, Mother, let them be of books. Something dark and ironic, like Hardy, will do. You'd be surprised how the lads fight over a good novel, although I still find comfort in poetry: Coleridge and Tennyson.'

'Poetry won't sustain you in the trenches.' Lady Fairchild tutted. Her job was to feed him up, keep him clean and make sure he didn't get ill.

'Oh, Mother.' Clarence's face displayed his frustration at her total lack of understanding. 'You have no idea.'

His veneer of politeness was starting to crack and, even though it was only six o'clock, he asked to be excused.

'Morpheus calls,' he explained.

'Oh, darling, you've only been home a couple of hours.' But all the poor man wanted was sleep.

* * *

The following morning, Lady Fairchild was anxiously trying to locate her oldest son. He'd gone out at the crack of dawn, according to the housekeeper, and no one had any idea when he would return.

'Let him be, Cynthia,' Sir Hugo said, looking up from his newspaper.

'But he's home for such a short time and it might be months before we see him again. It's too cruel.'

Olivia, who had also sought solitude after the death of her parents, understood. The effort of pretending everything was all right, combined with the effort of dealing with the fact that it was not, could be overwhelming at times.

So, she wasn't looking for Clarence but stumbled across him quite by accident, spotting him through the screen of bamboo at the edge of the Japanese gardens. He was on the bench with his back to her, and was holding a small, bone-handled folding pocket knife, twisting it round and round in his fingers, the blade catching the light and winking at her each time it completed a rotation.

She was about to walk away, leave him to enjoy the peace and quiet he so desperately craved, when she saw him grip the handle and turn his other wrist to the sky. Horrified, she watched him run the knife across his pale skin. A slow deliberate action, almost as though he was caressing his arm with the cold steel. A dark-red line appeared and began to swell and thicken, before gravity pulled the pooling liquid in a scarlet line towards the ground.

'Clarence?' Her voice was gentle as she stepped onto the gravel and into view. He quickly flicked the knife shut and licked at the blood, before tugging his sleeve over the wound. But she'd seen everything and he knew it. She came to his side and settled herself next to him.

He couldn't meet her eyes and stared at the stone dragon, saying nothing for some considerable time. A robin landed on the bridge, a fat worm in its beak, before taking flight again.

'Flesh and metal,' he finally said. 'You could not get two things more diametrically opposed. One forges the other into something that has the power to irrevocably damage itself.'

He held her concerned gaze for the briefest moment before the effort of it made him turn his head, even though his words continued to flow, as unstoppable as the water from the fountain before him.

'I once watched those under my command bathing behind the lines.' Olivia couldn't initially see the connection between this statement and his previous line of thought but didn't interrupt. 'They hadn't washed properly for weeks and took the opportunity to do so outside at an abandoned farmhouse in the fine weather. Their thin, white bodies were like dancing ribbons in the sunlight, larking about and splashing each other. I contemplated then how fragile the human body is. We have no natural armour, like the armadillo, or the thick fur of a grizzly bear. Nothing to shield us from the elements, and not even hooves or hard pads to protect our feet.'

He was focused on something in the middle distance but he wasn't really looking.

'One lad in particular caught my eye: his fair hair and lithe, pale limbs. There was not a mark on his perfect skin. Two weeks later, what was left of him was hanging on a thicket of barbed wire fifty yards from our trench in a place we could not safely retrieve his body. Machine guns and shrapnel from the shelling had shredded him to rags.'

The image was an unpalatable one, but she tried not to react as he paused and turned back to her.

'Why do we do it? As a species, why are we so destructive? God put us in charge of this incredible planet and all we do is destroy it. We are not fit to be on this earth, never mind presume to be in charge of it.'

There was a slight tremble of his hand as he slid the knife into his trouser pocket, and she tentatively reached for his knee. She didn't know what the right words were in such a situation so she said nothing, hoping her touch was enough.

'I've not been a kind big brother,' he continued. 'I wasn't even particularly welcoming to you.' She noticed the building tears in his eyes. One eventually spilled from his lower lid and tumbled down his unshaven cheek, hanging from the edge of his jaw like a tiny glass pendant. 'I could have been so much nicer to them but instead, I always had to be in charge, constantly reminding them that I was the one to inherit; I was the one born to rule. And now it's too late. If I die, they will always think of me as the bully – throwing my weight about. Constantly locking horns with the younger stags, to ensure they couldn't topple me as head of the herd. And yet, the truth of it is, I am jealous of them. Always have been.'

'Jealous? But you are set to inherit everything. If it was Louis or even Howard, I could understand it. You don't need to establish your superiority; you *are* superior.'

He shrugged. 'What if I don't want to be the oldest? What if I don't want to inherit? Imagine having your whole life mapped out for you. I know where I am going to live, what my job and my life will entail; even my choice of future bride was forced upon me. I do not doubt she'll make an excellent lady of the manor, but she doesn't make my heart sing. There was no magical moment when I knew she was the one, like the love stories you enjoy so much – not with her, at any rate. Perhaps it's why I enlisted so quickly; I saw a chance to do something that I had control over. It was almost a rebellion.'

He studied her face for a moment.

'Can I tell you something in confidence? Something I think only you would truly understand? And you must swear never to tell another living soul?'

'Of course.'

'The only person who has ever made me feel like that was someone who used to work here. Even though I'm certain they felt it too, I never acted upon it or even let them know how I felt.'

'Because it would cause a scandal?' she asked, imagining Lady Fairchild having an attack of the vapours at the thought of Clarence courting a maid – young, uneducated girls sometimes only stayed a year or two before marrying or moving on.

'You have no idea,' he replied.

Olivia contemplated what it must be like to be in love with someone you couldn't be with, and wondered if she had been in Clarence's position, whether she would have followed her heart. It was all very well in stories to sacrifice everything to be with the one you loved, but she couldn't see the heir to Merriford living with a former servant in a tiny, terraced house, having been banished from his home.

Poor Clarence. Now she understood. Or, at least, she thought she did.

'I envy the others, and maybe Benji most of all. He drifts around unseen, with few expectations placed upon him. If he wants to spend his life sitting in fields painting wildflowers, he will do so unchallenged. He is indulged by Mother and tolerated by Father.' His bitterness at this state of affairs was apparent from his clenched fists, curled lip and tone of voice. 'If anyone marries for love, it will be him.'

'And so you're cruel to him for something that is no more his fault than being born to inherit Merriford Manor is yours?'

He shook his head. 'I shouldn't have spoken to you so openly. This is my burden and you are too young to bear the weight of it with me. I'm sorry, Livvy. But facing your own mortality rather makes a man reassess his previous actions.'

She reached for his hand, sensing him flinch, but he allowed her to take it. This was a moment of unprecedented honesty between them and he'd trusted her with his deepest secrets. It was no use pretending that him dying wasn't a possibility, because of course it was. If he was going to treat her like an adult and trust her with these fears, then he deserved a mature and considered response.

She thought about what might have made her parents' passing a little easier. For her, it was the unexpected nature of their deaths that was the hardest. When her maternal grandmother had passed away several years ago, she'd been sick for months. Everyone knew what was coming and her own mother, whose relationship with the dying woman had been strained at the best of times, was gifted with the opportunity to clear the air between them. There had been an honesty at the end that, even as a child, Olivia had admired. But when her own parents had been taken from her, she'd had no such luxury. Their hopes for her future, any advice they might wished to have passed on, the opportunity to say the unsaid, was snatched from them.

'Write to your brothers,' she said, in a sudden moment of clarity. 'Explain everything. Apologise for the things you regret. Tell them how much you love them, what you hope for their futures and ask for understanding. You don't even have to send the letters. Keep them safe. They will find their way to us if anything should... happen.'

He shook his head. 'I'm not much one for words. That's your gift. Well, that and showing genuine affection.' He squeezed her hand. 'No one in this house really does that, have you noticed? We barely even touched each other before you arrived and began flinging your arms around everyone.'

She nodded. 'It was one of the hardest things about moving here. The only person who didn't flinch was Benji. Touch is incredibly healing; touch is everything.'

He reached his large hand up to place it over hers and, for a moment, they revelled in the warmth of the contact.

'Olivia Davenport,' he said, squeezing her fingers. 'How did one so young get to be so wise?'

'I had to grow up fast, I guess.'

'Of course – your parents. Come here, you strange little thing.' He threw his arm around her shoulders and pulled her close. 'I'm so glad you came to Merriford. Even though I wouldn't wish the reason that you did so on anyone. You've changed us all in subtle ways, but I've only just realised it. Mother actually hugged me on the driveway yesterday. I don't think she's put her arms around me since I was four. I wonder if it's because you're a girl and females in our house have always been outnumbered, or simply because you're you.'

She buried herself in his thick, wool coat and felt, for the first time, that there was something akin to a familial bond between them.

'Come back to us, Clarence,' she whispered.

'I'll do my best, if only to make sure Louis doesn't get his hands on the estate. But I just hope if my number does come up, I at least get to die a noble death.'

17

Howard had always been as keen as mustard to sign up, and announced his intention to do just this on his eighteenth birthday. Lady Fairchild was distraught. Initially, she tried emotional blackmail. Hadn't she given enough? Two sons had already volunteered. Surely, she begged, she should be allowed to keep her youngest children safe. Could God, King and Country not grant her that small kindness?

He was persuaded to wait, but everyone knew it would not be long until he was called up, regardless. And then three months later, conscription was introduced, in the January of 1916, when it became apparent that the numbers of voluntary recruits were not enough to replace the mounting casualties. God, King and Country had remained unmoved.

Within weeks of enlisting, Howard was sent off to train. Olivia didn't like it any more than his mother, but she understood there was a part of him that needed to do his bit. Besides, since the outbreak of war, the schools had instilled in these young men that it was their duty. Clarence and Louis had been in the OTC in case there was a war. Howard had been in it *because* there was a war. He had known this day was coming. His brothers, at his age, had not.

It was mid-April and Lady Fairchild and Olivia were parcelling up packets of cigarettes all morning for Louis, who didn't smoke but who'd requested some for his men. It had actually been Olivia's idea, after receiving a letter from him complaining that he'd overheard them calling him uncaring and aloof. She'd written back suggesting that bribery could be surprisingly effective in winning people over.

As the women worked, they talked of books. Olivia was astonished to learn Her Ladyship had not read much since her school days and so, after they'd finished, they went to the library to look out some novels. They were standing side by side, gazing out one of the huge windows and discussing Dickens, when they both spotted the telegraph boy cycling up the driveway.

Olivia's heart stopped.

The conversation dried up and they watched his bony, white legs pedal frantically up the gravel, as he hunched forward over the handlebars, focused on the road ahead. She knew him from Sunday School and dancing at the village fetes, but she had no desire to run downstairs and speak to him. He was a nice lad but he was not welcome here – not in this capacity.

Lady Fairchild sank into one of the upholstered sofas, all colour draining from her face. A few minutes later, the housekeeper, who had taken over the butler's duties since he'd signed up, entered the room with tentative steps and handed her mistress an envelope before discreetly departing.

The two women looked at each other and the room was unnervingly still for far longer than was comfortable. Olivia's eyes focused on anything other than the feared missive: the way the sunlight fell across the wooden floorboards in oblong strips, the steady ticking of the large, bronze clock on the mantel, the rows of gold lettering running up the book spines and glinting in the pale sun.

'Perhaps Sir Hugo has been delayed in London longer than he thought,' Lady Fairchild said with false optimism. 'Or maybe that aged uncle of his has finally passed away – the poor fellow must be about a hundred. Or one of my boys has unexpected leave.' She managed half a smile but they both knew it was none of these. Her hand visibly trembled as she finally found the strength to slide the silver letter opener under the flap and face the brutal news within.

Please God, let it be an injury, Olivia thought. Something that had taken Clarence or Louis away from the front lines and out of danger, but that they would make a full recovery from. Even losing a leg like the vicar's son was better than her worst fear.

She studied Lady Fairchild's face as the sheet of paper was slid from the envelope: intense concentration, a fleeting frown, and then the poor woman's whole face collapsed, along with her privileged, hitherto cushioned, upper-class world...

It was with regret that they were informed Lieutenant Clarence Fairchild had died two days previously.

Lord Kitchener expressed his sympathy.

* * *

One of the hardest crosses they had to bear was the news that followed. Five days after the telegram, they received a hand-written letter from Clarence's divisional commander, and learned that the eldest Fairchild son had not been killed in action, nor had he died from wounds sustained in battle. He'd been knocked down by a passing ambulance behind the lines as he helped to transfer one of his injured men onto the back of a truck and died instantly. His death was an accident and, in many ways, a tragedy even greater than had he died in battle. The noble death that he had so wished for, and that might have offset their overwhelming grief, even if only slightly, had been denied him.

For his mother, this was the knowledge that almost destroyed her. His death was avoidable. Unnecessary.

But for Olivia, the moment that hit the hardest was two weeks later when she walked into the drawing room, having heard that Clarence's personal possessions had been delivered to the house.

Because there, on one of the side tables, amongst the jumble of his pocket watch, fountain pen and books, was a bundle of letters, in the handwriting of the eldest Fairchild son, addressed to each of his brothers and tied together neatly with parcel string...

18

It was as if the air inside every room at Merriford Manor had somehow become denser. Every step took gargantuan effort; every breath was almost suffocating. The thoughts that lumbered through Olivia's mind, the inarticulate words she spoke, were all slowed by her palpable grief. She sensed the desolation hanging in the atmosphere, nestled in the shadows and crawling across the wallpapers. Even the servants, some of whom had already lost family members or friends to the war, bore the devastating news of the young Mr Fairchild's death in their deflated posture, dipped heads and whispered voices. Some of the older staff had known him since he was a baby and had perhaps even hoped to serve out their days under him as master. It was too much to bear.

Lady Fairchild took to her bedroom for a week and when she reappeared, she was shrouded in black. Sir Hugo didn't touch a newspaper for days. Olivia retreated to the tower and wondered if the awfulness of the situation would cause the voice to return, but there were no responses to her repeated whispers through the wall.

She did, however, find some comfort in writing her feelings and observations down, even penning a final letter to Clarence, which she tucked in her dressing table drawer. Grief was not new to her but experiencing it in a country at war was. It was not just her state of mind she had to wrestle with, but everyone's around her as well. Being optimistic and cheery was becoming wearing. Anxiety was etched across the faces of so many, and the absence of young men in the fields and in the towns was no longer worthy of note. Even the way people grieved was changing – for how could the previous elaborate and indulgent practices to honour the dead be conducted when the loss was on such a catastrophic scale? That Lady Fairchild would lose a healthy adult son was unthinkable barely two years ago, but now her circumstances were not unusual. Was it better or worse that she was not the first of her close circle of society ladies to go through this? And did it affect how much sympathy she could expect when everyone knew that she would not be the last?

However, the extent of the physical affection between Olivia and the older woman was slowly growing. The day Her Lady-ship had let the devastating telegram flutter to the floor, Olivia had dashed to her side and thrown her arms about the bereaved mother. For the first time in four years, her touch had been reci-procated. She felt herself gripped with a fierceness that had surprised them both. Olivia was not her daughter, nor was she even an adult, but the connection between them was real.

'We will get through this,' she assured Lady Fairchild several weeks later, when the grief wasn't quite as raw. 'Every day the pain will hurt a little less, and the sun will shine a little brighter.'

'But if it should happen to Louis, too, or Howard... I feel so guilty for doing so little when they are risking so much. Perhaps if I was younger and unmarried, I'd have considered training as a nurse, but neither my age nor my husband would allow it. And whilst Sir Hugo might permit me to potter about in our kitchen gardens, growing food for the table, he would not see me ploughing a field or chopping out mangolds.'

Olivia understood because she felt the same. Why was it only in her imagination that she could wield a sword or sacrifice herself for those she loved? Their sex restricted them both and, for different reasons, their age. And so, when Her Ladyship visited her in the tower a week later, the news she brought offered the young girl some consolation.

'After much deliberation, and possibly a degree of coercion from the powers that be, Sir Hugo has decided that Merriford Manor will serve as a convalescent home for the remainder of the war. I suspect he may have jumped before he was pushed, as several large houses have already been pressed into service as hospitals, but we are to give over a portion of the house to this end and can continue to live in the rest.'

She gave a small smile – the first Olivia had seen since Clarence's death.

'I know that the local cottage hospital has been struggling, and we are so fortunate to live here, with such beautiful grounds. It is the perfect place for our brave men to recuperate and heal, and I finally feel we are doing something practical.'

Olivia immediately had visions of herself as a modern-day Florence Nightingale and could not stop her rapidly spinning brain from picturing herself in a VAD uniform, mopping at the brow of some fevered invalid. Might she meet a gallant war hero whom she could dedicate the remainder of her life to, much as Ruth had done? Would her love story start at the foot of a hospital bed? She decided to write a short story about such a romance to cheer herself up, especially as it occurred to her that when Merriford Manor was full of strangers, it would prevent her wandering uninhibited around the grounds.

Perhaps when she was eighteen, she could look into training as a nurse.

'Clarence would have been pleased,' she said.

'I'm so glad you feel the same. It will mean a degree of disruption, but it's the least we can do.' Her Ladyship's shoulders relaxed and she finally took in her surroundings. 'It is so dark in here, Olivia. How can you bear it?'

'Sometimes darkness is a comfort.' She'd found such comfort four years ago by imagining herself to have a friend through the wall in the darkest part of the night.

The older woman's eyes alighted on the open notebook across the small desk, and she glanced at the words.

'Are you writing stories? Dabbling in fiction? Your governess always said your prose was exceptionally good for someone your age. Do you suppose it is down to your extensive reading? Or do you think it is something you have inherited from your father?'

Olivia shrugged. 'My head is always so busy, I guess I have to get some of it down on paper, or it would spill out of my ears.'

The older woman gave another fleeting smile. 'You should pursue it. It is one of the few acceptable professions open to our sex. And one that is compatible with marriage and motherhood. I, on the other hand, have always known myself to be purely decorative. With Clarence's death, the convalescent hospital will finally give me a purpose. That's the most exciting part of all of this; I've read of civilians volunteering at such places. Surely, even without nurses' training, there are things we can do? Write letters for the injured, visit those who have no family, read aloud to the troubled of mind?'

Olivia caught the 'we' and sat up straighter, as Lady Fairchild's announcement took on a new significance. Reading stories and writing letters were things she was exceptionally good at. Her Ladyship was quite correct: this could not have come at a better time. It would finally give them both a purpose.

* * *

To everyone's astonishment, within a few short weeks, Merriford Manor was successfully transformed into a serviceable convalescent hospital. The great hall and morning room were taken over, with the family retaining just the dining room and drawing room, both on the east side of the main house. Sir Hugo had overseen the removal and safe storage of various paintings, valuable furniture and fragile ornaments. After the rooms had been cleared, there were endless deliveries of iron beds and single mattresses, stacks of white hospital linen, boxes of enamelware, bed pans, and medical equipment. Folding screens divided the spaces and offered a degree of privacy, as the rooms were converted into dormitories. Part of the west wing was given over to hospital stores, and arrangements were made with the kitchen staff to allow for the provision of all the extra meals.

One hot June day in 1916, Olivia stood in the cluttered library, now home to several large tables and cabinets from elsewhere in the house. She looked down over the driveway as trucks arrived with the wounded – the sightless and the limbless managing with wheelchairs and crutches. This would be home for these unfortunate men for the foreseeable future. It would be a place they could rehabilitate, and do so in the green and peaceful English countryside.

Even though the family largely cocooned themselves in those areas of the manor that they had retained for their personal use, the sights and sounds of the patients invaded every moment of their lives. They quickly grew used to seeing the men seated outside on the formal lawns in their hospital blues. The ill-fitting, blue, single-breasted jackets, blue trousers, white shirts and red ties made convalescing soldiers distinguishable from men avoiding military service, but were not popular with those who wore them.

The house had been so quiet before, when the boys were away, but now, there was always something going on: the constant arrival of Red Cross staff and volunteers from the village, the tip and tap of endless games of ping-pong, and the occasional jolly tune coming from the upright piano in the music room.

Lady Fairchild was in her element, recruiting local volunteers to undertake various tasks such as serving meals, providing companionship to the patients, organising recreational activities, and helping with administrative duties. Olivia was one such volunteer and she made herself useful, setting up a library for the wounded with books that had been donated, and reading and writing letters for those who were not able to do so for themselves.

Her tendency to select fairy tales and romances, when the men expressed no preference, was tolerated because the skill with which she delivered the story was, as one soldier put it, 'enchanting' – a word that caused her to think back to the almost kiss from Ernest all those months ago. Such was her popularity, that one end of the library was set up with chairs for her performances, and the men were quite put out if they missed an instalment.

Lady Fairchild took it upon herself to remind everyone that Olivia was just seventeen, and the only downside of her popularity was that she was removed from the tower and given a bedroom in the main house to preserve her virtue. With no Ruth to act as guard dog, it was, the older woman told her, better to be safe than sorry, and having long accepted that Seth would never return, Olivia was not as upset as she might otherwise have been.

'I don't know how I would manage without you, dear girl,' Her Ladyship said, as they tidied up the library together after one particularly dramatic reading. 'The tragedy of the *Titanic* has, rather cruelly, been my saving. You mean a very great deal to me, and whilst I could never presume to replace your mother, it would be a kindness, make me feel a little less distant, if you were to call me Cynthia.'

And for those brave and long-awaited words, Olivia rewarded her with a bone-crushing embrace.

* * *

'Howard has written to say he's likely to be deployed in September and we've had news from Louis,' Lady Fairchild announced. 'I was so worried not to have had any correspondence from him for a while, but he's apparently been quite unwell with trench fever. The only silver lining to his letter being that, due to his recurring relapses, they are shipping him back to England for a time to fully recover.'

They had endeavoured to get him transferred to Merriford but, apparently, it wasn't that simple. His mother, however, was able to visit him twice that summer during his stay at a hospital in Buckinghamshire. The icing on the unexpected cake was when his father pulled some bureaucratic strings and Louis was allowed to come home briefly before returning to the front.

Unlike Clarence, he had no compunction when answering his mother's anxious questions, as he told of the bloated dead, the plagues of rats, the continuous roar of bombardment, and how on one occasion, he had handed out bags and ordered his men to collect up the pieces of their fallen comrades after a shell had dropped in their trench. Benji sat, wide-eyed, lapping up every detail, but the increasing horror was written across the faces of Olivia and Lady Fairchild.

'It's certainly no picnic, Mother.' His expression was serious, as was his desire to respond honestly and to the best of his ability. 'The lice get everywhere and the rats eat everything – from the tablecloths to the dead. My men are supposedly allocated one and a quarter pounds of fresh meat daily but the reality is that the only fresh meat in the trenches is the bodies of their friends...'

'Enough!' Lady Fairchild cried. Her face was white and Olivia threw Louis a frustrated look.

He merely shrugged. 'Well, you would keep asking. And the brutal truth is that I'm on borrowed time. I've done the maths. Subalterns, like myself, are not expected to live beyond a few weeks. We lead our men out onto the battlefield, and snipers are always on the lookout for the uniform of an officer, picking us off first if they can.'

'Louis!' Olivia's frustration was apparent, and he finally realised he'd overstepped the mark. Lady Fairchild didn't press her son on anything further for the duration of his visit. She did, however, give him the tightest embrace when he left the following day, which he endured admirably, as his mother told him all the things that she wanted to say without the need for words.

* * *

Just eleven short days after Louis Fairchild had left for foreign shores, the family received word that he had died at a casualty clearing station on 4 September 1916, from wounds sustained during battle.

Tragically, his maths had been correct.

19

Louis's death, so soon after Clarence's, hit them all viscerally hard. Howard, who was able to engineer a visit home before he was due to sail from Southampton, was particularly distraught as he'd not seen his older brother for months. It was small compensation, but he would, at least, overlap with Benji before he returned to school.

Olivia knew to expect a period of initial awkwardness whenever any of the Fairchild offspring returned home. Boarding school, university and then with the oldest two going off to war, there had been big gaps when she hadn't seen them, and she was often startled by how much they'd changed in the intervening periods. Benji, for example, had grown a whole inch over the summer term, and even he was leaving his boyhood behind, apparent from the occasional pimple and high-pitched squeak.

But the first time she saw Howard in his uniform was entirely different. Something inside Olivia changed – or perhaps it had been changing for a while and it was the first time she acknowledged it.

She was huddled over a pair of knitting needles with Cynthia, as Her Ladyship tried to unpick a disastrous row for her. Olivia had been thinking about Major Turrell – one of the patients at the hospital whose eyes had been damaged by a mustard gas attack. It wasn't that the major did anything to make *her* heart flutter; besides, she was only seventeen and he was almost thirty. It was more that she thought he deserved a happy ever after.

The man had a passionate and poetic soul – she knew this from the things he asked her to write to his mother – so she was imagining an uplifting end to his unfortunate circumstances, possibly with the stern nurse that she'd noticed cheered his spirits immeasurably every time she tended to him. But the lady in question was so matter-of-fact with her ministrations, and the strict overseeing eye of the matron would inevitably put an end to any untoward shenanigans of an amorous nature. As a way of coping with the devastating loss of Louis, Olivia liked to imagine a love blossoming for the major, and this had been at the cost of her knitting.

Howard was not expected until that afternoon, having cadged a lift from a friend who lived in another part of Norfolk. So, when he arrived early, loudly clearing his throat to alert those in the room to his presence, they were all taken by surprise – more so because he'd grown a moustache and Olivia almost hadn't recognised him.

Lady Fairchild burst into tears, allowing the tangled knitting to fall to the floor. Her husband walked over to his third-eldest son, now tragically heir to his estate, and shook his hand, but Howard's eyes were focused on Olivia, not leaving her face for a moment. She rose to her feet and began to wonder if she had something on her cheek – stray crumbs from lunch or ink from her writing.

'What do you think of me now, Livvy?' he asked. His hands swept across his uniform.

'Very smart and more than enough to turn some young lady's head.' But it was the wrong response and she didn't know why. His face had a dejected look about it.

Lady Fairchild walked to the doorway and kissed her son, much to his surprise, and then briefly embraced him, as Olivia took the opportunity to study him further. Her stomach constricted in an unexpected way. Howard, standing near the doorway in his khaki uniform and cap, looked so grown-up and yet so painfully young, all at once.

'Confined to the drawing room, I see,' he said, walking into the centre of the room. 'The old place feels very different with all these strangers bustling about.'

'We are doing what we can for the war effort,' his mother said. 'It's not much but—'

'It's everything, Mother. You're giving them a place to heal, some peace and quiet and the odd pretty face to cheer up their day.' He briefly flicked his eyes to the inexplicably nervous girl standing across the room from him.

'Young Olivia's been quite a hit with the men,' Sir Hugo said. This time, Howard met and held her gaze as his father continued. 'She reads for them and I've been told her passion really brings the books alive.'

'Major Turrell always asks for her specifically,' his wife volunteered.

'Now, now, she's far too sensible... far too young,' her husband said, 'to be getting involved with the patients.' Olivia was many things but perhaps sensible was not one of them.

'He comes from a distinguished line of Turrells... that's all I'm saying. Now give your sister a kiss and we can ask the house-keeper to bring in a pot of tea.' Lady Fairchild's determination that the little orphan they had taken in was a legitimate part of her family brought a lump to Olivia's throat. Her parents had chosen her guardians well and for that, she would be eternally thankful.

'She's *not* my sister,' Howard stressed, quietly under his breath, but Olivia caught his words.

'Oh, Howie, we have missed you terribly,' she said, putting out her arms to embrace him but his face registered panic. It was fleeting but she saw it so let her arms drop back to her sides. Perhaps he didn't want his two dead brothers replaced by a girl who was not related to him. He took a step towards her and leaned down to give her an awkward peck on the cheek, as his mother had requested.

The men waited for the ladies to settle themselves and then they all sat together in a cluster around the fireplace, Howard reluctantly taking the vacant space next to Olivia on the sofa, but placing himself as far from her as he possibly could.

The maid brought in a tray of tea, and she felt sad that the acceptance and closeness she shared with Cynthia, and had long shared with Benji, would never be shared with him. Things had always been difficult between herself and Howard but she'd hoped that would change as they got older. Or was there something else going on? Was he furious because he believed she was flirting with a blind major at the hospital? Did he disapprove that his mother was now treating her as one of her own? He'd certainly been displeased that Olivia had encouraged Cynthia to drive a motor vehicle, as she remained an absolute menace on the road.

Benji was summoned from the gardens to greet his brother, all gangly limbs and awkwardness, and then Lady Fairchild mentioned Louis and the mood dipped. Olivia's eyes flicked briefly to the photograph taken at Haven-on-Sea all those years ago, as the youngest Fairchild wedged himself between Olivia and Howard, and five bereaved people struggled to find things to say – all of them acutely aware that two faces were missing from their family gathering.

* * *

Whatever was rankling Howard, it became ever more apparent over the next couple of days. In recent years, whenever the Fairchild boys were home, Benji would walk by her side, keen to chat and be involved in whatever she was doing. Howard had often trailed behind, like a well-trained gun dog, but perhaps it hadn't been a desire to be part of their close friendship, as she'd always thought, and instead him observing her, checking that she didn't overstep. Now, he seemed to move away from her whenever they were in a room together.

Determined to avoid confrontation, and mindful that his imminent deployment abroad and recent death of his brother were understandably on his mind, she continued to throw herself into her volunteer work with the wounded, often spotting him on the edge of what she was doing. When she read for a group of the men in the library, Howard appeared in the doorway. When she took Captain Smith for a turn about the lawn in his bath chair, she caught sight of him looking out through the French doors of the music room.

Taking some time for herself, she retreated to the Japanese gardens, jotting down ideas for another story, when she heard the thud of feet and turned to see Benji racing towards her.

'Howard's got into trouble at the boating lake.' He was breathless and red-faced. 'Come quickly.'

Without a moment's hesitation, she dropped her journal to the ground and hitched up her skirts, running behind Benji over the bridge and down to the lake, all the time wondering what she was going to find. Had he been messing about in a boat and it had overturned? She knew he couldn't swim, and had always kept to the shallow areas when the boys had mucked about in the water in years gone by.

Please God, she thought to herself as her thumping heart almost burst from her chest, *do not let someone else I care about drown.*

But as she approached the water's edge, her eyes frantically scanning for signs of a distressed individual or, even worse, a floating-upside-down dead one, she was astonished to see Howard's auburn hair and freckled face bobbing about in the middle of the lake.

He raised a hand and gave a small wave.

'Ha! I reckon we had you there for a moment. But look, Livvy, I can swim.'

20

Olivia was incandescent with rage.

'You stupid, unkind, thoughtless boy,' she shouted, refusing to acknowledge his age, as this was a joke too far – something a child might do, unaware of the panic they had caused. He did not deserve to be recognised as a full-grown man. 'How dare you make me think you were drowning!'

Howard's smile slid into the dark water surrounding him and he swam towards the bank, climbing out and grabbing a towel from beside the pile of clothes on the little wooden jetty. He began to rub himself with the coarse fabric, hopping from foot to foot and casting repeated and nervous glances in her direction.

'I wanted to show you that I'd overcome my fear. One of my fellow cadets taught me at camp. It was supposed to be a surprise.'

Her hands were on her hips and she was breathing heavily through flared nostrils as she tried to calm herself. Her panic had been real and it would take time for her physical reactions to subside.

'And you honestly thought the best way to let me know was to make me think your life was in danger – that you might be drowning, like my parents drowned in the North Atlantic Ocean?'

All the colour drained from his face as he whipped up a cotton shirt and slipped his arms into the sleeves.

'Oh gosh, Livvy. I didn't think.' His face reflected his horror at the realisation of what he'd done.

'No, you didn't. Have you any idea what was going through my mind as I raced here?' She was shouting now and she could see the shocked look on Benji's face as he, too, realised what she was saying. 'Either of you? With all the death that we are dealing with?' She looked between the two of them, incredulity apparent in her wide eyes.

The youngest Fairchild was now red-faced and staring intently at his feet.

'It's not Benji's fault. Don't be cross at him. I gave him a shilling to fetch you down here. Go back to the house, Benji. This is my mess to clear up. I need to speak to Olivia alone.'

His brother nodded, mumbling sorrys and turned towards the manor, ambling up the path, as Olivia and Howard stood yards apart until his footsteps faded to nothing and the silence became too much.

'I don't understand, Howard. How could you do this to me? Of all the utterly stupid and irresponsible pranks you have ever pulled, this is absolutely the worst.' She could feel the tears pricking at her eyes but refused to let them fall. 'I thought we'd reached a truce. You've left me alone since that first summer I arrived at Merriford Manor and now you do this. What were you thinking?'

Howard avoided her eye and sunk onto his haunches. His head fell to his hands as his fingers started to tear at his hair. 'I'm such an idiot. I've gone about this all wrong and made you cry when it was the last thing I intended. I wanted you to be proud of me. You seemed so indifferent when I arrived in my uniform...'

Her anger began to subside as she realised that the man before her was genuinely repentant. She took a couple of breaths to calm herself. 'Of course I'm proud of you. I'm proud of everyone who steps up to defend the freedom of this nation. I'm angry with the power-crazed men who have allowed this war to happen, and worried sick for your safety. I've lost so many people I cared about and can't bear to lose anyone else.'

'But I'm only here for a few days, Liv, and you're spending all your time with the patients...' He dared to meet her eyes and swept his hand through his wet hair in his misery, struggling to finish the sentence.

'I've made commitments to the hospital and I take my role here seriously. I don't understand. One minute, you're avoiding me and the next, you're complaining that I'm too busy to spend time with you.'

'You really don't know?' Howard's face was now concertinaed into a frown. He got to his feet and took a couple of tentative steps towards her, as though he was afraid she might slap him, or otherwise vent her anger. To be honest, she'd felt like throttling him the moment he'd climbed onto the bank.

'And yet you've always had the measure of me and once pointed out, quite accurately, may I add, that my silly behaviour was always for attention.' He paused and raised his eyes to meet hers. 'You're no longer the annoying but intriguing thirteen-year-old girl, racing around the grounds, indulging in your ridiculous fantasies, wearing borrowed dresses that don't fit, and waving sticks about as you fight an imaginary foe. You're a beguiling young woman of seventeen and you've spent all your time – my precious few days at home before I'm shipped out to face an uncertain and dangerous future – with everybody *but* me.'

'You're jealous?' Her voice was incredulous. 'Of these broken men?'

'Yes.'

Olivia's heart began to accelerate, as she tried to make sense of what he was saying.

'I needed you to know... I wanted to...' He took a deep breath and tried again. 'Even when I was younger, there was something about you that fascinated me, but I had no idea how to speak to girls back then. I grew up with three brothers and went to an all-boys' school. The day that Ernest was holding you in the music room... Oh, this is impossible to put into words... I wasn't cross with him. Ernest is that sort: confident with the ladies, full of charm, and always says the right thing. He meant nothing by it and, of course, I could see you were thrilled by the attention. I... I was furious with myself because he had the courage to do something I'd been dreaming about in my stupid, immature mind for weeks but was too scared to act on. Turns out that even at nearly nineteen, I'm no better.'

He bit at his bottom lip, pausing for a moment to gauge her reaction, but she was calmer now and listened to him without interrupting. She was astute enough to realise, in that moment, he was scared, of both her temper and her reaction to the clumsy words he was stumbling over.

'Every time you're near, my stomach collapses and I feel as though I might heave up my last meal. My... my legs are shaky and my palms are sweaty. Quite frankly, I'd rather face a trench of Germans than stand before you now and admit the truth of my feelings, because the next few words that come from your lips could tear me apart as surely as any shell landing at my feet.'

She suddenly realised what he was trying to tell her and was confused and flattered all at once. How had she not seen the signs? Loitering in her shadow, with an inability to talk to her one minute and gushing nonsense the next. And then completely avoiding her. She'd thought he'd been holding on to some grudge when all the time, the complete opposite was true.

He was embarrassed by her hesitation to reply and his eyes fell to his feet.

'Remember the letters we received from Clarence after he...'

She nodded.

'He told me that it was important to say the things that mattered to the people you loved. It took a certain type of courage to be honest with yourself, he said, and one he didn't possess. Strange, really, how I'd always looked up to him as so strong, but he saw himself as weak. I guess, in a way, I'm doing this for him.' He swallowed. 'I wanted the attention that Clarence had for being the eldest and Louis got for being clever, but in recent months, the only person whose attentions I really wanted was yours. And now with Louis also taken from us, I realised I might not have the luxury of time. So... I'm probably making the biggest fool of myself, but I think I'm in love with you and I can't go off to France and not tell you, even if you don't feel the same.'

As she digested his words, she knew that she'd never thought about him in that way, at least not consciously. But, then again, she'd be lying to herself if she didn't admit she'd been acutely aware of his body as he'd stepped from the lake.

'This is all rather... sudden. I'm not sure what I feel.' Maybe there *were* feelings of a romantic nature, muddied by Cynthia's continued insistence that she was family. She'd been so slow to realise that he was no longer the awkward adolescent of four years ago and somehow, Benji had slipped into that role. Howard was a man now; one who was shortly to go to war, *and* one who was suddenly declaring his love.

'I realise this has come out of the blue but, it turns out, facing possible death rather forces a man to focus.' He stepped forward and put his hands on her upper arms, perhaps to steady himself, perhaps to stop her moving away. 'Let me show you how I feel and you can slap me afterwards,' he joked. 'I'm damn sure I'll deserve it.'

He hesitated a fraction, perhaps expecting the slap – she had form, after all – before leaning down to press his lips onto hers. Olivia instinctively tipped her head up and closed her eyes, thrilled by the contact of warm skin against warm skin. She could smell the lingering tobacco smoke and was surprised by the rough but strangely arousing sensation of his moustache brushing across her face. She considered the bewildering mix of sensations. Her chest rolled as he got better at what he was doing and she found that she had absolutely no desire to slap him – quite the opposite. She raised her hands to grip the cotton shirt covering his damp but surprisingly solid upper arms, and pulled him closer. Encouraged by her response, he slid his hands up into her hair, weaving his fingers between the strands, and she could hear his breathing intensify – almost feel the thumping of his heart.

Of course, she'd kissed the back of her own hand in her silly fantasies, dragging her lips across her skin as though she were caressing the mouth of a lover. Her accompanying thoughts had often elicited surprisingly arousing sensations throughout her body, considering the finer details of an intimate relationship with a man were as yet unknown to her. But it was nothing compared to this. Olivia's reactions to the taste of him, the warmth of his muscular arms around her, and the pull of all those parts of her that had suddenly burst into life, surprised her. Her body clearly knew something it had spectacularly failed to communicate to her brain. If she could have climbed inside his skin and nestled there, somewhere in the soft, safe cavity of his chest, she would have done so.

Eventually, he pulled back and studied her. He couldn't help but smile – that curling of his lip that she'd seen when he'd been up to mischief and cared not two hoots about the repercussions.

'I may not know much about girls, but I'm pretty certain that's an encouraging start.'

'Yes,' she acknowledged, feeling shy for the first time. 'Perhaps I have lived too much inside my head and should have paid more attention to the world outside of it.'

'You do know that there is a part of me that has been in love with you ever since you locked me in the privy? But Mother's damn insistence that we treat you as a sister has kept me at bay. Clarence's letter, Louis's death, and my present situation, however, were a call to action – one that I'm glad I found the courage to answer.' His voice faltered and his brow furrowed. This was the serious Howard who rarely surfaced. 'I... I don't expect you to promise anything, but say you'll think about all this when I'm gone? Let me go off to war with hope in my heart?'

She nodded.

'And then when you finally acknowledge what a topping idea this is, you'll kick yourself for not realising sooner what a smashing chap I truly am,' he pointed out, a wide grin forming on his freckled face. 'I can give you everything you ever imagined, Livvy. I am the fearless knight about to do battle. I have the castle, complete with towers. I would fight dragons for you and, although I would very much wish circumstances were not so, I will one day have the wealth and power to give you everything you desire.'

It was all galloping along rather too quickly, so Olivia felt the need to add a note of caution. 'Whilst I know there were times when I happily let the prince fight the evil witch and rescue me, please bear in mind that I was always just as willing to saddle up the horse and charge into battle myself. I need to slay my own dragons, achieve my own ambitions. Look how the war is already changing things for women. You might be taking on more than you can handle.'

It was only fair to give him warning. She had big plans for her life – plans to make her parents proud. She would write novels and travel the world – not stay at home and give birth to endless babies. Lady Fairchild's sole achievement in her unfulfilling but privileged life had been the production of four healthy sons, and they were now being snatched from her in the cruellest way imaginable. Olivia knew there was more to life than motherhood. God would not have given her such a wild imagination if he had not intended her to use it.

'None of this puts me off in the slightest,' he said, reaching for her soft cheek and tracing a line from her ear to her chin with his fingertip. 'It was obvious from the very moment that young Olivia Davenport arrived in our lives, she was always going to be a force to be reckoned with.'

21

The following year offered with hope when, in the April of 1917, America entered the war, but there was still heartbreaking tragedy to be found in Olivia's life. Major Turrell was shipped off to St Dunstan's Lodge in Regent's Park – an exciting new facility where blinded servicemen could learn how to adapt to life without sight – but died unexpectedly from an infection two weeks after leaving Norfolk. Even the seemingly no-nonsense nurse shed a tear when the news got back to Merriford.

As always, Olivia turned to her imagination to see her through. She wrote a short story about a romance between a blind soldier and the nurse who tended to him, knowing that the major was the man in her uplifting tale. What he had been robbed of in life, he would have on the page. Benji, who was the only one who really understood her need to indulge her creative soul, read it and told her it was 'jolly dramatic and soppy enough for any woman'. He encouraged her to submit it to a competition in a ladies' journal and, much to her surprise, she came first, entitling her to have her work published in the next edition.

Her mother had been correct: after the rain, the sun was sure to follow.

'It's suffocating, isn't it? Grief?' Lady Fairchild said to Olivia as they walked around the gardens, arms linked and looking for all the world like mother and daughter. Sir Hugo was away again overnight – the advent of war not curtailing his little trips to the coast.

'I can hardly bear to look at the photograph on the sideboard that we had taken in Haven-on-Sea during your first summer,' she continued. 'How can two of those smiling faces have been taken from us? And now Howard is out there too.'

He'd been in France for seven months and no one suspected the newfound intimacy between him and Olivia, least of all his mother. It was to remain their secret until such time as she was certain of her feelings. She wrote to him regularly, and had sent out a picture taken on her eighteenth birthday, which he told her was kept tucked into the small pocketbook he carried.

'I think back to when you arrived at the manor. I had no idea how to be a mother to you and was fully aware that Selina had raised you very differently to the way I raised my boys. She was so tactile and indulgent, whereas Sir Hugo insisted on firm discipline with our sons, and was adamant that excessive affection would weaken their character. I see now that you craved affection, space to breathe, and support in your creative endeavours.'

'Don't apologise. You were so kind to take me in and did your very best. By giving me the tower, you gave me all the space I needed. My mother would be so very grateful for everything you and Sir Hugo have done.'

'I dearly hope so but I am not convinced. She was so different to me, and such a joyful soul. I remember when Jasper first introduced her to us and she insisted on looping her arm through mine, which I found somewhat... invasive. Now I see that it's one of the best ways to truly connect with another.'

They stopped before a bed of red and yellow tulips and Olivia rested her head on the older woman's shoulder. For all their undoubted love and strong sense of family, the Fairchilds had displayed very little physical affection until her arrival. If she had taught them anything in return for their kindness, let it be that.

'If only I had put my arms about my boys more before they were snatched away from me.' Cynthia's voice started to crack.

'They knew that you loved them. It was more than enough. Besides, Louis really wasn't the embracing sort.' They both smiled at that.

'I could bear the pain of all this more if their bodies had been returned to me. Instead, they are buried hundreds of miles away. I have no graves to visit, nowhere I can lay flowers, and it feels so unreal, as though they aren't dead at all.'

'You can always talk to them,' Olivia soothed. 'They are both watching over you, even at this moment, and will listen to anything you have to say. I still find myself having conversations with my parents. I even wrote to them both after they'd died, imagining how they might respond.'

Lady Fairchild shook her head.

'I wish I could open myself up to such fancies. I envy you that.' She turned to her companion, planting a small kiss on the top of her head, and then Olivia tilted her face upwards and their eyes met.

'I'm so proud of the young woman you have become. You've long been like a daughter, and I know Benji and Howard see you as a sister.' Cynthia's words confirmed she was blind to the truth of her son's feelings. 'When loved ones are taken from you, those who remain become so much more important.'

Olivia nodded mutely. The Fairchilds could never replace her parents, but they were her family now, even though Howard's declaration of love had the potential to send all the apples in the cart flying into the air. The huge weight of carrying their secret was almost as dizzying as the kisses they'd shared by the boating lake, but the next time he came home for leave, she would know for sure what she truly felt and tell him as much.

* * *

Unhappily, Howard was not to return to the shores of his homeland for the whole of that year. In her frustration, Olivia threw herself into her writing and was met with moderate success. She had several further short stories published in ladies' journals. The money, which she had no need of, she donated to the convalescent hospital – another activity that took her mind off her troubles.

She had long since decided that her volunteer work was just as valuable as becoming a qualified nurse, especially as she'd discovered that she wasn't terribly good with blood. Besides, she couldn't, in all conscience, leave Cynthia, even for the few weeks it would take to train. She did make friends with the nurses at Merriford, however, and one, in particular, shared her love of reading. The woman's sweetheart was in the navy, so Olivia told her, in the strictest confidence, about Howard. She was relieved to finally speak about the conundrum out loud, and it gave them another thing in common.

Christmas 1917 was a muted affair for the family, for how could you celebrate with two Fairchild heirs dead, and a third stuck in waterlogged trenches abroad? It didn't seem right to be feasting on goose, drinking sherry and playing parlour games when Howard was fighting for his life and their future. But for

Benji's sake, and to raise the spirits of the wounded men, all those at Merriford Manor made an effort. There was usually someone proficient enough on the piano to entertain his fellow patients, and that December, they had the benefit of a young man who had worked in the music halls before the war.

The new year was ushered in, as the newspapers reported on the alarming number of merchant vessels being sunk by U-boats – and the ensuing shortages meant that rationing was finally introduced. Sugar was the first item, but meat, butter and cheese followed soon afterwards. Sir Hugo bemoaned the absence of marmalade on the breakfast table, and the increased costs of postage and tobacco. But all Olivia could think of was Howard and how unfair it was that they had been kept apart. Her letters were daily – his sporadic. It was no way to conduct a romance.

In the March of 1918, the Fairchilds were sad to learn that Ernest Dunn had been killed, and Sir Hugo and his wife attended a memorial service for him in the village. Everyone felt particularly sorry for his mother, especially as the father had passed away the previous year with heart trouble. Olivia had not been close to him but it was yet another young life cruelly extinguished.

Howard had now been in France for a year and a half with no leave, but this was sadly not uncommon. All that time when he had not seen his family or been able to hold the girl he had professed to love since he was fourteen. The strain of the war was becoming increasingly apparent through his letters but Olivia had long been angry that someone so young had been asked to lead men older and more experienced than himself into battle. His anguish and despair seeped into every page, and she became desperately worried about his state of mind.

And then, out of the blue, he was granted ten days' leave and she wondered if his obvious mental struggles had been apparent to his superiors and consequently a factor in this decision.

The nervous anticipation that Olivia felt over his impending visit was palpable. Would it be that their grand love affair was really not so grand after all? His declaration back in the autumn of 1916 had caught her off guard, and the remaining few hours they'd spent together had not been sufficient for her to establish anything with any certainty. And then not to have seen him for all that time – their letters simply hadn't been enough. She'd never been in love with anyone outside of her imagination and only ever been kissed by him. Her childish infatuation with the gardener when she'd first arrived had been misguided in the extreme, and her attraction to the butcher's son was just harmless flirtation. So how could she know if what she felt for Howard was real? She needed to be near him, to look in his eyes, feel his hands on her face, his lips on hers, to be certain.

When he landed back in the country, he telegraphed from London to say he would be at Merriford Lode station at ten past one on the Tuesday afternoon. Sir Hugo had planned to collect him in the motor car but it had been playing up all week, so Olivia offered to walk into the village and meet him. She was nervous that if they were to reunite in the presence of his parents, that her true feelings, whatever they proved to be, would be written across her face like the newspaper headlines on the sandwich boards in town. *It's Not Love After All!* would be embarrassing for her, a shock to the Fairchilds and devastating for Howard.

'We could all go?' she suggested half-heartedly, knowing Lady Fairchild wasn't really one for long walks and her husband had been having trouble with his knees recently. In the end, both were happy for her to go alone and she felt relieved that this long-anticipated reunion would not be witnessed by anyone else.

The day was warm, if gusty, and she changed into a pair of sturdy leather shoes and tied a pretty silk scarf, gifted from Cynthia, around her neck. The last thing she did before stepping away from her dressing table mirror was to pinch her cheeks and give her face a healthy, virginal glow. It only occurred to her as she set off down the long driveway, almost an hour before she needed to, that she would be a veritable beetroot by the time she arrived at the station, and she needn't have pinched her cheeks at all. Thank goodness she was giving herself plenty of time and could compose herself before his train pulled into Merriford Lode.

Cowslips and primroses covered the banks as she walked alongside the open fields and into the village. The chatter of birds and the smells of spring filled the air. The two-mile trip would have been quite pleasant, if only her stomach wasn't churning over nearly as madly as her mind.

The station was quiet and, looking at the clock over the entrance, she knew the ten past twelve had just been and gone. She had plenty of time to compose herself before Howard arrived and the truth of this thing between them could be established. But as she headed for the waiting room, she was shocked to see him sitting on a wooden bench, staring at the track. He jumped up immediately, hearing her footsteps, and looked at her with a mixture of wonder and delight.

'My God. Is that really you? Or am I dreaming?' He stepped towards her and she felt indescribably nervous. He was so much thinner than when she'd seen him back in 1916 and, like Clarence, he had an unhealthy pallor to his skin and a haunted look about his eyes.

They came to a halt a few paces apart.

'I wasn't expecting you yet,' was all she could manage.

He shrugged. 'I caught an earlier train. I wanted to get out of London. Too many military personnel buzzing about. The whole point of me being here is to leave that world behind for a while. Father said he'd pick me up in the old motor car and I was quite content waiting on the platform.'

'They've sent me, I'm afraid. The motor is playing up.'

'Infinitely preferable.' His eyes darted about, unable to settle on one thing, least of all her face, and she sensed he was as nervous as she.

'You'll have to carry your bag, though. I came on foot.'

'But the ground beneath my feet is dry. Besides, I much prefer a pleasant stroll through the lanes with you than listening to Father chunter on about the government and how he wishes he were young enough to fight.'

They exchanged a nervous smile and then set off together in the direction of Merriford Manor, walking barely two foot apart but not touching. Polite chatter ensued. How was Cook? Had Mother gone overboard with cake? Did Benji still hate school?

They'd just crossed the bridge by the ford and were in a quiet, tree-lined lane when he suddenly stopped.

'Damn this,' he said, throwing his kitbag to the ground and halting his steps. 'Come here.'

As soon as she was close enough, he grabbed her shoulders and crushed her frame to his. For a second, she couldn't breathe.

'You're all I've thought about in those moments when my mind had the space to do any rational thinking beyond keeping myself alive. And, after all those months, I started to doubt myself... Was I holding on to something that wasn't real? But here you are and I've never felt more certain of anything.' He cupped her chin with his hand and tilted her face to his. 'I love you. I've always loved you.'

She couldn't say it back, not because her feelings weren't powerful, but because the words wouldn't mean anything yet. What did she really know of romantic love? Looking at him in that moment, she certainly felt a dizzy, spinning something. But reading about it, daydreaming about it, wasn't the same as experiencing it.

He leaned forward and rested his forehead on her own to the backdrop of a highly agitated blackbird above their heads, and she suspected they were close to the nest. But the squawks of the bird started to fade as everything around them ceased to exist. She felt an intense connection with the man before her, as though he was the only thing in the world at that moment, and sensed his need, as surely as if he shook her by the shoulders and pinned her to the nearest tree. And to her surprise, she felt that need too.

It was *her* clawing at his hair, pressing her body close to his, wanting to anchor every part of her to every part of him. She heard him groan as her breathing became fast and feverish, but didn't stop to analyse what she was doing. Howard had now been a part of her life for six years and she knew him almost better than she knew anyone, save Benji and Cynthia. The clashes between them all this time had been masking the attraction. The lane was deserted but, in truth, neither of them would have cared should a whole regiment have marched by.

'Not here.' Just two words as he swept up the leather handles of his canvas bag with one hand and gripped one of hers with the other. He strode fifty yards to the edge of the trees and then took a path to their left, through a carpet of late bluebells, many past their best but beautiful nonetheless.

Olivia stumbled a couple of times, but his strong arm stopped her from falling as he marched forward with a grim determination. She knew what was happening – why he was leading her into the cover of tree canopies, and every part of her was willing it to be.

Finally, he threw his bag to the floor, slipped off his thick wool coat and spread it over a flat patch of ground. Out of the weak sunlight and in the gloom of the forest, she began to shiver.

'You're cold,' he said, his brow concertinaed into a frown, as he embraced her once again and rubbed at her shoulders.

'No, I'm nervous,' she whispered into the thick cotton of his shirt, glad he couldn't see her face.

He stopped rubbing and sighed. 'This is madness. What the hell am I thinking? You're so young, so innocent, so...'

He bent to retrieve his coat and she put out her hand to stop him, sliding her body under his and meeting his eye.

'I said I was nervous, not unwilling.' She tried to convey the sincerity of her words. 'No one knows what is ahead, or when I'll even see you again, and we must grab these precious moments. I want this too.'

Overriding his concern, he lowered her gently backwards and she wriggled her slim body to find a more comfortable space between the bumps of the woodland floor. They both knew time and the possible risk of discovery were against them, and this, along with the genuine feeling that her whole body might burst if this didn't happen, made everything more electric.

A million frantic kisses and the hasty loosening of clothing before their eyes engaged and, for the surprisingly short duration of their fumbled and frantic coupling, their gaze remained entirely focused on each other. Just at the point when he started to shake, losing all focus, he pulled away from her and turned to his side, a small cry following his withdrawal, before he returned his attention to her.

'I'm sorry. That was... over sooner than I expected. Did I hurt you?' One hand came to rest on her cheek and he lay his exhausted body next to hers.

'A bit, but it's fine.' And it really was. She wasn't completely sure what had just happened. It was nothing like she'd imagined, not better or worse, just incredibly intense, but she knew one thing for certain now – she loved him.

'Your parents will start to wonder where we are,' she pointed out.

He glanced at the new wristwatch that his father had sent out in the Christmas parcel Olivia had helped his mother put together.

'They aren't expecting us yet. Can we enjoy the peace for a little while longer? Mother can be so overwhelming.'

'Only because she misses you so desperately.'

She hitched herself up on her elbows and leaned over to kiss him, letting the rough hairs of his moustache graze across her lips, before reaching for a bluebell and threading the stem through his thick, auburn hair. He smiled at her action and then closed his eyes, not bothered by her frivolous attentions. He'd been exhausted before they'd lain together, but now he was truly spent. She continued to snap off flowers and weave them into a crown until he resembled a woodland sprite from her childhood picture books. Finally, she nestled back into his arm.

'How does it feel to have claimed a virgin?' she asked, a gentle smile playing across her lips. He was only a year older than her age-wise, but who knew how old in terms of experiences. Had she been a disappointment?

He turned to face her, his eyes twinkling as he raised both eyebrows. 'I don't know.' He grinned. 'You tell me.'

It took her a moment to realise what he was saying, but she merely shrugged. 'I left these shores an innocent and never touched the Frenchwomen behind the lines. I understood the desperate men, seeking an hour of solace, a few minutes of human touch, but I have always saved myself for you – the strange girl who appeared in our lives and turned my world upside down.' She was surprised and flattered all at once. 'It's I who should apologise, but we can learn together, can't we? We have a lifetime to get it right.' He paused, suddenly nervous and biting at his bottom lip. 'You *will* marry me, won't you?'

And that was his grand proposal – an anxious need to be reassured that what they had hastily and recklessly done together across a dying carpet of bluebells on the woodland floor that April afternoon, a halo of blue flowers woven through his hair, was as momentous to her as it was to him.

'Surely,' she said, the tip of her fingers tracing the deep furrows in his brow and a hint of mischief in her eyes, 'my body has already given you my answer, Sprinkles.'

22

'Such a shame you're not in the tower any more,' Howard said as they walked up the gravel driveway between the two wings of the house and towards the front door. Lady Fairchild and Sir Hugo were standing on the stone steps, anticipating the imminent return of their son. His mother would have been looking out from the library since Olivia had left to meet his train, so anxious was she to have him home. But, despite her eagerness to see him, if Lady Fairchild was going to cry, she would do it at the manor and not on a station platform for all to see.

'It was felt necessary when the wounded young men moved in.' One of the nurses had indeed been caught *in flagrante* with a young officer and been summarily dismissed, but Olivia had felt sorry for the young lovers, especially after the heartbreak of Major Turrell. 'They were protecting my virtue.'

'Exactly, because it's your virtue I fully intended to violate, but I can't do that creeping down the corridor that my mother may step into at any given moment.' Although they had been intimate only a short while ago, they were walking some distance from each other, not touching, and with nothing about their demeanour to indicate this was the case. 'Shall we tell them?'

Her eyes flashed wide. 'That we've been together in the woods?' She shared a close bond with Cynthia now, but they weren't quite *that* close.

'No, you silly goose. That we're engaged.'

'Your mother sees us as brother and sister. We need to tread gently. She's so desperately excited to have you home, Howie. Let today be for her.'

And as a highly emotional Lady Fairchild ran towards them, arms outstretched and tears streaming down her cheeks, Olivia stepped to the side and allowed Howard's parents to usher him into the house, wondering if everyone could now tell from her face that she was no longer a child, but a woman.

* * *

Howard was better than both his older brothers at tolerating his mother's overexuberance. He'd always had the most open personality and, perhaps the truth was, he finally had the undivided attention of his parents that he'd so desperately craved growing up. By nightfall, however, the young lovers had not been able to snatch one minute alone, and his desperation resulted in a note passed to Olivia under the dining table.

They met at the end of the top corridor at midnight and he led her to the boathouse. It was, he confided, a place Clarence had held assignations in the past. The gamekeeper had long since been ordered to turn a blind eye to any nightly activities going on within, so they would not be disturbed. Somehow, Howard had arranged for a bed of blankets to await them and liberated a bottle of something dusty and strong from the cellar. They made love, slowly this time, and it was an improvement on their fumbled efforts in the woods.

Shafts of moonlight fell across his pale, exposed flesh as he lay face down next to her, his head tilted, and eyes wide with wonder, caressing every inch of her face.

'This makes a change from picking lice out the seams of my uniform by candlelight.' It was said in his usual breezy manner but she detected the resentment within.

'Do you want to talk about it?'

He rolled over and sat up, staring out the window, and she wondered if he had heard her request, until finally he spoke.

'Was dear old Louis's candour not enough?' He closed his eyes. 'Because, even if I wanted to, and even with all the vocabulary I have at my disposal, it's a woefully inadequate dictionary to describe what's going on out there.'

She shuffled closer to him and threw her arms about his shoulders, no longer embarrassed as the blanket fell from under her arms. He was exposing himself emotionally. What did her nakedness matter?

'We got it so wrong, Liv. Thinking of it all as some great escapade – a chance for glory and sacrifice. There's no glory in the waterlogged pits of death I walk through. I pray to God that it's all over, one way or another, before Benji is dragged into it.'

'You'll be fine.' She tried to reassure, to soothe. 'You simply have to be. We've found each other now and I'll not have you leave me too.'

'Promise me that whatever happens, you'll pursue those plans you wrote out in your notebook? That you'll travel and have magnificent adventures?'

'I promise,' she said. 'But we can do it together. As man and wife.'

He put his head in his hands.

'I should have married you before I touched you. I've done my best to ensure that you won't fall pregnant, but it's never guaranteed. Assuming that you aren't carrying my child, which would rather change things, I think we should wait until this bloody mess is over before we tell my parents, though. Our American brothers stand beside us now and surely, it can't drag on much longer.'

Olivia nodded. 'Your mother won't like it. She insists I'm your sister.'

'And that's why I must be the one to do it. I can't have her angry with you, especially if there are whispers from some of the more sanctimonious villagers.'

'Until the war is over, then,' she agreed.

* * *

It was an anxious few days for Olivia after Howard returned to the front but she was relieved to find that she was not with child. The days stretched into weeks and she missed him like crazy. She tried to hide her listlessness and frustration, but she found it difficult to focus on anything other than those passionate few days together, and she lived entirely for his letters.

One early June afternoon, she returned to the boathouse to recapture precious memories of their time together. The wooden door had warped with the spring rains and it was with some difficulty that she opened it and stepped inside. It smelled of damp and the blankets that they had lain upon back in the April were still folded up on a wicker chair.

Olivia picked up an abandoned striped jumper of his, left behind from their illicit night-time encounters, and held it to her face. She could smell traces of him in the wool and decided to take it back to her room to remind herself that the whirlwind of their romance was real. Surely, the war couldn't last much longer and the need for their subterfuge would be over. Sir Hugo was convinced it was coming to an end – the Germans were exhausted – and then they could marry and be done with all the secrecy. She had every faith Howard would return to her, and that he would find the right words to soften the blow for his parents.

'You love him, don't you?'

Cynthia's voice startled her and she spun to face the older woman, who had entered the boathouse without her knowing.

'Who?'

'Don't treat me like a fool, Olivia.' Her tone was gentle but her eyes were sad as she looked at the distinctive garment in Olivia's hands. 'Everything was written across your faces as you returned up the drive together in the spring. The very fact you would not touch each other – you, who embraces everyone from the cook to the postwoman – or meet each other's eyes across the dining table, told me all I needed to know. But this afternoon, one of the hospital volunteers from the village mentioned she sat with him on the ten past twelve that day. So, I asked myself, why it took you both so long to walk back to the house and why you might lie about it.'

Olivia met the eyes of the woman who was all but a mother to her and swallowed hard.

'Howard wanted to be the one to tell you. He thought you'd be angry, but it is only a very recent thing.'

Cynthia sighed. 'I was shocked when I first suspected the truth – you know that I see you like a daughter – but then I thought about it all more sensibly. There is no blood link, so there is nothing improper about your romance, as long as my son's intentions are honourable and this is no casual dalliance.'

'We're engaged,' she confirmed, and Cynthia's face broke into a smile. 'Unofficially.'

'I'm hurt that neither of you felt you could trust me with this information; however, this news brings me joy, when I have been joyless for so long.' The older woman stepped forward and reached out to cup Olivia's anxious face with her soft hands. 'Leave Sir Hugo to me. Perhaps we can engineer a wedding before the year is out. I'm certain my husband can pull some strings. Get Howard back here as soon as possible. The war has taken its toll on my poor boy and they surely can't deny him this. What good is it knowing people in high places if you can't occasionally use it to your advantage? And, naturally, you must have my mother's ring...'

And, as the older woman flipped from thought to thought, Olivia smiled to herself. Her wedding would be organised to within an inch of its life and she doubted she'd have much say in the proceedings, but honestly didn't care. That their union could go some way to repairing all the damage and heartache that the war had brought upon this family was enough for her.

* * *

Lady Fairchild officially announced their engagement the very next day, much to consternation of the vicar and grumbles of the wounded men Olivia attended. Even Benji's congratulations were muted, despite her reassurances that it would change nothing between them. But he was young; he would adapt. Olivia immediately wrote to Howard to say that the cat was out the bag, and that his mother had taken it surprisingly well and, as the days went on, the spirits of the whole household lifted. Everyone was excited to be planning for such a happy event after four years of misery.

Sir Hugo set about tugging on those strings, attempting to engineer leave for his son, but Howard's commanding officer stressed that, militarily, this was a critical period and Captain Fairchild had not long been home. Consequently, no leave was forthcoming. The family eventually thought they'd secured leave for him at the end of the summer but he fell ill with pneumonia and spent three weeks in a French hospital.

Despite this, good things were on the horizon as, by September, everyone knew the war was coming to an end. The Allies were advancing and Germany was on her knees. Her army was disillusioned and her people were hungry. All Olivia prayed for was for Howard to stay alive until the end came.

How terribly cruel then, for a telegram to arrive one September afternoon to inform the family that their son was missing in action, having led a night raid in enemy territory.

All three members of the party had failed to return.

23

There was no body and so Olivia refused to accept that Howard was dead.

She got through the next few weeks doing the thing she did best: retreating to her imagination. There were a dozen different scenarios that could have played out: the men could have become disorientated and be hiding out somewhere, or perhaps Howard was recovering in a foreign hospital but had lost his memory, or the party had been captured by the Germans and were in a prisoner of war camp. It would, however, take time to establish if this was the case, especially as the enemy was now in a state of utter chaos, but Sir Hugo was calling in all the favours he could think of to discover the truth as quickly as possible.

She reconciled herself to the fact that being captured might be the best thing to happen to him. He would be safe until the conflict was over – away from the shells and bullets, and out of the rat-infested trenches. She was under no illusion that prisoners had it easy but, every day, she played out scenes in her head where her beloved Howard was returned to her. Surely, she would have known, felt *something* – a hole, an empty ache – if he were dead. It hadn't taken her long to feel an eviscerating void after the sinking of the *Titanic*, and her parents' bodies had never been recovered either.

She wondered if her photograph was being caressed and cherished by him in some distant land, a reminder that he was loved beyond measure and must survive the war so that they could be reunited? Or was it buried under several feet of earth, with his broken, lifeless body, waiting to be found and give them all the full stop they longed for? Or perhaps destined never to be found at all?

It was nearly a month of not knowing. A month of torture. And then the news came through that they'd all been waiting for, with Sir Hugo finding her in the library, listless and exhausted from lack of sleep. She looked up as he strode into the room, waving a sheet of paper at her.

'He's safe, Olivia. He's been in a German prisoner of war camp all this time.'

* * *

On the eleventh of November 1918, the armistice was signed in France, with all hostilities ceasing at eleven o'clock that morning. Church bells rang across the country; even Big Ben spoke for the first time in two years. The days passed in a blur of celebrations. The war was finally over.

Wedding preparations began in earnest, even though they had no idea when Howard would be able to get home. A three-tier cake had been baked, but not yet iced, and Olivia was fitted for a dress.

It was mid-December, Benji was back from school, and the household finally had a festive season to look forward to, when the housekeeper sought Olivia out in the library. One look at the woman's face and she knew something was terribly wrong.

'The Fairchilds have had a telegram. I thought you should know.'

An icy terror started somewhere deep inside and slowly spread outwards from her very centre, creeping like a deadly poison through her veins, and killing every part of her as it went. The war was at an end. The fighting had ceased. Surely, it could not be bringing bad news.

She rushed to the drawing room and flung open the door. Sir Hugo stood with a piece of paper in his hand and Her Ladyship was staring at her husband, pale as the moon, but they both turned to face Olivia as she entered. The look of bewilderment and unfathomable sadness in Sir Hugo's eyes, the exaggerated silence that hung in the air like a heavy, immovable fog, and the way Cynthia held herself – slumped, defeated and broken – told her all she needed to know.

Finally, he spoke. 'Oh, my darling girl. It's Howard.'

Olivia's knees went from under her as the world shattered into a million tiny, irreparable shards. First her parents, then Clarence and Louis, and now she'd been dealt the most wicked blow of all, just when she thought all the unbearable suffering and crippling pain was over.

Sir Hugo had not yet said the words but she didn't need to hear them. Howard was dead and the details didn't matter. He spoke of them regardless.

'Influenza. They think he was already quite weak from his ordeal and he caught it when he was being transported across France.'

Nothing in this world would ever matter again.

PART III

AFTER THE WAR

24

Olivia ran crying from the back of the house and stood on the damp lawns, not knowing what to do or where to go. She could not bring herself to take refuge in the boathouse. In fact, she didn't think she could ever step into that building again without wanting to smash every window or put a match to the whole place. Instead, she spun back on herself and ran for the tower, the place she'd found comfort once before.

As soon as she passed through the ground-floor entrance, a calm washed over her. She climbed the spiral stairs and returned to her old room to find the furniture remained, even though her personal belongings had been moved to the main part of the house. But even in that soulless space, she felt a connection to something – a heartbeat – that enabled her to breathe again.

Walking over to the south-facing window, she watched the sun start to go down to her right. The saturated colours that filled the sky were of fire and blood, and she thought of Howard, and only Howard, from the moment the white blazing ball of the sun sunk into the vibrant orange sky, until the last thin strip of gold was tamped down by the layers of deep purple and soot grey. In the darkness, she moved to sit on the edge of the bare mattress and, now that the light had drained from the day, all that was left was a room full of shadow and memory.

Grief was exhausting and so she curled up on the bed. Not many moments later, she heard the main door open below and the anxious voice of the only surviving Fairchild son call up the stairs.

'Olivia? Are you in here? Everyone's worried sick.'

Slow footsteps clumped up the spiral steps, followed by a knock at the door and she rolled to face the wall, not wanting Benji to see her tears. It swung open slowly and he came to her side, perching next to her and reaching out his hand to rest on her shoulder.

Neither of them spoke. Why articulate such desperate emotions? It wouldn't bring any of his brothers back or make either of them feel any better. If anything, to say it out loud would only make everything worse. It was almost as if speaking the truth would sever Howard from her entirely and she wouldn't even be able to reach him in her dreams.

Eventually, Benji removed his spectacles, swung his legs up onto the bed and lay beside her, and she rolled back to face him and nestled in his arms. He wasn't the stocky build of Howard or Clarence, but instead slender, like Louis, and much taller than her now, as she'd always predicted he would be. She found comfort in his embrace, nonetheless.

'I told my parents that I knew where you'd be.' It was the first thing spoken aloud for several minutes. 'And that I would sit with you. We can be here all night, if it helps. No one expects us at dinner. To be honest, I don't think anyone feels like eating. Mother has taken to her room and Father has shut himself in the library.'

She knew it was selfish to wallow in her grief. The three remaining Fairchilds were suffering every bit as much as her. Instead of hiding herself away, she should be with Cynthia, comforting the woman who had lost three of her four sons in unimaginably unjust circumstances. But her grief was an intensely personal thing and easiest to deal with in solitude.

'I need to move back into the tower,' she said. The calm of the last hour had at least given her thinking time. 'I've always been happiest here.'

'I'll see to it.' Benji spoke with the authority of a man, not a fifteen-year-old boy, and it occurred to her that he would one day be the master of Merriford Manor – something no one could have foreseen only five short years ago. His whole life was about to change in the most dramatic of ways, and she briefly wondered if it would see the end of his artistic ambitions.

'But you aren't to shut yourself away, Livvy,' he stressed. 'You must promise me you won't give up.'

It wasn't a promise she could make so instead, she closed her eyes to block out the world. She had no fight left in her. The cruelty of finding out that Howard had survived the raid, survived the war in fact, only to die from influenza was worse than any joke he ever played.

How many times was God to test her? Had she not been through enough in her short life? Had she not faced adversity with fortitude back when her parents died? But you could only repair a broken vase so many times because, if you repeatedly dropped it on the hard, stone floor, eventually, all that remained would be dust.

And now, Olivia Davenport felt all that remained of her was dust.

* * *

The new year stepped quietly over the threshold without a fuss. The photograph of them all at Haven-on-Sea disappeared from the sideboard and everything about the house that was related to the wedding was discreetly spirited away. The flag-waving, celebratory bonfires and drunken euphoria of Armistice Day seemed a lifetime ago. In many ways, the end of the war had changed very little; the dead remained dead, food shortages continued and the troops could not get home. It hadn't taken long for the unconfined joy of victory to segue into a bleak reality. The returning men found it a struggle to settle into their old jobs, the women resented being shuffled quietly back into the kitchens, and the victorious nations found themselves just as broken as those they had defeated.

Olivia had moved back into the tower two weeks after the telegram about Howard but shut herself away, much as Benji had feared, because the world outside was of no consequence to her. She prepared for a long and lonely winter, and in all probability, a long and lonely life.

In the end, Cynthia rallied before her. Perhaps having lost two sons had hardened her to losing a third. She was lady of the manor, patron of the church and there were still injured and despairing young men at the hospital in her house who needed support. She must lead by example. Her husband and her remaining son relied on her, but Olivia had no one. Why should she rally? What was left for her now? Even the wounded men she volunteered for would soon be patched up and sent back to civilian lives. The hours that she'd spent reading to the sick, helping the blind and illiterate compose letters, knitting socks and packing up parcels, would be at an end. She had no purpose, and that was clearer to her now than it had ever been. All the while Howard had been alive, she'd anticipated a future juggling marriage and her childhood dreams and, even briefly, after Louis's death, expecting to be mistress of Merriford Manor at some point. Now she had nothing and no one.

Even her writing was something she no longer took any pleasure in. Why had she been so convinced that escaping into other worlds was the answer? Her prize-winning story hadn't brought Major Turrell back, and no amount of fanciful fiction, however uplifting, would give her or Howard the happy ending they so deserved. What a naïve little fool she'd been to believe that her imagination could make everything better. To allow herself a fleeting dream of Howard lying amongst the bluebells after they'd made love in the woods, or to compose a story where they went on wild adventures in foreign lands, was only good for the few minutes it lasted. When reality returned, Howard was still dead and the body that she had so willingly and completely shared hers with was now far away, a decomposing mass of tissue and bone. This was the harsh fact that she could never run away from.

January.

February.

March.

April.

What did she care for the month when all her days were the same? Her only solace was found in the company of Cynthia, because she understood. They did not speak of the boys; they barely spoke at all, but they often embraced or reached for each other's hand. Olivia wasn't living; she was existing. She couldn't even rouse herself to say goodbye to the last of the patients when the hospital was closed and Merriford Manor was returned to what was left of the Fairchild family.

Benji found her sitting at the edge of the lake on a blanket that Easter. She would never step in the boathouse again, but being near the water was calming and she enjoyed watching the waterfowl.

'Benji?' Her mood lifted when she realised he was home. She was certain he was another inch taller and was trying to grow something across his top lip, but she made no mention of it.

'It's Benjamin, not Benji,' he corrected. 'You must appreciate that I am almost a man now.' At sixteen, he might have the physical presence of one, but Olivia recognised he still had a lot of growing up to do.

He flicked the tails of his jacket away and sat gingerly beside her.

'Mother says you really aren't the ticket – that you are drifting about like a ghost. I want the springy, unstoppable you back. The one I so looked up to in my childhood.'

'I'm fine, Benji... Benjamin, but the time for fairy tales has passed. I'm thinking about returning to Windy Acres. Merriford has been one phase of my life. I'll be twenty-one before the year is out and it is time to move on to the next.'

'That's rubbish, Livvy. This is your home, and there is *always* a place for fairy tales – you taught me that. The Grimm brothers made a living from them. I hate to see this quiet and withdrawn version of you. It's so wrong. You're our sunshine and without it, this family will wither and die.'

Olivia felt resentful. It wasn't her job to keep everyone going.

'You don't understand. I lost my parents, Clarence, Louis and then the man I loved. Who cares if I rot in my tower now?'

'Mother, Father... me. So many people care about you. We can't pretend that the war hasn't changed us. I don't know of one family who hasn't lost someone, or isn't struggling with the return of a soldier who will never be the same again. Even those who look fine on the outside hide wounds on the inside. One of my school chums said his big brother still suffers from shell shock. He doesn't speak much, cries an awful lot, and has violent flares of temper over the smallest things. He hit his own mother, apparently. Scary stuff.'

'But he's alive and with people who love him. God took three members of this family away – it's not fair.'

But it was Benji's turn to get cross.

'Life *isn't* fair, Liv, we all know that, but for you, of all people, to give up is absolutely crushing. My whole education these last few years has been tailored towards the expectation that I would be an infantry officer upon leaving education. And now I bear the shame that I never shall. I feel like shutting down, snapping every paintbrush I ever owned in half and running away, but I can't. I finally understand Clarence so much better because my life, like his, is mapped out for me now and I just have to get on with it. You have so many options, so many choices, and if you don't take them, I shall be unspeakably angry with you.'

His words made her feel guilty but she remained silent.

They sat together watching the coots and moorhens paddle about at the edge of the lake. After a while, a concerned Benjamin reached out his arm and pulled Olivia to him. She allowed her head, which barely reached his shoulder, to rest against him as he nervously cleared his throat.

'I can sleep in the tower with you again, if you like? You know, help you to feel safe?'

'No, it's fine. I can manage.'

There was a pause.

'Then start managing because, from what I can gather, you're doing a frankly dreadful job, old thing. Sort yourself out, Liv. Your parents, and Howard come to that, would be so very disappointed in you.'

And she wondered when he had suddenly become the grown-up.

* * *

That night, Olivia stared hard at the ceiling, knowing that Benji's words, as harsh as they were, were valid. But knowing a thing and doing something about it were two very different beasts and she had no idea if she had the strength to pull herself from the mire. Finally, she allowed the familiar tears to build, knowing that if she didn't let them out, she would suffocate under the weight of them. How foolish she'd been to think that life was like fiction – that as the heroine of her own story she would ultimately triumph, even if she'd had to undergo great adversity along the way. There was no triumph to be had.

She cried for the loss of her loved ones, but also the ensuing loss of herself. She rolled to her side, facing the deep red of the bricks and wanting nothing more in that moment than to smash her head against them and make the world go away.

Eventually, she stopped for air, and in that brief moment of silence, the voice of someone she had not heard from for years, came through the wall.

'Cordelia?' The voice was clear, questioning and familiar.

Seth was back.

25

'Seth?' she whispered. Her tears immediately halted. She knew without question that the voice was not a concerned visitor at her bedroom door, but a bewildered enquiry not two foot from her head and directly the other side of the wall. Everything was still for a few moments and she realised that her reply had not been heard. She repeated the name, saying it louder the second time, as she stared at the bricks before her in disbelief.

'*Seth*?'

Of course, she thought to herself, this was inevitable. The voice had returned as a product of her grief. She was only surprised that it had taken so long. Where had her imaginary friend been back in December when her world had totally collapsed for the second time? The inner voice of her own creation from before the war, who had helped her to cope with the death of her parents, had failed to return to help her navigate the unthinkable: the death of her fiancé. She'd spent all this time alone. He was five months too late.

'Is that really you?' Seth queried, and she thought she detected a half-chuckle in his tone. 'The voice I spent two years thinking was a ghost until you made the wild claim that your parents died on some ship that never even sunk?'

She wiped the back of her hand across her wet cheeks. 'My parents *did* perish aboard the *Titanic*. Why would I make something like that up? You're the one with fanciful tales of living in a world I don't recognise.' She groaned. 'Oh, how I curse my vivid imagination. I have relied on the fantasies in my head as an escape for so long, but the real world has dealt me crushing blow after crushing blow and I sometimes feel there is no point to anything any more.'

Her breaths were still catching in her throat and she twisted around to reach for a cotton handkerchief on the nightstand, before returning her head to the pillow and the position she had always heard the voice the clearest.

'Ha, I'd forgotten what a dramatic soul you could be. Well, now, I can't tell you how much I've missed our silly bickering and your nonsense that you were a medieval, lovelorn princess who'd launched herself from the tower after being jilted. Course, I dint believe it for a second and spent weeks trying to work out how you'd got in the tower. But whatever the truth, I'm delighted to hear from you again. So much so, that I don't care if you're a bored girl from the village who's ribbing me, you're in my head or even if you are talking to me from another version of my own world – although that last one is the most nonsense of all, obviously.'

'Obviously,' she echoed.

'And I'm mightily disappointed to hear you sounding so glum at such an uplifting time of year. Can you not see Mother Nature bursting into life all about? The titty-totty shoots, poking their bright-green heads through the soil? Do you not smell the good, clean air hereabouts? A smell to gladden a man's soul, I can tell you. And have you not heard the sweet call of the cuckoo, announcing its arrival and a sure sign that summer is on her way?'

'Someone sounds more cheerful than I remember,' she mumbled, still bewildered that her brain had conjured up the hallucination of her adolescence, and thinking that she hadn't heard her first cuckoo yet, but she knew that the head gardener, Rowe, had told Her Ladyship he had. The return of the voice must be because she was back in the tower, she reasoned. There had always been something odd about this place.

'I wouldn't say I'm exactly skipping about, full of boundless joy, but I'm generally a more chipper soul and look for reasons every day to be so. It's good to be back at Merriford after my time away, and even better to reconnect with an old friend.' He chuckled to himself. 'I dint expect to hear from you ever again,' he said. 'I'd rationalised you away. You dint come to me in my darkest hours so I decided p'rhaps I'd got my head sorted and you'd served your purpose.'

Olivia felt a prickling sensation crawl across her skin. There was something not right about this whole situation; she just couldn't put her finger on what it was. It was certainly strange that he talked of being away, as though he were a real man who had the ability to leave the tower.

'But I'm glad that you're back,' the voice continued, 'so that I can say thank you, if nothing else. God but I was a miserable sod back then, wrapped up in my own misfortunes.'

She shifted over onto her tummy and sniffed.

'You were,' she agreed. 'But I was merciless in my teasing.'

'No, I needed to hear it, even though it took a couple of years for it to all sink in. I thought my life was at rock bottom, back then. Ha,' he scoffed. 'I had no idea how bad it was about to get. And in my quiet moments, I often thought back to our strange conversations. Your joy shone through, and your determination that life was for living. How you regretted tossing yourself from the tower because you could've gone on adventures and written books about them.'

It was uncomfortable for Olivia to hear him talk of her positivity, especially as Benji had told her off for barely coping. Where had that daredevil, carefree child gone? All her plans to follow in her father's footsteps and to forge new paths of her own had evaporated, along with her hopes of marriage and happiness. How utterly patronising of her to assume she could tell another to shake himself off, dust himself down and step forward to embrace life.

'Where have you been, then?' she asked, narrowing her eyes. 'You said it's good to be back as though you've been away.'

'Doing my bit for King and Country. The history books'll call it the Great War, and I doubt we'll ever see the likes again – not in my lifetime, at least.'

Olivia felt her body go cold at his words. 'You want me to believe you were a part of it? Out there in the trenches of France, fighting against the Ottoman Empire, or enduring the harsh climate of East Africa?'

'Wasn't every patriotic soul of fighting age? I signed up back in the August of fourteen, not many days after I'd got merry with the lads in the bothy and you came out with that strange tale about the ship sinking.' There was a contemplative pause. 'Guess I was trying to give my life a bit of meaning. I saw action in Belgium and northern France and was discharged last month, when the Fairchilds kindly took me on again.'

'*The Fairchilds*?'

Those creeping prickles intensified. Had he been playing her all this time? Was he some local lad who had conducted an elaborate prank on her all those years ago and was now outside, speaking to her through a pipe and making her think he was in the tower? Her mild curiosity side-stepped into anger. Her fists became balls, gripping at bunches of the linen sheets, as her nostrils flared. To play such a prank as this, when everyone knew what the Fairchilds had gone through, was beyond cruel.

'Who *exactly* are you?'

'I told you, back when we first started talking. My name is Seth – Seth Tanner. I'm one of the undergardeners here.'

26

Olivia's body stiffened with shock and she allowed her head to fall back against the rough bricks, trying to better hear Seth's bemusing words and make sense of what the voice was saying. Her stomach was churning faster than a spinning top and she thought she might be sick. Everyone knew the tragedies she'd experienced in her short life, from the death of her parents, to the loss of the three eldest Fairchild sons. The upcoming wedding had been the talk of the village and she couldn't believe that anyone could be so unkind as to put her through this. Why would this man claim to be the very person she'd initially suspected of being the voice? And someone she had such an uncomfortable past with, to boot?

Everything that had happened in the summer of 1912 came rushing back to her. As far as she knew, Tanner had moved to Cambridgeshire and hadn't had a connection to Merriford Manor for years. And yet, she'd always thought Seth's manner of speaking was similar to the prickly lad she'd had her silly, infantile crush on. Whoever he was, he was delusional, assuring her that the events that had so devastatingly altered the course of her life had never happened. It was simply too much for her to cope with in the middle of the night, alone and in her current state. But perhaps that was the truth of it – she was so unhappy that she was lost to her own mind and no longer had any control.

'Seth Tanner hasn't worked at Merriford Manor for years,' she said, her tone quite sharp.

'I know, I've been serving abroad—'

'No, I mean he left to work in Cambridgeshire back in 1912.'

'Well, I most certainly didn't. Why would I leave a job I love to go halfway across the country?'

A guilty pang shot through her and she avoided his question.

'This is all nonsense,' Olivia said. 'You insisting that you are someone I happen to know doesn't live in Norfolk any more, and trying to persuade me that the *Titanic* didn't sink...'

She heard a long sigh drift through the wall. It was the weary impatience of a person repeating himself to someone who wasn't listening.

'May God strike me down if even one word coming from my mouth is not the truth. I'm Seth William Tanner and that ship *did* hit an iceberg head on, but was able to sail onward for repairs. There were a lot of red faces at the White Star Line and huge public outrage,' Seth continued. 'We heard a lot about it at the time because Sir Hugo had friends on board when it happened. Have you heard of the famous author Jasper Davenport?'

For a moment, Olivia wanted to laugh, but nothing about this situation was funny. Her parents were dead and this whole conversation was ludicrous. It was at that moment that she realised Seth had no idea who she was. He didn't even know her real name.

'Of course I've heard of him!' She spat the words out. 'He was my father and I am Olivia Davenport. I was orphaned when that boat went down, and Sir Hugo – as my godfather and legal guardian – took me in. I gave my name as Cordelia because I was pretending to be the ghost you kept insisting I was.'

If her tone was angry, his was simply incredulous.

'Olivia Davenport? The tree-climbing tomboy who was always so kind to Master Benjamin when she visited?' He snorted. 'I remember her asking if I'd ever seen fairies in the woods and whether I thought people's dreams floated around in the air and landed in other people's heads – or something equally dizzy.' The questions sounded like something she might have asked but never had – not of him, at any rate. 'Darn good shot with a catapult, as I recall.'

She frowned. 'That sounds like me.'

'If you're her, then tell me the title of the book your father published last year.'

But it was the wrong question to ask.

'The last book my father wrote was published at the end of 1911 *and then he died*,' she reminded him. 'And it was a cruel and wholly avoidable death. I know this because I've thoroughly researched the events of that night over the years, even though it wouldn't bring my parents back, but because I mistakenly thought understanding it all might help.'

It hadn't helped at all, of course, and the very fact that the whole disaster was preventable had made everything a million times worse.

'We talked about the *Titanic* before the war – remember?' she said.

'I do, as it happens. That was an odd night. You mentioned some names – members of the crew that I'd never heard of – but jigger me, if they didn't turn out to be real people. Never could quite get my head around that.'

'Equally, I thought about your version of events, where the ship telescoped, and it made sense.' She sighed, calmer now. 'There were details in your explanation that I didn't know, like the fact that many of the crew slept in the bow of the ship.'

'Well, I can assure you, Jasper and Selina Davenport didn't die. The poor woman broke her leg, though. Thrown from the bed when it smashed into the iceberg. She still uses a stick, I was told, although I've not seen her since the start of the war. I didn't make this stuff up. It wouldn't be a nice thing to do and I'm not a nasty person.'

'No,' she agreed. 'I know you're not.'

Neither of them spoke for fully a minute but eventually, his voice drifted through the bricks. His tone was softer – further proof of his kind nature.

'When I heard you tonight, you were sobbing. What was that all about?'

Olivia couldn't bring herself to mention Howard by name. She'd have to talk of their engagement and it was all still too raw. Although she realised that the stream of startling revelations from the other side of the wall that night had distracted her from wallowing in self-pity.

'We've all been hit very hard by the deaths of the Fairchild boys,' she explained. 'It catches me by surprise sometimes and I simply can't bear that they aren't here any more. In fact, I don't think I can talk about them, if that's all right with you, because it opens me up to more pain than I can bear. As I'm sure you can appreciate, they've been like brothers to me in the last few years and even saying their names is a twisting knife to my stomach.'

'I understand, and that's a sorrow we do share. The war has destroyed so many families and I don't think Her Ladyship will ever get over such a loss,' he said. 'Parents should not outlive their children. It in't right.'

'And equally, children should not lose their parents before they reach adulthood.'

There was a considered pause on both sides of the bricks.

'I'm sorry that your Davenports died on the *Titanic*,' he said. 'It's a terrible thing that you are in some world... some other place... where it sunk.'

It was the only explanation. He was somewhere similar to this world but not quite the same, and instead of a looking glass between them, it was a wall.

'Thank you,' she replied, resting her hand on the cold bricks and leaning in close to whisper her gratitude, 'for believing me.'

* * *

'Whatever happened to Tanner? The undergardener?' Olivia asked, as she joined Cynthia in the dining room the following day.

'Good morning, my dear. You look well.' The delight across Her Ladyship's face that the girl who had shut herself away for four months was up and about was plain to see.

'I am feeling a little better,' she agreed. 'And Tanner?' She repeated her question.

Cynthia avoided her eye and continued to survey the range of breakfast options, lifting the lid of a serving dish and allowing the smell of smoked fish to pervade the room.

'Goodness, dear, that's going back some years. You were very young and I felt a duty of care for you. We sent him to work for Sir Hugo's first cousin, Jonty, who has an estate in Cambridgeshire.' A thought obviously occurred to her and she looked across at Olivia with concern. 'He didn't touch you, did he? I'll never forgive myself if something happened. Howard told me you had a special friendship with the lad. That he'd said how pretty you were and invited you to spend more time with him in the gardens. And I'd seen you together in the greenhouse. Such attentions made me uncomfortable. Tanner denied it all, of course, but it was my duty to keep you safe.'

Olivia's stomach constricted as she realised what she'd done. Her silly lies to Howard had been reported back and had unimaginable consequences.

'The things I told Howard were untrue,' she admitted. 'I was cross with him for spying on me and I had a silly, childish infatuation with Tanner at the time. It was me who was bothering him and he never did anything untoward. I was curious and he was kind. He was Benji's friend and would humour us if we came across him in the grounds. My mind was always full of handsome princes and swashbuckling pirates, and I think I confused the two.'

Cynthia frowned. 'Oh dear, then I feel terrible for not believing him. Although, in my defence, I made sure he went to a good position. He was a hard worker and life had not been easy for the poor man.' She took a single slice of toast and sat down at the long table across from Olivia. 'You've always been quite a wild thing and attracted attention. People, and more latterly men, have always found you captivating, from Benji and Howard, to the patients at the hospital. There is something about you – your optimism, your determination, your spirit. Even I have long since admired your vivid imagination.'

The older woman wouldn't envy her if she knew what turmoil she was currently experiencing. Where did her imagination end and the disembodied voice beyond the wall begin?

'And he was a lovely-looking lad,' Cynthia acknowledged. 'If somewhat moody. Of course, we knew all about the girl when we took him on, but I felt sorry for him what with his father and everything.'

'What girl? What about his father?' She vaguely recalled Benji saying something about an Amy or an Annie all those years ago.

'He was sweet on one of the girls from the village but she ran off with a travelling lad, they say. Tanner was understandably devastated. Not long afterwards, he witnessed his father die a rather unpleasant death. The vicar spoke to me about it all at the time, quite concerned about his welfare. His grandfather had given the estate many years of excellent service, and I persuaded Sir Hugo to take him on.'

'Is there any way Tanner could have returned to Norfolk before the war without you knowing? Not taken up the new position after all and worked somewhere locally?'

Lady Fairchild frowned. 'No. His mother moved to Cambridgeshire to be with him not many weeks afterwards. I only know because she was on the rota for the church flowers back then and I had to find a replacement. What's all this about, Olivia?' She peered quizzically at her companion, who decided to backtrack and not cause too much alarm.

'I've been having some strange dreams and sometimes hear voices in my head, but it's perfectly understandable after everything that's happened. My parents, the war... Howard.' The two women exchanged an understanding glance. 'Perhaps the guilt of kicking the poor gardener out of the tower and the knowledge that my foolishness cost him his job is playing on my mind.'

'It is not normal to hear voices, Olivia,' Her Ladyship ventured, reaching for the butter dish. 'Maybe you should move back into the house if you find the tower unsettling. I never did like you out there. Sir Hugo's grandfather had a dog who refused to enter, but people don't sense these other-worldly things as keenly as animals. In fact, quite the opposite was true with my husband, who was always pulled to it as a child and used to enjoy haring up and down the stairs with his brother.'

Olivia jolted her head towards Cynthia. 'I didn't know Sir Hugo had a brother.'

'He was always a sickly child and he's... gone now.' Cynthia waved a dismissive hand. 'Apparently, the builders had the Devil of a job with the east tower because the seam of iron that runs through the estate is directly beneath the foundations and continues all the way up to the coast. You can still see the shrieking pits in the village, where they dug it out in times gone by.'

Olivia knew about the pits from when she'd gone on bicycle rides to the coast with Benji – she struggled to think of him as a Benjamin. Could this geological phenomenon be in some way connected to what was going on? She thought again of the world that existed the other side of the mirror in Lewis Carroll's book. It might all be nonsense, but she was determined to investigate the tower, the strange geology of the local landscape and perhaps even see if she could track down Tanner.

It wasn't that she'd got over Howard's death – she knew that if she lived to be a hundred, the pain of losing him would never truly leave her – but the return of the voice was enough of a distraction to give her a focus and divert her from her self-pity. It didn't mean her grief had evaporated; she was curious, not cured.

_____

27

Despite having conducted the same investigations all those years ago, Olivia spent that afternoon examining the physical structure of the tower. Was it possible for someone to access it at night? Her childish, thirteen-year-old mind had allowed her to accept that a voice floating through a brick wall was either a spirit or the subconscious invention of another imaginary friend, but her much better informed twenty-year-old self was more sceptical and wanted to rule out the practical before she embraced the fantastical.

Everyone was surprised to see her around the house and grounds, after having shut herself way for so many months, but no one commented as she carried out her investigations. She visited the head gardener's cottage and asked him to put ladders up to the east tower windows and check for signs of tampering. She also took the opportunity to quiz him about Tanner and he confirmed Lady Fairchild's version of events. The lad – a very promising individual, despite the melancholy – had been sent to work elsewhere and, to his knowledge, had never returned to Norfolk. The mother had followed a few weeks afterwards and all contact with them had been lost. He had no idea if Tanner had even survived the war... which hadn't even occurred to Olivia. Perhaps she would ask Sir Hugo to speak with his cousin – although this might lead to questions she didn't want to answer.

Satisfied no one had set up pipes or been opening windows from the outside, she needed to rule out the voice being in her head. Had the cruel death of the man she loved driven her to grief-induced auditory hallucinations? She found a book on clinical psychiatry in the great library that suggested 'affections of the temporal lobes' might be to blame. But most of the case study patients reported snippets of speech, the calling of a name, or indistinct mutterings – not complete and reasoned conversations. And when the voices *were* more reasoned, doctors theorised these were merely echoes of the patient's thoughts. Olivia, however, knew she could not have come up with the alternative scenario regarding the *Titanic*.

She returned to the tower that night, checked it for signs of an intruder, secured the windows and locked the main door. Leaving her lamp on, she started to read an adventure novel to while away the time – the first book she'd picked up in months. Thoughts of Howard, as ever, swept over her with the dark cloak of evening. Every so often, she whispered Seth's name but got no reply.

It was almost ten o'clock when a call of, 'Olivia?' made her jump.

'I'm here.' She shuffled closer to the bricks and his voice was only inches from her face.

'So, our conversation last night was interesting,' he said. 'Half-thought I'd dreamed it all, but I asked the other staff a few questions about Olivia Davenport. She's not been to Merriford since I've been back but the Davenport family stayed here for a week the summer of 1912, after their horrible experience, and apparently they have visited from time to time throughout the war.'

Was there really an Olivia out there who still had both parents? A girl cherished and nurtured, who did not know the pain of losing people she loved? Even the death of the three Fairchild boys would not affect this young woman in quite the same way, for she would never have become as close to them in a world where she was only an occasional visitor to Merriford Manor.

'And I'm supposing I'd better be calling you "miss" from now on – on account of you being a lady.'

'Not a bit of it,' she stressed. 'It never mattered before and it shouldn't matter now. We're friends and equals, Seth. In this tower we are, at any rate.' It would feel awkward if he started addressing her as such and put a distance between them that she didn't want. 'Tell me more about the Davenports...' she said.

Even if this was all fantasy, she couldn't help but indulge herself. Was it wrong of her to escape, even if only for a moment? She closed her eyes – a picture forming in her mind's eye of them sitting on fancy wicker chairs in the formal gardens at the back of the manor, her mother's leg perhaps resting on a footstool, enjoying afternoon tea on the terrace with the Fairchilds. All of that had been taken away from her and it still hurt.

'I know very little about them. Their lives, and the lives of the Fairchilds, are far removed from mine. Most of what I picked up was through servant gossip, or what I saw as I went about my duties. I know that the newspaper coverage of the *Carpathia* rescue helped sales of Jasper Davenport's later books and I gather he's done well in recent years, but I don't read novels.' He laughed. 'I don't have the time. If I read at all, it's the *Gardener's*

Chronicle, as I'm always keen to learn about new plants and hybrids, and the latest fertiliser mixes. I might not sound particularly educated to you but I've even had a piece published on lady's slipper orchids. Sir Hugo's late father—'

'Has a collection in the conservatory. I know.'

'Ah, there I must correct you. It's in this tower and the reason I sleep here. Some are extremely valuable, and determined collectors will stop at nothing to get their hands on them.'

Olivia remembered that the orchids had been moved when she'd been given the tower. Her subconscious might create a world where her parents had survived and her father had gone on to have success with his writing, but she had forgotten this detail, and wouldn't have conjured up the name of an orchid, or a gardening publication, because she had a limited horticultural knowledge. It made her think.

'Tell me something I couldn't possibly know – something about the orchids – that I can check on, so that I can rule out you being a figment of my imagination.'

There was a considered pause. 'Well, now, I can tell you that they have three petals and the biggest is called the labellum – see, I know some fancy words.' He chuckled. 'And this big old petal should be at the top but as the bud grows in the plant, the whole thing spins about so by the time it's in flower, it's standing on its head.'

Olivia couldn't have fabricated such a thing, she acknowledged to herself.

'So, if you really are Seth Tanner, and I really am Olivia Davenport, how does this make sense? You aren't here with me, but you are. There appear to be two different realities, as ridiculous as it sounds, and we overlap somehow.'

She expected him to laugh but he didn't.

'We don't understand how a woman can give birth to two

identical babies, but it happens – two things created by God that are the same in every way. Only He understands how and why.'

'He didn't mention anything about creating two worlds in the Bible,' she huffed.

'Perhaps He did that on the eighth day,' Seth joked. 'It probably dint take long because He knew what He was doing – having made one a few days before.'

'I beg to differ. He did a rotten job the first time around. He should have put a nicer species in charge – sheep, for example. I suspect they wouldn't have instigated a war over the assassination of an Austro-Hungarian archduke.'

'No,' Seth agreed, and they were both silent for a while. The war was still so raw that it couldn't be mentioned without a period of reverence and, for Olivia, the wretched heartbreak of losing Howard twisted her insides into tight, constrictive knots, so that she still could not bring herself to mention him by name.

They considered the possibility of overlapping worlds for a long time, comparing what was going on in each of their lives and, if her abstract theory was to be believed, their worlds. All major events in history they agreed on: from the existence of ancient civilisations and the chronological order of the monarchs of England, to the major battles in the war and the current prime minister. But smaller details after April 1912 were subtly different. What had happened to make them diverge? And was it linked to the lode?

It was bittersweet for her to hear that Jasper Davenport was as famous as Joseph Conrad, but that Margaret Brown, an outspoken survivor of the *Titanic*, had been killed in an automobile accident just outside New York City recently. The war had followed a similar path and the armistice had been signed on the same day. But when she talked of Lord Kitchener's death aboard the HMS *Hampshire*, he insisted the man was still alive.

Things closer to home were at odds too. Miriam Peterson, a lady from the village, had lost her son in Africa, but Seth said he was now the Merriford Lode police constable.

Olivia tugged a blanket around her shoulders and wondered at the things she was being asked to believe. Was it the chill of the night air or the chill of her circumstances that was creeping across her skin?

'The tiniest pebble dropped into the middle of a big lake makes surprisingly large ripples,' Seth said. 'If just one man of fighting age died aboard your ill-fated *Titanic* but didn't die here, then a subtly different battalion would have been formed when the war broke out. Different men would have stood in different places when the shells dropped and changed everything – who survived and who died. And for each of those men, this affected who they married and what children they had. Some people born here will never exist for you, and the other way about.'

The implications were immense. It made her realise that every single event in life had the potential to lead to a million different outcomes. Over time, their worlds would diverge at an increasing rate. Eventually, there would be different political leaders, different heroes, different villains. Two totally separate histories would play out.

The conversation moved on to talk about themselves, even though they both avoided mentioning the Fairchild boys. She admitted that, at twenty-one, she would inherit a large house and a considerable sum of money, and he countered that his only prospects would be what he could achieve by hard work and determination. There was no judgement on either side.

She also learned that a hard-working but unhappy Seth Tanner had signed up in the August of 1914, looking for something to give his life meaning, which explained why the voice had disappeared for fifteen-year-old Olivia. He'd spent the duration of the war trying to stay alive, writing letters to his anxious mother, dreaming of his future, and doing his best to keep his feet clean and dry. Much of this time, he swung from either being bored out of his mind, or in a stomach-churning state of anticipation, awaiting orders for the next push. Like Clarence and Howard, he would not be drawn on details of the fighting, but instead focused on those moments of stillness or beauty that touched him in all the chaos and misery. Moments of joy, he reiterated, that a bossy Princess Cordelia had ordered him to hold on to.

In return, she told him of her work with the wounded men once the manor had been requisitioned as a convalescent hospital – which had also happened in his world. She even mentioned the publication of her short stories and articles in the ladies' journals. Impressed, he questioned her further on her writing and she was forced to admit it had fallen by the wayside, so he encouraged her to pick up her pen again.

They were still talking when the birds began their tweeting in earnest and the colours started to saturate her room.

'I'm increasingly convinced that our strange situation is all connected to the lode,' he said. 'I read something in the newspapers just before the war about the Cleveland ironstone mines, up in Yorkshire, and how a lot of them miners thought the pits were haunted. They'd been hearing voices for a couple of years – which makes sense with our thinking this all happened the year the ship sank. And then one poor man claimed he'd been talking to himself in the mine – except it was a version of himself that had just become a father to a baby boy—'

'Let me guess, and his wife had just had a little girl?'

'Exactly that. Those ripples that we talked about. We know that an iron seam runs under this tower, so I'm now wondering if whatever caused the world to split had travelled along them metal deposits, and they're the fragile link between the two. I'm not much of a scientist, but I know that we use copper wire for electricity because it's a good conductor. What if the metal in the earth was conducting... something? Electricity? Heat? Rays of a nature I couldn't hope to understand?'

'I'm not much of a scientist either, but it's a good theory,' she acknowledged. 'The metal conducts our voices like a telegraph wire, but can't conceivably conduct our bodies?'

It occurred to Olivia that without the physical barrier of bricks between them, they might be able to sense each other, or somehow see *something*, even if it was just a shadow or a ghostly form. They both crept outside in the half-light of morning and followed the assumed line of the lode from the tower and across the back lawns, but were to be sorely disappointed. She thought perhaps she heard a faint something, but in the gardens, they had no sure way of knowing exactly where the seam ran. Nor could they pinpoint where each other was standing, since all contact was lost as soon as she stepped from her room.

'How will you get through the day with so little sleep?' she asked, as they returned to their beds, and aware he had a whole day's work ahead of him.

'Had it worse,' he reminded her. Of course, she remembered with a stab of guilt, he'd been to war. 'But let's talk again tonight. Maybe not for so long, though,' he joked.

'Until tonight, then.'

'Until tonight.'

She settled down under her covers feeling guilty that she could sleep in, but Seth had to work a long day. As she closed her eyes, she thought she heard the door to the tower but couldn't be certain. And then a further, swelling wave of guilt swept over her as it struck her she'd hardly thought of Howard since Seth had whispered her name through the bricks all those hours earlier.

* * *

'I have arranged for you to see a top London doctor,' Sir Hugo said to Olivia. 'Old university chum of mine. He knew your father too. Thoroughly decent bloke. Lady Fairchild is concerned about you and he's done some ground-breaking work with all these poor fellows suffering from war neurosis. Thinks hearing voices and the like is just the old brain trying to make sense of things. We know you've rather been through the mill.'

She'd been called to the morning room but felt somewhat ambushed to find Sir Hugo present, especially as she was running on so little sleep.

'I perfectly understood the need to isolate yourself over the winter,' Cynthia said, leaning forward to put her hand on Olivia's knee. 'And am delighted that you seem a bit livelier, but these odd questions about Tanner, and your request for Rowe to examine the tower are giving us cause for concern. Then, this morning, Benjamin tells me he heard you talking to yourself in the night.'

She'd been right; someone had been in the tower the previous evening. Benji was spying on her and reporting back to his mother. But if he'd stood at the bottom of the staircase, only her voice would had travelled out, because Seth wasn't technically in the adjoining room. He wouldn't have been heard in the same way.

'You're so far from the people who care most about you out there – the people who want to look after you. I talk to my boys, and it is a comfort, my dear, but they never answer back. I don't have conversations with them. I'd hoped all that imaginary nonsense was behind you.'

But it wasn't her imagination. The things that Seth was saying to her through the wall were too detailed for her to have fabricated. She knew nothing about varieties of orchid or their petals – and the lady's slipper did exist; she'd looked it up. Rowe had also confirmed that William was Tanner's middle name. There was no way Olivia could have known any of this information.

'If I've been heard talking aloud, then it will be me running through story ideas.' This was untrue; she had absolutely no desire to write again but she didn't want them worrying about her. 'Returning to the tower is helping me to deal with the grief. I realise that I've been cooped up for far too long and will address that immediately.' She glanced over to one of the tall windows. 'As the weather looks so promising, perhaps I shall bicycle into the village this very afternoon.'

Cynthia's face registered her shock before she rearranged her features to express delight, but the truth, which even surprised Olivia, was that she did feel better. She had something to distract her from the pain of it all now. She wanted to know more about Seth Tanner and she intended to start by asking questions in Merriford Lode.

28

When you lose someone, it's the little things that feel like a vicious kick to the gut. As Olivia cycled down the winding lanes of the flower-dotted Norfolk countryside and approached the ford, it was seeing the last of the bluebells that opened up a gaping chasm inside her. It seemed impossible to her that it was only a year ago, she'd walked down these roads, anxious and unsure, to meet Howard and decide what her feelings for him truly were.

She dismounted and rested the bike against the cold stone of the bridge and took a moment to recover from the sudden rush of memories. Closing her eyes, all she could see was his face as he lay beside her, the ridiculous flowers threaded through his hair, and him not minding a jot. She could almost smell the fustiness of the soil and feel the roughness of his khaki uniform as she'd nestled in his arms afterwards.

He had been so careful to ensure that she wouldn't fall pregnant, but now she wished more than anything that they'd been careless. Had she fallen, even though it would have been out of wedlock, he would have left a proper legacy behind – a child.

Something remaining in this world that proved he had once walked amongst them and he had been truly loved.

Olivia stood by the bridge for quite some time until she was able to move on, mentally and physically, wheeling the bike beside her as she walked into the village. She'd been to Merriford Lode a thousand times – to visit the shops, attend village events and sit in the church pews every Sunday – but never had reason to ask questions about the Tanner family before. The head gardener said they'd lived in a small cottage in Brick Lane, but that Tanner moved out to the bothy when he'd first been given the job at the manor. Would any of the neighbours even remember them?

An older woman was outside the end terrace whacking a row of small rugs strung over a line with a rattan carpet beater. She recognised Olivia immediately, well-dressed and attractive young ladies not being commonplace in such a small village.

'Always felt sorry for them,' she said, after Olivia had made her enquiry. 'Nice people who minded their own business, but were there if you were ever in need. They didn't deserve what happened. That poor lad had to deal with his sweetheart disappearing without a trace, and the sudden and violent death of his father, all within the space of a week.'

'How long ago was this?'

'Let me think... 1911. The year of the coronation.'

So, Tanner had been carrying all that heartache for a year when she'd first met him. No wonder he'd worn a permanent frown.

'He went from a cheery soul to a broken lad in days. Pitiful to see, and his only salvation was that job of his – always did love nature. Remember him growing a few flowers in tins and old saucepans as a youngster in that dreary little backyard of theirs, and how happy he was when he got a job at the big house and could follow in his grandfather's footsteps.'

Another pang of guilt shot through Olivia as she was yet again reminded how much Tanner had loved working in the manor gardens. The very fact *her* Seth (and she thought of him as such purely to differentiate between the two Seths she now felt certain existed) had chosen to come back to Merriford after the war was proof of this.

'Who was the young girl he was sweet on?'

'Annie Taylor. Nice enough, but her parents were devout church people and she had a tough upbringing.' Olivia knew Mrs Taylor through church but hadn't realised she'd had a daughter. The woman didn't ever talk about her.

'There was never going to be anyone good enough for their Annie. Even when the pair started stepping out, they were never left alone or allowed to go anywhere together. And then she broke it off without giving him a reason, but everyone knew she'd been seeing someone else. My Frank saw her creeping through the village in the dead of night on a couple of occasions, out towards Widow Larwood's, but we never said nothing. Didn't want her getting thrashed by that puritan father of hers.'

The widow's house, Olivia knew, was a tumbledown building their side of the woods that had been unlived in since the old woman had died nearly twenty years ago. It was halfway between Merriford Lode and Merriford Manor. Often an overnight stop for tramps, it was also a shelter to several stray cats. Sir Hugo regularly complained about the travellers who occasionally pitched up in the Larwood fields and had once mentioned that the house had been left to a distant relative of the owner who had never bothered to claim it but did not want to sell. Consequently, it had stood empty all this time.

'And then she disappeared. My Frank reckoned she met

some traveller there and they got friendly – if you know what I mean.' The old woman shook her head. 'Must be eight or nine years back. There were a couple of possible sightings of her in Norwich and Yarmouth, but nothing was ever confirmed. And then a few days later, young Seth's father died. Fancy watching your father practically burn alive and not be able to do a thing about it. The poor fellow's coat caught when he was tending to a bonfire. In the scramble to remove it, he tumbled back into the flames. Dreadful, it was. He took three days to die.'

Olivia's shock at this horrific detail was apparent across her face and her heart went out to Seth a little bit more.

'Always said to Frank it was a blessing when the young lad was given the other job in Cambridgeshire. He could make a new start. His mother followed him down there a few weeks later. I miss her; she was a good neighbour and much more respectful than the mouthy lot who moved in after her. She couldn't write much beyond her name though and Seth had no reason to keep in touch with anyone here, so I don't know no more, unless you do?'

The older lady looked at her with hopeful eyes, but Olivia shook her head.

'Did anyone ever hear from Annie Taylor again?'

The woman shrugged. 'Not to my knowing, and even the traveller thing was a guess. Everyone had a theory. Some thought there was a babe and she'd run off with whoever had fathered it. Being the hellfire and brimstone sorts, her parents would have cast her out anyway. Mind you, I always think those brought up strict are the ones most likely to rebel.'

'Did anyone else disappear around that time?' Olivia asked.

The woman shook her head. 'That's why many think it was a traveller lad – someone passing through. But I always wondered if the chap responsible was already married and wealthy

enough to set her up somewhere as his mistress. It happens.'
She shrugged as she gave the rug another almighty whack and
stepped back from the erupting cloud of dust. 'If you want to
know more, you'd best speak to Freda. She was Annie's friend
and girls tell each other everything.'

'Freda?'

'Freda Howells. She's one of your housemaids.'

Olivia hadn't realised the connection, but decided when
there was an appropriate opportunity, she'd quiz the girl. Armed
with this new information, she thanked the woman and took her
leave. At least she understood better now the reasons the Tanner
of eight years ago was so cross with the world.

29

Gardening staff, Olivia learned through talking to Mr Rowe, worked long hours. And junior gardeners, in particular, had duties that extended well into the night. In order for Lady Fairchild to enjoy fresh peaches and pineapples, someone had to keep the hothouse stoves burning around the clock, which explained why Seth was often late to the tower. The poor man retired after a ten- or twelve-hour day, before rising with the sun and heading out at the crack of dawn to start his duties again. It was merely a place to lay his weary head and act as protector to stop thieves from stealing Sir Hugo's prize orchids.

That evening, sitting with her back to the wall and a book resting on her knees, she heard faint noises through the bricks. It was eight o'clock and Seth was only now returning from a day's work in the Merriford gardens. There was a big sigh and the squeak of bedsprings as someone considerably larger than herself lumped down on a bed in the adjoining room – a bed that was not there.

'You sound tired,' she said, confident it was Seth who had joined her. 'Did someone keep you up all night?'

'Hello, there.' He sounded weary but faintly amused. 'Someone did indeed, and the things we talked about have been on my mind all day. I've been so distracted, I watered five seed trays before I realised I hadn't planted any seeds in them.'

She smiled at the image.

'I cycled into Merriford Lode today and asked a former neighbour of yours if she was still in touch with you or your mother, but she wasn't.'

'I'd forgotten that you said I work elsewhere. Still don't understand why I'd do that.' She could almost imagine him shaking his head. 'Guess this is one of those ripples we talked about.'

She couldn't bring herself to tell him that she had, to all intents and purposes, got him fired back then. This job was his life, and all he'd wanted to do after being discharged from the army was return to Merriford.

The talk of ripples led them to discuss which of his fellow servants were present for both of them and it was surprising that, apart from a housemaid who had left to get married in Seth's world, and that Seth was absent in hers, the members of staff were almost identical. She knew Sir Hugo was short of gardeners, as there simply weren't the men available that there were before the war. Many big houses were struggling, and even women were turning their noses up at working in service. Why be at the beck and call of some demanding master all hours of the day, when you could walk out the factory doors at the end of your shift and not have to worry about anything until you turned up for work the next morning?

'How did you persuade Sir Hugo to let you return to the tower after the war?' she asked.

'They initially offered me a bed in the bothy, but people have generally been accommodating of us returning servicemen.

There have to be some advantages to nearly getting my guts spread across the fields of Flanders. And I've long had a strange affinity with this place. Made a friend here several years ago – a spirited little girl who told me she was the ghost of a fancy princess. Someone I've since learned lost both her parents at sea, was living in a dreamworld, but still managed to have a sunnier outlook than me.'

'You weren't exactly a ray of sunshine,' she agreed.

She wondered if he might justify his previous dour self with talk of his sweetheart running off or the death of his father but he said nothing, so she didn't mention her investigations into Annie Taylor.

'And for that, I apologise, especially as I seem to recall that one of our earliest encounters involved me using some pretty choice language.' She thought back with amusement to the evening when she'd heard him swear through the wall. 'Master Howard had put a hoppin' toad in my bed. I'd asked him quite sharply not to trample over the flower beds and was sure he'd say something to his father and get me into trouble, but he never did. Instead, he sought revenge in his own way.'

Hearing Howard's name brought her up short and she struggled to respond for a few moments. He'd always had a grudging respect for those who stood up to him and called him out on his silly behaviour, and she was the prime example. But she couldn't talk about the man she'd loved to Seth; she couldn't talk about him to anyone. Just thinking of his face made her insides collapse, so she moved the conversation on.

'Equally, I must apologise for my childish nonsense back then. A princess indeed...'

'Not at all – it's because of that nonsense I owe you a debt I can't never repay. I think you may've saved my life... certainly my sanity.'

She shuffled closer to the wall. 'I don't understand.'

'Even though I wasn't in a good way back then, the girl through the wall was always so positive and forward-looking and I often thought back to our conversations during the war. Even on that first journey to the front, as I trudged through a landscape of lush, green fields, confetti-covered cherry trees, smelt the scent of damp soil, I remembered how you always focused on the positives. So many of the men thought we were headed on some great adventure but I was under no such illusion. And, so many times, as dusk fell like a soft blanket on the jagged world below, I thought of you, always telling me that after every raincloud, the sun was sure to follow. And so I held on tight to the beauty of that afternoon and thought about it often.'

'Your words are surprisingly poetic for a—' She stopped herself. How patronising of her to assume that because he was a servant, he couldn't articulate his feelings.

He chuckled. 'What? An uneducated gardener?'

Thank goodness he couldn't see the glow of her cheeks.

'No, I—'

'I read a lot of poetry during my time in the army, mainly because I'd come by a copy of *The Oxford Book of Verse* and kept it with me always. Mum occasionally sent out horticultural journals, but there weren't a lot of call for my gardening expertise in the waterlogged trenches and barren wasteland of no man's land.'

'No, I suppose not.'

'I'm not saying I always understood what I was reading, but I was keen to learn. Better men than me fell into the mud and I realised I'd wasted my youth being angry with the world. I could have met a nice girl before the war but I'd shut myself off to the possibility. Bit of a slap in the face to realise there was every chance I would die a wretched death, far away from home, missed only by my mother. So, I determined that if I returned, I'd try to make something of m'self and not end up miserable and alone. And I'm fairly certain that the ladies are more amenable to young men who have a smile on their face and know a bit of fancy poetry.'

She didn't want to think about the young women working at the manor or living in Merriford Lode who might currently have their eye on the handsome returning undergardener, and instead questioned why she had failed to pull herself around after losing Howard. It was clear that Seth had suffered as much as her in his lifetime – if not more. He'd witnessed the deaths of men first hand. His pain must be so much greater. Why had her childhood optimism been able to pull Seth from his self-pity but deserted her?

'I thought about all them plans you had,' he continued. 'How if you hadn't been so foolish as to launch yourself from the tower that you'd have been off around the world and trying new things. How you believed nothing should stop people from fulfilling their dreams. Began making notes in my pocketbook and allowing myself to make plans of my own. Why shouldn't I become a head gardener of a place such as Merriford? There are no limits – the sky goes on forever, right?'

Now she felt really embarrassed for her 'do as I say, not as I do' attitude. How arrogant of her to spend her childhood dispensing such bossy advice to him and then fail to take any of it on board herself.

'So, Princess Cordelia, what *have* you done with yourself? Did you write those books? Have you still great plans to travel and go on wild adventures? Will you learn to fly an aeroplane? Or study at a university?'

There was a pause. All those dreams had died with Howard. Her plans for family, fortune and fame.

'The war put everything on hold—'

She heard his derisive snort through the bricks.

'Don't use the war as an excuse to close your world down; use it as a reason to live your life to the fullest. Nothing should stop you putting pen to paper or escaping in your head. You taught me that.'

But she had no reason to throw herself into her books any more. At twenty-one, she would reach her majority and planned to return to the Davenport family home in Suffolk to lead a quiet life. Travelling no longer appealed because so many of the people she'd cared about had left for foreign shores and never come back. Benji would eventually marry and she would still be a spinster. Not even being related to the Fairchilds, she would have no place living at the manor. She didn't *need* to work, and she certainly didn't need to marry. Thanks to the efforts of the suffragettes and Lloyd George, at thirty, she would even have the vote. Olivia could live as an independent woman and please herself without having her heart broken again. But if she couldn't have her happy ending, why should she write them for others?

Of course, she didn't say any of this. Howard's death, and her love for him, was something intensely personal to her, much as Seth had avoided giving her any details about Miss Taylor.

'It's not that easy.'

'Course not, but in't that the whole point? Imagine if you were a honeybee and destined to die within a month. Such a tiny, hard-working little insect, flitting from flower to beautiful flower, part of a community, experiencing the colours and scents of Mother Nature at her best, but only living a handful of days. Yet, the giant oak stands in the landscape for a hundred years and never moves from the spot it first fell to the ground as an acorn. Why live all that time if you only ever see the same view and have no one to share it with? Personally, I'd rather be a honeybee.'

And as she contemplated Windy Acres, as charming as it was, being her only view for the next fifty years, she wondered if she shouldn't like to be a honeybee, after all.

30

Over the following few weeks, as the dull, cold and wet of a depressing spring stepped aside for a better-behaved summer, Olivia's melancholy slid slowly away from her without her even noticing. The Treaty of Versailles was finally signed in the June, seven months after the end of the war, by a defeated German nation on its knees. Even Sir Hugo, with three dead sons to avenge, proclaimed the terms somewhat harsh, but it was a full stop to the war, and would hopefully allow everyone to move on and rebuild their lives. She had now blindly accepted that somehow, the wall in the tower connected her to a man living in another version of her world. Perhaps it was naïve of her, but she needed to believe in something good, and this friendship had dragged her from her destructive introspection. It was certainly beyond rational reasoning but, as Sir Arthur Conan Doyle had his fictional detective, Sherlock Holmes, say in his novels: 'Once you eliminate the impossible, whatever remains, no matter how improbable, must be the truth'.

Olivia briefly wondered if there was someone she could take up to the tower at night who would hear Seth's voice and confirm it was real. Benji was unlikely to volunteer again after the disappointment of before the war, but in the end, she realised that by exposing the truth, she would be opening them up to outside interference. What if journalists got wind of it and this precious secret was taken from her? No, that would not do at all. Seth was the only thing that had brought her any joy since Howard's death.

She still had moments of overwhelming grief that caught her unawares, like when the memorial cross was erected in the parish church of Merriford Lode at the start of August. The Fairchild surname was chiselled into the granite three times, far more than any other family in the village, and probably the reason Sir Hugo had funded the cross almost in its entirety.

Cynthia unexpectedly gifted Olivia a small selection of pretty, leather-bound notebooks in the mistaken belief that she'd rekindled her writing. It made her feel guilty and so she picked up her pen again, knowing Seth would be pleased. She began to outline a novel during her afternoons, putting every emotion she could dredge up from her harrowing experiences and charting the doomed romance of the two lead characters. Unlike her story inspired by Major Turrell, the ending would be more realistic and art would imitate the harsh realities of life. But each evening, as soon as Seth spoke to her through the wall, she put her pen down and gave him her full attention. Not being able to see his face made it easier to be honest and lay her soul bare. He'd not chosen to share confidences with a child, but now that they were both adults, their discussions were often surprisingly frank because Seth could not see the colour in her cheeks, and nor could she see whether he was studying her in earnest or rolling his eyes at her whimsy. It didn't matter.

'I saw you today,' he said, one evening as they started their night-time chatter. He didn't sound overly pleased with the announcement.

'Through the wall?' She was excited for a moment. If he could see her, perhaps they could meet.

'No, Olivia Davenport of Windy Acres, Suffolk, blessed with both parents and a sunnier disposition than you.'

'Oh.' His Olivia had not lost a fiancé in the war, she'd wager, and said nothing. She was finding her way back, but it would take time.

'Your family was visiting the manor. I dint realise it was you at first. I ha'n't seen you for years.' There was a considered pause. 'You've grown into quite the young lady.'

It hadn't occurred to her before that he had no image of her as an adult, because she had seen him at nineteen, already a man, back in the spring of 1912, and she doubted he had changed much in the intervening years. She could remember every detail of his dark hair, green eyes and sullen face and, from the day he'd been clearing the pond in the Japanese gardens, more than she had a right to know about his body. The last time he'd seen her was in the summer of 1914, when the Davenports had visited, and she hadn't even been sixteen. Everything about her had changed, from her height, to her body shape, even her unruly, blonde hair, which she now wore pinned up.

'And?' Where was this leading.? Had they held a conversation?

'Nothing really. Watched you for ages as I was edging the formal lawns, but you dint pay me much attention. Servants are invisible to the likes of you.' There was a definite edge of resentment to his voice. Had their differing social positions in life now been made obvious to him by the encounter that day?

Olivia felt uncomfortable. Two people making friends either

side of a wall had no reason to make assumptions or pass judgement, but she didn't want to be lumped in with Sir Hugo, who demanded that his housemaids turned to face the wall as he passed. It didn't make him an unfeeling master, just an old-fashioned one. Servants were ranked lower than children, and were expected to be neither seen nor heard.

'I can assure you that you weren't invisible to me when I moved here after the death of my parents. Benji and I would often chat to you in the gardens and I even helped you in the greenhouse. There was no judgement from me.'

'You were children. That's different. The Fairchild boys often came into the east wing when I first started working here, stealing cakes from the kitchens and chatting to the housemaids, or popping out to the stables to see the horses and talking with the stable lads. But as they got older, the distance between staff and family became greater. Master Benjamin barely acknowledges me now.'

Perhaps Seth was correct. Benjamin was acutely aware that he would be the next master of Merriford Manor. He could no longer have a relaxed relationship with the men and women he would eventually be in charge of. The same was also true of her, she realised with regret. She'd learned the names of the housemaids when she'd first arrived, perhaps because they were often girls not much older than herself, but as time had passed, and she'd become more like a daughter to Lady Fairchild, she'd had no interest in the duties or lives of the young girls scuttling about. She still hadn't even sought out Freda to ask about Annie Taylor. Her world and theirs so rarely overlapped.

'Being honest, without this rum ol' thing happening through the wall, we'd never have formed a friendship,' he continued. 'Gardeners have nothing in common with the daughters of gentlemen. And yet our circumstances have proved, to me at least, that you're just a young woman and I'm just a man. The trappings of our lives, or lack of them, have let us find out about the things we have in common, without being self-conscious of how we dress, our stations in life or our wildly different expectations.'

'I wonder what I'm like,' she mused, almost to herself.

Growing up with her parents around must have shaped her differently to the girl she'd become since their loss. The Olivia that Seth had encountered would have lived through the same war but it would not have broken her in such a way. She would not have volunteered at the hospital and spent so much time with those damaged men. Her war would have been spent at Windy Acres.

It was also in that moment that she realised she wouldn't have fallen for Howard because their childhoods would not have coincided in the same way. The deaths of the Fairchild boys would undoubtedly have upset her – she'd known them all her life, after all – but his would not have destroyed her. They were the children of two old school friends, who saw each other a handful of times each year and it was unlikely, although not impossible, that Howard would have fallen in love with her. And she almost certainly would not have willingly given her innocence to him in a bluebell wood. But then, she knew nothing for certain about this other version of her. Perhaps she had fallen in love. Perhaps she had lost a sweetheart.

'We hardly embarked on a lengthy chat about the weather or took tea together, but you seemed nice enough.' He was still smarting; she could hear it in his tone. 'You smiled at me and commented on the colourful show of late delphiniums, which was kind. I'm rarely acknowledged by visitors to the house unless they want something.'

Pleased to hear that the Olivia he'd met had been polite, she pondered how much of who we are at our very core is always within us and how much is a result of the things we live through and the people we meet. Were we born kind or unkind, in the same way that our height, intelligence and eye colour were inherited from our parents?

She assumed that this other her had the same dreams, and would want to find love and to marry. It had been her desire since she was about seven years old, even though she knew that motherhood alone would not satisfy her. Olivia had always hankered for a bit of privateering, dragon-slaying or nation-conquering on the side. It was therefore highly likely that this other version of her *would* find love and lead a happy and fulfilled life. This woman knew nothing about the bond she'd shared with Howard – the annoying, attention-seeking third son of her father's oldest friend. But she would also not know that there was an attractive, ambitious undergardener at Merriford Manor who had the potential to make her heart race and her breath catch. Because the truth suddenly hit her in that moment; she was jealous of Seth talking to Olivia Davenport.

Every day since he'd reappeared in her life, she'd counted down the minutes until she could sit one side of a brick wall in the east tower and hear his soft, Norfolk accent, because being with him made her feel safe and happy. But was there more to it than that? Was there a reason she hadn't asked Freda about Annie Taylor? Whilst she was interested to know what happened to Tanner, she certainly didn't want to track down his sweetheart.

Why had she not realised until that moment that he was stirring up feelings in her that she'd forgotten existed: the dry mouth when you're near someone you want to impress, the flutter of your heart rate when someone pays you a compliment and, most ridiculous of all, the desire to make yourself look attractive when you're in the company of that other person?

Why, she belatedly asked herself, did she arrange her hair so carefully, pinch her cheeks to give them colour, and spray herself in lavender before she retired for bed, given that Seth couldn't see her?

Because she'd just stumbled on the answer, even if she would not admit it out loud.

31

The country experienced an Indian summer that September and Olivia allowed herself to delight in the good weather, abundance of food and opportunities to reconnect with nature. Benji helped her to sort the puncture in her front wheel and she persuaded him to undertake one last trip to the coast together before he returned to boarding school. He was a young man of sixteen now and shy with girls, even her, but reluctantly agreed.

It proved to be a delightful expedition. They took a picnic, bathed in the sea, and even stopped at the shrieking pits on the way home to listen for the fabled ghost. He was no longer afraid of it and instead almost eager to encounter the axe-wielding maniac – but, of course, no ghost was to be found, even in the twilight of a September evening, and they only heard the birds sharing the exploits of their day from the lofty treetops.

As they whizzed through the ford on their bicycles, feet held aloft to save them from being splashed, she realised that it was now Seth she thought of in her quiet moments, and not Howard. It was the excitement of relaying her exploits through the wall that occurred to her first, not the sadness she so often associated with the bridge. When she wrote of a dashing hero in her stories, she pictured Seth; when people talked to her of a future, she pictured Seth; and when she closed her eyes at night and thought about the coupling that had taken place amongst the dying bluebells, occasionally and unintentionally, she pictured Seth.

The guilt that came with this she boxed up and put away in a part of her brain she refused to access, but it sat there gathering dust, nonetheless.

The Fairchilds, in their capacity as the land owners, were always part of the harvest celebrations and, that year, the night of the supper was unseasonably hot. Olivia had drunk some ale but not felt much like dancing, even though she'd stayed until the end. Back in the tower, she wondered if Seth had been a part of the same estate gathering in his world. His stumbling steps and loud hiccoughs through the wall sometime later made her suspect that he had. She told him about her evening and he reciprocated, giving an impromptu and hearty rendition of the song, 'John Barleycorn'.

'I made cider from the apples my grandfather planted,' he said, explaining his inebriated state. There had been no Seth and no cider at the harvest supper in her world. 'And I danced my feet off,' he continued, 'even though the one face I wanted to see in the barn wasn't there...'

Was he saying what she thought he was?

Silence.

'You do know, don't you, Olivia, that the only girl I wanted in my arms was you?'

She froze at his unexpected words. What could she possibly reply to that?

'I shouldn't have said nothing. I'm sorry. It's the drink. And now you've gone quiet so I've probably embarrassed you.'

Every square inch of Olivia's skin felt on fire and she found herself tracing her fingers across her body as he talked, the tiny beads of sweat enabling them to glide across her skin as though it were made of silk.

Another hiccough.

'It's just... it's just I hadn't realised until the other day how beautiful you'd become... or maybe, it's not even that... how hypnotising you are as a person. There's something about you that completely zings – I can't describe it any better. Talking to you through the wall all these months, even before I saw your face, I wanted to spend time with you and now I can't stop thinking about you when we're apart,' he blundered on.

She wasn't classically beautiful but she was spirited and had what her mother had always described as an expressive face. But she also knew that the men at the hospital had always been drawn to her. She certainly had a 'something' and it appeared Seth found that too.

All this talk of attraction and being held in his arms made her tummy flip. She dragged her fingertips across her lips and a shiver ran through the length of her body, despite the heat, as she shuffled closer to the wall. How could he make her feel this way when she couldn't see him or touch him? It was extraordinary. Or perhaps it was just the ale.

'The last time I saw Tanner, he was about nineteen,' she said. 'But I'm afraid I've got no closer to finding out if he survived the war.'

'I'm not sure I want you rootling around in the other Tanner's life.'

'You don't want to know if you're alive?' She didn't understand.

'Imagine if you find me still working at this other house – a strapping young man of twenty-six, handsome, tanned and a mighty interesting and amusing chap to boot, then he'll be the one you'll talk to, befriend, look at... be able to touch...' He was half-joking but he was also half in earnest. She could tell by his tone. Her stomach clenched. 'Because I'm all those things, you know, and quite a catch about these parts. Women throwing themselves at me when I go down to the village, with the vicar's daughter paying me particular attention.'

Now it was her turn to be jealous. Even if he was teasing her, she knew that a young, healthy war veteran would be as rare as hen's teeth. Look at the baker. He may be the wrong side of thirty, but every young girl for miles around had taken a sudden interest in collecting the weekly groceries from the village, particularly the bread, since he'd returned from service.

'I think of you all the time too,' she finally admitted.

The silence that followed could not have been more pregnant if it was a springing heifer about to calf.

She pressed her forehead to the rough bricks and spread her fingers out, over the wall, willing it to dissolve, like a morning mist burnt away by the sun, but it was going nowhere.

A loud thump made her jump.

'What was that?' she asked.

'Just frustration. Sorry, but I can't bear that you are standing not a foot from me, and even though I can picture your face, I can't touch you, or even, if I was brave enough to risk dismissal, kiss you.'

She jolted at that.

'It's nonsense though, isn't it?' he said, moving on from his brave words quickly. 'Because you wouldn't be alone in the tower with me under any other circumstances, and you certainly wouldn't let me kiss you, even if we were.'

Her heart was bouncing around like a wildcat, and she felt clammy and uncomfortable. The almost suffocating heat of the night was cloying and she felt shaky and sick all at once, but suspected there was another, less meteorological-related reason for that.

'Why would you want to kiss me?' she whispered.

'You know why. The young girl I befriended all those years ago has grown into a woman over the years I've been away. She was always a comfort to me but now she's become something more. Seeing Miss Davenport recently only made me realise how much I care about you. And I can only be this bold because you can't reach out and slap me.' She heard him groan in frustration, followed by his heavy footsteps as he paced, and then the squeak of the bedsprings as he threw himself back onto the bed.

'Eurgh, this heat and far too much drink makes it hard for a man to think properly. Words are slipping from my mouth like butter melting in the sun, and I can't do a damn thing to stop them. My apologies.'

Olivia sat back on her knees, still facing the wall, and determined to be equally bold. Besides, she'd spent a lifetime negotiating with marauding armies, wrestling with fire-breathing dragons, and seducing foreign princes. Courage she had in spades.

'What are you wearing?' she asked.

'You can't ask me that.'

He sounded indignant but as she looked down at her glistening arms, tiny droplets of sweat sitting like diamond shards on her pale-pink skin, she couldn't help but wonder what Seth's view was in that moment.

Shafts of bone-white light cut across the room and one lay across her bed, as though the moon had chosen her in that moment. Was he similarly illuminated? He must surely be shirtless in this heat, and she pictured the light falling over his chest as he stretched out. She felt exactly the same as he did – hearing him was no longer enough. She needed to see him, touch him, smell him... but it was an impossible wish.

Was it worse or better that she had been with a man? She knew what it was to have someone trace his lips across her face and push them down on her mouth, to have his hand slide up her body and press into the small of her back to guide her closer. To be as one. She should be married by now, but the war had taken that from her, and the man she now cared for – and she did care deeply for Seth – was out of her reach yet, ironically, barely a yard from where she was kneeling.

'I mean,' she blustered, 'it's a hot night and I'm struggling in a nightdress that is determined to smother me. The window is open but the air outside is so still, it's made little difference.'

There was a longer than expected pause. She knew he occasionally went quiet if he didn't like where the conversation was going, so inched nearer to the wall.

'Take it off, then,' he finally said. 'No one can see you.'

She swallowed. 'You didn't answer my question,' she pointed out. 'Are you wrapped in an equally sticky nightshirt in this unsufferable heat?'

Another pause.

'I'm in my cotton underpants.'

She slid back and sat on her feet, closing her eyes, trying to recall the memory of his naked torso from all those years ago. Was his skin also covered in a million pinprick beads of sweat? Had military service enhanced those already well-defined muscles? Or was he thinner now from the poor nutrition and harsh conditions of war? At least he was safely back at Merriford Manor where he had access to good food, fresh fruit and a comfortable bed.

A further rush of bravery swirled inside her. Had he

suggested she remove her nightgown as a joke or a challenge? She swung her legs to the floor, pulling the damp cotton over her and shook her head so that her loose, wavy hair fell to her shoulders.

'Well, it's off but it's not made that much difference, to be honest. The air is so still and humid that I don't feel any cooler.'

There was a squeak of bedspring.

'You removed your nightgown?' he said, surprise evident in his voice.

'It was your idea.'

'I didn't think you'd actually do it. If only all the young ladies that I came across disrobed so easily.'

Those dratted women again – the ones who could see his face and make eyes at him. She swallowed, every nerve ending rippling across her body like the meadow grasses being toyed by a gentle breeze.

'But we're good friends, Seth. We've known each other for years and shared our darkest secrets and deepest fears. I'd do anything you asked me to do...'

The silence that followed was unsettling. She leaned closer to hear what was happening the other side of the wall. Damn those bricks – they muffled the quieter sounds that might have given her some indication of what was going on. What was he thinking? Was he imagining her without her nightdress? And if so, was that having a similar effect on his body as the thought of him naked was having on hers?

'You're right.' His quiet voice finally mumbled from the other side. 'Taking off your clothes doesn't make much difference, does it?'

The implication of his words made her heart thud alarmingly. Two people separated by the thickness of a house brick and an entire universe, baring their flesh, together and yet they could not be further apart if he was on the moon. What were they doing? This was madness.

She kneeled on the bed and faced the wall. Every inch of her clammy skin felt alive and, even though he couldn't see her, her body reacted as if his gaze was travelling all over her exposed flesh. She closed her eyes and reached out her hand to trace the tips of her fingers along the indents of mortar – a surprisingly erotic sensation.

'Are you still there?' His voice was hoarse and anxious.

'I'm here, kneeling on the bed, facing you, with my hands on the wall, wishing there was nothing between us but an empty space.' It came out as a shaky whisper.

'And I'm barely a foot away from you, wishing the same.' She could tell from his voice he was nervous. 'Do you think you'd slap an impertinent undergardener if he kissed you?'

'Would you think less of a forward young woman who knelt naked on a bed before you, wishing more than anything that you *could* kiss her?'

She heard the frustrated groan come from his room.

'I can't touch you, but *you* can touch you.' His voice was unsure but she knew exactly what he was suggesting. It was something she did from time to time, especially since her sexual awakening, on those lonely nights when she missed Howard and found herself thinking back to how he'd made her feel in the boathouse. But, more recently, when she'd thought of Seth.

'And *you* can touch *you*,' she said.

'If my hands were yours right now, where would you want me to put them?' But she was ahead of him and was already tracing a line around her breasts with her soft fingertips, and then sliding her hand down her side, over her hip and round to her inner thigh.

Not afraid to say the words out loud, mainly because he

couldn't see her hot cheeks or quivering body, she told him what she'd done and he immediately responded with details of what his hands were doing. Every caress, every intimate exploration, they described to one another. But their words quickly dried up, their breaths became more jagged, their movements more feverish, as everything became too much and all that pent-up longing was released on both sides of the wall. Seth cried out her name and it was followed by the noise that Howard had always made as he'd rolled away from her. She lay breathless, hotter than ever, and the occasional uncontrollable judder rippling through her body, like the aftershocks of an earthquake, as she let her jelly limbs fall to her sides.

After a minute or two, when she finally had control of her body again, she turned back to the wall.

'I know it makes no sense, and I'm not sure I can do anything about it, but I love you, Seth,' she said.

'That, Olivia, was a given,' he replied. 'I may be just a gardener but I'm still a gentleman and I would not have been intimate with a lady if we were not in love.'

32

'I go back tomorrow,' Benji said, as Olivia sat opposite him at the breakfast table the next morning. 'But I'm not as worried about you as I was back at Easter. You seem brighter, somehow. Almost radiant.'

They were alone in the dining room as his parents had stayed later at the harvest supper and not surfaced yet. Olivia reached for his hand and squeezed it. His cheeks coloured like the banks of willowherb that ran down to the village, but he was at the age when it didn't take much to make him blush.

'I feel better,' she said. 'I will always miss Howard but I recognise that I have to move on.' What she couldn't admit to the young lad across from her was that she had moved on already. Ten months after his brother's death and she had fallen in love with another man. One who, to be utterly factual, she had never even met, and more than that, she had been intimate with. Although she had no concerns that she might be carrying Seth's child.

'Mother says you've started writing again?'

'Yes, a novel, but it will take me months to complete. And you? Did you find any time this summer for your sketching?'

Benjamin avoided her eye and she saw his jaw tense as he gripped the handle of his knife even tighter. 'Pa's not so keen any more. Made some comment about painting being for children. I was indulged when they had a litter of sons, but my future is no longer going to include studying at The Slade. Clarence said some things in the letter he left after his death, which strike an uncomfortable chord with me now. He was apologising for being such a pill, and trying to explain why he was the way he was. Honour, duty, obligation… all things he had to uphold but that came with so much pressure. I was not given the opportunity to fight so I must do the right thing and step up instead. Art can only ever be a hobby, whilst I feign an interest in hunting, shooting and fishing.' He sighed. 'Although everyone's appetite for such things is waning now.'

'The war has destroyed so many people's hopes and dreams,' she agreed. 'But at least we are alive to have those dreams. We have a future – something denied to so many.'

'Look, about that, I overheard Mother talking to Father.' He sat up straighter, pulling his shoulders back and scrunching up his brow. 'She was bandying some names about – fellows who've come back from the war and are looking to settle down… She means well but she doesn't understand that it's far too early for you to be thinking about that when Howie is barely cold.'

Olivia cast her eyes to her plate, looking at, but not focusing on, her devilled kidneys.

'She believes that the distraction of running a home and motherhood will help, whereas I'm of the opinion that marrying in haste could lead to a lifetime of regret. It comes from a good place, but she's interfering—'

'And you wanted to warn me?'

His pale face looked serious and his young eyes shadowed and intense. He pushed a spoonful of scrambled eggs about his plate.

'Not exactly.' He swallowed and cleared his throat, pink spots flashing briefly on his round cheeks. 'I wanted to get in first, so that I don't come back at Christmas and find you're engaged again.'

Olivia frowned.

'I know you aren't going to take what I say seriously but I need you to understand this isn't a sudden, impetuous gesture. You mean the absolute world to me, Livvy, but you never saw me – not like that – and I suspect I will always be a boy to you. But I'm old enough to know my own mind.' He swallowed hard. 'I'm not about to drop to one knee and propose, I realise that would be ridiculous, but if you could hold off for a bit. Maybe we could reach an understanding... Wait and see how the land lies when I've finished my education?'

Olivia watched the horrifying scene unfold before her. How had she not seen this coming? What clues had she missed?

'Oh, darling Benji... Benjamin,' she said, being careful that her tone in no way mocked his sincere gesture, and reached her hands out across the tablecloth again, but his fell to his lap.

She placed her napkin by her plate and pushed the chair back to stand. Manners dictated he do the same. He took a step towards her and it was immediately disconcerting, because despite her being four years older, he was considerably taller. In that no man's land between being a boy and an adult, he was hurtling towards the latter at an alarming rate. And there was no denying that, despite the spectacles, he was a handsome young lad. Those cobalt eyes of his retained their earnestness, which was as attractive in its way as the cheeky twinkle of Howard's. Their features were so similar that she could almost imagine it was her fiancé standing in front of her now.

Benjamin studied her face, absorbing every tiny detail in the hope it would give a clue to her imminent response.

'You are the sweetest man I know.' She deliberately used the word 'man' so as to be sure not to patronise, but couldn't he see this was ridiculous? She didn't love him in that way. She wasn't even certain that his feelings were of a romantic nature, despite his declaration. He was being noble – perhaps feeling it was his duty to take care of the woman his brother had loved now that she was alone again. Or simply confusing their very special friendship as something more because she'd come into his life and given him the affection he was lacking at a critical age.

'It's kind but—'

'Don't tell me it's a kindness. I love you, Olivia.' He held her gaze, finding an inner strength to brazen it out. 'This is nothing to do with Howard. Do you have any idea how devastated I was when Mother told me the two of you were engaged? How it cut me to the quick that I'd been trounced by an older brother, again. All my life, I trailed in their shadows, not big enough, strong enough, old enough to be part of their gang. I was teased for my spectacles, mocked for my stature, had my art derided, and consistently underestimated. But you saw me, you stood up for me, you cared for me.'

'Absolutely and unconditionally. And my response is nothing to do with your age, nor am I in any doubt of the sincerity of what you say, but it wouldn't be fair to either of us. I love you beyond measure, but not like that. I'm so sorry.'

'But the night we spent together in the tower? I thought it meant something. I thought...' His voice trailed off and she realised her foolish error. It had meant something different to him because, like her infatuation with Tanner before the war, when your body was changing, and your emotions were heightened, any small gesture could be misinterpreted. It was easy to latch on to an older figure and imagine yourself in love.

'I'm sorry.'

'I can wait.'

Could he not see she was serious?

And yet there was a part of her that recognised that her adolescent feelings for the gardener, and Howard's adolescent feelings for the strange orphan girl who had dropped into their lives, had both proved to be genuine. And the words 'pot', 'kettle' and 'black' were foremost in her mind.

* * *

As if being ambushed by Benji wasn't enough, later that day, Lady Fairchild pounced on her as she sat at the piano. Her playing was mediocre but being in love made her feel capable of anything.

'You know that I love you as one of my own, and nothing would have made me happier than for you to step into my shoes one day, but it was not to be. I am, however, conscious that you don't have a close circle of friends. I know that you missed Ruth when she married, and many of those who you kept company with are gone: my darling boys, the nurses and wounded men who befriended you during their time at the hospital...'

'I still correspond with one of the nurses. She has invited me to stay with her if I should ever find myself in Lincoln.' Olivia closed the lid over the ivory keys and wondered where this was heading.

'I don't say this to get rid of you, God knows my heart will break to see you go, but I want the best for you. Sir Hugo has an aunt who lives in Whitechapel and I thought you might like to stay with her for a while – go to the theatre, drink cocktails at a nightclub, listen to this new-fangled jazz music that all the youngsters are talking about...'

It was an exciting prospect, and one of the things she'd promised Howard was to have magnificent adventures. If she was going to have a serious stab at this writing lark, she should be embracing every opportunity that came her way. But going to London would mean leaving Seth behind.

'I'll think about it,' was all she could say, because now they'd realised exactly what they meant to each other, there was no way she could do that. Their connection couldn't extend beyond the tower, never mind beyond the county.

33

As always, Seth was late to join her at night, particularly given the season. Olivia knew that it was when the land and the gardens needed the most attention. Like a needy child, just before they were put to bed – everything had to be tidied away and tucked in for the winter.

He asked how she was and, grateful for a listening ear, she told him.

'Oh, one of those days, you know, when you all but get a marriage proposal from a very unexpected quarter, and an invitation to live in London, with the idea that experiencing the nightclubs, cocktails and the music will somehow make the misery of the last four years go away.'

Silence.

She'd been trying to make light of both offers but quickly realised that it was unfair to talk of these things to a man who she knew had feelings for her, even though there was nothing they could do to be together.

'I hadn't thought that you'd be so in demand, but of course

you're as eligible as me – more so. However, you're not tied to a place of work, as I am, but a lady of leisure, with a whole world of experiences open to you. Whereas I'm just a working man, grateful for a job.'

It seemed to Olivia that their difference in class was still preying on Seth's mind. It hadn't mattered before the war when they'd been two friends keeping each other's spirits up, and she thought it a shame that society divided people so.

'It was unkind of me to be so flippant but I'm not about to marry anyone. You know how I feel about you.'

'Ah, but if I stepped through the wall now and fell to one knee, would you say yes to me? A member of Sir Hugo's staff, the summit of whose ambition is to have regular articles published in the *Gardener's Chronicle*, and achieve the dizzying heights of head gardener at Merriford, with an eye on the tied cottage?'

'Of course I would. Do you not know me at all? Did you not listen to my daydreams as a child? Yes, there were princes and castles, but also ordinary people achieving extraordinary things. Not everyone's happy ever after is about riches; sometimes, it is completing a journey, finding love, becoming part of a family or defeating an enemy.'

How she hated these moments when she couldn't see his face to work out what was going on in his mind, but it wasn't her explanation of fairy tales that he focused on.

'*You'd marry me?*' His tone was incredulous.

'In a heartbeat.'

'Why?'

She didn't even have to think about her answer. The words came tumbling from her lips.

'You have a kind soul, and never once overlooked or under-valued Benji when he was younger. You're passionate about the things you love and always looking to educate yourself further. You treat me as an equal, value my opinions and encourage my passions. Many men don't like the thought of independent women, yet you've always supported my plans to be exactly that. We share a sense of humour that was apparent even when you were at your lowest ebb. You listen to my ideas for wild adventures and I know you would travel with me anywhere I wanted to go, if only in the hope of learning about new species of plants,' she teased. 'And, if truth be told, because you also happen to be quite easy on the eye – even Lady Fairchild admitted to that.'

He snorted at the last piece of information. 'And yet, she let me go...'

Olivia said nothing. His good looks had been part of the problem.

'A willingness to travel the world and a pleasing face. I see.' He chuckled to himself.

'But I've had an opportunity to interact with you in the real world, and you have barely exchanged a few words with me,' she pointed out. 'I should be questioning why you would want to propose in the first place?'

'Oh, I'm purely attracted to the money,' he said. The bed squeaked as he adjusted his position and she could just imagine the huge grin across his face. 'You'll inherit when you come of age, which I understand is imminently, and I can put my feet up and be a kept man.'

His answer proved her point about the sense of humour, if nothing else.

She pulled back the cotton bedcover and climbed into bed, resting her head on the soft, feather pillow and positioning herself to face the bricks. The room was still, save the ticking of her small bedside clock, and the moonlight had gone, doubtless obscured by cloud.

'What are you doing now?' he asked.

'Facing the wall and imagining you next to me.'

'I *am* next to you. We've all but shared a bed for years.'

Another silence.

'To hell with this.' Seth's bed squeaked and she heard his feet hit the floorboards with a thump. 'I need to see you, to hold you in my arms. I'm coming through.'

'You're what?' She sat bolt upright.

'If our voices are travelling through the wall, why can't we?'

'Erm, because we've firmly established that we can't be together. Neither of us has the ability to float through solid brick, despite our rash assumptions of years ago, as we are not spirits of the departed. We tried to meet and it wasn't possible.'

'Then I'll remove the damn bricks. They're the only barrier to us being together.'

Olivia's heart was both panicked and thrilled by his suggestion. She felt there was some logic to what he was saying; if sound could pass from one room to the other, why couldn't they?

Was this the answer? Breaking down the wall?

'If I chisel the mortar out, I can push one through. Don't move.'

He disappeared for a few minutes, she assumed in search of the appropriate tools. When he returned, he worked quickly and she could hear every whack of his hammer, although, interestingly, she couldn't feel any vibrations. He eventually informed her that he'd loosened a brick sufficiently to remove it, and warned her to stand well back. She grabbed one end of the iron bedstead and swung her bed out so that it no longer sat against the wall. If he was coming through, she wanted to clear a path for him.

'If I hit the brick hard enough, it should shoot through into your room,' he said and there was a loud thump.

Nothing.

'Where are you?' The frustration in his voice was evident.

'I'm here.'

'I should be able to see you. I don't understand. Can you see my hand?'

The wall hadn't changed. There was no missing brick, no wiggling fingers. Nothing. Disappointment flooded her heart.

'Where the hell are you?' He was angry now and as frustrated as her. 'This can't be!' It was almost a shout. 'I won't have it. Stand well back,' he instructed. 'I can't have you hit by flying masonry. I've got a sledgehammer and will destroy the whole damn tower if that's what it takes to get to you.'

She reassured him that she was safely out of harm's way. The first crack of the sledgehammer made a deafening sound but she saw nothing, not even the flutter of disturbed dust, which she would have expected even had his first swing been gentle – and it was far from that.

With each thud, she heard him let out a ferocious growl, but the wall in front of her didn't change. There was an almighty crash, which contrasted deeply with the eerie silence that followed.

'How can this be? I've made a three-foot-wide hole in the damn wall and you aren't there.'

She moved closer. 'But I am. I'm standing before you.'

'Then there is nothing for it but to step through. Keep talking to me and I'll keep talking to you.'

And as they spoke simultaneously, a babble of reassurance from her and grim determination from him, her brain separated her words from his, until he stopped talking mid-sentence.

'Seth?'

After a minute, his voice returned. 'This is hopeless, isn't it? It doesn't matter what we do; we can never be together.'

But Olivia would not be beaten.

'Where will I find a sledgehammer?' she asked. 'Perhaps both walls must be destroyed.'

'The gardener's tool shed attached to Rowe's cottage. We use them for driving fence posts into the ground.'

She raced out into the night and along the edge of the lawns, down to the cottage, trying to be quiet so as not to attract attention. The shed was latched, but not locked, and inside, she found what she was looking for. It was heavy and cumbersome – the weight of the iron head making it hard for her to run fast, but she returned to the tower, wrestled it up the spiral stairs and entered her bedroom, out of breath but optimistic.

'Careful,' he warned. 'Legs apart. Dominant hand near the head.'

Her first attempt was feeble. She didn't have the strength in her arms to lift it properly. But she managed to twist her body round so that the handle was over her shoulder and, using every ounce of strength, she launched it at the wall. Dust flew everywhere but nothing gave. A primal growl came from deep within and grew in volume as she repeatedly struck her target, and eventually, a small section fell away from her and into the adjoining room. She worked on making the hole bigger until, abandoning the sledgehammer, she could clamber through, coughing and spluttering, as her lungs filled with the settling dust.

But she found herself alone in the dressing room.

There was no Seth.

She allowed herself to sink to the floor, sitting amongst the broken half-bricks and not caring, as her tears left clear streaks down her dirty cheeks.

And then the sound of pounding feet up the metal staircase.

'What the hell?'

Benji stepped into her room, frantically looking around for Olivia, until he noticed the hunched, nightgown-clad and sobbing figure through the hole in the wall.

'Oh, Livvy. I don't think you're well. You need help.'

34

'We all thought you'd turned a corner,' Cynthia said, her arms wrapped around Olivia as she held the pale and silent young woman close.

Benji had guided her into the main house and woken up Lady Fairchild's personal maid, who had washed her and found a clean nightgown. Olivia had said very little but couldn't stop her eyes from leaking. No sobs came from her mouth, no explanations; it was as if she was in a trance as she allowed herself to be tended to. And then she'd been taken to one of the guest bedrooms and instructed to sleep.

She'd woken up to find Cynthia on a low chair beside her, the older woman's face a mixture of concern and confusion. At first, there were no words from either of them, as Lady Fairchild did what the young *Titanic* orphan had taught her. She moved over to the bed and embraced her so that touch could begin the healing. It was enough just to be held and they sat intertwined for quite some time before the inevitable questioning.

'What's going on, darling girl?'

'Surely, you have bad days,' she mumbled into the older woman's shoulder. 'Yesterday was a bad day.'

'Of course I do. The loss of three sons is unbearable, and sometimes, I can hardly drag myself from my bed, but I don't start demolishing buildings. You've destroyed a wall, Olivia... I really think a spell at a private sanatorium might do you good. Sir Hugo knows people and you would be well cared for. Howard wouldn't have wanted to see you like this – he would want you to embrace life, be happy, find love. Please let us help you.'

The jagged blade of guilt sliced through her, leaving a raw and open wound, because her weeping had not been over the tragic death of the third Fairchild son, but instead her despair at not being able to reach the man she now loved. How could she have moved on so easily? What sort of shallow, insincere person did that? Queen Victoria had mourned the death of Albert for a lifetime. Howard had not even been dead for a year.

She allowed more tears to seep into the soft silk of Cynthia's blouse, knowing full well they were tears of shame, not of grief, and then realised she had to compose herself. Absolutely the last thing Olivia wanted was to be shipped off somewhere. She had to be allowed to remain in the tower, and to do that, she must prove that she was well.

She pulled away from Lady Fairchild and sat up straight, wiping the last of the tears from her hot cheeks with the back of her hand.

'I was tired and overly emotional last night. You know me: always one for drama.' She forced out a small smile. 'It's not good to bottle things up; we both know that. I was angry at the world and lost my temper.'

'But you went to the gardeners' sheds for a sledgehammer.

You love that tower – you always have – I don't understand why you'd want to destroy it.'

She reached out for Cynthia's pale hands and gripped them tight. 'I can't explain it. Everything came rushing at me like a swirling tornado. But I can promise you that if I ever feel overwhelmed like that in the future, I'll come to you. I'm begging you to trust me when I say that it won't happen again.'

One of the maids entered with a tray of tea and toast, bobbed a curtsey to Her Ladyship and set it down on a small table.

'Come, eat.'

Olivia swung her legs to the floor and trailed over to the breakfast. Her mind was racing. It was imperative that the Fairchilds realised this was a minor hiccough and that everything returned to normal as quickly as possible.

'I'll clear up the mess.'

'Benji has already seen to it. The housemaids are sweeping up the dust and laundering the bedding. Luckily, it is not a supporting wall, so he's gone down to the village to enquire about getting it repaired. If it can all be done without too much fuss, I see no need to mention it to my husband when he gets back.'

'Back?'

Lady Fairchild sighed. 'Haven-on-Sea calls to him more and more, and I try not to mind.'

Olivia poured herself some tea and then set about eating the toast, forcing out a bright smile, as though nothing was wrong. She saw Cynthia's shoulders relax as a consequence.

'Please trust that it's all out of my system. In many ways, I feel happier now than I have done since we heard of Howard's death. I *am* healing. I *will* get through this.'

'Very well, I won't talk of the sanitorium again, unless you give me cause to think otherwise.'

'And on an unrelated note,' Olivia said, fully aware that what she was about to ask was utterly and wholly related, 'in an effort to sort out my life, tie up the loose ends and move on from all the things that have caused me pain, I want to ask again about Tanner – the gardening lad who was moved to Cambridgeshire when I first arrived. I still carry a degree of guilt that he was uprooted when he did absolutely nothing wrong, and wondered if it might be possible to trace him? I'd like to find out if he survived the war. It will give me peace to know the ending of his story.'

Cynthia smiled, gave an understanding nod of her head and squeezed Olivia's hand.

'Of course, dear girl. I will see what I can find out.'

* * *

Later that day, Olivia sought solace in the Japanese gardens, as she always had. She watched a daring squirrel dash along the handrail of the bridge as she inhaled the sweet scent of the late-flowering honeysuckle. The steady trickle of water spewed from the dragon's mouth, and its euphonious backdrop allowed her to order her thoughts. Seth had removed the physical barrier between them and still they could not be together. It made no sense – their voices passed through the wall but their bodies could not.

They'd talked of marriage but she recognised now that it was impossible. Perhaps it would be better that she should remain a spinster, because if she couldn't be with Seth, then she didn't want to be with anyone. Even *she* could not fall in love so completely a third time. And she wouldn't marry without love. As long as she could still communicate with him at night, she would happily see out her days finding other things to fill the void a marriage might have plugged. She was already earnestly pursuing her writing, and that would keep her busy enough.

It then occurred to her that Seth might one day fall in love with someone else – someone he could hold in his arms. And how long could she remain in the tower anyway? Especially when Benji inherited the manor. And with Seth aspiring to head gardener, and Rowe hurtling towards retirement, would he still be able to access his old room if he moved into the cottage?

Benji interrupted her thoughts by striding over the bridge and waving at her.

'What ho! Thought I might find you here.' He came to her side and studied her face. 'Mother says we're not to worry about you and that it was just a temporary aberration.' Bless her, Cynthia had her back. 'She says you're keen to move back in. Give it a few days for the mortar to set but there's a chap from Merriford Lode bricking up the hole as we speak. I know you've always had an affinity with that place, even if I don't understand it, but what I'm struggling with is why you should try to destroy it.' He tipped his head to one side. 'Is it still connected to this nonsense about ghostly voices coming through the wall?'

Before the war, she would have welcomed Benji being in on her secret. The only Fairchild with an imagination to match hers, he would have been as much in awe of the situation as she was. But things had changed. She was in love with Seth, and Benji professed to be in love with her. She could not have the two men talking to each other. It wouldn't be fair on either of them.

'I'm fine,' she reassured her concerned companion. 'But you must stop creeping around the tower at night.'

'I'm keeping a concerned eye on the girl I love,' he defended. 'No one really likes the idea of you out there alone, and we both know that you talk to yourself more than is healthy.'

She leaned towards him, trying to express her sincerity. 'What each of us do in our own bedrooms should be private. I doubt that you would want me to stand sentry outside your door at night, listening in. I merely ask for the same consideration.'

He coloured and dropped his eyes. Young lads of sixteen certainly did not want eavesdroppers loitering nearby when they thought themselves alone.

'And you aren't in love with me, Benji – not really. I know that you care for me, as I care for you, but it's not romantic love. One day, someone will come along who makes you feel as though you are the most important thing in their universe, and you will wonder how you can even breathe without them.'

'I do love you, Livvy. I always have. And I'll happily wait until you realise what I say is true.' His jaw was set with the determination of one who was about to conquer an unconquerable mountain.

There was no point in arguing with an adamant adolescent. She'd been one herself not that long ago. Let him discover the truth of her words over time, she decided. Instead, she turned the conversation to other things. He was returning to school the following day and she said she would miss him. In response, he encouraged her to hurry up and finish writing her book – which she said she would.

Resigned now to the fact that being with *her* Seth was not possible, she also told him of her wish to track down Tanner and he agreed that he should also like to know what became of the chap. And so Olivia decided to focus her energies on finding out about their former gardener's past and establishing that he had at least survived the war.

* * *

Later that week, Olivia tracked Freda down to the still room, where she was making jam. The housemaid had married at the start of the war, but her husband had been killed on the Somme. Struggling to find household staff, the Fairchilds had been only too happy to take her back. Olivia asked her about Annie Taylor, something she'd been putting off because she now realised that she was jealous of the girl who Tanner had fallen for.

'She was my best friend at school,' the woman confirmed. 'I was always sore that she disappeared and never thought to drop me a line and let me know she was all right.'

'Did you know anything about the man she was seeing?'

Freda shrugged. 'She never would give me a name, so I wondered if he was married, because something wasn't right. P'raps she was worried that I'd set my brother on him, because she knew I weren't happy about how she was treating the Tanner lad.' She shook her head as if to confirm Annie's behaviour was not acceptable in her eyes. 'He didn't deserve to be cheated on, and I know for a fact she did things with this man that she'd never done with young Seth.

'Maybe that was the problem,' she continued. 'Seth was old-fashioned and honourable, and Annie, well, her parents were very strict and I guess she was seeking adventure and thrills. Turns out those thrills came back to bite her. You ain't going on no adventures with a babe on the way. To be honest, I think it's the only reason she finally told me when she did. She was in the sort of trouble you can't hide for long and she knew it.'

'She was expecting?' There had been talk of a child, so was Freda confirming it?

'Expecting a babe and hoping for a ring on her finger. To my mind, she either eloped or the man in question paid to set her up somewhere – nice little cottage where she could pretend to be a widow and he could still visit if the fancy took him.' Freda almost sounded jealous of the scenario. 'Last time I saw her, she was in a right state because Seth had proposed. She told me, she may have done a stupid thing but she weren't out to trick a good man. Turned him down flat, gave no reason and then disappeared.'

Freda clearly didn't have much time for the actions of her former school friend, and Olivia couldn't say she blamed her. But she did know this: if Seth had proposed marriage, then he really had loved this girl. Whether she'd deserved his love or not was irrelevant.

35

Olivia returned to the tower a week after destroying the wall, but over the next few nights, her calls for Seth were in vain. With her ear pressed to the newly laid bricks, she was repeatedly met with nothing but silence, and she wondered what sort of trouble he'd landed in over the sledgehammered wall. She had members of the Fairchild family on her side, able to order the damage to be fixed and willing to overlook her mental collapse. He could easily have been fired for his actions and that uncomfortable thought nestled beside her on the pillow as she settled down to sleep. If he didn't return, she'd get no resolution – never find out any more about his life, or even her other life for that matter. She realised now that she hadn't asked enough questions about his Miss Davenport, swanning about with both her parents and never having lost a fiancé in the war – although she couldn't be absolutely certain a young man hadn't come into her life at Windy Acres. The point was, she would never know.

Refusing to give up hope, she was confident that he would find a way of returning to the tower, if at all possible. It was beyond cruel to suppose that he'd be taken from her too, so whilst she awaited his return, she channelled her restless energies into her writing. The novel was coming along nicely – a tragic tale of a young woman who loses her beau in the war. It wasn't autobiographical, in that the two main characters were nothing like herself or Howard, but she was drawing on her experiences and those of people she knew. She poured her heart into the prose, often crying as she worked, and mindful not to let her tears smudge the ink. *If I am moved, an editor will be moved,* she decided.

Exactly two weeks after Seth had smashed through the wall to try and reach her, Olivia heard noises she knew were not coming from *her* dressing room. She sat upright, even though seconds before, she had been dancing around the edges of sleep. Everything inside her willed it to be Seth because, apart from her desperate desire not to lose him, she had some exciting news.

'Olivia?' His voice was anxious.

'Oh, thank the Lord.' She was now sitting on her bed with her face turned to the bricks. He was back. How long would she have continued to wait for him had he not returned? Years, probably. 'What happened?'

'Sir Hugo was all for firing me, but Mr Rowe spoke up on my behalf. He appealed to Lady Fairchild as a woman who had lost sons in the war, and who had seen the mental state of those at the convalescent hospital. Even Master Benjamin put in a good word before he left, I believe. But the upshot of the whole episode is that I'm on a warning. The cost of the repairs are to be deducted from my wages which, considering half my wage packet goes to my mother, means we'll both be short for a while. But something like this cannot be allowed to happen again or I'm out on my ear for good.'

'And they let you return to the tower?'

'I told them that I talk in my sleep and often have night-mares since the war, so it was likely that I'd disturb the others in the bothy and, much like before, they felt sorry for me.'

'Is that why they allowed you to have it in the first place? Because they felt bad when your father died?' she clarified, wondering if he would also admit his heart had been broken by young Annie Taylor.

He hesitated a fraction too long. 'Yes.'

It seemed he would never open up to her about his former sweetheart and, in a way, she understood. She was keeping the truth of Tanner's dismissal from him, after all. It wasn't some-thing he needed to know about – her childish infatuation – and he might not want to speak of a first love to someone he had all but proposed to.

'I heard Benji's voice on the day you smashed down the wall, telling you that you needed help,' he said. The change of topic did not go unnoticed by her.

This link through the wall was bigger than just them, she realised, but Benji hadn't said anything to her about hearing the voice.

'Did you speak to him? Make your presence known?'

'I thought about it, but I rather like that it's our secret.'

She didn't comment because she knew exactly what he meant.

'How did you explain the destruction your side?' he asked.

'Considering I was found with the sledgehammer in my hands, there wasn't much I could say. I certainly couldn't pin the blame on anyone else. Lady Fairchild was all but ready to cart me off to a sanatorium...'

And she told him how she, too, had manipulated her way back into the tower by using her childhood trauma to justify her actions and elicit sympathy. She still didn't mention Howard, who had been her trump card.

'I have news,' Olivia said, now keen to change the subject herself. 'You'll be glad to know that you aren't dead.'

'I'm fully aware of that,' the voice came back. 'I can hear my beating heart and see the rise and fall of my ribcage as we speak.'

'Not you, silly, the you that is here.'

'You've seen me?' Seth's voice was suddenly excited. 'Although now I'm downright jealous of myself.'

'No,' she admitted. 'Lady Fairchild contacted Sir Hugo's cousin and we have been told that you are living somewhere in deepest, darkest Cambridgeshire. Would you like me to investigate further, visit Tanner and find out how he is?' She still thought of Seth and Tanner as two separate men.

'About that,' he said. 'With everything that has happened in the last few days, and the obvious futility of our situation now apparent, I've been thinking...'

Olivia's heart rate slowed to a wary amble. Why did she suspect she wasn't going to like what he was about to say?

'Your world and mine clearly overlap, like two sheets of paper lying on top of each other. What if our voices were like the wet ink, the imprint of which can transfer across from one page to the other, leaving a mark, but we're the words themselves, written on the page? We can't leave the paper, Olivia.'

His analogy made sense.

'As much as this destroys me to admit, I don't think we can ever be together. How can I enter your world when I am already there – living somewhere in Cambridge? It's a biological impossibility. And, if that's the case, we must look to lead fulfilling lives without each other, and accept that this link we have, however precious, can't go on forever.'

'Don't say that.' This couldn't be snatched from her as well. She was teetering at the edge of the pit she'd clambered out of after Howard's death. One gentle push and she'd plummet to the bottom again. 'Surely, the world somehow replicating itself is impossible, yet it's happened,' she pointed out. 'There must be a way. And, even if there isn't, I'll happily see out my days as a spinster, living in this tower, writing ridiculous books that will probably never get published, but don't tell me that we have to part.'

'But it's not realistic, or fair, on either of us. It's a kindness that the Fairchilds let me sleep here, especially after I smashed down the wall, but they could ask me to move out at any point. We both have dreams and we owe it to ourselves to at least try and achieve them. Besides, Sir Hugo won't be the master of Merriford Manor forever.'

She knew there would inevitably come a day when Benji would inherit and who knew what plans he had for the place. In both her world and Seth's, there were so many scenarios out of their control.

'You always told me that you wanted to travel,' he reasoned. 'You'll soon have the money and no commitments. The world is slowly opening up again, now we are at peace. Go to the fjords of Norway and the jungles of Brazil.'

She was reminded how similar their existences were. Germany had still lost the war and Spanish flu had swept the world, regardless or not of whether an ocean liner bound for America had sunk seven years ago. The differences were much smaller, and it was only with time that what seemed insignificant now had the potential to make their worlds diverge on a more dramatic scale. Vincent Astor, for example, had inherited astounding wealth after his father had gone down with the *Titanic*, and it remained to be seen what he would do with it, but what was Jacob Astor, the American business magnate, doing in Seth's world with that money? And what ripples would two different uses of that wealth have in their different worlds?

'I can't leave you and gallivant around the world, Seth. You're my voice of reason, the person who brings me the most happiness. The man I love.'

'Yes you can. I left you to fight the war and I came back, and I'll be here when you return from your travels. All I'm saying is we don't know how long this will continue, and we can't rely on always being in contact. I love you, too. God only knows how I love you, but we have to face reality.'

'Not a strength of mine,' she acknowledged.

'Nonsense, your wild and vivid imagination is part of your charm. But one of us needs to be sensible about this—'

'And it's going to be you,' she finished for him. She looked down to find she'd crossed her arms without even realising.

'Yes, because I realised something else when I was holed up in the bothy waiting for the tower to be fixed – there's a way we could be happy. And your news makes me think it might be possible...'

She knew what he was going to say before his words drifted through the wall.

'I can find happiness with Olivia Davenport and you can be with Seth Tanner. We can find each other in our own worlds. I know it's a huge risk, with only a small chance of success, but it's an adventure, and you taught me that life is an adventure, waiting to be had.'

Silence.

'Are you sulking?' His soft chuckle broke her heart a tiny bit more.

'Tanner doesn't love me like you do and I doubt he's thought of me in seven years. And the other Olivia Davenport, as lovely as she may be, will not consider the romantic advances of a gardener she barely knows.'

'Won't she?' he questioned. 'The young girl who believed in fairy tales, challenging the rules and true love overcoming all the odds? Perhaps if we dint know much about the people whose hearts we hope to capture, we might not stand a chance, but we've got each other as guides. Navigating through stormy waters without a compass is madness, but I'm your compass, and you're mine. We can steer each other true.'

He was suggesting that there would be tricks they could employ, tactics they could use which would give them an advantage, but she remained unconvinced.

'I'm not in love with Tanner. I'm in love with *you*.' She inadvertently snorted her indignation.

'He's still me, he just doesn't have the memories that we share or the benefit of befriending a happy-go-lucky, overdramatic young girl in his youth who gave him a more positive outlook on the world. He's lived a different life, away from Merriford and without you, but he's the same man inside. I'm not saying it will be easy, but I know me, and you know you, and I'm certain that your Seth Tanner will welcome your sunshine into his life as much as I have.' He paused. 'But maybe the reality is you don't want to settle for a servant... someone who—'

'That's not it at all. You know that if it were possible, I would marry you in a heartbeat. Windy Acres may not be Merriford Manor, but it will shortly be mine to do with as I wish. It's a place you could make your mark, grow your favourite plants and write articles for the *Gardener's Chronicle* to your heart's content. And if we were shunned by society, we'd simply move to America, start again, and have a whole other adventure.'

'That sounds more like the Olivia I know,' he said. 'And there's a version of her at Windy Acres as we speak, to my knowledge not leading a particularly adventurous life and waiting for someone who understands her, supports her and is happy to indulge her whimsical nature.'

She snorted. 'And somewhere in Cambridgeshire is the man who will treat me like an equal, encourage my dreams and make my heart sing?'

'Maybe.'

'But what if you're married, Seth? What if—'

'What if you'd never lost your parents and insisted on sleeping in the east tower? What if one of the other gardeners had been asked to guard the orchids. What if I'd been killed in the war? And that's the one that really makes me grateful, because there were times when I dint think I'd make it, but I promised myself if I did, I'd live my best life. So, shouldn't we at least try?'

Olivia wondered when he'd become the optimist. The adventurer. The one who leapt over obstacles like they were mere scratched lines in the dirt between them. And she realised that she had been the turning point for him and how he thought about life, as much as he had enabled her to move on from the utter desolation she felt at losing Howard.

She looked over to the small south window, a scattering of stars across the black like a handful of pale seeds tossed onto a patch of freshly ploughed earth, and wondered if there really was an Olivia out there who hadn't been through what she had. Who'd never cried herself to sleep or spent four months hiding herself away in a tower wholeheartedly wishing she were dead. Without the encouragement from Seth and Benji, had that Miss Davenport even put pen to paper? And, equally, was there a grumpy undergardener in her world, still wallowing in his unhappiness, content to see out his days on a couple of pounds a week, pining over a lost love and struggling with the horrific death of his father?

Seth was right. They had to at least try.

36

'Sir Hugo's cousin wrote back again saying Tanner doesn't work for him any more but still lives in a tied cottage on the estate with his mother,' Cynthia said. 'Apparently, he came back from the war, to quote Jonty, "a bit worse for wear" and is managing on a war pension. The silly man never says quite what he means but I don't believe anyone who lived through what those poor men did can have remained unaltered. We saw it ourselves at the convalescent hospital.'

Olivia was helping Her Ladyship collect the seed heads of the dahlias and poppies from the borders along the front driveway. It was a job Cynthia had taken on herself, knowing how busy the garden staff were, and she was no longer a woman to idle her days away with embroidery and society ladies.

'If he's struggling with nervous exhaustion, could we not offer him employment here?' Olivia asked, handing her a small paper bag. 'We could do with extra hands, and I still carry the guilt of his move to Cambridgeshire. Surely, we are better placed to support him, after our experiences with the patients?' She felt strongly that this was one way to right the wrongs of the past.

'Of course. I can speak to Sir Hugo, and I know Rowe would not object.'

'Thank you. I need to know that he's happy,' Olivia said. 'It will give me peace of mind.' If he were to accept and move back to Merriford Lode, it would also give her the opportunity to see if Seth's wild plan had any chance of success.

'Why don't I drive us both over there tomorrow afternoon and you can see the man for yourself? He still lives with his mother and never married, apparently. We can take the motor car and call on one of my maiden aunts afterwards. There's definitely some batty old dear on my mother's side who lives in the area and I'm sure she would welcome a visit. I would call on Jonty but he irritates me beyond reason.' She rolled her eyes. 'I'll give you space to speak to Tanner, make the offer, and atone for your perceived transgressions, and then we can drop in on Aunt Dorothea for afternoon tea.'

Even if Tanner refused the job offer, it made sense to at least visit the man. Perhaps he *would* stir in her the same emotions as Seth. And she genuinely wanted to see for herself that he was all right. Had she not come to the manor that summer, disrupting everything, he would still be there, tending to the orchard that his grandfather had planted, and his mother would not have been forced to leave her friends or, more poignantly, her husband's grave.

They set off bright and early, with Cynthia only hitting the one pheasant, and wove through the long, leaf-strewn lanes of Norfolk and skirted the open fens of Cambridgeshire. Olivia was in charge of navigation and they managed the journey tolerably well.

They'd been given written directions to a row of terraced houses not far from Jonty Fairchild's more modest estate and, after being dropped off by Cynthia, Olivia tentatively knocked on the door of the middle cottage. A tiny woman of about fifty, whom she assumed was Mrs Tanner, opened it and eyed her well-to-do visitor with suspicion.

Olivia introduced herself, half-expecting to have the door slammed in her face, but it was not. Perhaps he'd never enlightened his mother as to why he'd changed employer. She politely enquired if Seth was at home.

'With no job, where else would he be?' Mrs Tanner sighed. 'What do you want him for?'

Olivia reassured the older lady that it was nothing to worry about, quite the opposite. She was there on behalf of the Fairchilds to see how he was faring and whether there was anything they could do for him.

Slightly mollified, the woman swung the door open a little wider.

'You'd better come through. He's out the back.'

Olivia stepped straight into the low-ceilinged living room and followed her through a narrow kitchen and out the back door into the yard. It was a small, cobbled space, with a tin bath leaning up against the wall of a brick privy, and a few empty flowerpots dotted about. Two kitchen chairs were outside, one of which Tanner was sitting in, as it was still mild enough to sit in the sun.

It was a shock to see him at first and time had played tricks with her memory. He'd seemed so big to her back then, and he remained an imposing figure, even seated, but not the giant she remembered from her childhood. His face was tipped up to the weak sun and he still had the same handsome profile. It was an image she'd carried around in her cluttered head for seven years, and had so desperately tried to recall every detail of, once she'd realised it was Seth behind the wall.

'A Miss Olivia Davenport to see you,' she said. 'All the way from Norfolk.'

'Olivia Davenport? The *Titanic* orphan from Merriford?' He tilted his head slightly to look at the woman his mother was introducing. 'Well, she can turn straight back around. I've nothing to say to her.'

She'd expected no less but it hurt just the same.

'That's no way to treat a guest, love.' The woman looked at Olivia, lowering her voice slightly. 'He's never been exactly what you'd call a sociable lad,' she tried to explain. 'Life's been mightily unkind to him over the years.'

'I *am* here, Mother, and can perfectly hear what you're saying.'

'Well, it's true and manners cost nothing. So, I'm going to put the kettle on and make Miss Davenport a cup of tea. I, for one, would love to hear about all our old friends in Merriford Lode, and any gossip from the manor. We don't have many visitors now and life is a bit quiet,' she explained and gestured to the empty chair. 'Make yourself comfortable, my dear. Take my seat and I'll fetch another from the house in a bit.' She turned back to her son. 'At least hear what the poor woman has to say. She's travelled all that way, in a motor car, no less.'

He huffed and shrugged his shoulders.

'I'll give the two of you some privacy and see if I can't find a bit of fruit cake in the tin.'

Tanner got to his feet as Olivia approached. There was something off about the way he stood up and kept his body facing away from her but she understood he wasn't about to welcome her with open arms. They both sat down and stared at the plain wooden fence before them.

'What can I do for you, Miss Davenport?'

'Oh, Tanner—' she gushed, wanting to reach out and

embrace him but held herself in check. He looked so forlorn and lost, somehow – just as he always had. There was no hint of the strength and humour that *her* Seth continually displayed. 'I came to apologise that you were moved from Merriford before the war. I said some things that were untrue and Lady Fairchild was overprotective. I'm sorry if my behaviour led to her rash actions. I was lonely and you were kind.'

He shrugged. 'Some of us are just born unlucky. Bad things follow us wherever we go.'

'I won't have that.' She sat upright and turned to him. 'We make our own luck in life. Some people have a better start than others, granted, but things only break us if we let them. Don't forget, when I first met you, I'd just lost both parents on the *Titanic*. I admit it took me time to rally but I was determined to grow up and become someone they could be proud of.' She didn't mention the swerve that determination had taken after Howard's death because, with Seth's help, she'd got back on track.

He huffed. 'You had a wealthy guardian to take care of you and a good education. You've never wanted for a new pair of shoes, never worked for a living or been sent out to a foreign country to kill men you had no quarrel with.'

'Wealth does not guarantee happiness, nor protect you from the cruelty of life. You do know that the Fairchilds lost Clarence, Louis and Howard, I suppose? Howard was reported missing in action and his death wasn't confirmed until after the war. It was all very traumatic.'

He was quiet for a moment.

'No, I dint and I'm sorry for that. I can't think of Howard as being old enough, somehow. He was just a lad when I left, and a mischievous one at that. Used to pick on Benji and I often wished one of his brothers would have stood up to him. I was hardly in a position to give him the thrashing he so often deserved.'

'Oh, don't worry; I gave him a taste of his own medicine. Do you not remember the time I locked him in the gamekeeper's privy? I even punched him on the nose once. He quickly learned not to mess with me.'

Tanner snorted. 'You certainly struck me as a feisty one – even if you did run around playing the princess or daydreaming in the Japanese gardens.' He rubbed at his stubble-dusted chin and she noticed that his appearance generally was a little neglected. 'Taken on by a girl. I wonder how that went down?'

'He forgave me eventually.' She took a deep breath and resigned herself to talking about the things she found difficult. 'We were engaged to be married.'

'I'm sorry.' His face briefly crinkled into a frown.

She shrugged. 'The princess in the tower found her prince, but then he was taken from her, so you aren't the only one who is followed about by bad luck. I seem to have lost so many of the people who were close to me, but I try not to let it bring me down.'

Howard's death had, of course, completely destroyed her, but she was proof that you could pick yourself up from the furthest of falls.

'If you're trying to compare my life to yours, you're way off, miss.'

'I'm offering an olive branch. It's perfectly obvious you are struggling, and the Fairchilds have had trouble replacing staff since the war, so I have been sent to enquire whether you might consider returning.'

Olivia realised she had her work cut out if she were to try and have any meaningful connection with this man but, if he would only agree to return to Norfolk, she could begin to peel back the layers of hurt and distrust, and uncover the heart that she hoped still existed.

'Well meant, I'm sure, but no.'

'No? Just like that without asking anything about the job? And yet I understand you are currently unemployed. Would you not even consider it? Sir Hugo even has a vacant tied cottage that he would rent to your mother.'

'You know nothing about my life or what I've been through. I lost the woman I loved when I was about your age, saw my father die before my very eyes and then gave four years of my life to a country that has no use for me now. I don't have your ability to see the world as a great big adventure – been on one of those and I can't say I liked it much. My world's smaller now. I won't be climbing trees and pretending they are castles or beating invisible Roman soldiers in sword fights.'

'Goodness me, Mister Grumpy. I'm not saying it's a magical solution that will make everything all right again, but there is a job waiting for you – a job you love, in a place you love...' She wanted to add, *with a woman who loves you*, but she wasn't sure that she did love this bitter version of him so she thought carefully about how to finish the sentence. 'Perhaps there is even another woman out there for you, if you would only open yourself up to the possibility.'

'Hah. Everything seems so easy to you, but you explain to me, miss, exactly how I can work in the gardens with only one arm?' He reached his right hand across his lap and pulled an empty sleeve towards her.

Olivia was very good at not registering shock – something she'd learned in her time volunteering at the hospital, so was able to keep a neutral expression. Besides, she'd known something wasn't quite right in the way he held himself and had kept side-on to her the whole time.

'A shell landed in our trench to my left. Killed two men outright and I was caught in the blast. There are days when I wish it had taken me too. You tell me who'd want to marry this?'

And for the first time, he turned his head all the way around so that she could see the other side of his face. That shell had cost him an arm and, she realised with surprise, an eye, leaving him horribly scarred.

Now she finally understood why he remained so bitter.

37

This time, Olivia couldn't hide her shock and looked at his damaged face for longer than was polite, knowing that her cheeks had flushed pink, before she dropped her gaze to the ground. But during that intense moment, she'd seen something in his remaining eye, felt a frisson flutter across her body when he'd finally looked at her properly, as they'd sat facing each other in that tiny backyard. She was no Gibson Girl but she also knew there was something about her men found attractive – even if it was just her spirit. Howard had fallen in love with her, so had Seth, even poor Benji thought he had, in his own misguided way. Tanner could see she was no longer the child of before, but instead a young woman – she sensed it in his body language and the way he'd assessed her figure when she'd first arrived.

He'd stood firm with his refusal to return to Merriford Lode, but had, at least, been polite and, after the promised tea and cake, Mrs Tanner had shown her out. Olivia took the opportunity to quiz the diminutive lady as they returned through the house.

'It's sad to see him so lost. Why did he not marry? He must have had interest before the war?'

'There's never been anyone since his first girl, Annie,' she said. 'I don't think he ever truly got over her.'

'But she left him for someone else. Surely he doesn't still hold a candle for her?'

'I don't reckon you ever met her, but she was uncommonly pretty, that girl. All the lads in Merriford Lode thought so. Never seen eyes so blue. And such a kind soul, always helping out at church and doing good. Perhaps there's part of him that thinks she might come back one day – he's the loyal kind.'

Olivia felt deflated and chided herself for momentarily believing *she* was some sort of Mata Hari, beguiling young men wherever she went. Her wild hair and tendency to drift off into a dreamworld would be no match for the sparkling sapphire eyes of an angel, who the whole village was apparently in love with.

She thanked Mrs Tanner and left.

* * *

'Jonty failed to mention that the man was *quite* such an invalid,' Cynthia said as they sped down the chalky lanes towards Newmarket. Olivia had filled her in on the visit and his reaction to the job offer. 'You've done your best but if he won't be helped, there's an end to it.'

'I'll persevere, if only because there is nothing I can do for Clarence, or Louis, or Howard. But if I can help even one man who went through what they did then, in a funny way, I feel I've helped them. Imagine if it was one of your sons who had returned injured? You'd be overjoyed to have them alive, but broken-hearted if they felt that they were worthless. He seems to have given up.'

Lady Fairchild was wearing leather driving goggles and was focused intently on the road ahead. They had the top down and Olivia had unpinned her hair and let it fly loose behind her, determined to blow all Tanner's defeatism away. She felt the older woman briefly glance her way and they consequently swerved rather erratically to the left, before she got control of the motor vehicle again.

'He was always a good worker. Not the most cheerful button in the box from what I heard through staff, but pleasant enough, and always happy to help me with the cut flowers for the house. Leave it with me, darling. I'll see what I can do.'

* * *

'And?' Seth asked through the wall that night. 'Am I still dashingly handsome, built like one of them Greek gods and unbelievably witty?'

Olivia had considered the best course of action on the long, and occasionally perilous, journey home. How would she feel if he told her that the other Miss Davenport was not faring so well? It was not news she would want to hear, so she decided to be economical with the truth. The disabilities and disfigurement didn't bother her, but Tanner's state of mind did. In the end, she decided to pretend that things were proceeding nicely. After all, there was no way he could ever find out about himself unless she told him. He could hardly pop by.

'He was pleased to see me and is currently considering the Fairchilds' offer of employment.'

'And how did you feel about him?' he asked, a touch of anxiety evident in his tone. 'Do you think you could love him? Because I'm certain he could love you.'

'Honestly!' She laughed at his eagerness. 'I talked to the man for barely half an hour. I'd like to see how you get on when you visit Miss Davenport and try to convince her to elope with a gardener she's never formally met. These things take time.'

'With a bricklayer to pay for and only one afternoon off a week, it's not so easy for me. I'll have to get the train to Windy Acres, but I'll pursue the young lady when I can.'

'Annie Taylor was mentioned...' She let the name hang between them, suspended somewhere in the fabric of the wall until he answered.

'What did he say?'

'Tell me about her?' She didn't answer his question, curious as to his response.

'She was just a girl from the village who stepped out with me for a while when I was a young lad.'

'*Just* a girl who you felt strongly enough about to propose to.'

'Ah.' A deep sigh floated into her room. 'I should've told you about her – I'm sorry.'

She agreed and her silence spoke for her, as she plumped up one of the pillows and placed it behind her back. She was settling down for a long story.

'I forget how involved you are with everyone's life at the manor,' he said, 'when you are only a fleeting presence here. Did I talk about her to you when you came to live with the Fairchilds?'

'No, Benji mentioned her years ago, but your mother seems to think you never got over her.'

'I can assure you that I have.'

'Tanner hasn't.'

'Poor chap. I guess there's nothing like your first love; it stays with you forever. When you're young, you're passionate about everything from cricket matches to workers' rights. You fall so much harder, and I couldn't believe she'd chosen me, out of all the lads in the village. I think me being a regular at church and her father being somewhat of a zealot was in my favour. She was widely admired.'

'And extraordinarily pretty?'

'Yes,' he begrudgingly admitted. 'That too. Her home life was difficult, though. Not sure her father trusted me, as though I might defile his daughter if he left us in the parlour for more than a minute. She reminded me of you in many ways – desperate to break free of Merriford Lode and to try new things.'

Olivia tried not to mind that 'extraordinarily pretty' was not one of the comparisons.

'But the difference was she cajoled others to go along with these grand schemes, whereas you were always prepared to undertake them alone. She was forever suggesting that she escape her house at night and we meet up, but I was worried what that might lead to.'

His worries, as it turned out, were entirely justified. It was obvious to Olivia that Seth had been too sensible, too morally sound. Annie had gone in search of excitement elsewhere. And that excitement had landed her in trouble.

'To begin with, I didn't mention her because you were just a child, and the things I was dealing with back then were too heavy to lay at your feet. And then, more recently, it was because she didn't matter no more. Someone else had filled the hole she left. Someone who was so much more than a pair of bright-blue eyes.'

She had to smile. He'd dug himself nicely out of the earlier hole.

'Who was *your* first love?' he asked, and she heard the bedsprings groan as he jiggled about, making himself comfortable. 'The first man who really captured your heart?'

She thought for a moment that this could be the time for her to be honest about Howard, but then she realised that her *first* love, the first real person she had dreamed of, made future plans about and had awoken tantalising sensations in her body had been a nineteen-year-old undergardener back in the summer of 1912. He was right about the strength of adolescent feelings.

'You,' she replied, knowing she meant Tanner, but allowing him to think otherwise.

'Well, now, that does wonders for the old ego. Thank you.'

And they made love again, through a wall, together but entirely separately.

38

Olivia was now determined to get to the bottom of the Annie Taylor mystery, although she was nervous as to what she might find. Was resurrecting a blue-eyed siren really such a good idea? She also realised that wherever the woman was in her world, didn't necessarily mean the same things had happened to her in Seth's. However, Annie had run away before the universe had apparently cleaved their worlds in two – which they were pretty sure was the April of 1912.

Freda had confirmed Annie was seeing another man and had consequently found herself in the family way. No men had disappeared from the village at that time, so Olivia considered what her friend had suggested: the man was married. Ernest Dunn had seen her with a carpet bag, so she was planning to make a home somewhere, and there had been a handful of possible sightings in various parts of the county for a few weeks afterwards.

Her parents had kept such a strict eye on her that Olivia doubted she could have conducted an affair away from the village. She was meeting this man at night, possibly in the

Widow Larwood's abandoned house... because it couldn't be at the house of her lover, if he had a wife. She toyed with various possibilities... unless the house and extended buildings were so large that they could find a place to be alone, like, say, a boathouse...

Her insides began a slow merry-go-round. The Larwood house was a dump, crawling with rats, damp and unclean. A gentleman would conduct an assignation somewhere more salubrious. Maybe somewhere that held bedding and lamps, and that gamekeepers were instructed to ignore. There was a married man at Merriford Manor who fitted the bill but she did not want to accept he was a possibility. Someone who had enough money to support a mistress should that be his wont, and who often took trips to the coast...

The thought that Sir Hugo could be behind Annie's disappearance was sickening. He was an entitled man who generally got the things he wanted, but surely not an adulterer. Although, wasn't that what the wealthy did? Married for either land or the money, and took a mistress for the thrills? Could he have had another woman all this time, and found excuses to travel to Haven-on-Sea because that's where Annie and his illegitimate child, or children, now lived?

Olivia couldn't ask anyone about this directly. These good people had taken her into their home and she must be mindful of leaping to wild and unsubstantiated conclusions. Instead, she began to ask innocent questions about Sir Hugo's trips to the seaside town, pretending that she was planning a visit there. Did he go often? Had Cynthia ever accompanied him? What sights would he recommend?

That Sunday, when everyone was attending the service at the Merriford Lode parish church, she feigned a headache and cried off. When the house was quiet, she went to Sir Hugo's study and methodically searched for clues. It felt wrong to be prying through his private papers but she wanted answers. She laboriously leafed through every page of the large crocodile-skin diary on his desk and noted monthly entries that said:

Visit A – Haven

Opening the drawers beneath, she came upon an address book and found two for Haven-on-Sea, which she noted down, before returning everything to how it was, slipping out into the hallway and back to the tower, awaiting the household's return.

It was quite by chance that Sir Hugo's next visit to Haven was the following Thursday, so Olivia told Cynthia she was going off for the day on her bicycle. She wrapped up warmly and headed westwards but, once out of sight, circled back for the train station. It was a forty-five-minute journey to the resort and she'd only been on a handful of occasions, the first time being that summer she'd come to live with them all. Although things had changed since the war, and it was no longer unusual to see young ladies travelling alone, she still felt uncomfortable in the carriage and was thankful when an elderly couple joined her.

Once in the town, she asked directions to the first of the addresses. It proved to be an expensive guest house but no one had heard of an Annie Taylor. Perhaps it was where Sir Hugo stayed when he visited.

The second address was for St Walstan's Lodge, Pebblebank Lane. It took her longer to find this but when she did, she could see that it was, in fact, some kind of hospital. Sir Hugo had written *two o'clock* by the diary entry so she hung about until ten minutes to and then entered the busy lobby, taking a seat with her back to the desk and burying her nose into a newspaper that someone had abandoned in one of the high-backed chairs.

A plaque on the wall caught her eye, which explained that the building was a sanitorium, founded in 1864. She began to wonder if poor Annie Taylor had ended up here as a patient. Nurses in grey dresses, white aprons and starched caps scurried about and other people started to arrive. Visiting hours must start after luncheon.

It wasn't long before she heard Sir Hugo's voice, but she didn't turn around or let her presence be known.

'Good afternoon. I'm here to see Andrew.'

'Of course, Sir Hugo. You'll be pleased to hear your brother is having a better day than on your last visit. Follow me.'

His brother? She almost dropped the newspaper in her shock.

The pair walked past her and down the wide, vaulted corridor and Olivia remembered Cynthia mentioning a younger brother – one who had been sickly. It would appear that his sickness was of the mind and he had been conveniently squirreled away all these years in a sanitorium.

The pieces of the puzzle slowly fell into place and she realised how mistaken she'd been. Olivia's guardian had not been secretly visiting a mistress all these years, but a relative he was ashamed of. She had let her imagination run wild again and could only be grateful that she hadn't flung unfounded accusations out that would have damaged his reputation and her relationship with the family.

39

The evenings were drawing in and soon the trees would be reduced to spiky silhouettes, bare of leaves. Olivia turned twenty-one and the legal guardianship of Sir Hugo came to an end. She knew that she could return to Windy Acres, if she chose, and manage her own affairs, but had decided to stay because the Fairchilds assured her she was family and she was not prepared to part from the man she loved. At night, Olivia spent far too much time whispering through the wall to him, making the most of their situation whilst they could. During the day, she continued her writing and finally finished the novel.

Encouraged by Seth, she approached her father's former editor and he agreed to read her manuscript, more out of compassion, she suspected, than any genuine belief that he was about to discover the next Mary Elizabeth Braddon.

Whilst she awaited his verdict, and after a week of driving rain, when venturing outside held little appeal, the weather finally broke and she was finally able to continue with her enquiries regarding the disappearance of Annie Taylor.

One of the problems she had was that the girl had run off so long ago. Memory was an issue with those she spoke to as details were now blurred and dates were muddled. Olivia hung around the kitchens and talked to Freda again, who couldn't even be certain of the last day she'd seen her friend. She asked the staff if any traveller families had been in the area at the time, but no one could remember if any were camped out at Widow Larwood's cottage or not. Ernest Dunn, Clarence's childhood friend who had so nearly kissed her that day in the music room, had been killed in the war, so she couldn't question him about what he'd seen in the lane, and others had died too – the old woman who'd employed the young girl as a housemaid, and even Annie's father. He'd succumbed to pneumonia the previous winter, although she doubted he would have volunteered information about the daughter who was such a disappointment to him. She decided to pay Mrs Taylor a visit, and also talk to Ernest's mother and see if she could remember anything about the day her son had seen Annie walking to the station.

Mrs Dunn had worked at the bakery since the loss of her son, so Olivia waited until after three, and then called on her. She was invited in and offered a cup of tea, and to share the tin of broken biscuits the older woman had been sent home with.

'I'm so sorry about Ernest,' Olivia said, as they sat together in the back porch.

'And my sympathies to you too, miss. Her Ladyship was so excited about the wedding. It just ain't right that all these young men have been taken away from us. I've still got my girls, but for the Fairchilds to lose three was unthinkable.' She had two older daughters who were now married with children and lived elsewhere. 'And yet the postmaster sent two sons out and they both came back.' She shook her head, lost in her melancholy. 'My lad had such big plans for life. Humble beginnings weren't going to stop him from achieving marvellous things. Had a way with people and bags of charm, did our Ern, positively brimming with it.'

'I remember,' Olivia said, thinking back to the handsome young man who had danced with her and called her enchanting.

'And Master Clarence was so kind. Strutted about a bit, like his father, but the gentry can be like that,' Mrs Taylor said. 'Passed lots of things down to our Ern, although that was part of the problem really.'

'Oh?' Olivia wasn't aware of any problem.

'He started aspiring to greater things once he was asked to spar with Master Fairchild up at the manor. "One day I'll have a big house, Mother," he'd say. "With my own man to dress me and a wife to be proud of." And he was a clever lad.' She tapped at her forehead to indicate that he had brains. 'Had a gift of saying the right thing and using a bit of flattery to get what he wanted.' She chuckled to herself at the memory. 'I'm not saying he was an angel, mind. Had a bit of a temper when he was riled. But everyone loved him.'

Whilst every mother thought the very best of her children, this wasn't quite true. Benji hadn't liked Ernest much, and Howard hadn't been overly keen after the almost kiss – even though she now understood why.

The two women looked out over the fields at the horses pulling the harrow across the Fairchild land in preparation for the planting of winter wheat. Olivia brought the subject round to Annie and asked if Mrs Dunn could recall anything from the day Ernest had seen her leaving.

'Not really. He said she was heading north, carrying a carpet bag, and he assumed she was off to catch a train.' The Dunns' thatched cottage was one of several houses on the main street that led to the station. 'I was surprised not to see her myself as I was washing all the front windows that day, but I guess I had my back to the road.'

A carpet bag made sense if the young girl was leaving town, but then Mrs Dunn said the stationmaster couldn't remember Annie buying a ticket. Perhaps she hadn't left by train, after all, but by another means of transport. Which brought Olivia back to the traveller scenario, although Widow Larwood's was in the completely opposite direction, on the way to the manor.

After eating far too many broken biscuits, Olivia thanked Mrs Dunn and decided to visit Annie's mother. It wasn't far to the Taylors' small house. Olivia knew her from church but the woman kept herself very much to herself, even before her husband's death, and Olivia wondered how she would be received.

'I don't know why you're dredging all this up.' Mrs Taylor invited her inside but did not offer her so much as a seat or a cup of tea.

There was a pinched look about her face, as though she was sucking a lemon, and a very dated way of dressing, so that the widow's weeds she wore made her look like a lean version of Queen Victoria.

'Isn't there a tiny part of you that wants to know what happened to your daughter? Where she is now? If she's happy? You might even have grandchildren. Wouldn't that be a small comfort after losing your husband?'

She could see the widow narrow her eyes at the thought, and she finally gestured for Olivia to take a seat. 'I don't know where we went wrong.' She wrung her hands and looked as though she might cry. Olivia shifted uncomfortably in her chair. 'My Annie attended church twice every Sunday and learned her scriptures from a young age. She was taught right from wrong and we kept her away from temptation and yet, I've heard whispers that she was with child.'

This strict upbringing probably contributed to the young girl's desire to seek out adventure, Olivia thought to herself, but she was not here to judge.

'Did you know anything about the man she ran off with?'

Mrs Taylor shook her head. 'My husband wasn't happy with her seeing the Tanner boy but he was a good Christian lad, and a hard-working one. I persuaded him that he would make our girl a decent husband in time. It was only after she fled that I remembered occasionally hearing noises in the night, which I now suspect was her sneaking out to meet someone, but you know how old houses creak? The afternoon she left, she packed a bag and took all the essentials with her. And, I'm ashamed to say, the next day we discovered the rent money was missing. To think that I bought up a wanton woman and a thief.' She shuddered.

The decision to run off had not been on the spur of the moment then. Again, everything was pointing to a planned elopement – but with whom?

'Someone recently remembered occasionally seeing her heading in the direction of the Larwood house at night. Perhaps she really did run off with a traveller,' Olivia concluded.

Mrs Taylor slapped at her bony thighs. 'Then there we have it. I did wonder for a while if the Tanner boy had us all fooled. If my Annie was heading south to meet with someone at night, then I doubt the widow's run-down house was her destination, but beyond that. She was clearly heading for the manor!'

Olivia had suspected this to be the young woman's true destination when she'd mistakenly considered Sir Hugo as the culprit, and she circled back to it now. There had been over twenty men working there before the war, but servants risked instant dismissal for such conduct. A member of the household, however, could do as he damn well pleased. Her thoughts kept returning to the boathouse. Hadn't Howard told her that theirs was not the first romantic liaison conducted there? Perhaps it wasn't the lord of the manor who was toying with the blue-eyed beauty in the village, but instead a man who would one day become exactly that...

* * *

As Olivia was wheeling the bicycle up the long drive, Benji stepped from the house and she nearly dropped it to the ground in surprise as he strode across the gravel to meet her. There was more swagger in his walk now, she realised, and he still looked alarmingly like Howard from certain angles.

'What on earth are you doing home?' She'd not been expecting him until the end of term.

He shrugged. 'Measles outbreak in the dorm but I've got no symptoms as yet. Mother pushed for me to come back until I'm clear. The headmaster knows what she's been through, so he didn't put up much of a fight.'

Poor Cynthia, Benji was even more precious to her now, and Olivia's heart went out to the woman.

'I've been waiting for you all afternoon. Since you've already had the stupid disease, I thought we could take a walk together or play a game. But Mother said you were out. She told me you'd both been to see Tanner recently and that you'd gone down to the village today to dig about in his past – ask about the Taylor girl and whatnot.' He graciously took the bike from her. 'But it was all before your time. Why the sudden interest, Livvy?'

'The poor man has been dealt some unfortunate cards in his life yet he always struck me as the decent sort. Look how he encouraged your sketching and let you help him in the greenhouse when you were young? He never got over Annie's disappearance, so I thought I'd try to track her down. It's guilt, mainly. I feel so rotten that the job he loved was taken away from him. I can't do anything about his war wounds, or what he witnessed with his father, but thought I could help to heal his broken heart.'

She couldn't admit that part of her wanted to eliminate the competition. Tanner's reception of her had been cold and indifferent, but she had felt *something* that afternoon, in his tiny backyard. She'd already fallen in love with his words, his spirit and his kindness through the wall, but there was something about his body, his face and the smell of him that had elicited a reaction from her too. Seth was correct, and she knew that now. If she couldn't be with the man she loved, she could so very easily love the version of him that she was with. Finding a happily married Annie, or even a kept one, with numerous children clinging to her skirts, might take the shine off those sapphire eyes for her heartbroken former beau.

They entered the west wing of the house and Benji propped the bicycle up in one of the empty stalls in the stables, as Olivia took her shawl from the front basket.

'Your mother has offered him his old job back. I think she feels guilty that she was so quick to find him other employment when I caused all that trouble. The gardening staff here could certainly do with an extra pair of hands.' There was a moment when she realised what she'd inadvertently said and the colour drained from her face, but then she caught Benji's smile.

'Livvy!' he laughingly chastised, as they walked back outside. 'I'm sure Tanner's remaining hand would be most welcome. And in all seriousness, it would be great to have him back here. Maybe I could even pop and see him – have a word.'

They climbed the shallow steps to the front door.

'I spoke to both Mrs Taylor and Mrs Dunn today.' She paused, wondering how to word her suspicions. 'Finding out who Annie was seeing back then is obviously key to where she is now.' She swallowed hard. 'Is it possible that Clarence...' She couldn't finish the sentence.

'Olivia! No. What did Ernest's mother say? That friendship was damnably odd and I never much liked the Dunn boy – the way Howard used to suck up to him, and how Clarrie was always so keen to do things for a postal worker's son from the village. I know that makes me sound like a dreadful snob. But it should have been the other way around.'

Olivia narrowed her eyes and considered this as they both stepped through the door. Benji sat down on the long bench and began to remove his boots.

'He caused Clarence's scar, did you know? Ernest thumped him so hard in a temper that he cut his chin open. They told everyone it had happened during one of their bouts, but it wasn't true.'

'But everyone liked Ernest,' she said, frowning.

'Liked him, or was scared of him,' Benji said, raising both eyebrows. 'He was so full of charm and flattery but, just occasionally, there was a flash of something darker. I never thought much of it when I was younger, but he was an ambitious man, Liv, and I guess his lack of fortune made him feel weak. He often tapped Clarrie for money. In fact, I don't think I ever saw my brother say no to anything he asked. Had an extraordinary way with girls too.'

Olivia's heart began a slow but definite pounding, and she lumped down on the bench.

'As did Clarence. Inheriting all this made him an attractive prospect.' She gestured to the house. It was Howard telling her about the rendezvous in the boathouse that had made her consider him as Annie's secret lover.

Benji shrugged. 'He talked about girls a lot, but it was bravado. He never seemed particularly interested in any – spent more time with the horses than he did with women – and he certainly didn't love his fiancée. That was all Mother's doing.' He rolled his eyes.

Yes, she realised, because Clarence had been in love with someone who'd worked at the house, but it was a love that could never be. Had he told Ernest about her? Did it give the Dunn lad some sort of hold over the future heir to the manor? Olivia's mind was racing now.

'I was so sure Annie Taylor was meeting Clarence at the boathouse. She was spotted coming this way in the middle of the night.'

'Crikey, Liv. The boathouse? You do know Ernest was the person who crashed there most often? Usually if he'd been over for the day and couldn't be bothered to walk back to the village. It's why the blankets were kept out there.'

Two pairs of eyes met and locked in the entrance hall in Merriford Manor as Olivia tried to work through the muddle in her brain.

Ernest had supposedly seen Annie walking towards the train station just before he disappeared, but his mother, cleaning the windows, hadn't seen the young girl. He was a handsome lad, charming all the girls for miles about, and Annie was a real beauty. Yet he had a temper... a scary thing when coupled with his great ambitions.

'But Ernest couldn't have been the man Annie was running away with because he never left the village,' Benji pointed out.

A spear of realisation pierced Olivia's body.

'*What if Annie didn't leave it either?* You said yourself, he revived the story about the shrieking pits being haunted? The biggest of which is on his family's land. What if he did that to keep people away?'

Finally, Benji understood what she was getting at, and his eyes became saucer-wide.

'Because he was out to enjoy everything life had to offer,' he said. 'He intended to be someone – and that someone would not want to be tied down by a village girl with a baby on the way... Oh my God, Livvy, you don't think...?'

She turned to Benji and she knew that they both most definitely *did* think.

What if Annie had sometimes met with a man at the Merriford Manor boathouse back then, and what if it had been a charming young lad from the village? What if Clarence Fairchild had been sufficiently intimidated by this young man to let him use the boathouse for these liaisons? And then she had another thought. What if... what if Clarence's secret was even bigger than she'd first assumed? He'd never been one for the ladies, nor had he expressly stated the sex of the servant that so enchanted him. Perhaps it wasn't the horses that drew him to the stables. Ernest was the sort who might use such information against him. The sort to smash his fist so hard into his friend's cheek that the friend was left with a lifelong scar. The sort to flirt with a fifteen-year-old girl one minute, and the lady of the manor the next.

But was he the sort to revive a long-forgotten ghost story with the sole aim of keeping locals away from his land? Because maybe, she considered, in the murky depths of the largest shrieking pit lay the body of a pregnant young girl who had tried to force him into a marriage that did not suit his ambitious plans.

40

Olivia and Benji decided to be creative with the truth in order to convince the local police to investigate the shrieking pits. They had no proof that Annie Taylor lay beneath the stagnant waters of a medieval iron ore excavation site, but the more they talked about their theory, the more they both convinced themselves it was a possibility.

'You weren't here in 1911, so I'll say I saw something,' Benji offered. 'Ernest is hardly here to disagree with me. I was only eight years old so it's plausible that witnessing suspicious activity – perhaps a figure dumping a bundle in the water when I was out playing in the fields – might not resonate with me until now. And with all the questions you've been asking, I can say it jogged my memory.'

'But what if they don't find anything?'

'Then the little boy of years ago got muddled.' He shrugged. 'No one's going to blame me.'

'Mrs Dunn will never speak to us again if we're wrong.'

'She'll never speak to us again if we're right. She cherishes Ernest's memory and talks about him as though he was the very best of sons. I feel desperately sorry for her, but we both want Tanner to make peace with the past.'

It was an uncomfortable couple of days for the pair of them. Constable Peterson either didn't care much about the fate of a young woman whose morals were questionable, as though it made her some lesser being, or didn't want the hassle of organising such a search when, to his mind, the whole thing was so long ago and everyone had accepted the girl had run off. But Olivia felt passionately that Annie's mother deserved the truth, even if her theory was correct and justice could not be administered.

In the end, the whole thing spiralled out of control, as gossip and whispers abounded. By the time the search was organised, it had become a frenzied circus. Curious locals and, indeed, at least two journalists gathered on the public right of way, in view of the shrieking pits, as volunteers in waders began the unenviable task of looking for something that might not even be there.

Rather tragically, within the first hour, and going on the theory that anyone dumping a body, particularly on their own land, would deposit it at the nearest accessible spot, human bones were found wrapped in a quilted bedspread, and weighted down by rocks. Not long afterwards, they also found what was left of a carpet bag.

Annie Taylor might have been led to believe she was starting a new life somewhere with her lover, but the man in question had never intended to honour any such agreement.

* * *

Olivia felt desperately sorry for Mrs Dunn. She hadn't suspected for a moment that the last resting place of tragic, young Annie Taylor was on her land, and now Ernest's precious memory had been tarnished. He would not be remembered as the charming and clever son who'd died gallantly fighting the Germans, but instead as the man who'd got an innocent young girl pregnant and then killed her because she stood in the way of his aspirations. His childhood friendship with Clarence had shown him a tantalising glimpse of a world he wanted to be part of and he'd been determined to rise to the top, through fair means or foul. Annie, a mere housemaid, however beautiful, would never have been enough.

None of the finer details could be proved, of course, and Ernest could never be made accountable, but when the inquest was held at the local police station, the body was firmly established to be her because of the approximate age and sex of the bones, and the discovery of a small crucifix, that Mrs Taylor identified as belonging to her daughter.

Benji, who had returned to boarding school mercifully free of measles, was not asked to testify, possibly because he'd been a child at the time. A couple of people came forward to say that they had occasionally seen Annie with Ernest but had not thought it particularly relevant until now. Others talked of being on the receiving end of his temper, and the coroner considered why Mr Dunn claimed to have seen Annie heading for the station when she'd clearly never left the village.

But one thing was certain: Annie had met a violent end. The skull was crushed one side. Her former sweetheart, Mr Seth Tanner, had been called to give evidence, and possibly be ruled out as a suspect. Mrs Dunn, in her misery, had suggested that he could have killed Annie in a jealous rage and planted the body on their land to frame her beloved Ernest, but when it was determined that the bedcover she was wrapped in had belonged to the Dunn household, there was little doubt in everyone's mind what had occurred.

The coroner duly recorded a verdict of unlawful killing by person or persons unknown.

Many of the villagers had been shocked by the former gardener's appearance when he gave his evidence, although he wasn't the only one in Merriford Lode to bear the ugly scars of war. One of the local farmers had been so badly burned that no one, apart from his immediate family, had seen him since he'd returned. Tanner, however, did not seem to mind the stares and pitying looks. They washed over him like the ford that swept across the Merriford road. He gave the impression of a man who simply no longer cared. Life had thrown so much at him and he couldn't fight it any more. And yet, Olivia knew that he had the capacity to care, and care deeply.

She found him after the inquest, sitting near the recently erected memorial cross in the churchyard. He would know every single name carved into the stone, and probably went to school with most of them. Ernest Dunn was the third name down.

'May I join you?' she asked.

'I can't stop you, Miss Davenport. The church belongs to everyone.' It wasn't said unkindly, just stated as fact. He absent-mindedly gestured for her to take a seat, and briefly got to his feet as she did so.

She sat to his right so that he had to look at her.

'Always thought of Ernest as a decent bloke,' he finally said. 'Grew up with him, although he was a bit older than me. Was in awe of him, truth be told. He had big ambitions, whereas I was taught to do my duty, know my place and be grateful that I had a bed to sleep in at night.'

'Nothing wrong with ambition,' she said. 'As long as you aren't hurting others. You have a love for nature and an enquiring mind. There is no reason you couldn't eventually become a head gardener at a place like Merriford. Even boot boys become butlers, you know.'

'Excuse me for my bluntness, miss, but that's a ridiculous notion. With one arm?'

'One arm doesn't stop you managing staff, planning garden designs or overseeing cultivation, crop rotation and expenses. Surely, the whole point of being at the top in any sphere of life is to direct those below you to do the physical work?'

He huffed at that, but it was a considered huff.

'Don't forget, I was the young girl who thought anything was possible – even women fighting Vikings.'

She saw the corners of his mouth turn up, like they had all those years ago. He was a man who wanted to smile but didn't want to be seen to. And yet the number of times she had shared a hearty guffaw through the wall with Seth proved that, deep inside, he had the potential to enjoy life and revel in its magnificence.

'I remember.' His face became more serious as his thoughts returned to Annie. 'I had no idea she was carrying a child. No idea she was even seeing another man behind my back until she disappeared and the rumours started.'

'I know.'

He swivelled on the bench to face her, even though he would get no better view from a missing eye. She admired him for not attempting to hide his injuries at the inquest or subsequently. That took courage.

'How do you know?' He leaned towards her. 'What is it about you, Miss Davenport, that makes you think you know me? That makes you suddenly want to contact me and atone for your behaviour as a child, interfere in my life and pursue some inexplicable desire to see me succeed? I've had Her Ladyship corner me earlier and all but beg me to take up my former job. And then an old neighbour told my mother this morning that you've been asking about Annie for weeks. Your interest in me makes no sense.'

She spun him the same tale she'd spun Cynthia: that she wanted to help the veterans of the Great War. It could be any one of the Fairchild sons sitting before her now, with similar injuries, and she owed every returning soldier a debt of gratitude. The whole country did.

He seemed to accept this and turned back to the stone cross.

'I'm not the same person I was before the war, and I weren't in a great place even then. I'm afraid I can't help but question God when he allows some of us to bear more sorrow than others. Or allows a murderer to escape justice.'

'This enduring melancholy isn't you. There's a much more optimistic version of yourself deep inside that you need to find,' she insisted, frustrated by his attitude.

'I have nothing, *nothing*,' he stressed, 'to be happy about. The girl I loved was unfaithful to me, my father died a horrific death, I lost the job I loved...' he gave her the side-eye '...I lived through a war of unparalleled magnitude, and now find myself of no use to anyone. I'm neither wanted nor needed.'

'Can you hear the words coming from your mouth?' She was angry now, jumping to her feet and raising her voice, despite herself. 'You've been offered employment when there are thousands of returning servicemen who would give their right arm for such an opportunity. And offered a small cottage in the village, to boot. Yes, there's a two-mile walk every day, but there is absolutely nothing wrong with your legs – so don't even start complaining about that.' She'd done all of this for him – secured him a position, found him a house with his mother, *and* solved the disappearance of the girl he'd loved – and all he could do was feel sorry for himself.

Tanner looked bewildered by her outburst and frowned as she crossed her arms, her flared nostrils finally relaxing.

'If I gave my right arm for the cottage, I really would be no use to anyone,' he commented – a trace of his humour resurfacing, but she was too angry at that point to acknowledge it.

'Mr Tanner, I'm afraid I have no time for your self-pity. Do you think you're the only one who has suffered? I took myself to a dark place for many months, but I fought my way back out again because life goes on. And being here, standing in the dappled sun of this late-October day, is a privilege that my parents, Annie Taylor and the three oldest Fairchild boys do not have. How dare you waste your life when you are still alive to make a difference to the world. *How dare you not even try.*'

And she spun on her heel and walked away.

41

That evening, before she returned to the tower for the night, Cynthia told her that Tanner had accepted the job offer. Whether this was down to her outburst, or he would have accepted anyway, she wasn't sure. He would start work at Merriford Manor the following week, just as soon as he'd settled his affairs in Cambridgeshire.

It would take time to win him over, and she wasn't even sure that was what she wanted. She had feelings for him, undeniably, but he wasn't a joy to be around, did not make her laugh, or feel wanted. But then Rome, she concluded, was certainly not built in a day.

Olivia still hadn't told *her* Seth anything about the horrific discovery of Annie's remains. Initially, she'd kept silent because she could not even be sure the missing girl was in one of the pits. And when the bones had been found and her identity confirmed, it seemed a cruel thing to do. Why should he have to grieve his first love when he believed she was alive? Her Seth had moved on and fallen in love. Nothing would be gained by telling him to have the shrieking pits trawled in his world.

Ernest was dead. He could not be made to pay for his crime. And perhaps it was kinder for Mrs Taylor to believe her daughter was still alive.

As if to prove the contrast in personality of the two versions of the same man, Seth was full of beans and good humour that night. She heard the springs creak as he bounced onto the bed the other side of the wall.

'I've paid off my debt, saved the train fare, and researched the route. My next free half-day off is a week Wednesday and I shall travel down to Suffolk and pay the enchanting Miss Davenport a visit. It will be interesting to set eyes on you... her again. I'll present her with a cutting of *lonicera japonica* – the vanilla-scented honeysuckle that you tell me you so love, at which point, she'll fall into my arms and declare undying love.'

Olivia gave a tiny snort. 'I admire your optimism but suspect it will take more than a little green-leafed twig in a flowerpot.'

'Then I'll keep trying. You, young lady, are not made of wood. There's no doubt in my mind you will succumb to my working-class charm eventually, much as I'm sure Tanner is already flattered by the attentions of the newly wealthy Miss Davenport.' He paused. 'How are relations with the Cambridgeshire version of me?'

'Proceeding slowly.'

She told him that Tanner had accepted the job, if not the circumstances surrounding it.

'You are a work in progress – a half-finished Hadrian's Wall.' She deliberately picked a construction of colossal proportions, knowing the task ahead was not easy, and then she considered the implications if she could win him round.

'It won't be the same, will it? If we find love with the others?'

'It won't be better or worse,' he reassured her. 'It'll be

different – an adventure. And adventures, as you've always said, are there waiting to be had.'

* * *

Tanner started work at the manor and Olivia decided to give him a wide berth to begin with. It wouldn't be wise to over-whelm the poor fellow or scare him off. She made no special enquiries with either Sir Hugo or Mr Rowe as to how he was getting on, but occasionally watched him surreptitiously from the tower windows, pleased to see that he was coping admirably. He may not be able to use shears or push a wheelbarrow, but he could deadhead, weed, rake gravel and, most importantly, read. She politely but briefly acknowledged him if she came across him in the gardens, and realised he had a sizeable stump that he was able to manipulate to pick up objects, like flowerpots. It had not been obvious how much of his arm had been lost when he was wearing a jacket but the amputation had taken place just below the elbow.

She did, however, make sure she always looked her best when she was out and about in the grounds and knew, because Tanner had to turn his whole head to the left to see anything, that there were occasions when, equally, he was watching her. Schooled by *her* Seth as to what he found attractive, she wore a lot of pink because, surprisingly, it was his favourite colour. She would hum 'The Rose of Allendale', because he confided it was something his father had sung to him in his childhood. She wore a heavy rose-scented perfume because, coincidentally or otherwise, they were his favourite flowers.

Meanwhile, Olivia received a letter back from the editor she had sent her novel to, and rushed up to the tower to read it, launching herself across the bed in her excitement. But it was not the opening paragraph she'd hoped for; he was sorry but he was not interested in publishing her book. Her heart slid out through the soles of her buckled shoes. She twisted her body to lie on her back and stared at the ceiling. All that work, all that emotion...

She was downhearted but read the letter to the end and was mollified when he said that her writing was surprisingly rich for one so young. Perhaps it was a kindness, perhaps he really meant it, but his last sentences said there were traces of Jasper Davenport in her style and she shouldn't give up; she could tell a story, but she was not telling the story he wanted to publish. People had lived through the war and it was still too raw, he said. They wanted to escape.

Right, she thought, swinging her legs to the floor and striding over to her desk. She sat down and rolled up her sleeves, scrunching up her eyes and letting her mind wander down unexplored and hidden paths, before grabbing a clean sheet of paper and lifting the glass stopper from her ink bottle. Flashes of the young girl she had once been began to resurface. *If you want escape, I'll give you escape...*

42

SETH TANNER. A WORLD AWAY...

Seth knew that he was a miserable sod back in the spring of 1912, too self-absorbed, nursing his miseries and putting all his energies into his job. And then his life took an unexpected turn.

One minute, he was trying to get to sleep after a long and exhausting day working in the gardens, and the next, he was having a bizarre conversation with a young girl through the brick wall – even though he was pretty sure there was no such girl in the tower with him.

For the first few days, he thought Master Howard was behind it all. The young lad had always been a handful and had plagued the poor undergardener for years, knowing that someone in his father's employ could not bite back. Seth would find newspaper stuffed in watering can spouts, chalk on the garden seats and had his bed short-sheeted on two occasions.

But the voice wasn't a boy, instead a young girl, so Seth wondered if Howard had put one of the maids up to it. Every night, he locked the tower door and checked all the rooms, but her scolding words still came through the brickwork. Eventually, he learned to live with them. Over time, her relentless optimism, her love of life and her stern reproaches forced Seth to reconsider his outlook on life.

His mother had long since pointed out that he wasn't a lad for changing, but instead the loyal, quiet sort. He knew he hadn't been put on the earth to lead and had no beef with that, but the war had proved a time for introspection. So, when he returned to Merriford, found his friend still in the tower, and they finally worked out the truth of their unusual situation, it made him reassess everything he thought he knew. And then, he fell in love, wholly and completely, with a woman he'd never technically set eyes on and could never have.

But the Seth Tanner of after the war was a very different man and he determined that he could be one for changing after all.

He arrived in Stowmarket on his afternoon off, alighting from the train and embarking on a chilly six-mile walk. Windy Acres, a house of some size, was easy to find but his courage, less so. Considering he'd charged at a trench full of Germans in the spring of 1917, it was strange how walking down the driveway of the Davenports' house was one of the most frightening experiences of his life. Having pushed Olivia to pursue Tanner, he couldn't back out, but, despite his bravado through the wall, he knew that actually convincing Miss Davenport to view him as a romantic prospect would be a challenge.

He rang the bell, apologised that he had no invitation, and wondered if Miss Davenport would receive him, explaining that he worked for Sir Hugo and that they had met before, if only briefly.

The maid kept him waiting a few minutes but finally directed Seth to the drawing room, where a cheery fire crackled in the hearth.

'Good afternoon.' He removed his cap and turned it

nervously in his hands. 'Please pardon the intrusion but my name is Seth Tanner and I—'

'If it's my father you're after, he is in London for the week.' She got to her feet. 'You're one of his avid readers, no doubt? Hoping to procure his autograph or get some insight into his next book?'

'Not at all. It's you I'm here to see.'

'Me?' She looked surprised. 'Do I know you?'

'My name is Seth Tanner and I work for Sir Hugo Fairchild. I'm one of his gardeners.'

He stuffed the cap into his pocket and slipped his canvas bag from his shoulder.

'Ah, I thought you looked familiar. Have you worked there long?'

'All my working life, apart from the time I served in the war.'

She gestured to a chair, which he took as soon as she was seated. 'Now I remember seeing you about the grounds recently and believe we spoke briefly.'

Flattered that she remembered their previous meeting, he was, however, increasingly tongue-tied as he studied her face and reconciled this Olivia with the woman he'd fallen in love with. Through a wall, the lack of eye contact had made him brave, but the reality of her world being so far removed from his was never more apparent.

'What can I do for you, Mr Tanner?' she asked.

His mouth went dry and his palms clammy. Her eyes flicked to his legs as he wiped his hands on his trousers.

'I have a gift for you.' He took the Japanese honeysuckle from his bag and handed it to her. 'It has the most delightful vanilla fragrance.'

'Oh, my favourite. We have something similar here at Windy Acres.'

She took it graciously but it was obvious from her expression that she didn't understand why a member of Sir Hugo's staff would undertake such a journey to deliver her a gift.

Seth cleared his throat. 'The thing is, Miss Davenport, I have been an ardent admirer of yours for some time, and whilst I appreciate our very different stations in life, I'd ask that you don't dismiss my overtures of friendship out of hand.'

'Naturally, I am flattered by your attentions, Mr Tanner but they are rather... unexpected.' There was a nervous flash across her face.

'If I could appeal to anything in you, it would be your imagination – something I saw in you when you visited Merriford Manor as a child and that I hope you've kept hold of as an adult. Your optimism and joy for life, your determination to not let your sex stop you achieving things, your plans to travel the world and not conform to society's expectations – all of these draw me to you. I suspect you are a woman who knows that there are things in this world that can't be properly explained, and you are open to them. You always have been; from the time you first read *Alice's Adventures in Wonderland* – a book your father gave you on your fifth birthday.'

Miss Davenport's eyes expanded as she listened to what he was saying.

'The truth of it is, and please don't dismiss me out of hand, that we are connected in a way I don't rightly understand. You've been speaking to me in my dreams for years – and, no, I'm not drunk or mad. Perhaps you'd be so good as to confirm the following things? When you were young, you were convinced a woodland fairy lived in your wardrobe, who only ventured out when you were asleep. That you have a doll hidden in the attics because at nine, you believed it had evil powers. And, in the winter of 1910, you secretly packed a bag, intending to run away to sea.'

Her face paled as he listed the secrets his Olivia had passed on to him.

'Are you professing to be some kind of medium?' she asked.

'Hardly, miss. Apart from anything, you aren't dead.'

'You must appreciate how unnerving it is to have a man I barely know show up at my house uninvited and talk of things that I haven't shared with anyone? I shouldn't have entertained you. Even though my maid is only the other side of the door, there are elements of our meeting that could easily be construed as improper.'

'You were never one for snobbery, so I was hoping that the little girl who so enjoyed the fairy tale of a princess marrying a swineherd would treat a gardener as an equal.'

'Again with the insights that you have no business knowing. I think I may have to ask you to leave, Mr Tanner. This is all very unsettling.' Her face, at first anxious, quickly changed to one of sympathy. 'Did you suffer terribly in the war? Did you find it affected your state of mind?'

'If you think I've developed a neurosis from battle, then you're wrong. The things I saw will haunt me forever, but I've been able to move on from them. I'm here today to ask that you get to know me. We have a special connection that I can't explain. And whilst I understand that any personal association with me will lead to gossip, I don't think that matters to you as much as it matters to others.' Her eyes narrowed. 'But know that I'm here to support you, to never belittle you because of your sex, and will help you get your books published—'

'My books?' She looked perplexed. 'I've written no books. That is my father's preserve and I merely edit for him.'

This was a surprise.

'Goodness, then what are you doing with all the story ideas bursting to escape your cluttered head, miss? How are you filling your days and making your mark on the world? Have you kept up the notebook you started with your father of all the places across the world that you intend to visit?'

Her face clouded over. 'I believe that my role as a wife and mother will give me all the fulfilment I need.'

'Nonsense,' he scoffed, unable to help himself. 'That's not the real you, Miss Davenport, and anyone who says otherwise don't know you at all. Look, I appreciate this is all very sudden but all I ask is that you give me a bit of time. I've blundered in here today and taken you by surprise, but if I've learned anything from the war, it's that you must seize life and wring it for every drop of joy that you can. Time may not be in our favour.'

'Indeed, Mr Tanner, and it is my painful duty to inform you that, even if I believed your fanciful story of some mysterious connection, and wished to pursue your flattering attentions, I'm afraid you're too late. I'm engaged to be married.'

She raised her left hand and he saw the ring at once – a thin, gold band with a flower-like setting of diamonds around a central emerald. It announced to the world that she was promised to someone else.

'You're quite correct. It would not have been your position in life I would have objected to. I'm not like that. My future husband was not born into great wealth and I have based my decision on his other attributes. The war has been a great leveller in many ways. Perhaps you do know me a little better than most, as my parents were certainly hesitant when I announced my intentions, but I'm marrying for love.'

Seth was too late. The Olivia Davenport of his world had fallen for another man. He'd always known it was a long shot, but the injustice of it all was frustrating. His Olivia had known that she was no snob.

It was with a heavy heart that he caught the Stowmarket train back to Merriford Lode, and watched the flat, East Anglian landscape scamper past his third-class window. What would he tell Olivia through the wall? All he could do was console himself with the knowledge that at least Miss Davenport had a bright future ahead of her.

* * *

Seth was late retiring that night and found small tasks to keep him from the tower. He stood for a long time in the kitchen gardens, smoking a cigarette and contemplating life without either Olivia. He suspected that he'd rally, because it was now in his nature to do so, but it would take a while. There would be some pleasant girl from the village, or a young war widow, who would make him a good wife and support his endeavours. Men were, after all, in demand since the culling of his generation.

Olivia must have been listening for him because, even though he undressed and washed silently, the springs gave him away as soon as he lumped on the bed.

'How did it go? What did I say? Do you think you stand a chance?' Her voice was eager but anxious. Sweet, sweet Olivia of the hazel eyes and earnest stare. He could almost picture her in the room beside him – more so because he'd been in her company that afternoon and absorbed every detail of her face and her figure – from her wavy curls down to her delicate ankles.

But Seth couldn't bring himself to lie and hoped that his news would be taken well. Miss Davenport might not end up with him but she was happy. Her excitement over the upcoming wedding had been plain to see. She'd insisted that he stayed for a late-afternoon tea, probably to offset her guilt at having disappointed the young man, and ordered her maid to bring them some sandwiches.

'She was definitely confused by my visit, but polite and friendly. Her life seems settled and she's content. Jasper Davenport is a worldwide success and I understand that your parents are in good health, even though they were both in London, visiting his publisher, when I called, so I didn't get to see them.'

'But?' She knew him too well. He swallowed hard.

'She is engaged to be married.' He gabbled on, not allowing her a chance to offer sympathy. 'And you were right; it's not with a man of high rank or exceptional wealth. In fact, I could hardly believe it myself, because it's someone we both know – an ordinary man from Merriford Lode, although admittedly, he's done quite well for himself since the war. Someone you first met at the manor, when your father visited Sir Hugo back in 1914... By the spring, Miss Olivia Davenport will be Mrs Ernest Dunn.'

43

'Ernest Dunn?' Olivia's voice rose by an octave, such was her distress at the news.

She'd spent a restless day wondering how Seth's visit would go, and keen for him to return. Had Miss Davenport seen Seth's worth? She'd expected things to take time but been confident he could lay the foundations, especially with all the information he had about her at his disposal.

What she had not expected was the revelation that she was imminently to be married to a man who had a short temper, was handy with his fists, and likely a murderer.

It was a double blow. Ernest had survived the war and somehow wormed his way into Miss Davenport's life. None of it made sense until she remembered that her father was an international success. It was the money, she realised. The money and perhaps the fame. Her stomach contracted even further. This was the man who had got poor Annie Taylor pregnant, likely promised her things he had no intention of delivering, and then killed her. *And this other Olivia was to be his wife.*

A feeling of nausea washed over her and she leaned against

the wall, her hands scrunched into tight fists, indicative of her despair.

'What's wrong?' Seth knew from her tone that the news he'd delivered wasn't welcome. 'I can assure you, you looked radiant and were full of chatter about the wedding. Your father's going to buy you both a house in London so Ernest can pursue his business ambitions. He was discharged much earlier than me and is currently renting somewhere near Bethnal Green. Course I'm disappointed but I'll bounce back. There are plenty more dandelions in the meadow.'

But she couldn't raise a smile at his efforts to find a bright side to this miserable situation.

'Ernest died in March '18, and I wrongly assumed the same was true in your world. You never talked of him.'

'Why would I? I've never had much to do with the man and haven't seen him since I signed up. He never had time for his family and has largely been in London. We know that different people are alive and dead in our worlds – think of Lord Kitchener – the ripples, remember? Besides, he's an all right fellow. Bit of a charmer but a handsome chap and quite the social climber. Clarence introduced the pair of you just before the war, apparently.'

Olivia shuddered. The other Jasper Davenport had been an extremely wealthy celebrity by 1914. Had Ernest seen an opportunity to marry well, playing on her sympathies, and knowing that she was not a girl to conform?

'He's not a good man. Your Miss Davenport has made a terrible mistake. He is manipulative and violent. He's done bad things, and was responsible for the scar across Clarence's chin – a vicious swipe because the young master of the house upset him. Living here and being part of this family, I've had more to do with him. He's marrying for money – not love.'

'Come, now. No one's perfect – least of all me, but you genuinely seemed happy. Maybe he's changed? Maybe the spirited Olivia Davenport has worked her magic on him?'

Her stomach began a slow churn. She had to tell him the truth about Annie Taylor and then he'd want to know why she'd kept it from him all this time. But how did you break such horrific news?

'But he's... You don't understand the magnitude of this, Seth... Annie was... You need to get the police to search the shrieking pits,' she finally blurted out.

'What?'

'There are three pits, one of which is on the edge of the Dunn land—'

'Yes, I know them. They follow the line of the lode up to the coast. Nobody ever goes near them. They're supposed to be haunted. Ha.' He snorted. 'Or perhaps it's just another poor soul trying to bridge the gap between my world and yours. He was spotted several times before the war, waving an axe.'

'I'm almost certain Ernest resurrected an old legend and is the source of those sightings. He wanted to keep people away from the pits, specifically the one nearest to their farmhouse.' She sucked in a deep breath and allowed her head to fall back against the cold bricks. 'Ernest was the man Annie was seeing. He got her pregnant and... I don't know how to tell you this... When he found out, he killed her. I don't care what you do, but get me away from him. He is calculating and dangerous, and the only way you'll stop the wedding is by proving him to be the murderer that he is.'

'Jesus, Olivia, you knew all this and didn't tell me?' Seth's voice bellowed through the wall and Olivia jerked her head back in surprise at his anger.

'I didn't think—'

'No, you dint. How can you have kept this from me? How long have you known?'

'A few weeks. The police searched the pit here, and her body was found at the bottom.' She didn't admit that the whole investigation had been down to her. 'The inquest concluded Annie was killed by a person or persons unknown, but everyone in that room knew he'd done it.' She explained how all the evidence pointed to Ernest. 'But he's dead, Seth. In my world, he could not be made accountable for his crime. I thought there was no point upsetting you.' She couldn't stop her tears from falling but kept her voice level.

'But he can be made accountable in mine! I'll make the bastard pay – with his life. If I can't have you, I might as well sacrifice myself for a noble cause, and seeing that man wiped off the face of the earth is good enough for me.'

She heard him thump or kick out at something.

'Calm down, Seth, and listen to me. We must be clever about this. I know you're angry right now but I've seen this play out. His mother even twisted the facts to try and pin it on you at one point. Shouting accusations might put you in danger. He's killed once and could do it again.'

The other side of the wall went quiet so she pressed her ear to the bricks. Had he run from the tower in his fury to do something stupid? But it was the middle of the night, and Ernest was in London. She assumed Seth was composing himself and tried to make him see sense.

'Besides, don't you see, if you can get him put away, and refrain from getting yourself into trouble when you do, Miss Davenport will be free.'

She heard a huff.

'Don't blame her. She didn't keep the truth from you; I did.'

'And yet, I've kept nothing from you,' he pointed out. 'I've been honest about everything. It's not my fault that Ernest never came up in conversation.'

'And it's also not your fault that he's managed to trick Olivia Davenport into marriage. I should have told you about Annie. I shouldn't have assumed he'd died, just because some things were the same, like the loss of the three Fairchild boys.'

'Three?' he queried. 'Clarence and Louis were killed but Howard survived. Poor lad, I don't think he expected he'd ever be the heir of Merriford Manor, not that he's been home much since the war.'

'What did you say?'

He repeated his words and she felt her entire world collapse for the second time that evening. Of all the pranks Howard had ever been party to, this was the absolute worst – even though it was a trick he'd had no control over.

Not only had Ernest survived in Seth's world, but so had Howard.

44

Olivia was in absolute turmoil. She'd never told Seth about her engagement to Howard and now was certainly not the time. He was furious enough that she'd kept the discovery of Annie's body from him. This was the man she loved and he already had cause to be disappointed with her. But worse than that was the knowledge that this other misguided version of her – who was all set to marry the duplicitous Ernest Dunn – had both the men she'd truly loved in her lifetime available to her, and she couldn't honestly say who she wanted the other Miss Davenport to be with. It was an impossible situation.

She had wrongly assumed, when Seth had first mentioned the deaths of the Fairchild boys, that he was talking about all three of them, but clearly he'd just meant Clarence and Louis. And it was at her insistence that they didn't talk of them because their loss had simply been too painful. But to find that Howard had also survived the war... What a mess.

The tears she spilled that night were silent. She didn't want Seth to know how much this news had affected her. Some part of her was overwhelmingly happy; Howard was alive and there was a Fairchild family somewhere in the universe whose losses, although unbearable, could have been so much worse. In his world, one of Cynthia's boys had returned and perhaps Benji might even be allowed to pursue the life he wanted.

But the wall, yet again, was preventing her from being with someone she cared deeply about. This time, however, the man in question barely knew she existed. This Howard had not spent a large part of his youth with her; she'd not stood up to him and shown him what a force of nature she was. He would not feel the same about her as she did about him.

And so she cried herself to sleep, lamenting the two men she loved, neither of whom she could ever have.

* * *

In the morning, her thoughts were more ordered. Seth had calmed down and asked her to trust him. He knew that it was his duty to make sure that Ernest Dunn paid for his crime and her priority was Tanner because, if she was honest with herself, he was the only man who could ever be truly hers.

She found the gardener in the disused stable block in the west wing. One of the maids had told Olivia that she'd seen him heading there. As she swung the wide wooden door open, he was leaning over a butler sink that the hospital had installed, with his shirt undone, trying to wash his remaining hand and stump together.

'I'm so sorry,' she gushed. 'I didn't know you were—'

'No problem, miss. I dropped a pot of creosote.'

Her first instinct was to rush over and help but he was coping admirably. The soap was inside the toe of a stocking and tied to the tap so he didn't have to chase it around the sink.

Aware that she should have stepped back out the room and

allowed him to complete his ablutions unobserved, she was instead fascinated by his injury and opened her mouth without engaging her brain.

'Does it still hurt? Sorry, that is absolutely none of my business.'

He shrugged. 'I'd rather people asked than speculated. Yes, it hurts, and as ridiculous as it sounds, sometimes I forget it isn't there. And then I get days when I feel as though someone is crushing my hand, even though it dunt exist, and I can barely focus on anything.'

'May I see?' she asked, wondering how he would respond to this request.

'If you like.' He shrugged off his shirt, revealing his white cotton vest, and she noticed how the undulations of his muscles were visible through the fabric, before focusing on his damaged arm.

He slowly turned to her, as her heart began thumping wildly. It was an intimate moment, and one they should not be having. If anyone were to walk in on them now, with him in such a state of undress, he would be fired on the spot, and this time there would be no reprieve.

She stepped through a beam of light that fell from one of the high windows behind her, as dust motes drifted down to the uneven cobblestone floor. He was in the shadows and it was there she joined him, closer now, to see the arm. Apart from the stump itself, there was scarring on his shoulder, indicative of the shell fragments flying at him from the left, and her overriding emotion in that moment was compassion. Without stopping to think what she was doing, her hand reached out to touch the wound, but she hesitated, expecting him to pull away or snap at her. Instead, he twisted his head to the left to enable him to see what she was doing, but otherwise remained motionless. She let her fingers delicately trace a line down his forearm to the brutal, bumpy full stop to the limb.

'It's not pretty.' He broke the silence. 'Put my hand up to shield my face.'

'I've seen far worse. I helped at the convalescent hospital. Not in a medical capacity, but I read to the patients and helped write letters to family... that sort of thing.'

She lifted her face and met his good eye, fully aware her behaviour was verging on unacceptable. All the things she knew about him came rushing at her in that moment. Things that had shaped him and that he had done long before the cleaving and replication of their world. Things that Seth had told her about.

Here stood the man who had hand-reared a baby bird as a boy and cried when a neighbourhood cat had killed it as a fledgling. Who'd picked wildflowers for his mother every year on her birthday and carried this tradition on, even when he was in the trenches of France, by pressing poppies, cornflowers and lily of the valley in his pocket notebook and enclosing them in the letters he sent home. Who'd fallen in love for the first time with a pretty, blue-eyed girl from his village and behaved honourably towards her, even when she had pushed for more. Who'd befriended the youngest of the Fairchild sons and looked out for him, encouraged his sketching and allowed the child to help with his planting. And even though he was bitter about many things, he still had the capacity to love, a sense of humour and an obvious determination to overcome his injuries and adapt. He had spirit and, underlining everything, she knew he was a good man. Why had she continued to separate the two men in her head? They were one and the same.

This was the man she'd fallen in love with.

She briefly studied his mouth before returning her gaze to his eye. The rumbling sound of an automobile outside suggested that Sir Hugo had returned from somewhere. There was an exchange of voices and then they faded, highlighting the tense silence within. The only movement was the slow rise and fall of both their chests, as she managed to keep her breathing steady, despite the frantic somersaulting of her insides.

The stillness between them in this moment was more arousing than any touch. It gave her the time to focus on what she was feeling, contemplate every nerve ending across her skin, revel in every heightened sensation within. He felt all of this, too, she knew, because his stare remained penetrating, deep, uncomfortable.

Of all the things she'd done with Seth through the wall, with all the things he'd made her feel, she'd never kissed him and, suddenly, the possibility of physical contact became the most important thing in the world to her. Lifting herself up on to her toes, she leaned forward and tipped up her chin. It was what he wanted too, wasn't it?

But his rough hand went for her shoulder, pushing her gently but firmly away.

'Oh no you don't.' He stepped back from her, shaking his head. 'I won't let you do this to me a second time. Swanning around the grounds, just like before, saying I said things when I dint, watching my every move and following me about. I see you, at the windows.' She was embarrassed that she'd been caught spying. 'As if the likes of you and the likes of me have anything in common. You're a picture-book fairy, floating about in a make-believe world, where you really think if you wave a stupid wand, you can magically give everyone a happy ending. The real world ain't like that.' He snorted. 'Because there's only one way this ends, miss, and that's with me moved on from this job again.'

'*I was thirteen years old, Tanner.* Will you not let that go? I'm twenty-one now and perfectly aware of who I am, what I want, and the consequences of any actions I undertake.'

'And you fancied a bit of the gardener, did you? The poor chap missing an arm, with the scarred face, who's indebted to you for helping him get his old job back? He'll be grateful of any attention. Have some fun with him and let him deflower you in the stables.'

But Olivia was angry now.

'This little plant was deflowered a long time ago.' It wasn't meant to shock him but it did. 'And if that's really how you feel then I'm sorry for you. You've learned nothing since we first met. You're afraid to be honest with yourself. I know you like me, I can feel it. And I like you. I've had disappointments and heart-break in my life and they've just made me even more deter-mined to grab the wonderful things and pull them close when they come along. You, on the other hand, are afraid of reaching out for anything in case it's snatched away. As though my love for you is some kind of trap – luring you forward only to turn about and bite your—'

'Hand off?' he volunteered.

She'd inadvertently said the word 'love' but he didn't seem to notice. His eyebrow rose a fraction.

'You, young lady, are still living in the fantasy world of your childhood, where princes and paupers run off into the sunset. Where there are no obstacles to Cinderella marrying a prince, and falling in love solves everything.' He snatched his shirt up and tried to put it back on but he was rushing and the task was not easy with only one fully functioning arm. The faster he tried to dress, the more of a muddle he got into.

'Let me?' She moved to help but he shrugged her away.

'You're mad. I don't want any part of this. How can you talk of loving me when you don't even know me?' Ah, so he had heard, then.

'I know you better than you think. I know about the black-bird you hand-reared when you were seven years old, the wild-flowers you gave to your mother every year, even when you were in France, how you were always kind to Master Benji...'

His face went from embarrassed and angry to, quite frankly, astonished.

'You frighten me, if I'm totally honest, miss. And I'm not sure you're quite the full ticket. Always were one for ridiculous flights of fancy, and the extraordinary sense of entitlement that comes with money. If you want something, you assume you can just take it. Well, you're barking up the wrong tree. I'm not interested.'

But Olivia was on solid ground. 'How can you deny it when you've been watching me as much as I've been watching you? You happily removed your shirt and let me touch you, because you know as well as I do that there is something electric floating about in the air between us, and it terrifies and excites us both. Believing yourself not worthy is another matter, but you look me in the eye and tell me that you feel nothing for me and I'll back off,' she challenged, hands on hips and head tipped to the side in expectation.

'I don't want no part of this. If you talk such stupid nonsense again, I'll hand in my notice. You see if I don't.'

And she saw Tanner's jaw clench before he stormed from the stables, his unbuttoned shirt flapping about his body as he left.

45

SETH TANNER. A WORLD AWAY…

Olivia's revelation had been a stab to the gut. Seth was furious. Ernest Dunn, who had even patted him on the back after Annie went missing and offered words of sympathy, had damn well known where she was all the time.

It took him a whole day to calm down as he went through a whirlwind of emotions. At first, he was angry with everyone and everything: himself for not realising that Annie had been unfaithful in the most intimate way, with her for giving herself to someone else, with Ernest for taking her life, and even with Olivia for keeping it all from him. Finally, he allowed himself to grieve for Annie – not doubting for a minute that she was lying in one of the shrieking pits on the Dunns' land. She hadn't deserved such a fate.

And then he began to think rationally. Olivia was right: he couldn't rush headlong into ill-thought-out acts of revenge. But how would he explain his conviction that there was a body in the pit? Especially given that he was making this bold claim so many years after her disappearance. He didn't want to become a suspect and had to think of a way around it.

* * *

'Constable Peterson's mother, Miriam, said that an anonymous letter has been delivered to the police station,' his mother told him, as he stopped by for some of her delicious home baking one afternoon. 'It claims that the body of poor Annie Taylor is at the bottom of the largest shrieking pit. Someone was seen throwing a bundle in all those years ago and Peterson has asked Mrs Dunn if he can search it.' Her excited face lit up like a street lamp. Nothing much happened in her mundane life, so the potential for such scandal was thrilling. 'Difficult position for her to be in, really. If she refuses, it suggests she has something to hide, but no one wants a body dragged out of a pond on their land – especially as she's wanted to sell the small-holding for years.'

'Oh?' This he didn't know.

'Ernest won't let her. He doesn't want to live in the old house himself, but won't sell the plot. Can't think why. She'd like a smaller place now that it's just her, somewhere in Essex maybe, nearer to him and the Davenport girl. There'll be babies there before long.'

The thought made his blood boil.

'Anyhow, she's written to him, asking what to do.'

Ernest wouldn't want the pits drained, or the land sold, for increasingly obvious reasons. It only added to Seth's conviction that Olivia was correct about Annie's whereabouts and he was more determined than ever to see Dunn pay for his crime.

'I just don't understand why the author of the letter waited all these years to speak up,' she said.

Because he only found out a couple of days ago, he thought to himself but shrugged.

That Sunday, he visited his mother again. She always

prepared a nice roast for her beloved son after the church service and filled him in on village gossip – which was now rife with the news of the anonymous letter. Miriam Peterson was a woman who couldn't keep anything to herself and, living at the station, had access to all sorts of information she shouldn't have, so Mrs Tanner was quite up to date with events.

'Miriam said Ernest got all angry over the accusation – well, you would, wouldn't you? If someone said there was a body in your garden,' she said, placing four large roast potatoes on Seth's plate, always worried that he wasn't eating enough at the manor. The delicious smell of lamb drifted from the small kitchen range, and his stomach rumbled.

'Apparently, he said they couldn't come on his land without a warrant, but the constable said his reluctance to help was suspicious, so Ernest eventually agreed to let them search tomorrow, but has insisted on being present because his mother lives alone now. If the police are going to trample all over their land, he wants to make sure they don't do any damage.'

She walked over to the oven to retrieve the small piece of mutton she'd got in, knowing it was Seth's favourite, as he stirred the little cut-glass dish of mint sauce in anticipation.

'The search is tomorrow?' he clarified, his stomach constricting at the thought of Annie being discovered after all this time.

'Yes. He's due in Norfolk this afternoon. The Davenport girl and her mother are coming with him, but staying with the Fairchilds. The Dunn house isn't really fit for entertaining wealthy young ladies.'

Mr Rowe had asked Seth to cut some mistletoe and holly to decorate the big house, and now he understood why – the Fairchilds were to have overnight visitors. His heart skipped at the unexpected news that Olivia would be at the manor and, whilst time with his mother was precious, he was suddenly keen to return. Here was an unexpected opportunity to press his case further. After a hurried meal, he took the time to think about the revelations as he walked from Merriford Lode to the manor.

He was up in the tower, changing out of his Sunday best and back into winter work clothes, when he spied a smart motor car sweep up the drive. It was chauffeur-driven and undoubtedly Jasper Davenport's. Ernest Dunn, just as self-assured as he remembered, helped Olivia and her mother from the vehicle, as Seth stopped himself from haring down the spiral stairs and running outside to punch him.

A little while later, he was asked to help carry extra table leaves up to the dining room, often finding that his duties overlapped with the household now that the male servants at the manor were significantly reduced. Able-bodied men in service were, as his mother so often pointed out, like hen's teeth.

He was carrying the last one through when he met the party in the corridor. Miss Davenport's cheeks tinged pink as she recognised him but she said nothing, just met his eyes and smiled. She looked drawn and tired, as pale as a jasmine flower, and he heard her mention to her mother that she had a headache. Perhaps the strain of the accusations against her fiancé were getting harder to hear.

'Thank you, Tanner.' Lady Fairchild nodded in Seth's direction, as he stepped to one side.

'There's chamomile and feverfew overwintering in the greenhouse that would help with the head, if you have time to come by later,' he said, in a low voice, as Miss Davenport passed him. He was working in the kitchen gardens for the rest of the day, and hoped she might escape outside, if she could.

She nodded.

Sure enough, barely an hour later, as the sun started to dip below the west wall, he heard the iron gate squeak. It needed oiling, but was not something he'd got around to, as they were so short-staffed.

'Miss Davenport.' He nodded. The temperature was dropping fast and his breath was condensing before his face, but he didn't feel the cold, because his heart was racing. He handed her two small bunches of herbs from a small trug, that he'd prepared in anticipation.

'I apologise again if I spoke out of turn when I came to Windy Acres—'

She raised her gloved hand to silence him. 'No need to say sorry, Mr Tanner. I was flattered. Never apologise for honesty, even if you worry that your words will be badly received.'

He shrugged. 'I'm a man who follows his heart. I smile at the daffodils and embrace the sunshine.' Seth quoted her own mother's words back to her. 'What you see is what you get. I've never pretended to be someone else.'

'No,' she said thoughtfully. 'I understand. Howard – Master Fairchild,' she corrected, 'is much the same. Lady Fairchild told us that he has returned to France because he believes himself in love with some French nurse who cared for him during the war. It may be a foolhardy quest, but it may equally make him the happiest man on God's earth.'

Master Howard had barely been discharged from military service when he'd set off to find a young woman who had captured his heart the previous summer. It would be like searching for a needle in a haystack, but Seth admired the young man for trying.

'Do you mind if I take a few moments on this bench?' Olivia asked. 'The atmosphere in the household is suffocating. Everyone is trying to avoid mentioning the real reason my fiancé has returned to the village, but it is the elephant standing in the corner of the room that I find staring at me intently.'

Knowing he was the reason for the investigation, Seth merely nodded and returned to his work. She took a seat and he embarked on activities that showed off his build to good advantage. If a lady could flutter her eyelashes, a strapping gardener could flex his muscles. All was fair in love and war, and this was war.

He worked silently for a while, pulling up leeks for the kitchens, as he watched her crush some of the feverfew leaves and inhale the pungent perfume in his peripheral vision. After a while, she spoke up again.

'Are you local, Tanner? Did you grow up in Merriford Lode?'

'That I did.'

'Then you perhaps know of the Taylors and have heard rumours as to the circumstances surrounding our visit? Such a dreadful accusation to make, even though I have repeatedly reminded Mr Dunn that no one has suggested his family is responsible for anything. Who even was this missing woman? Lady Fairchild said she'd run off with a traveller years ago.'

He briefly explained his relationship with Annie, and her embarrassment at not realising there was a connection was apparent.

'S'prised me too, when I heard she might be dead,' he said. 'I'd no reason to doubt she'd left Merriford. Mr Dunn must be horrified.'

'He is quite at sixes and sevens,' she confirmed. 'As am I, and wish he were staying here with us. The invitation to sleep at the manor extended to him but he decided to spend the night with his mother. Perhaps he is more fond of her than he gave me cause to believe.' She sighed and rose to her feet, rubbing her arms to keep warm. 'I apologise for my frankness. I shouldn't have spoken to you so openly. And I am sorry that such a painful time in your life is being raked over.'

And as she left through the squeaky gate, it occurred to Seth, knowing Ernest of old, that his behaviour was highly suspicious. He'd never had much time for his parents when they'd been younger, and wasn't a man to turn down an opportunity to mingle with elevated company, or enjoy fine food and good wine. Which meant only one thing – he'd returned to his family home to move the body before the search.

* * *

Seth headed to Merriford Lode as soon as he'd finished his duties, calling at another cottage on the way, and setting himself up in the field that edged the Dunns' land to wait...

It was well after midnight when he finally saw a lamp bobbing about in the black, but was too far away to see who was holding it. The figure placed it on the ground and, cast in shadow, there was no doubting their purpose. They were searching for something in the waters of the largest pit, and Seth suspected he knew exactly what that was.

The man splashed about for a while, poking at the bottom with a shepherd's crook he'd brought with him. Eventually, he pulled out a mass from the waters that was far too small to be a body, but Seth had seen enough. He leapt over the fence in his uncontrollable anger, and wasn't spotted until the last moment, just as the object was swung into the barrow.

'What the...?' Ernest was caught off guard as Seth swept the lamp up from the floor, shouldered him out the way and held it aloft.

The carpet bag.

Part of him was relieved. He'd been expecting worse –

although he suspected much worse remained in the pit. Perhaps Ernest only needed to dispose of the bag before the imminent search as it was the thing that would identify any possible body as Annie's. If she truly was in the pit, only bones would remain and it would be difficult to prove they were hers. But a bag of her possessions could prove hard to explain.

'You absolute bastard!' Seth shouted and pushed him to the ground. 'You killed her. You got her pregnant and then you killed her. What did she ask of you? That you do the decent thing and marry her? But you wouldn't do that, would you? Because she was too poor. She was a bit of fun but it wasn't going anywhere, and you had your sights set higher than a village servant girl. You wanted to marry money and I bet you couldn't believe your luck when the Fairchilds introduced you to the Davenports.'

'I don't know what you're talking about, Tanner.' He got to his feet, the twist of his top lip visible in the gloom, knowing he had a height advantage. 'Don't push me about with your filthy, garden-soiled hands.'

Ernest shoved at Seth's chest with one hand before swiftly grabbing his left wrist with the other, pinning one arm behind his back, now in total control of the situation – physically, at least.

'Anything you say I will deny. In fact, I shall keep you here until the morning and claim that it was you poking about in my pits tonight. No one knew about Annie and me because I made her swear not to tell a soul. It'll be my word against yours and who will believe a gardener over the son-in-law of a gentleman?'

'You didn't need to kill her, goddammit. I'd have supported her. Brought up the child. She was a sweet thing.'

'Stupid girl would make threats though, and I couldn't trust her not to blab eventually. But come the morning, I shall point out that you had more reason to kill her. She was screwing another man because you wouldn't give her what she wanted, and she'd backed a better horse. Or maybe I'll just walk you back to the house now and get Mother to run over to the station and notify the police that you were wading about in the pit.'

'No need, Mr Dunn.' Constable Peterson stepped from the shadows and nodded at the young gardener who had called on him earlier that evening. Seth took the opportunity to wriggle from Ernest's grasp, taking advantage of his shock, and placed him in a hold. 'The police have been here for some time. I heard your exchange quite clearly and took note.' He peered towards the barrow in the gloom. 'And you appear to have an item of interest in here. Do you mind if I take a look, sir?'

And Ernest Dunn sunk to his knees, knowing that he was beaten.

46

Olivia was disappointed but not overly concerned when Seth failed to come to her that night. He'd asked her to trust him, and trust him she must, hoping that in his world, Ernest would be made to pay for his crime. But patience was not one of her virtues and she was desperate to ask his advice regarding Tanner. She knew she'd rushed the man, and that her behaviour in the stables had been ill-thought-out, but Impulsive had long been her middle name and that would never change.

Instead, she spent the time working on her new novel, infusing it with joy and magic, a dash of peril and, this time, giving her heroine a happy ending. Art imitating life, she'd decided, was not the way to go. The publisher was correct: everyone was looking for their sunshine. Even her.

The following day, she turned her attentions to the Christmas dance that the Fairchilds were laying on for the servants. It wasn't that they had anything to celebrate – far from it – but, in the end, everything came down to duty. It was Sir Hugo's duty to lead by example. He must look after those in his employ and make sure they knew they were appreciated, hoping that by hosting such an event, he would foster loyalty and gratitude. The world would shortly be ushering in a decade that everyone hoped would mark a fresh start and it was time to put the past to bed. Men had died so that those they cared about might have a brighter future and people were slowly embracing this. Even Cynthia was determined that her boys should not have sacrificed themselves in vain.

The dance was to be held in the servants' hall and, as the preparations got underway, Olivia felt the atmosphere of the household palpably brighten. She overheard some of the maids tittering about their dresses, even though there would be only a handful of young men to appreciate them in their finery. From her window in the tower, she observed Rowe and Tanner ferry greenery into the east wing, as she sewed, rather haphazardly, beads onto the dress she planned to wear for the evening. The head gardener had long since cultivated a small grove of Norway spruce for this time of year, and she'd witnessed them wrestle a sturdy ten-foot specimen, which had been felled for just this occasion, through a door that was far too small. A recently purchased gramophone was also moved from the main house to the hall to provide lively music, and the family were even providing some bottles of champagne.

She cared more than she should about this gathering because Tanner would be there. The family would only attend for a short while at the start of the evening, hand out small gifts and then retire to allow the servants the freedom to enjoy themselves. But Olivia was determined to make a point and catch the eye of a particularly infuriating, self-pitying young man. Sir Hugo would be expected to dance with the housekeeper and cook, and Cynthia to let the butler take her for a spin about the room. Some of the younger maids had even been overheard expressing their desire to be waltzed by Master Benji. But would

Tanner ask her for a dance? And if he didn't, then hopefully he would at least start to appreciate what he was missing out on.

The dress she wore that evening was quite extraordinary. Cynthia had gifted her an old evening gown and she'd added a diaphanous layer of tulle, which she embellished with glass beads and tiny silk bows. She'd threaded pearls and ivy through her loose hair and attached a tiny pair of wings, fashioned from thin wire and a length of delicate net curtain, to her back. In her hand, she held a silver wand.

With her shoulders straight and head high, she entered the hall, and was rewarded by compliments from many of the older servants, their crinkled faces breaking into smiles of delight, heartened that the bereaved fiancée of the third Fairchild heir was finding joy in the world again. The staff of Merriford were long used to her eccentricities and occasional forays into costume, but Tanner was not. He couldn't tear his gaze from her, and his eye burned into the back of her head and the side of her face as she did *her* duty and made sure to talk to each and every person in the room, thank them for their service and wish them all the best for the festive season.

The dancing began and the boot boy, a young lad of barely fourteen, cheekily asked Miss Davenport if she would partner him for a two-step. She hadn't danced since Howard's death but cautiously embraced the simple backwards and forwards to 'Alexander's Ragtime Band', knowing that Tanner was still mesmerised by the strange young woman he had never fully understood. She whirled about the room, growing in confidence, and lost herself in the music, letting go of her pain for those few minutes and unable to prevent her face breaking out into a smile of pure joy. She hoped that Howard was looking down on her from above and smiling, too.

When the song came to an end, she walked purposefully

over to where Tanner was standing, next to old Mr Rowe. She saw the young man stiffen as she approached, almost readying himself for a confrontation.

'Gentlemen?' Her tone was questioning. This was his chance to ask her to dance. She'd made it easy for him. It was the one time and place when no one would bat an eyelid at such intimacy. Could he not smell the rose water she was wearing? Was he not tempted to put his arm about her and pull her close?

Her stomach rolled over slowly as the silence stretched before them. Rowe gave a nervous cough and Olivia finally acknowledged that Seth was not going to step up. Instead, she thrust her wand into his hand – a length of hazel that she'd wrapped in silver ribbon – before turning to the elderly head gardener and leading him onto the dance floor.

Tanner frowned, staring at the curious object, as she cast a backwards glance over her shoulder.

'Keep it,' she said. 'You need the magic more than I do. I have learned to make my own.'

* * *

It was not long after that waltz that the family retired and left the servants to their fun.

'Wings?' Cynthia exclaimed, her eyes twinkling, as they settled in front of the drawing-room fire and Sir Hugo poured them all a nightcap. 'Dear girl, you never cease to astound me.'

'You look beautiful,' her husband said to Olivia, as he handed her a small port. 'It's so lovely to see the old Olivia back. I hope you will always be whoever and whatever you wish to be. The old ways are changing and we must embrace the new, my love,' he said to his wife. 'It's what we fought for – a bright future.'

They toasted each dead Fairchild son in turn, and then Sir Hugo raised a glass to Benji, who was still flushed from the overexuberant attentions of the slightly tipsy household maids.

'To Benjamin. My son. *My* future. I know he will do me proud.'

* * *

The euphoria of the night continued when Seth's reassuring voice drifted through the bricks of her bedroom wall half an hour later. Strangely, there was no Christmas dance in his world, and she wondered how much her presence at Merriford Manor had altered the path of events. Olivia understood Seth's Lady Fairchild to be a lonely and unfulfilled woman. She did not drive, she rarely laughed, and she had lost all interest in her gardens.

Seth bounced down on the bed with exciting news: Ernest had been arrested and things were moving fast.

'The housekeeper told us in the servants' hall that she'd never seen the master so angry,' he said. 'The Fairchilds feel responsible as it was Clarence who introduced Miss Davenport to Mr Dunn. Master Benjamin then told his parents the truth of Clarence's scar, which made Lady Fairchild cry, and Mrs Davenport insisted that her daughter break off the engagement immediately.'

Olivia was more relieved than she could say that there would be no wedding. If this crossover of worlds hadn't existed, there would be a version of her out there somewhere marrying a manipulative and dangerous man.

'I can't thank you enough,' she said. 'You've served a justice that this world will never get to see and, whilst I know that it's something you can't rush, you will eventually be able to pursue your romantic interests. I know me, and I know that your declaration will have piqued her interest and be simmering away in her mind. If nothing else, I am a curious and romantic soul.'

'I'm only thankful that you told me the truth.' There was no accusation in his voice, just genuine relief that disaster had been avoided. 'Oh, Olivia.' He sighed. 'I can't tell you how much this turn of events has given me hope, even though it will take weeks for all this unpleasantness to die down.' She heard him wriggle about on his bed and settle himself. 'But sometimes, it's hard, isn't it? Being in love with two people who are really the same person? I've accepted that I can't have you, but I also know that she *is* you – so why does it feel she's a second choice, a substitute for the real thing?'

'I understand completely. My Tanner doesn't have your joy for life or desire for adventure. He's the same but frustratingly different.'

'How *is* the poor man? I've been so swept up with everything that I forgot to ask how you were getting on.'

The eagerness in his voice made her feel obliged to soften the truth.

'It will take time here too.'

47

Christmas came and went, with little progress made on either side. Tanner largely avoided Olivia, despite their brief encounter at the dance and, with the weather deteriorating rapidly, she had fewer reasons to be outside. It was Benji who told her that the undergardener had been fitted for a wooden prosthetic arm, one with articulated joints, no less, but that he'd found it cumbersome and never wore it. Apparently, the stubborn man had announced that prosthetics and face masks were as much to protect the sensibilities of others as for the benefit of the veteran. She thought Tanner had a point and yet again admired his stoicism.

It took Olivia three months to finish the novel. She'd had one book rejected and was fully prepared for it to happen again. Everyone had a period of apprenticeship, in whatever field they worked in – from the surgeon to the artist – and she realised that her earlier effort had been a necessary part of her training. What had made her think that she could get it right first time? She'd accepted that there was unlikely to be a husband to fill her forthcoming years, so 'merry spinster attempting to get published' it was. She had nothing to lose by writing the story that she wanted to tell – only time, and she had plenty of that. This one was for Seth, for her father and, ultimately, for herself.

In the March of 1920, she received a visit from her father's former editor. Not a letter but a visit. He had called, he explained, to offer to publish her manuscript. Her wild yarn of space aeroplanes and travelling in time, spellcasters and clever, futuristic machines was good. So good, in fact, it could have been written by a man. She bit her tongue. They negotiated terms, but it was never about money for her, and he asked if she would consider writing under a pseudonym – a male one, so as not to put men off buying the book, but she dug her heels in and persuaded him that the Davenport name would help sales. He accepted that she may have a point. Besides, she said, feeling brave and adventurous, there were other publishers she could try...

Seth told her he hadn't seen his Miss Davenport since the discovery of human remains in the shrieking pit, as she'd apparently returned to Windy Acres with her parents. The trial of Ernest Dunn was to be held at Norwich Crown Court and he would be called as a witness, as would Miss Davenport, so she knew the paths of the two would cross again.

Absent for several days, he finally returned to the tower to fill an anxious Olivia in on the proceedings. Spring hadn't quite sprung and she had a thick shawl wrapped around her shoulders. The fire in the room was blazing away but the single-brick structure of the tower had always been difficult to heat.

'Guilty of manslaughter,' he announced through the wall, his tone reflecting his disappointment with the verdict. 'There was no doubt he killed her but, in the end, it couldn't be proved that it was premeditated,' he said. 'He had a good lawyer and managed to charm the jury and convinced everyone that she'd become hysterical and attacked him. He claimed he'd been forced to defend himself. I'm old-fashioned, however, and have always believed in an eye for an eye. He'll be out in eight years, but Annie'll never get to walk this earth again. How is that fair?'

They were both silent for a while and Olivia felt equally dispirited. Perhaps justice had been better served in her world where Ernest had died.

'Do you think we'll ever find happiness?' he eventually asked. 'I want to believe that it's our destiny to be together and that's why all this happened through the wall. Two happy Seths and Olivias? Because all I feel at the moment is anger and injustice. I'll find my joy again but right now, I feel so glum.'

She decided to lift him from his unusual, but perfectly understandable, mood by being creative with the truth, all the time remembering she mustn't mention Tanner's injuries – something else that would bring him down.

'Then perhaps I have news that will cheer you up. I stumbled across Tanner working by the lake today and he finally admitted that he does feel something for me.'

She closed her eyes and imagined the scenario that she had so been hoping for these past few weeks, where he would be bold enough to cast his worries aside and fight for love. Even at the dance, she'd sensed his attraction to her. Men were not as good as women at hiding their feelings. And yet still he had done nothing. The words she'd just spoken to Seth were her greatest wish, but they were an absolute lie.

There was a pause and, as always, she was frustrated not to be able to see his face. So much of their conversations relied on the tone of their voice, which meant when she heard no sound, it was impossible to know what he was thinking. Was he happy or jealous?

'He did? That's so good to hear. I've news, too, as it happens, but was worried how you'd react. Now I know you'll be as happy as me.'

He had something else to tell her? She shuffled to face the wall.

'You've spoken to Miss Davenport? Has she decided to shock society by running off with a gardener and sailing around the world? Perhaps she will finally do something with her life now that she's got rid of her insincere fiancé.' Olivia was frustrated that it had taken the death of her parents and the loss of Howard to push her to write. In Seth's world, she had led a charmed life by comparison, and somehow that lack of drama and heartache had removed her childhood desire to achieve.

'Not quite, but I was so despairing of the verdict that I forgot to tell you that she sought me out afterwards. Came over to me in the corridor to offer her sympathies and wondered how she'd not known of Mr Dunn's temper. She's asked me to visit Windy Acres on my next afternoon off. I think we're at the start of something.'

This was a pleasant surprise for Olivia as she'd expected her other self to take longer to warm to someone who was, after all, practically a stranger, and who worked for the Fairchilds. With this new information, she couldn't admit to him that Tanner wanted nothing to do with her. The encounter in the stables had pushed him too far, too fast, and even the sight of her dressed as a fairy, after his admonishing description of her as exactly that, hadn't moved anything within him.

'And my... her parents didn't mind? My father was not protective so soon after his prospective son-in-law had been exposed as a liar?'

'Quite the opposite. He shook me by the hand and thanked me for saving his daughter from a dangerous marriage. For such a wealthy, famous and highly educated man, he's very down to

earth. Mind you, he was the reason the trial became so sensa-
tionalised – he was within a cat's whisker of becoming the
father-in-law of the accused. You wouldn't believe how much
has been written in the newspapers. Sales of his books have only
got better, and they were damn impressive before.'

'And Howard?' she asked. 'Was he present?'

Her former fiancé had been on her mind, ever since Seth
had told her that he'd survived the war. It was possible to love
two men equally, much as she imagined a mother would love
two children, but there was a part of her that wanted Miss
Davenport to at least have the chance to choose between the two
great loves of her life.

'Master Howard's a sorry fellow. He dint have a good war and
he's far from the joker he was in his youth, but he wasn't around
for the trial because he's still in France. I forgot to tell you that
he's finally tracked down his French nurse and now plans to
bring her back to the manor.' He chuckled. 'Her Ladyship's in a
right muddle there; wants her son to be happy but is quite
alarmed at the thought of some French chit in charge at
Merriford.'

That was it then; Howard had found someone. Why would
Seth think this information would be of any interest to her? He
knew nothing of what had passed between them. She shook her
head as if to dislodge her former sweetheart from her mind. He
was alive and he was in love. She couldn't wish more for him
than that, and it was not her place to interfere. In Seth's world,
he had never been Miss Davenport's to lose.

'So, it would seem love might be on the horizon for everyone,' he finished.

Olivia couldn't bring herself to answer and rolled away from
the wall. She tried desperately not to mind that whilst everything was going so well in Seth's world, it was far from good in

hers. Strangely, neither of them made any further comment, and she eventually drifted off into a troubled and melancholy sleep.

* * *

Even though Olivia didn't think her heart could take another battering, a few days later, Seth had one further announcement through the bricks. They had both been more reticent with each other of late and conversations through the wall had been stilted and fleeting. He was undoubtedly reflecting on his imminent romance, whilst she wallowed in self-pity, frustrated by Tanner's inaction.

'You're not going to like what I'm about to say, but I've given this a great deal of thought.'

She braced herself.

'We gain nothing by continuing to meet and I feel a dishonesty about being in touch with you when I'm pursuing the attentions of another. It's a betrayal of a sort to Miss Davenport, because when I give myself to someone, I give myself completely.'

Olivia knew this to be true. Look at his loyalty to Annie.

'The visit to Windy Acres went well, then?' she concluded.

'Yes, we had a lovely afternoon. I've high hopes but, much like your efforts with Tanner, it'll take time. It may not be written in the stars, but I reckon our love stories have always run through the seam of metal that lies beneath this tower.'

'Then we have done the very thing we set out to do,' she agreed. 'Find each other in our own worlds to enable us to move on from the happiness that we've had together here.'

In truth, she couldn't bear to hear the details of his courtship as it progressed over the following weeks. Severing all ties might be the kindest thing she could do for herself. They'd both always known that neither could remain in the tower forever. It was a twist of the knife every time he talked of a Miss Davenport who, it now seemed, might one day be his completely, and in every sense of the word.

Tears started to trickle down her cheeks but she kept her voice level, not wanting him to know how much she was suffering in that moment. Things with Tanner were worse, if anything, and she knew it was time to move back to Windy Acres. She was of age and, if Seth was imminently to desert her, there would be no reason for her to remain.

'Then we part now – tonight.' She was surprised by her clarity of thought in that moment. 'I will ask to move back into the house tomorrow. Cynthia will be delighted.'

'Yes,' he agreed. 'When I'm with her, it's not fair to be thinking of you. She deserves all my love and all my attention. I can only have one Olivia Davenport in my life, and you must only have one Seth Tanner. I'm glad you managed to get him to swallow his pride, and for myself, I feel fortunate that a lady such as Miss Davenport has taken a chance on someone like me.'

Someone like me. His words echoed around her head. If only Tanner *had* chosen her. Miss Davenport was the lucky one – he was everything. The only time the self-pitying undergardener of her world would hold her close, or kiss her lips, would be in her imagination.

'Then this really is the end?' she asked, her heart thumping wildly.

'I reckon it's for the best.'

'Then please accept my thanks,' she said, 'for everything you have done for me over the years. Your friendship has shaped me in so many ways, and has seen me through some incredibly difficult times. I love you. I will always love you.'

Letting him go was the only option.

'And I will always love *both* of you,' he replied.

And as they said goodnight to each other for the very last time, she silently acknowledged that she, unfortunately, would only ever be loved by one version of him.

48

SETH TANNER. A WORLD AWAY…

Sir Hugo Fairchild could be a demanding master but he was a fair man. When Annie's body had finally been recovered and the news broke that the daughter of the world-famous author Jasper Davenport was engaged to a man now suspected of a historic murder, the newspapers went wild. Journalists besieged the manor but Sir Hugo looked after his own. He even took the time to speak to Seth personally, acknowledging how trying the whole episode must have been. He gave his undergardener leave to attend the trial and allowed him to stay in Norwich for the week to save him undertaking the long journey every day.

Being at court, looking at Dunn's indifferent face and smug expression, was infuriating, and equally tough on the Davenports. Seth got glimpses of Olivia across the courtroom and in the corridors. She looked pale and ill, and he wondered at her parents for letting her attend once she'd given her testimony. But then he knew she would not shy away from this, regardless of society's expectations.

On the final day of the trial, he realised it was his last opportunity to speak to her before she returned to Suffolk. Who knew when, or even if, she would ever return to Merriford Lode. With all its horrific associations, she might choose never to head to Norfolk again.

'I understand that you're wary of me, miss, but you must appreciate that we have this connection now, however unfortunate. Your fiancé and my sweetheart were known to each other.'

He spoke to her in the corridor, pulling her to one side, and anxiously twisting his cap in his hands.

'Is this what it has been about the whole time?' she asked, her eyes narrowed. 'Did you know that Mr Dunn was acquainted with Miss Taylor? Were your overtures to me in some way connected?'

'Course not, miss. What are you even suggesting? That because he stole my girl, I can claim his?'

'Is that not your thinking?' she said. 'Your bewildering attentions might make more sense.'

Seth shook his head. 'Then you really don't know me at all.'

'No, I don't, and that's rather my point. Please forgive me, Mr Tanner. I should not have entertained you when you came to Windy Acres. I fear it's given you false hope, particularly given the turn of events, when all I intended was friendship. This whole episode has been overwhelming and I would prefer that you didn't try to contact me again.'

He was crushed by her words, despite her kindly tone, and nodded.

'I understand and am sorry if I made you feel uncomfortable.' He turned to go but hesitated and swung back to face her. 'I appreciate I have no right to ask this, but please promise that you'll remember the young girl you once were – so full of courage and daring. If you choose not to marry, then I wish you all the best, but it'll be a mighty shame if no one gets to share their life with such a spirited young woman. Don't let go of them dreams you once had just because one man wanted to marry you for your money and not your soul. Write the books. Go on the travels. Live the most fabulous life.'

She frowned at first, but then nodded, and he walked away, carrying the knowledge that he'd probably never see her again.

Because Seth had lied to Olivia through the wall. Miss Davenport would never be his. He'd been foolish to think he stood a chance with her, but hearing that Tanner had admitted his feelings, he couldn't bring himself to stand in the way of their happy ending.

And he knew that Olivia would never let him go unless she thought he'd also found his.

He was a broken-hearted man but also remembered the relentlessly chirpy voice of Princess Cordelia through the wall all those years ago, and would instead throw everything into his career. Seth Tanner would become a figure of note in the horticultural world. In fact, who knew what he might achieve, because he would impose no limits on himself.

The sky, after all, went on forever.

49

Olivia asked Cynthia if she could return to her former bedroom the following morning, knowing the older woman would be delighted to have her back in the main house. It was strange at first, sleeping in a bed where she was truly alone. The absence of sounds through the wall was unsettling, and she missed the comfort of knowing someone else was nearby. Since Seth's return from the war, they had almost been as a married couple at night, with the companionship and intimacy that entailed. She missed him badly and could hardly believe that after eight years, he was no longer in her life, and never would be again.

After a few days, but more especially nights, of feeling sorry for herself, and several prolonged periods of contemplation in the Japanese gardens, the knowledge of Seth's success with Miss Davenport forced Olivia's hand. Not that she would ever know how his story ended, but she had her suspicions that if Miss Davenport had invited him to Windy Acres, he'd already successfully wormed his way into her romantic heart. His status would be no barrier to her. Love paid no attention to irrelevant details, like class. It overcame everything.

Unless you were a stubborn gardener.

'You are a difficult man to find,' she said, tracking him down to the orchids in the conservatory, and determined to have one final attempt to win him over – even if it meant he made good on his threat to leave.

'Her Ladyship generally prefers me to keep out of sight if she has visitors.' He lifted up his good arm and waved it across his face. 'This puts them off their hors d'oeuvres.'

Olivia felt cross with Cynthia for being so insensitive, especially as *she* only saw the man and hardly paid any attention to his scars.

'So, what exactly is it I can do for you, miss?' He was determined to continue in his subservient role.

'There was nothing specific I wanted. I was just seeing how you were getting on. Rowe tells me you have been asking about taking on greater responsibility, and that you've submitted an article to the *Gardener's Chronicle*, and I wanted to say how pleased I was to hear you were making an effort.'

'Forgive me, but do you know how patronising that sounds?'

'Forgive me, but when you act like a child, there is a tendency for people to treat you like one.' She was starting to lose her temper. Despite her resolve not to force his hand, she couldn't help herself, and got straight to the point. 'I honestly believe that you do like me, Mr Tanner, but for some unfathomable reason will not admit it.'

He took a step closer to her, as she stared at him and dared him to deny it. He was taller than her and she had to tip her head up as he approached. There was another excruciating silence as he looked down at her lips, but he did nothing and she spoke to ease the awkwardness.

'You could have danced with me at the Christmas party. Did you not wonder, just for a moment, what it might feel like to hold me? I know that you were mocking me when you said I was a picture-book fairy, but I took it as the most enormous compliment. I have always believed that I can be anyone I want to be and I can fall in love with whomever I want: rich man, poor man, beggar man, gardener. And I chose you, Tanner. I will always write my own story but I cannot force you to be in it.'

Kiss me, she thought, *just goddam kiss me*.

He tipped his head briefly to one side but then pulled back. Her chest, which had tightened in anticipation, released and her disappointed heart slid to her shoes.

He shook his head before speaking.

'I covet Sir Hugo's motor car but am realistic enough to know that I will never have the means to afford one. I'd be lying if I said there weren't something about you, but my reasons for not acting on such feelings are hardly unfathomable. You fascinate and terrify me all at once. But you're an independently wealthy woman – the servants' hall is full of talk about the success of your book – and I'm in the employ of your guardian and will never be a rich man. You are perfect and healthy and full of joy, and I am damaged and far too introspective for my own good. I will never understand why you pursue me when you could have any man you wanted.'

'And yet I care not one jot for any of the attributes you are so convinced you are lacking. All I care about is how you make me feel. I have enough money for the both of us and am not embarrassed to be seen with you or worried about pitying stares – and I certainly wouldn't tuck you away if I was serving hors d'oeuvres on the terrace. You'd be standing by my side always. I don't want to be married to anyone else; *I want to be married to you*.'

There followed a moment of excruciating embarrassment for both of them as it was apparent she had practically proposed to him, before he stepped away and returned to watering the orchids, periodically narrowing his eyes as her words played back in his head.

'Oh, have it your own way, you foolish man,' she said, when he made no effort to respond to her declaration. 'I shall make plans to return to Windy Acres – my parents' house in Suffolk. If you won't fight for me, then I don't wish to constantly encounter a man who finds a dozen reasons to deny himself something that would make him happy. And God alone knows, you deserve some happiness in your life.'

Olivia wasn't sure she would actually go through with this threat, but she was resorting to drastic measures to force his hand.

He stopped his task and jerked his head in her direction. 'You're leaving?'

She shrugged.

'But, Miss Davenport, how do you not see that this sudden attachment to me makes no sense? I feel like there's something you're not telling me and I just want the truth.'

His good eye locked with hers and she could see he was expecting a proper answer. She gave a resigned nod of the head, knowing that if she told him about the wall, he would think her crazy, so she frantically searched for another explanation. There wasn't one.

In for a penny... She took a deep breath.

'What I'm about to say will sound ridiculous but I swear on Howard's memory that every word of it is true. And you must listen to what I have to say, without judgement or interruption, until I've finished.'

He shrugged and settled himself against the counter as she told him everything: from the moment her thirteen-year-old self had heard a voice through the wall, to Seth's idea that they find each other in their own worlds. He tried to interject on a couple of occasions but she raised her hand to silence him. She wanted to get through the explanation in full before he pulled it to pieces and made her feel even more of a fool than she already did.

By the end, Tanner's face was full of pity, not for her impossible situation, she realised, but for her state of mind.

'This is dizzy fantasy, miss. Something you wish to be true but in't: your parents, Howard and even me, all alive and well, whole and perfect.'

'Believe me—' she crossed her arms '—the world through the wall is *not* a perfect world. Ernest Dunn survived the war and, in my ignorance, I nearly married him. Not something I would ever fantasise about, I can assure you. It's also a world where my lack of adversity has made me compliant, and it would appear my ambitions amount to editing my father's work, rather than producing any of my own, and I was seemingly content to marry and settle into a life of domestic bliss. I prefer the stronger, more adventurous me who doesn't give a damn about conforming. The me who stands before you now.'

He said nothing for a moment.

'Then we go to the tower right this instant and we talk to this Seth,' he said, challenging her to prove her nonsense tale.

'We can't. You've gone.' She explained the tough decision that they'd come to as her heart sank and she was reminded that she would never speak to him through the wall again. The man before her was her last chance. If he rejected her, then there would never be a Seth and Olivia – not for her, at any rate.

'Very convenient, that.' The sarcasm dripped to the floor between them as he spoke.

'Oh, have it your way, Tanner.' She'd suddenly had enough. 'Think me a child, think me deranged, think whatever you choose, and live in your closed-off world. I hope it keeps you warm at night. I shall go to Windy Acres and write fabulous stories, travel abroad and have breathtaking experiences. Maybe one day, I'll even find someone who wants to do all these things with me. But whatever I do, I shall be happy.'

Tanner shook his head. 'God preserve the man who takes you on,' he said, and he scooped up his watering can and walked out on her for the second time in his life.

50

SPRING 1921

A whole year had passed and Olivia Davenport was the talk of the small village in Suffolk where she lived, and not for the first time. Nine years ago, the gossip had centred around her tragic orphan status and the newsworthy nature of her parents' deaths, but now, the scandal of a young woman, only just twenty-two, returning to her family home, Windy Acres, *alone* had been sufficient to fan the flames of local gossip. And then, when the curious young lady began to indulge her whimsical side by building the most outrageous treehouse in the gardens, *and* adding a large circular tower to the front of the property and painting the render pink, of all things, the tittle-tattle really took off. There were even rumours that she had asked a cabinet maker to make her a throne upholstered in red velvet with *Princess Cordelia* embroidered into the fabric. That was the whisper that made her smile the most – because it was true.

She was an eccentric. An oddity. And far from upsetting her, it made her happy. She found she didn't mind the intrusion into her private life as much as she thought she would. Her publisher was delighted with all the attention she attracted and actively encouraged her quirkiness, because the newspapers and journals lapped it up. Olivia found that becoming a dotty spinster at such a young age was no bad thing. She had a lifetime ahead of her where she could do what she liked and people would just roll their eyes and say, *Oh, that's so like Miss Davenport – such a queer fish, but a likeable one.* If just one young girl read about her in the *Girls' Own Paper* and decided to follow her heart, embrace her imagination, be brave or step outside society's ridiculous boundaries, then she'd achieved something worth far more than the healthy royalty cheques that were now dropping through her letterbox at regular intervals.

Cynthia had been heartbroken to see her leave, until the older woman was told that she was welcome to stay with Olivia whenever she liked. Purchasing a second motor car and enjoying the hedonism that the decade was chasing, Lady Fairchild found she was hardly ever at Merriford Manor at all. Benji was also accepting of Olivia's decision and had, as she predicted, fallen in love with the outspoken twin sister of one of his school chums. It wouldn't last, mainly because his mother disapproved, but it was a start.

Her debut fantasy novel had been a huge success, with her second book looking to outsell the first. Her way had been lit by women who'd written similar stories, like Mary Shelley and Jane Webb-Loudon, and her publisher played on the fact that her father was Jasper Davenport, and used one author to sell the other. She was proud to be associated with him and to continue his legacy, even though her stories were far more wild than his had ever been.

The questions she asked in her work were not 'what if the prince married the chambermaid?' but 'what if there were creatures living amongst us on this planet that had come from Mars?' and 'what if someone really could become invisible?' She even had an encouraging letter from H. G. Wells himself. Science fiction was not to everyone's taste, but then, nor were female novelists – however good their books proved to be. She was content to make a living from her imagination and spend her days doing something she loved. Olivia accepted that she may only ever find love in her vivid dreams or vicariously through the heroes and heroines she created on her brand-new, black Remington typewriter.

The books were such a triumph that she was invited to do a series of public talks across East Anglia, and the first stop was the printers and stationers, Jarrold and Sons, in Norwich.

The weather was frustratingly changeable that day but it had not deterred the eager audience listening to her read from *The Starbound Woman*. She was well received, always having had a talent for the dramatic, and a small group of enthusiastic young women gathered around her afterwards – full of gushing questions and lauding her with praise.

As she gathered up her papers, someone approached the table she was seated at and slid a copy of her book in front of her.

'Can you sign this one for me, please, miss?'

Without looking up, and half-listening to the ladies to her left, she opened it to the title page.

'Of course. I can add a dedication, if you like? What would you like me to say?'

She dipped her pen into the glass bottle of ink on the table before her and hovered it above the page.

'Well, now, if you could put something like: "To the stubborn idiot who mayn't properly understand me, but who read my books and decided that whilst such a vivid imagination may well be in need of medical investigation, by God, does it offer an escape from life". In retrospect, that's a bit wordy. Let's keep it simple: "To the stupid idiot begging for a second chance..."'

Her eyes travelled up the long, lithe body before her, taking in the empty sleeve and finally coming to rest on the damaged face.

'They've been talking about you in the servants' hall for months,' he said, shrugging. 'One of the housemaids, Freda, has been following your success since you left Merriford. She showed me an article about your treehouse and the tower that you've added at Windy Acres. You're totally off your rocker but, I guess what I'm saying is, I'd rather live with you in your crazy, fantasy world, than alone in mine.'

It had taken a lot, she realised, for him to come. There were already whispers in the room and one child had pointed to his face and said in a startled voice, 'Mummy, where has that man's eye gone?' And it was never easy to admit when you were wrong, especially for a stubborn man like him.

There was a cough from her publisher, probably anxious to wrap the event up and get home to his wife. Dark clouds had moved overhead and the interior of the store was suddenly gloomy, but Olivia's heart had never held so much sunshine.

'Miss Davenport?' the man prompted, and she realised she'd been frozen like a fool for several seconds.

'Of course.' Her cheeks coloured and she returned her focus to the page and began to write.

> *To the man I've loved since I was thirteen years old.*
> *Thank you for finding your way back to me.*
> *Here's to a shared lifetime of adventure.*

She rolled the blotter over the ink and looked up at him. 'Wondered if you had any jobs going at Windy Acres,'

Tanner said, awkwardly retrieving the novel and clutching it to his chest with his only hand.

'No, but I have a vacancy for a husband; if you feel you might be suitable, then please do consider applying. Send me a list of your attributes and any relevant qualifications and I will give it some thought and get back to you.'

'I'm pretty certain that's the second marriage proposal I've had from you, Miss Davenport. Did you not know it is usual for the man to propose?'

'Oh, I've never been one for worrying about the rules.' She batted his comment away with a lazy hand. 'Who cares for convention?'

'I used to, but not so much any more...'

He smiled then and his whole face changed in a heartbeat. She saw in him at that moment all the joy that she'd felt Seth impart through the wall. There. There was the man she'd fallen in love with.

He'd been inside Tanner all along.

* * *

Three days later, somewhere not of this world, but of a world very much like it, a young lady sat in her favourite window seat at Windy Acres and looked out over a garden bursting with green shoots, the drooping heads of violet bluebells, and the lemon-yellow trumpets of the daffodils.

It had been a particularly trying year. A dark secret had been uncovered in her former fiancé's past, and he was now serving an eight-year gaol sentence for manslaughter after the rather forward yet fascinating Seth Tanner, the former sweetheart of the victim, had exposed the crime.

That particular young man had been on the periphery of her

life for many years, but only stepped from the shadows after the war. His ridiculous romantic advances had come out of nowhere, along with his impertinent but resolute conviction that she was not living her best life. He had insisted that she should be writing and travelling, and she knew that without his encouragement, she would not have picked up her pen in the last few months. Perhaps she should have mentioned his strange behaviour to her father's oldest friend, Sir Hugo, but she didn't wish the man ill. There was something about him... something that intrigued her, put fire in her belly and made her heart race. He had a ready smile and a cheery disposition. But could she really trust her judgement after being so wrong about Ernest?

She gathered up the loose sheets of paper on her lap and placed them on a small tripod table that was to her left, returning her focus to the garden. The pages were notes for a novel that she'd been playing about with. Mr Tanner had been quite correct to assert that she had story-writing in her veins, only she was not sure what she wanted to write about yet. If he had been correct about that, she pondered, looking out at the small honeysuckle bush he'd given her the previous year, what else had that astute young man been right about?

Her father entered the room and wandered over to her, kissing the top of her head and glancing at the papers by her side.

'What are you up to?' he asked, peering at the top page. 'Giving your old father a run for his money?'

'Just ideas.'

'But you're a girl,' he teased. 'I'm not really sure you're up to such a serious undertaking. Besides, I don't want to lose my best editor.'

'Oh, you're so terribly old-fashioned. Girls are just as good as boys at most things, and better at some.'

He scooped up her papers and began to flick through them.

'Daddy?' she said, after a pause. He looked up from her words. 'Would you do something for me?'

'Of course, if it's in my power to do so.'

'Would you offer Mr Tanner a gardening job here? The young man who exposed Mr Dunn and saved me from a terrible fate? Johnson will retire next year and Mummy so adores her roses.'

'Not sure Fairchild will appreciate me stealing his staff, and I think it's highly unlikely the young man would want the job anyway. Why would he leave the impressive grounds of a large estate like Merriford for our more modest acreage in Suffolk?'

The thing of it was, she hadn't been able to get Mr Tanner out of her mind. He was a handsome lad, to be sure, if a little rough around the edges, but he seemed to carry with him such joy, when so many who returned from the war had lost theirs in the mud-filled trenches of countries far across the sea. She still didn't understand what had prompted his trip across two counties to visit her on that spring day, but it was flattering, and she regretted her cold dismissal of him after the trial.

Olivia had bumped into Howard Fairchild through mutual friends a few weeks ago. He'd not long returned from a grand European adventure, and had a shy French girl on his arm and a skip in his step. At one time, she'd thought the heir to Merriford Manor had taken a shine to her, but in his darkest hour, he'd fallen for a woman who'd tended to him in a field hospital. Olivia, however, could only ever think of him as the annoying prankster of her occasional visits to see Sir Hugo during her childhood. Besides, the thought of becoming another cold and distant Lady Fairchild, swanning about the house looking decorative but touching no one, certainly did not appeal to her.

'Tanner's a solid chap,' Howard had confirmed. 'Went from

dour-faced misery to extraordinarily jovial fellow after he returned from the war. Our head gardener rather rates him and says he's a man who is going places...'

'Please, Daddy, for me?' Olivia appealed to her father with wide eyes.

Jasper Davenport nodded.

If he comes, I will know, she thought. *And then we shall have all the time in the world to get to know each other.*

Olivia curled her legs under her bottom and studied her reflection in the windowpane. Two Olivia Davenports, she mused. One sitting heartsore but determined, in the window seat, and another, staring back at her – somehow more confident and at peace.

She smiled and her reflection smiled back.

* * *

MORE FROM JENNI KEER

Another book from Jenni Keer, *The Ravenswood Witch*, is available to order now here:

https://mybook.to/RavenswoodBackAd

ACKNOWLEDGEMENTS

First, a brief note about the shrieking pits. I came across them during my research into the area of North Norfolk that I have set the book in – so they really do exist! Mine are fictional because Merriford Lode is fictional, but they are scattered around areas like Aylmerton and Gresham, and are remnants of ancient, man-made excavations, dating back to the prehistoric or medieval period. Some have ghostly associations, and some are linked to strange noises, but I have taken liberties with them. However, with a name like that, how could I resist making them a part of my story? Do look them up if they are of interest.

And now on to the many thank yous... Everyone knows how highly I rate my publisher, Boldwood Books, because I wax lyrical about them whenever I get the opportunity, and four books in and two years down the line and I'm happier than I've ever been. Thanks especially to Iso, my editor, for her continued kind words about my writing and brilliant mind. To Marcela for her marketing expertise, Helena Newton for the copy editing, and Emily Reader for the proofs. Alexandra Allden – you did it again! Another breathtaking cover. Thank you.

To Hannah – my incredible, hard-working, maths-loving, detail-orientated, quick-responding and mildly amusing (sometimes on purpose) agent. If I could adopt you, I probably would.

To beta readers Clare Marchant, Suzanne Hull and Kate Smith, who gave of their time, even though they were writing books of their own. Thanks especially to Suzie for her WW1 research help, her series of calm and instructive video calls when I was getting in a muddle with the OTC information, and for recommending the book *Six Weeks* by John Lewis-Stempel – which, as a mother of four young men, totally broke me.

To the Famous Five. You guys!!!!! Stargazing will never, EVER be the same again. Can we go on a writing retreat every week? With gin. And, just in case the aliens land, metal pants.

To the Romantic Novelists' Association. Best conference ever. I always learn something new, and the community and friendships I have built here over the years are priceless. Long may romance rule.

I could not, of course, do any of this without the love and support of my family. Anthony – you are my life. Harvey, Evan, Peter and Leo – you are my biggest achievement... unless, of course, someone makes a film of one of my books. Then you will drop a place in the charts. #suckitup

And extra thanks to my little pea, for introducing me to the awesomeness that is Machine Gun Kelly – whose songs proved to be the soundtrack to this book. Weirdly. And to Harv, who knows more about my books than I do, because he is a good listener and an even better rememberer! (I'm referring, of course, to the fact that I swore there had never been a dog in any of my books. A house point to any clever readers who can tell me his name.)

One last mention. Emma Jane Lambert – thinking of you often and sending love.

Finally, to all my friends, extended family and dear, dear readers. You keep reading and I'll keep writing. Deal?

Jenni x

ABOUT THE AUTHOR

Jenni Keer is the well-reviewed author of historical romances, often with a mystery at their heart. Most recently published by Headline and shortlisted for the 2023 RNA Historical Romantic Novel of the Year.

Sign up to Jenni Keer's newsletter to get a free short story

Visit Jenni's website: www.jennikeer.co.uk

Follow Jenni on social media here:

- facebook.com/jennikeerwriter
- x.com/JenniKeer
- instagram.com/jennikeer
- bookbub.com/authors/jenni-keer

ALSO BY JENNI KEER

Letters from
the past

Discover page-turning
historical novels from
your favourite authors
and be transported
back in time

Join our book club
Facebook group

https://bit.ly/SixpenceGroup

Sign up to our
newsletter

https://bit.ly/LettersFrom
PastNews

Boldwood

Boldwood Books is an award-winning fiction publishing company seeking out the best stories from around the world.

Find out more at www.boldwoodbooks.com

Join our reader community for brilliant books, competitions and offers!

Follow us

@BoldwoodBooks

@TheBoldBookClub

Sign up to our weekly deals newsletter

https://bit.ly/BoldwoodBNewsletter

Printed in Great Britain
by Amazon